HEAVEN'S
SHADOW

David S. Goyer is a screenwriter, film director and comic-book writer. He has written several screenplays based on numerous comic-book series, among them *Doctor Strange*, *Ghost Rider*, *Batman Begins*, *The Dark Knight*, and *The Flash*. He is currently working on writing the third instalment of Christopher Nolan's *Batman* film series.

Michael Cassutt is a television producer, screenwriter, and author. His notable TV work includes producing or writing, or both, for *The Outer Limits*, *Eerie, Indiana*, *Beverly Hills, 90210*, and *The Twilight Zone*. In addition to his work in television, Cassutt has written over thirty short stories, predominately in the genres of science fiction and fantasy.

HEAVEN'S
SHADOW

David S. Goyer and
Michael Cassutt

TOR

First published in the US 2011 by Ace, an imprint of The Berkley Publishing Group

First published in Great Britain 2011 by Tor
an imprint of Pan Macmillan, a division of Macmillan Publishers Limited
Pan Macmillan, 20 New Wharf Road, London N1 9RR
Basingstoke and Oxford
Associated companies throughout the world
www.panmacmillan.com

ISBN 978-0-230-76031-8

9 8 7 6 5 4 3 2 1

A CIP catalogue record for this book is available from
the British Library.

Printed in the UK by CPI Mackays, Chatham ME5 8TD

To Michael Engelberg

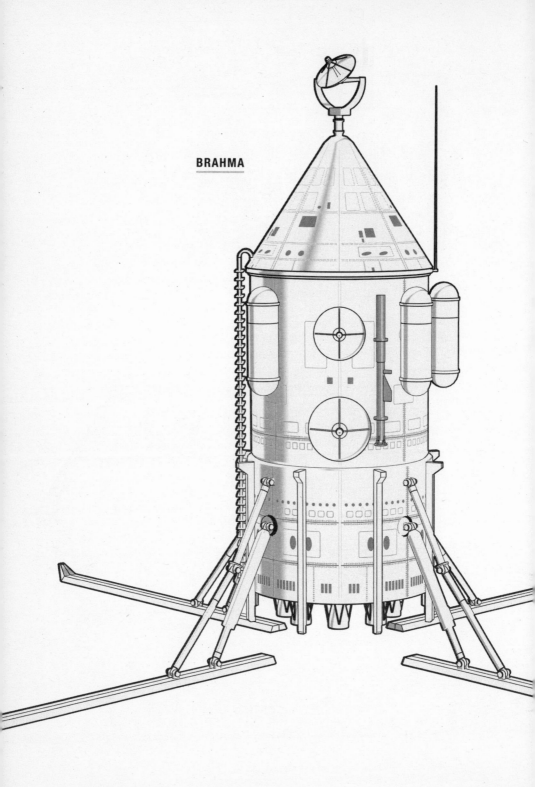

BRAHMA

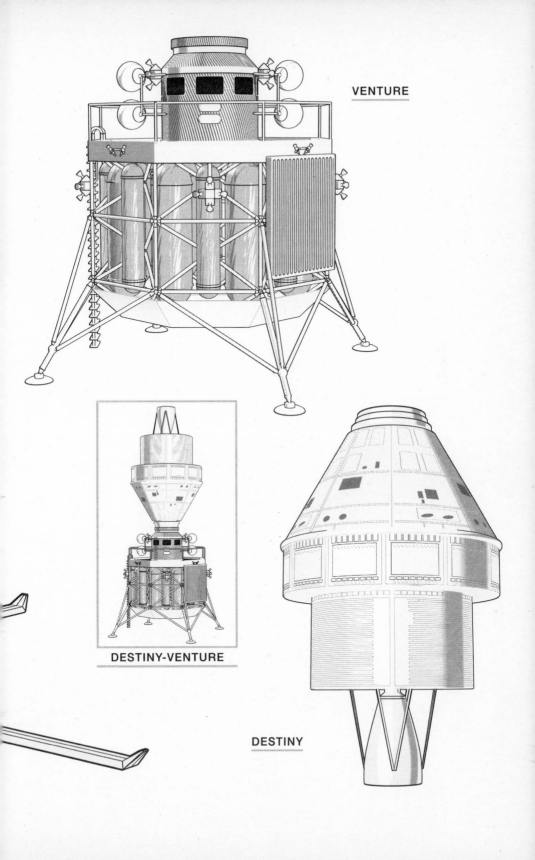

VENTURE

DESTINY-VENTURE

DESTINY

Dramatis Personae

ZACK STEWART, astronomer and astronaut, commander of *Destiny-7*

MEGAN DOYLE STEWART, journalist

RACHEL STEWART, their daughter

AMY MEYER, Rachel's friend

SCOTT SHAWLER, NASA public affairs officer, the "voice" of the *Destiny* missions

TEA NOWINSKI, *Destiny-7* astronaut

PATRICK "POGO" DOWNEY, *Destiny-7* astronaut

YVONNE HALL, *Destiny-7* astronaut

TAJ RADHAKRISHNAN, vyomanaut, commander of *Brahma*

NATALIA YORKINA, exobiologist and *Brahma* cosmonaut

LUCAS MUNARETTO, engineer and *Brahma* cosmonaut

DENNIS CHERTOK, aerospace physician and *Brahma* cosmonaut

HARLEY DRAKE, former astronaut, head of the Home Team

GABRIEL JONES, director of the NASA Johnson Space Center

SHANE WELDON, former chief astronaut, now *Destiny-7* mission director

BRENT BYNUM, deputy national security adviser, White
   House staff

JOSH KENNEDY, *Destiny-7* flight director

LINDA DOWNEY, Patrick Downey's wife

JILLIANNE DWIGHT, crew secretary, Johnson Space Center

KONSTANTIN ALEXANDROVICH FEDOSEYEV, Russian, now a
   Revenant

CAMILLA, a Brazilian child, now a Revenant

VIKRAM NAYAR, lead flight director at Bangalore

THE HOME TEAM
   SASHA BLAINE, Yale astronomer
   WADE WILLIAMS, popular science and sci-fi author
   GLENN CREEL, creator of Cartoon Network's
      Escape Velocity
   LILY VALDEZ, professor at University of California, Irvine
   STEVEN MATULKA, president of the Planetary Society

JASMINE TRIEU, astronaut, capcom

TRAVIS BUELL, astronaut, *Destiny-5* commander, capcom

JAMES and **DIANE DOYLE**, Megan Doyle Stewart's parents

TOBY BURNETT, Wackenhut security officer at JSC

LEE SHIMORA, *Destiny-7* Stay-3 flight director

Part One
"TO FIND THE SEA"

Near-Earth Objects are comets or asteroids that have been nudged by the gravitational attraction of nearby planets into orbits that allow them to enter the Earth's neighborhood.

NASA JET PROPULSION LAB, NEAR-EARTH OBJECT PROGRAM FAQ

What if it comes from farther away?　　　POSTER ALMAZ, JULY 7, 2016

KEANU APPROACH

Blue planet Earth and its seven billion human beings lay 440,000 kilometers below—or, given the arbitrary terminology of orientation in space, off to one side. If the sheer magnitude of the distance failed to provide a mind-boggling thrill, Zack Stewart could, by looking out the window, cover his home planet with his thumb.

That small gesture got the point across: He and his three fellow astronauts were farther away from Earth than any human beings in history.

Farther than the Moon.

Yet . . . they were still dealing with its politics, dragged down as completely as if trailing a 440,000-kilometer-long chain with anchor.

It irritated him. Of course, the fact that he had now been without sleep for thirty hours meant that *everything* irritated him. He was forty-three, a compact, muscular man with considerable experience in spaceflight, including two tours aboard the International Space Station. And now he was commander of *Destiny-7*, responsible for four lives and a multibillion-dollar spacecraft on a mission unlike any ever attempted.

He knew he should be pacing himself. But the stress of preparing for today's unprecedented maneuvers—440,000 kilometers from Earth!—had robbed him of sleep. Mission control in Houston had been uploading scripts for burns that would adjust *Destiny*'s flight path, but the computer code was too fresh from some Honeywell cubicle and kept crashing. NASA called these commands *e-procedures*. To Zack, the *e* stood for *error*.

The process reminded him of the time he had tried to load Windows onto a laptop in Antarctica . . . with dial-up. Then as now, the only choice was to grind slowly through it.

He pushed away from the forward right window of the *Destiny* spacecraft and turned toward the lower bay ten feet away, where Pogo Downey had his 20/15 eyes pressed against the lenses of the telescope. "See anything yet?"

Pogo, born Patrick but rechristened in flight school, was a big, redhaired Air Force test pilot wearing a ribbed white undergarment that made him look like a Himalayan snow ape. "Nothing."

"There should be *something*." Something, in this case, would be a faint point of light against a field of brighter lights . . . *Brahma*, a crewed spacecraft launched toward Keanu by the Russian-Indian-Brazilian Coalition . . . *Destiny*'s competitors. "We've got two tracking nets looking for the son of a bitch," he said, as much for his own morale as for Pogo Downey's edification. "It's not as though they can *hide*."

"Maybe *Brahma*'s pulling the same stunt—your gravity whatever."

"Gravity gauge." *Destiny* was about to make an unscheduled and unannounced burn that put the American spacecraft closer to Keanu than its Coalition challenger. "The wind is at your back, your opponent is in front of you. For him to attack, he's got to tack against the wind." Pogo still seemed unconvinced. "Didn't you ever read Horatio Hornblower? Where they mention weather gauge?"

"I'm not a big nautical fan, in case you haven't noticed." Pogo was fond of referring to astronauts with Navy backgrounds as *pukes*.

"Okay, then . . . it's like getting on their six." That was a fighter pilot term for getting behind—in the six o'clock position—an opponent.

Now Pogo smiled. "Does that mean we can take a shot at them?"

"Don't get any ideas," Zack said, not wishing to broach that particular subject at this time. "Besides, they can't pull the same stunt. *Brahma*'s too limited in propellant and they're too nervous about guidance." The Coalition craft relied on Indian and Russian space tracking systems that were far less capable than the NASA Deep Space Network available to *Destiny*. "Just keep looking," he told Pogo, then floated back up to the main control panel.

The *Destiny* cabin had twice the interior volume of the Apollo spacecraft, which still wasn't much, especially with the tangle of cables and the two bulky EVA suits.

"Gotcha!" Pogo used a touchpad to slide a cursor over the image, clicking to send the image to Zack's screen. Only then did the pilot turn his head and smile crookedly. "RCS plume. Dumb bastards." The Air Force astronaut's contempt for the competing vessel, its crew, and its politics was well known. It had almost cost him a seat on this mission.

"Everybody's got to tweak their traj," Zack said. He actually sympathized with *Brahma* commander Taj Radhakrishnan and his crew. An experienced flight control team would *not* need to fire reaction control jets—RCS—at this stage. But the Coalition had flown only three piloted missions total, and this was the first beyond low Earth orbit. Its control team, based in Bangalore, was naturally cautious.

Now the fuzzy image of *Brahma* appeared on Zack's screen, trajectory figures filling a window. "Houston, *Destiny*, through Channel B," Zack said, touching the send button on his headset. Without waiting for an acknowledgment, he added, "We have *Brahma* in the scope." *Destiny*'s 440,000-kilometer distance caused a four-second lag for each end of a conversation. That was going to be increasingly annoying.

Sure enough, mission director Shane Weldon's reply was out of sync. "Go ahead, *Destiny*." It took several seconds to give Houston the information that *Brahma* had been spotted, and for Houston to confirm that the burn was still go.

Zack relinquished the left-hand pilot seat, then floated down to the telescope. To hell with *Brahma* . . . what he wanted to look at was Near-Earth Object Keanu.

Three years ago, a pair of amateur astronomers—one in Australia, the other in South Africa—had spotted a bright Near-Earth Object high in the southern sky . . . literally over the South Pole.

The NEO was designated X2016 K1—an unknown ("X") body sighted in the first half of July 2016—but, to the horror of professional astronomers, quickly became known by its more popular name, Keanu, after the actor who had played the iconic Neo in the *Matrix* movies.

Within days, as Keanu's size (more than a hundred kilometers in diameter) and trajectory (originating in the constellation Octans and heading sunward, passing close to Earth in October 2019) became clear, imaginative elements in the space community began to talk about a crewed mission to the NEO. A spacecraft already existed: NASA's *Destiny*, designed for flights beyond earth orbit, to the Moon and Mars—and to Near-Earth Objects.

But with budgets tight and benefits uncertain—what would a crewed mission learn that a fleet of uncrewed probes couldn't discover for a tenth the cost?—enthusiasm for the idea faded away as Keanu grew in brightness in the southern sky.

Until the Russian-Indian-Brazilian Coalition announced that it was diverting its first planned lunar landing mission to Keanu. The first flag planted on its rocky, snowy surface would not be the Stars and Stripes.

That announcement triggered a frantic amount of replanning by NASA comparable to its fabled 1968 decision to send *Apollo 8* around the Moon ahead of the Soviets. "It's going to be like NASCAR," Pogo Downey liked to say. "Only this time we might actually be swapping paint."

In search of an edge, NASA's great minds had cooked up several disinformation gambits. At this moment, the two other astronauts in Zack's crew, Tea Nowinski and Yvonne Hall, were talking on the open loop, visual and audio of their preparations from the *Venture* lander being fed through the NASA Deep Space Network. Meanwhile, Zack and Pogo did their dirty work on an encrypted loop transmitted via military satellites.

The last-minute gravity gauge prank had been forced on the *Destiny* crew when bad weather at the Cape allowed *Brahma* to launch a day ahead of them.

Much as he enjoyed the challenge of spoofing the Brahmans, it killed Zack to be looking for another spacecraft instead of the hundred-kilometer-wide bulk of Keanu, now less than two thousand kilometers away.

And invisible! Both *Destiny* and *Brahma* were approaching Keanu's dark side, just as several of the early Apollo missions had sneaked up on the Moon—the crew hadn't even seen the cratered surface until moments before making the burn that put them into lunar orbit.

If the gravity gauge maneuver echoed the age of sail, so did this night-side approach . . . it was like sailing toward a rocky coast on a moonless night in fog . . . undeniably dangerous.

And ten times as complicated. Zack was not a specialist in orbital dynamics, but he knew enough about the mind-boggling complexities of the intercept to make his head hurt.

Destiny and *Brahma* were falling toward Keanu a thousand kilometers and twenty-four important hours apart. Without this added burn, *Destiny* would arrive a day later.

Arrive where? Keanu was actually approaching Earth from below, almost at a right angle to the plane of the ecliptic, where most planets of the solar system orbited. Both *Destiny-Venture* and *Brahma* had had to expend extra fuel to climb away from Earth's equator toward a point where Keanu *would be* in 4.5 days.

Complicating matters further, *Destiny-Venture* was now slowing down after having been flung out of Earth orbit by the powerful upper stage of its *Saturn VII* launcher.

And Keanu itself was speeding up as it fell toward its closest approach to Earth, passing just outside the orbit of the Moon—the brightest thing humans had ever seen in their night sky.

In order to sneak past *Brahma*, *Destiny* had to essentially hit the brakes . . . to fire *Venture*'s engines directly into the path of flight. The burn would cause the vehicle to take up a lower orbit around Earth, where it would then be going much faster than *Brahma*.

The cost in fuel was immense, eating up six thousand of the vehicle's nine thousand kilograms of gas. *Destiny-Venture* would have zero margins for error in landing or eventual liftoff. But if it went as planned, twenty-four hours from now, Zack's crew would be on the surface of Keanu in time to welcome the crew of *Brahma* as they landed.

At which point, Zack fervently hoped, everyone's attention would turn to exploration of this unique body and the arguments would be over its nature and not issues as pointless as who got there first.

"Thirty minutes," Pogo announced, startling Zack out of a momentary reverie—or nap. One more like that, and he would have to hit the medical kit for Dexedrine.

He blinked and took another look into the scope. The fuzzy white blob that was *Brahma* seemed to swell, then fade in brightness. The Coalition vehicle was cylindrical, so even if rotating it shouldn't be waxing and waning. "Pogo, do you see a hint of a halo around *Brahma*?"

"Sorry, got a different screen up at the moment—"

"How's the prank coming?" Yvonne Hall emerged from the docking tunnel between *Venture* and *Destiny* in her heavy white EVA suit, minus the helmet.

"Careful!" Zack said. "We've got half a dozen different mikes going." He waggled both hands with index fingers extended. "You never know what's going to get fed where."

Yvonne's eyes went wide. An African American engineer who had worked with the *Saturn* launch team at the Cape, she was clearly not used to being corrected. It was another reminder to Zack that Yvonne, Patrick, and even Tea were not originally Zack's crew.

"Hey, sports fans." Tea joined them, a candy bar and a bag of trail mix in hand. Blond, athletic, the all-American girl, she was one of those types found—and, Zack suspected, deliberately selected by NASA—in every astronaut group, the big sister who wants everyone to play nicely. "Do we need any snacks before the burn?"

Yvonne took the trail mix and pulled herself toward Pogo's floating EVA suit. "Any time you're ready to don your armor, Colonel Downey . . ."

Meanwhile Tea launched a candy bar at Zack. "Here," she said. "Take a bite and get dressed."

Zack allowed Tea to literally tow him and his suit through the access tunnel. He tucked and tumbled, orienting himself properly inside *Venture*'s cabin, a cylinder with a control panel and windows at the front end, and an airlock hatch on the back. "What's our comm situation?"

"You'll love this." Tea smiled and touched a button on the panel, allowing Zack to hear NASA's public affairs commentator. *"—Due to tracking constraints at the Australian site, direct communications with Destiny-7 will be unavailable for the next fifteen minutes. The crew is in no danger and will accomplish the burn as scheduled—"*

"Those guys are good," Zack said.

"We're all good, baby. And you'll be better if you get some rest." Tea knew he was operating without sleep.

"So now you're my nurse?"

"Just noticing that you're getting a little scope-locked." This was a term from Houston mission control, when some engineer would work a problem to death, ignoring food, sleep, and common sense.

But Tea knew better than to prolong the argument. She also had to concentrate on the tricky business of helping Zack into his EVA suit, a process that required gymnastic flexibility and brute strength and could rarely be accomplished in less than ten minutes. "And you're all buttoned up."

"T minus fifteen," Pogo called from the other side of the tunnel. "Are we gonna do this gauge thing or what?"

It was only when strapped to his couch in the second row next to Yvonne, behind the two occupied by Pogo, the actual pilot, and Tea, the flight engineer, that Zack allowed himself to relax.

Tea reached a hand back and took his, squeezing it. A simple gesture that triggered tears . . . partly from fatigue, partly from tension, but mostly from the memory of the strange events that had put him in this place, at this time. The events of two years past—

Where was Rachel now? Was his daughter watching *Destiny*'s flight from mission control? What was she thinking about her father? Zack could picture the look on her face, the unique mixture of love and exasperation. More of the latter than the former. He could almost hear her the way she would stretch the word *Daddy* across three syllables.

"Five minutes," Pogo said.

"How close are we?" Tea said. "I'm the navigator and I have a right to know."

"Fourteen hundred clicks from Keanu, give or take a few."

The four screens that dominated the *Destiny* cockpit were alive with spacecraft systems data, range and rate, timelines, numbers, images.

They would do this burn in the dark, without talking to Houston through either the open network or the encrypted one. Mission control wasn't worried about being overheard . . . but the Coalition had systems capable of detecting raw communications traffic, and even if the other side couldn't decrypt a message, just the heavy traffic load might give the game away.

"One minute," Pogo said.

The cockpit was now completely silent except for the hiss and thump of oxygen pumps.

The figures on the panel ran to zero.

Zack and the others heard a thump and felt themselves pressed forward into their straps, their only experience of gravity since launching from low Earth orbit.

"Thirty seconds," Pogo said. "Looking good."

Only now did Zack allow himself the luxury of looking ahead. Humans had been to the Moon eight times now, half a dozen during Apollo, two more since.

He and his crew would be the first to land on another body entirely . . . one that hadn't even been discovered until three years ago. It would have lower gravity, but water in the form of ancient snow and ice—

"Ninety seconds. Still good."

And what else? From years of studying Keanu, he knew that it was pockmarked with deep craters and vents that occasionally spurted geysers of steam. Their landing target would be next to one such feature known as Vesuvius Vent.

It would be the adventure of a lifetime, of several lifetimes . . . if the equipment worked.

And if politics didn't interfere.

"Shutdown!" Pogo called. "Right on time, three minutes, sixteen seconds!"

It was Zack's job to make the call. "Houston, commander through Channel B," Zack said. "Burn complete, on time."

It took five seconds to hear, "We copy that, *Destiny*," from Weldon in mission control. "You are good to go. We'll be sending you updated figures ASAP."

Laughing nervously, the crew began to unstrap.

Then Tea said, "Oh my gosh, look at that."

Even hardened Pogo Downey gasped. Outside *Destiny*'s three forward windows, Keanu's daylight side rose, its snowy, rocky surface flowing past below them. Zack thought, *It's like hang gliding over Iceland—*

"Zack," Pogo said, refocused on the controls. "Houston's giving us an update on *Brahma*."

Zack felt a surge of alarm. "Did they make a burn, too?"

"No. Pretty pictures."

Zack looked at the image on the control panel.

It showed the cylindrical *Brahma*—the height of a six-story building—half in shadow.

And sporting what looked like a *missile* attached to one side. "What the fuck is that?" Yvonne said.

"More to the point," Tea said, "how come we didn't see it before now?"

"They might not have deployed it before leaving Earth orbit," Zack said.

"And God forbid we should actually be looking at them when they were close," Pogo snapped. He was convinced that America routinely underestimated its rivals.

As Zack tried to comprehend the startling but real possibility that he could be in a space war, he heard Weldon's voice in his earphones. "Shane for Zack, Channel B. Did you notice anything funny about your burn?"

The phrasing was highly unusual, especially for Weldon, who was the most precise communicator in space history. *Funny* was not a word he would normally use. Tea and Patrick exchanged worried glances.

"What you do mean by *funny*, Houston?" Zack said, looking at Yvonne for support.

She gestured to the displays, nodding vigorously. "It was on time, proper orientation. If we had champagne, we'd pop the cork."

There was a moment of relative silence . . . the carrier wave hissing. Finally, Weldon said, "DSN noted an anomaly."

Anomaly? What the hell would the big dishes in Goldstone or Australia see that *Destiny* herself wouldn't see?

"Don't keep us guessing, Houston."

"There was a major eruption on Keanu."

Hearing this, knowing his crew was listening, too, Zack said, "Keanu's been venting periodically since we started watching." He was proud of himself for not adding, *That's why we wanted to land here, assholes.*

"This was substantially larger. Note the time hack."

"What the fuck is he talking about, the time hack?" Pogo snapped, clearly rattled. Not that it took much to set him off.

Zack looked at the figure uploaded from Houston. "Keanu started venting at 74:15.28 MET." Feeling a bit like a doctor delivering bad news to a patient's loved ones, he waited for the reaction.

"That was our burn time," Tea said, her eyes as wide as a six-year-old's.

"So some volcano on Keanu farted at the same moment, so what?" Pogo said. "The universe is full of coincidences."

"The same *second*?" Yvonne said.

The burly Air Force pilot loomed over her. "What are you saying?"

"Something on Keanu reacted to our burn."

Pogo's face went red. "Like what? Some alien anti-aircraft system?

What are you going to hit with steam?" He pushed himself as far away from Yvonne as he could get without actually leaving *Destiny*.

Yvonne turned to Zack and Tea. "This *is* significant, isn't it? I'm not crazy."

"You're not crazy," Zack said. If she was, then he was, too. He was resisting a connection between their burn and the venting on Keanu, but only in the sense that a cancer patient is reluctant to accept a fatal diagnosis: He had experienced a sickening chill the moment he heard the time of the event, as if his body and his unconscious mind were simply better informed than his intellect.

Now his cool, rational, scientific, astronomically astute intellect had had time to do the math:

Destiny was hours away from beating *Brahma* to the first landing on a Near-Earth Object.

And they had no idea what they were going to find there.

The prospect was as terrifying as it was exciting.

Far below the solar plane, at a distance of 1.4 million kilometers—closer than the orbit of the planet Saturn—Keanu now becomes visible to even the most low-powered Earth-based telescopes, first as a point of light, then, at higher power, as a resolvable disk. Which is to say, a definable body.

One year after its discovery, Keanu's nature is still the subject of a violent debate in the astronomical community . . . Is it a comet? A planetesimal? A visitor from the Oort Cloud or Kuiper Belt? Most astronomers agree that Keanu originated far beyond our solar system. . . .

NEOMISSION.COM, JUNE 20, 2017

TWO YEARS AGO

God, it's hot.

It wasn't even ten A.M. on this June morning, and already the temperature on the Space Coast was ninety and climbing. Megan Stewart's hair—normally straight—was frizzed into a Bride of Frankenstein do. Under her arms, behind her knees, everywhere she could be damp, she was. Even the backs of her bare thighs had somehow stuck to the fabric of the car seat.

It's like being in a broiler. The metaphor was tired—she needed something punchier if she was going to use it for her documentary.

She adjusted her Sennheiser webset. Five years old, the digital camera and mikes were already obsolete yet retained ease of use while still producing webcast-quality images. She looked directly at her twelve-year-old daughter in the backseat. "Rachel, how would you describe the weather here today?"

The girl blinked her brown eyes, making the now-familiar adjustment back to real time from her own Slate-based reverie. "Better than Houston."

"Really? How?"

"Florida's just as hot as Texas, but it doesn't smell as bad." Rachel's whole lifetime had been blogged by Megan for one site or another, from New Baby to Terrible2s to TweenLife and now for Megan's half-hour documentary for GoogleSpace. She had grown skilled at uttering answers that were just good enough.

Behind the wheel, Harley Drake laughed. "Why don't you just call it 'The Sixth Circle of Hell'?"

"I presume that's the one with fire."

"Yes, as opposed to blood or mud or being pummeled with heavy objects." He smiled. "It's for heretics."

"For a guy who calls himself a space cowboy, that's a lot of literary reference." Megan made sure to apply an exaggerated version of the Houston accent she had been absorbing over the past nine years. It was also a joke: Drake was an astronaut, but he had a master's in literature to go with four engineering and science degrees. Unlike Megan, he had likely read Dante's *Inferno*. Probably in the original Latin.

"'I am large, I contain multitudes.'"

"Which is a quote from Whitman. Thank you, astronaut Drake. God, this is uncomfortable." Megan killed the feed and removed the webset so she could swipe a tissue across her face.

Rachel said, "Why are all these people here so early? The launch isn't until next week."

Megan looked out the passenger side window of the Tesla. The southbound traffic on Highway 95 from the house in Nova Villas through the grimmer stretches of Titusville toward the 407 interchange—never easy—was truly terrible today, thanks to the addition of several thousand cars, pickups, and RVs heading the same direction, or parked on the shoulders.

"They want a good view," Harley said. "And a launch is an excuse for a party. It beats tailgating at a football game."

"Well, the view from here isn't actually very good, is it?" Rachel said. She disliked Harley so thoroughly she took every opportunity to contradict him.

It was certainly true that on this June morning, the view toward the twin gantries that hid the giant, three-barreled *Saturn VII* rockets was hazy and indistinct. Still, it made a serviceable backdrop for Megan's doc—which still lacked a title. *My Husband's Going to the Moon* sounded dated, like a filmstrip from the Apollo days. Another challenge.

Megan glanced back at Rachel. She was a small girl, favoring her father, bright, a bit too verbal at times, usually friendly and easy to get along with, though not this trip. Megan was relieved to see that she had momentarily transported herself back to her communal e-space with her Slate. "Ah, the teenage years . . ." she murmured, just loud enough for Harley's ears.

Or so she thought. Rachel's eyes opened and she uttered, "Oooo, the teenage years," in a perfect, contemptuous imitation of Megan.

Ordinarily that sort of challenge would have triggered a corrective response from Megan, but today she let it pass. Rachel's snippiness and her dislike of Harley was caused by fear that her father, Megan's husband, Zachary Stewart, would be killed on *Destiny-5*, the first crewed flight to the Moon of the twenty-first century.

Five years ago, when Zack first rode a Russian *Soyuz* into earth orbit, Rachel had been too young to truly appreciate the dangers. But no longer. Even if being a teenager in the close-knit astronaut community in Houston didn't provide reminders—such as the grown-up neighbor whose father had been killed in the *Challenger* accident—this trip surely had. They were presently driving on a stretch of State Road 405 known as Columbia Boulevard, named for another fatal NASA tragedy. And had Rachel noticed the turnoff to Roger Chaffee Street? He had been one of the Apollo astronauts who died in a fire in 1967—

Just to their right, as they crawled past the airport and slowly approached the causeway across the Banana River, sat the Astronaut Hall of Fame and its space mirror monument—a thin black slab with names of all the astronauts who had died on missions or in training. At last count there were thirty.

Megan had briefly considered a stand-up in front of the mirror, with the twin launchpads in the distance, but not this trip. Not with a terrified Rachel.

Besides, she had her own night sweats and tremors to deal with. She would dream that Zack was falling ten miles to smash on the smooth face of the Atlantic. Or stumbling on some rocky outcrop at Shackleton Crater, his oxygen and life seeping through a tear in his suit. Or incinerating on reentry (the interior of the *Destiny* suddenly going yellow, then red, then disintegrating in agony). Or any of the seemingly endless ways you could be killed in spaceflight.

The true horror would be confronting those last moments and wondering, *Is that it? Is that my life? It went so fast! What did I do?*

"You're getting that look again," Harley said.

"What look is that?"

"You suddenly go silent. Your eyes go wide." He nodded toward her hands. "And you start digging your nails into your palms."

"I'm allowed to show a little stress."

"Agreed. My job is to distract you when you do."

"Even though it doesn't change the situation."

"It only makes it less terrifying. And keeps you from giving your competitors some YouTube moments."

Megan's mouth formed the words *Screw you*. She liked Harley better than most of Zack's often insufferable, smug astronaut colleagues. But not today, not this week. Harley was serving as the Crew Assist and Casualty Officer—the astronaut designated by Zack and Megan to help with mundane matters like travel and housing during the week leading to the *Destiny* launch. It was a rule in NASA: Every crew member selected a CACO.

And so far, Harley had been a great travel agent, finding Megan and Rachel a family friend's condo in Titusville.

But should something go terribly wrong, Harley would also handle the funeral arrangements and insurance questions. He would be the one holding Megan's hand at . . . well, it wouldn't be Arlington. Zack was a civilian.

It would be at a graveside in northern Michigan, in Zack's hometown of Marquette. Megan had managed to wrench that much if-things-go-wrong information from Zack in the past week.

So, now, every time she looked at Harley, she saw herself in black, with smudged face, weak knees. Too bad she wasn't profiling Harley, because she had a title for him: He was her *Escort to Widowhood*.

"Do you believe in God, Harley?"

"Is that a comment on my driving?"

They had crossed the Indian River Lagoon and reached the Orsino gate to KSC proper, where the traffic had eased a bit. Of course, getting through the main gate didn't mean the trip was over; the Kennedy Space Center spread over hundreds of square miles of coastal Florida swamp, with the Indian River to the west and the Atlantic to its east. Harley Drake clearly wanted to cover the route in ten minutes.

"Well, you could slow down a bit," she said. "But the question remains." Megan was used to asking pushy questions. She was spending time with Harley; might as well get to know more about him. He was younger than Zack, though he'd been an astronaut longer and came from a military background. He'd been an Air Force test pilot, so presumably he was conservative, possibly Evangelical, though Megan had never seen evidence of it.

"Meg, I most certainly do not believe there is a white-bearded guy who tells angels what to do, but I'm a superstitious flyboy, and I can tell you from way back in my flight school days—there are guys who just bear the, what the heck is it? The mark of Cain? A black cloud over them. You just know that somewhere, somehow, the universe is going to get them. It won't be their fault, it's just . . . well, God's will. Whoever God is.

"Zack, by the way, is not that guy. The way good old Harley Drake reads the universe, your husband is destined to walk on another planet, then come home to give you a big wet kiss. How about that?"

He had such a goofy smile on his face beneath aviator sunglasses that Megan couldn't help laughing. "Consider me reassured."

But still she wondered. Based on what she'd learned from other astronaut spouses—female and male—Zack was high on the scale of personal openness. Not that the astronaut scale permitted him to be what a normal human would consider emotionally open.

She remembered how painful it had been to get basic burial information out of him—forget theological revelations! Questions about God and an afterlife had never been part of their marriage to begin with . . . pro forma attendance at a church, fine, both agreed on that. Both had been lapsed Catholics, so returning to Mass was easy—and good for Rachel. "At least she'll know what she's rejecting," Zack liked to say.

But get her husband to tell her what he expected to experience after death? Nothing doing.

Not that she had ideas or confidence, either.

Rachel emerged from sleep, or distraction. "God," she said, "how much longer before we get there?"

Harley slowed as traffic stacked up around them. "Here comes the last checkpoint. IDs, everybody!"

"I can't find mine," Rachel said. Then Megan handed the badge to her, trying not to smile. One point to Mom. She'd pay for it—

And here it came: Rachel sat up and announced, "I have to pee." Megan wanted to laugh; it was impossible to actually win against a girl who kept changing the game.

"You can go when we get to the press site."

"I can't wait."

"Do you see where we are?" At the moment they were in a line of cars and buses crowding the final gate into the compound where the gigantic white block of the Vehicle Assembly Building loomed over the launch control center.

"The whole left lane is open!" Rachel said. Sure enough, even Megan could see that the incoming lane was open and appeared to be barricaded at the gate ahead.

"Good point," Harley said. With his famous smiley wave, he backed up the car slightly, then eased into the left lane.

"Hurry," Rachel said, visibly squirming in the seat.

"For God's sake," Megan snapped, unable to help herself. "Are you five years old?"

"You treat me like I am."

"Only when you act this way."

"Which is never—"

"—Let's just stop at the guard shack," Harley said, turning to his left just long enough to miss seeing an official NASA pickup truck approaching at a right angle.

But the truck's grill and cab filled Megan's view for a fraction of a second before all sensation ended in a thunderclap of metal, light, violence, death.

CAPE CANAVERAL—The four astronauts in the crew of *Destiny-5*, the first scheduled piloted lunar landing mission of the 21st century, will hold their final prelaunch press conference at 10:30 A.M. EDT on Tuesday, June 6, 2017.

U.S. reporters may ask questions in person from NASA's Kennedy Space Center.

Non-U.S. reporters are not being accredited at this event.

NASA PUBLIC AFFAIRS

Most of the time, Zack Stewart thought being an astronaut was the best job in the world.

For one thing, he was living a childhood dream. Growing up just outside Marquette on the Upper Peninsula, he had often watched the shimmering northern lights and wanted to touch them, or—if that proved to be impossible—fly beyond them. And in years when the deep snow still fell and temperatures still plummeted below zero in January, he had bundled up in boots and a snowmobile suit and pretended to be an astronaut taking the first steps on a distant planet. It was such a pleasant, compelling fantasy that, well into adulthood, he still felt a thrill whenever he heard the crunch of boots on snow.

Zack had studied planetary astronomy and done research at Berkeley with Geoff Marcy's team, searching for extrasolar planets, refining the existing models of what habitable worlds must be like. From there it was a natural step to NASA—he'd put in his application the moment he learned the agency was planning a return to the Moon. It had taken him a decade and two rejections to reach the astronaut office—"I just plain wore them down," he would say, half-believing it.

He enjoyed the shameless ego boost of answering a casual question—"And what is it you do, Dr. Stewart?"—with, "Oh, I'm an astronaut."

And he had experienced the wonder and stress of Earth orbital flight, twice spending several months aboard the International Space Station, the first voyage beginning with the launch of *Soyuz* from Russia, the second in a *Destiny* much like the one on Pad 39-A right now. There had been lowlights to the missions, of course. During Zack's first stay, he had been forced to have a crew member removed. But the bad memories were lost in the euphoric glow of his first spacewalk, when, during one nightside pass, he had floated at the end of his tether with no communications and no tasks. It was like being in a sensory deprivation tank—but with ten times the danger and intensity.

And far more spiritual than any church service.

The unique visions and sensations to one side, Zack also found pleasure in the day-to-day aspects of the job, even when it meant driving into the Johnson Space Center early every morning to sit through endless meetings or simulations. So what? He was training for a flight to the Moon!

There were, of course, some drawbacks to being an astronaut. Having to stay in shape, for example. Zack had been a pretty fair athlete as a kid, winning letters in track and cross-country. But running had lost its appeal for him in college. Nevertheless, when he applied to NASA, he took it up again, dragging himself two or three miles three times a week, and learned to appreciate the endorphin high, and the pounds that melted from his waistline. But he never liked it.

Then there were the hours and travel, which were tough on his marriage to Megan and his relationship with Rachel. If it wasn't weeks in Arizona, simulating lunar EVAs, it was more time in Nevada working with the rover and various trips to the Cape. Even ordinary work days at the Johnson Space Center started early and ran late.

Another burden was dealing with the e-mails, the phone calls, the autograph hounds, the casual encounters Zack faced whenever he did something as mundane as go to a McDonald's drive-through or rent a car.

And the press conferences.

"Are we ready?" Scott Shawler, a chubby young man who happened to be Kennedy Space Center's public affairs officer for *Destiny-5*, had finished rearranging microphones and running tests on the huge video screen behind the rostrum.

"Will it matter if we say no?" Zack smiled as his crewmates laughed. Shawler was too nervous for humor, however. Zack had to give him a reassuring nod of his head.

Shawler's hands shook, but his voice was strong as he said, "Okay, good morning, everyone! Welcome to the NASA Kennedy Space Center and the L-minus-six event—"

In spite of the preparations, the first words from the PAO disappeared in a squeal of feedback. The reporters in casual polo shirts plastered to their skin by heat and humidity literally flinched. "Christ," Tea Nowinski snapped, not bothering to hide her annoyance, an unusual outburst for the leggy, beautiful astronaut. "Can't you guys handle basic comm?"

"Sorry!" Shawler blushed and reflexively put his hand over the microphone. "Let's try this again . . ." While Shawler and another member of his team rebalanced the audio, Zack looked at the man seated between him and Shawler, an African American man in his late fifties, who was dressed in a dark suit, white shirt, and tie—all too hot and heavy for the circumstances. Gabe Jones overcompensating again. He was the most nakedly emotional official Zack had ever met . . . capable of tearing up at the most basic expression of tragedy, or, his specialty, the wonders of space exploration. So he armored himself with formal clothing.

Shawler was finally ready. "I'd like to introduce Dr. Gabriel Jones, director of the Johnson Space Center . . . chief astronaut Shane Weldon, and astronauts Zack Stewart, Tea Nowinski, Mark Koskinen and Geoff Lyle. Ladies and gentlemen, the crew of *Destiny-5*, the first piloted lunar landing mission of the twenty-first century!"

There was a surprising amount of applause. It swelled to an actual roar and went on so long that Weldon, sitting to Zack's left, tilted his smooth round head and said, "Maybe y'all should quit while you're ahead." Zack had always been bemused by Weldon, who was three years younger but had the manner of a man a decade his senior.

"Ah, as all of you can see," Shawler continued, stammering, "the *Sat-*

urn VII carrying the *Venture* lunar surface activity module is scheduled for launch next Monday afternoon at twelve forty-two P.M. Eastern Daylight Time. Once it has completed one orbit, *Destiny-5* will follow with the second launch. Weather is expected to be good . . ."

As Shawler droned through his boilerplate text, Zack glanced at the three astronauts to his right, all of them wearing the same sky-blue polo-style shirts with the *Destiny-5* logo. The three of them had so much in common—hell, they were all within four years of each other in age—and had spent thousands of hours working as team since their assignment in December 2015. For a moment, however, they looked to Zack like strangers.

He turned to the people facing him . . . the usual mix of veteran reporters and ambitious bloggers, NASA and Cape officials, and, in the back row, family and friends.

But not Megan and Rachel!

Zack's slow boil was interrupted by the first questioner. "For Commander Stewart—why is *Destiny* important? Why bother going back to the Moon?"

The groans from the regular beat reporters gave Zack time to turn to Shawler.

"Scott, can you bring up the Goddard website?" Shawler was happy to show that he was, indeed, competent, clicking away at his laptop to change the image on the large screen behind the podium.

A white blob appeared on a black background.

"This is Keanu, our newest Near-Earth Object," Zack said. "If you look at the site, you'll see that Keanu is almost a billion and a half kilometers out from the Sun, and heading in fast. Earth will be in its sights twenty-seven months from now.

"Our best calculations show that Keanu will *not* hit Earth, which is good, because it's around a hundred kilometers in diameter and the devastation its impact would cause would kill everything larger than a bacterium."

He turned to Jones, who was, as expected, blinking back tears of wonder at the thought of such horror and tragedy. "We're going to dodge the

Keanu bullet, but one of these days we *will* spot an object we can't dodge. And when that happens, we need to be prepared two ways:

"First, we need to know how to operate around and on NEOs, in case we can do something to change their trajectory. Second, and slightly more important, the human race needs to have a permanent presence on another world, a pocket of humanity that can go on. If a NEO like Keanu hits Earth someday, seven-point-something billion people are gone! Wouldn't we be happier knowing that the human race won't vanish from the universe like the dinosaurs?"

The press conference had settled into the expected questions about *Venture*'s pressurized rover and the likelihood of discovering ice at Shackleton Crater when an Indian man of about forty stood up and asked, "What do you say to your Indian and Russian friends who fear a possible American claim to Shackleton as the first step toward interplanetary *manifest destiny*?"

It was Taj! Taj Radhakrishnan, an Indian "vyomanaut" (the Indian space program insisted on its indigenous terminology) who had been part of Zack's space station team. Zack had sent pro forma invites to all three of the internationals, but given the rising tensions between the United States and the new coalition of Russia and India, he hadn't expected any to actually show up, least of all Taj.

And now here he was—with his fourteen-year-old son, Pav, sitting next to him, obviously unhappy—asking the question half the world wanted asked. Zack's answer: "The plaque on *Venture* says, 'We come in peace for all mankind.'"

"So it does. But what happens when our *Brahma* lands at Shackleton?"

"If we happen to be home, we'll bring over a cup of sugar."

Taj smiled and made a perfect bow. "As long as you don't make us pass through an immigration check. I just had the experience at Orlando. It was humiliating in the extreme."

There were scattered boos from the press and onlookers—those who didn't recognize Taj. Shawler stepped forward. "If that concludes the, uh, questions, I want to have a few words from Gabriel Jones—"

The JSC chief started into one of his standard sound bites as a member of the KSC security team vaulted onto the stage and began talking to Scott Shawler.

"What now?" Tea asked, close to whispering.

Zack saw the look on Scott Shawler's face as the security guard delivered a message. So did Mark Koskinen. "Somebody's getting bad news."

Then Zack saw Shawler looking directly at *him*.

KEANU APPROACH: TERMINAL PHASE

"Houston, we're at fifteen thousand . . . coming up on powered-descent
initiation in five."

Zack waited for Shane Weldon's reply as he stood—tethered, since
Venture was still in microgravity—at the forward control panel next to
Pogo. He was still in his helmet, wearing gloves, feeling like a child bun-
dled up for a day in deep snow.

Houston and Weldon seemed more remote than ever, their signal
hissing and breaking up. "Copy that, *Venture* . . . still go for . . . descent at
78:15:13 MET." Mission elapsed time . . . had it really been seventy-eight
hours since the *Saturn VII* lit up, rattling Zack and his crew into Earth
orbit?

Tea and Yvonne were strapped in directly behind, but effectively invisible and, for the moment, silent.

The last word from mission control on that subject had been, "We've
got the Home Team on it," the Home Team being a panel of Keanu specialists led by Harley Drake, who was no doubt phoning and e-mailing
all over the world, contacting a broad spectrum of experts on NEOs and
venting.

And what was Rachel thinking? What had she heard? Zack had not
spoken to his daughter since launch. They had exchanged text messages—
her preferred means of communication—during the first sixty hours.

Nothing since then. She had sent them; he could see a queue in his personal message file. But he had had no time to compose even a two-word reply.

Well, he would send her the first message from the surface of Keanu.

Which was now closer than ever. They were under fifteen thousand meters altitude, roughly the same as an airliner crossing the United States. Three minutes until the twin RL-10 engines on *Venture* lit up, slowing the vehicle enough to drop out of orbit and head for touchdown—

"Houston, from *Venture*. Any word on our Coalition neighbors?"

"*Venture*," Weldon said, after more than the usual lag, "*Brahma* is in a lower, more circular orbit . . . plane diverges from yours . . . twenty degrees. Data coming to you."

The gravity gauge burn had put the combined *Destiny-Venture* vehicle in a wide, looping orbit around the NEO. Within twenty minutes, on Houston's orders (encouraged no doubt by Tea's report), Zack was injected with a sedative, zipped into a sleeping bag, and stashed in the *Venture* airlock. While he dozed, Patrick, Yvonne, and Tea completed the tedious work of configuring *Destiny* for a week—or a month—of uncrewed autonomous flight while transferring gear, food, water, and other supplies into the lander.

Zack had been awakened for the separation maneuver, which Tea and Yvonne handled, half an hour ahead of the terminal burn. *Destiny* had been left behind, and now the four-legged collection of tanks that was *Venture* flew on its own.

Meanwhile, the crew of *Brahma* completed its burn, winding up in a relatively circular orbit that had the advantage of allowing them more frequent landing opportunities. *Destiny*'s crew, in going for broke with the gravity gauge and jumping to a far more eccentric orbit, would have the first chance to touch down . . . but if unable to start descent this go-around, would have to wait another day.

While Brahma would swoop in ahead of them. And it would be Zack's old space station comrade, the excitable-yet-capable Taj, who would take the first steps on Keanu.

"Three minutes," Zack said. "Kids, you okay in the backseat?"

"Yes." "Fine." Both voices were so clipped and tense that Zack could not tell them apart.

"Okay, there's the *Brahma* data," Pogo said, pointing a thick gloved finger at the display. It showed an image of the big ball that was Keanu and two rotating planes representing the orbits of the two spacecraft, along with columns of constantly changing figures.

"Houston on Channel B," Zack said, clicking to the encrypted link. "Did you or the Home Team happen to note one of those venting episodes when *Brahma* did its burn?"

"Now there's a good question," Pogo said.

The lag stretched beyond the normal six seconds. Finally a new voice came on the line. "Zack, Harley. The answer is *no* . . . and *yes*—"

"Fucking A!" Yvonne blurted, clearly annoyed. Zack wanted to smile. Pogo Downey had the classic military mind—get 'er done, give me an answer. Yvonne, an engineer by training, had even less appetite for nuance.

But even Tea Nowinski, usually the mediator, the finder of middle ground in any group, joined the chorus. "What's that supposed to mean?"

"Okay, everyone!" Zack used the command voice. "Hey, Harley . . . interesting news." He wondered if the sarcasm traveled across the 440,000-kilometer distance. "Care to elaborate?"

"We can tell you this much, my man. There has been a second eruption on Keanu, but it took place approximately half an hour *after Brahma*'s burn. There was no apparent commonality. In fact, there has been a third event since then."

Zack found that news fascinating—and soothing. "So it's possible the first venting was a coincidence? That we're just looking at some kind of volcanism." Keanu had been venting ever since it was first observed—indeed, *Venture* and *Brahma* were both targeted to the same spot on Keanu's surface, a circular crater nicknamed Vesuvius that had been the source of several plumes of steam over the past two years.

Harley confirmed Zack's thinking. "So far that's the most logical theory."

"Yeah, well," Yvonne said, "the other theories are freaky . . ."

"Good to know," Zack radioed. "We'll keep our eyes open." He set aside the question of what—if anything—was strange about Keanu to wonder instead what *Brahma* would do when it arrived. What was that missile-like thing it carried? It didn't appear in the *Brahma* schematics available on the Web.

"*Venture*, we show one minute to PDI," Weldon said from Houston. "Everything's looking good from here."

"Is it okay if I say that I can't fucking believe we're still going to land?" Tea said.

In spite of the apparent anger, the whole exchange was pro forma, its very familiarity allowing the crew to feel as though they were back in their Houston simulator and not attempting the first piloted landing on a Near-Earth Object.

It was ten times the challenge faced by Armstrong and Aldrin on the first lunar landing—yes, *Venture* had far better guidance systems, but the Apollo crew had been aiming for a world that had always been in the human mind . . . had been studied for centuries, and in the years prior to their launch, been probed a dozen times.

Keanu had been unknown until three years ago. It had since been the subject of exactly two distant flyby space probes. (There wasn't a government or corporation on Earth capable of conceiving, funding, building, and launching a probe to Keanu in less than five years, by which time the NEO would be long past its closest encounter and heading back into the interstellar darkness from which it came.)

Zack Stewart's *Destiny-7* and *Venture* crew would indeed make the first human contact with this world.

"Thirty seconds," Pogo said.

It didn't seem to take that long for the numbers to reach zero. With a rumble that Zack found startling—he had never experienced a burn from the *Venture* cabin—the twin RL-10s ignited, ramping up from twenty percent of thrust to a full one hundred.

Zack was technically the commander of the *Destiny-7* mission, something he found especially absurd at the moment. Hot pilot Pogo Downey was flying this landing.

Of course, Pogo wasn't actually flying it yet. True, hundreds of hours of simulations had prepared him to manually steer *Venture* to a flat spot on the surface of the Moon . . . and several dozen hasty, postdecision sims had concentrated on the challenges of accomplishing the same thing in Keanu's lesser gravity.

But *Venture*'s incredibly sophisticated and rugged guidance system was really making the decisions, its radar pinging the surface of Keanu, recording range and rate of descent, then making the delicate adjustments in the tilt of the engines, whose combined axis of thrust—tweaked by the smaller reaction control jets spaced around *Venture*'s exterior—determined where the vehicle was going.

Two booms rattled the cabin. "RCS," Zack said quickly. He could actually hear the startled gasps of Tea and Yvonne on the communications loops.

He grinned to himself. He hadn't been selected as commander for his ability with a joystick. As much as he joked about Tea's "big sister" mentality, he had an even more acute case of wanting everyone to be happy. This personality trait had guided his professional life—he couldn't count the number of people with whom he'd nursed violent disagreements who took his low-key assents and gentle arguments as signs of genuine friendship. If he had to work late hours, fine. If an apology was called for, he would make it. If being charming was what a situation required, he could be very charming.

And, if the greater good could be served by a display of temper, he could boil over with the best of them.

After his second space station tour, one of the NASA doctors had told Zack he rated highest among every astronaut studied in one key interpersonal factor: not technical skills (though his were superior) or even emotional control (though he obviously stayed on an even keel).

He simply *played well with others*. Shared his toys. Helped pick up. Did more than his portion of dirty jobs.

Making the first landing on Keanu was, in many ways, a dirty job. Training time was short, danger was great, the crew had been shuffled at the last minute. And there was a good chance of conflict with the *Brahma* crew.

NASA wanted the people of Earth to be happy. And who better to keep them that way than Zachary Stewart? Not only was he an experienced space flier who had spent two years training on *Destiny-Venture*, he happened to be the astronaut office specialist in all matters Keanu. Best of all, he actually knew—and liked!—the rival *Brahma* commander.

"Coming up on pitchover," Pogo said, the first words he'd uttered since the start of powered descent.

Although there was no sense of motion—nothing like the banking of an aircraft—the view out the forward window changed, black sky giving way to Keanu's gray-and-white horizon.

It was as if *Venture* had clambered to its feet—which, in technical terms, it had. Within moments they were heads up, *plus Z* in NASA terms.

"What's that?" Pogo said.

Since burning into orbit around Keanu, *Destiny-Venture* had made two low passes, but both on the night side, where visibility was almost non-existent. Now, for the landing, *Venture* was heading toward the sun-lit side, like a transatlantic airliner flying toward the European dawn.

Only this dawn showed a *giant geyser flaring thousands of feet* into the black sky. Unaffected by winds—Keanu had no atmosphere—it looked like a perfect tornado funnel out of Zack's childhood nightmares.

He had to force himself to say, "Houston, are you seeing what we're seeing?"

Houston was receiving the same image, of course, from *Venture*'s cameras, but controllers wouldn't experience the same awe and majesty . . . or barely contained terror.

"I hope that's not from Vesuvius," Zack said, and immediately saw the answer to his own question, as the plume slid off to the left—clearly from another vent, which Weldon calmly confirmed.

As Buzz Aldrin had, while Neil Armstrong flew the first lunar landing, Zack concentrated on his job as commentator. "Okay, Pogo, there's three hundred, down at twenty." Three hundred meters altitude, down at twenty meters per second, both figures diminishing at different rates. "The field below looks smooth." They could see their landing zone from the forward windows, whose lower halves were angled inward. But glare from Keanu's snow and ice washed out the view—better data was coming from a radar image in the head-up display, which showed scattered boulders, though so far none big enough to topple *Venture*.

"Copy that," Pogo said, in a voice that was basically a grunt. Zack had once flown in a NASA T-38 jet that Pogo had to land in bad weather. All during the approach, the pilot had fallen essentially silent, his eyes locked on displays, hand on the stick.

Scope-locked.

Venture's landing on Keanu was different from that dark, threatening approach to Cape Canaveral in a T-38—the computer was still flying the vehicle, something pilots never liked.

"Two hundred, down at fifteen. Horizon looks close." Now, at a height of less than two hundred meters, the NEO still looked *round*! For a moment, Zack had the feeling *Venture* was edging sideways up to a giant white ball. He literally had to shake his head.

His twitching must have been visible even in the thick EVA suit. He felt a reassuring pat on his shoulder. Tea. There was no way to acknowledge it—which she must have known.

"Coming up on one hundred, down at ten," Zack said. "Electing manual."

According to the flight plan, manual landing was the backup mode, but Zack and Pogo had privately decided that human eyeballs and reflexes were better suited to the delicate task of accomplishing a safe landing than a computer. Zack's words gave Pogo the go-ahead to click the "pickle switch," making his hand controller come alive, while also telling Houston that this was a decision, not a systems failure.

"*Venture*, go for manual." Zack knew that Shane Weldon would agree with the decision. Besides, if they were wrong, they were dead.

"Hovering," Pogo said, just as Zack was about to note that *Venture* was at forty meters with zero rate of descent. Instead he said, "Will you look at that!"

Twice as far across as a football field, Vesuvius Vent lay in front of them, a big black hole in the ground, its bottom lost in shadows.

"Do I turn on the windshield wipers?" Pogo said, stunning Zack—

and no doubt millions of people listening, for years to come—with his coolness.

"Just set her down," Zack said, entirely unnecessarily. "Fuel at eleven percent." They'd burned almost ninety percent of *Venture*'s liquid hydrogen and oxygen, but had enough for a safe landing. (Fuel for takeoff was in separate tanks and fed a separate ascent engine.)

Gently, the snowy field rose to greet them. Zack could see individual rocks now—again, none tall enough to be worrisome.

"Ten meters." He wasn't bothering with rate of descent now. "Making some steam!" The invisible but hot four-lobed plume of *Venture*'s engines was vaporizing Keanu surface snow. Wisps of vapor rose, reminding Zack of Lake Superior on a winter day.

"Shutdown," Patrick announced, as the RL-10s quit abruptly, and the shuddering and vibration inside *Venture* ceased.

"Contact!" The traditional blue indicator lit—

—Then went dark. "Shit!" Patrick said.

Zack could feel it in his stomach, the roller-coaster sensation. "We're bouncing!"

Suddenly they were shaken by three quick booms—Pogo manually firing the small reaction control rockets spaced around the *Venture* cabin. "Keep her upright!" Zack shouted.

"Coming down again—"

Zack watched *Venture*'s squat, four-legged shadow rushing to meet them. There went the contact light—

"Goddammit!" They bounced again.

"It's lower this time," Zack said, almost convinced himself.

Sure enough, this time *Venture* settled and slid.

And stopped, safely upright on the surface of Keanu, fifty meters from the well-defined edge of Vesuvius Vent.

"Houston, Vesuvius Base here—*Venture* is on the surface and, ah, tied down."

He patted Pogo on the forearm. He could see his pilot grinning, making a quick sign of the cross. Only now did Tea and Yvonne speak, letting out whoops of relief.

Then Weldon finally responded. "*Venture*, Houston. As they said the first time, you've got a bunch of people about to turn blue here. Next time, drop the anchor."

Zack pointed to Pogo, who said, "Copy that, Houston. Tell ops I want credit for three landings."

For the next few minutes, they ran through the postlanding checklist, making sure not only the two main engines but the RCSs were shut down, that *Venture* was level and not settling into a pool of water now turning back to ice. "I think we've got rock under the pads," Yvonne said. "That's a good thing."

They also removed helmets and gloves, though two of them would be donning them again for the first steps on Keanu.

Zack stepped away from forward position and slipped past Tea and Yvonne. The *Venture* cabin was cramped—it would be very close quarters for the weeklong mission—but designed to be divided in two.

He pulled the privacy curtain, creating a vague "room." With his gloves off, he reached for the keyboard to tap out a private message to Rachel: MADE IT—INFLIGHT MOVIE TERRIBLE BUT HAD A WINDOW SEAT XOXO DAD.

He hit send. Then the tension of the past several hours, the past four sleepless days, the past two years, slammed him like a sudden squall. He buried his chin in his chest and shook with sorrow over the miracle of what he'd just lived through . . . the looming challenges ahead of him . . . and the fact that his wife would never know any of it.

Worst of all, that it was her accident that gave him this opportunity. She had to die so he could risk death.

Megan . . . we made it.

When he thought back two years, he still found himself angry—at God, at the universe, at whoever or whatever was in charge. He was crying from sorrow, but also from fury.

"Zack, how are you doing?" It was Tea, having slipped behind the curtain, speaking so quietly that Patrick and Yvonne couldn't hear.

The typical male response would be to shrug off the question with a noncommittal answer. But he and Tea knew each other too well. "Been better."

"It's been a tough road." She patted Zack's arm, then turned away, leaving him in this brief bubble of privacy.

He took a breath and wiped his eyes. They had made the landing; now they had to explore a whole new world.

Oh, yes, and wait for whatever *Brahma* might pull.

Well, he had been able to establish one important scientific principle: Tears don't fall in a NEO's gravity field.

Part Two
"LONG, GENTLE THUNDER"

In the sweat of thy face shalt thou eat bread till thou return to the earth, out of which thou wast taken: for dust thou art, and into dust shalt thou return. GENESIS 3:19

TWO YEARS AGO

Tropical Storm Gregory was approaching the Houston area the day Megan Stewart was buried. The hot rain fell in sheets rather than drops, sweeping across the roiled waters of Clear Lake, obscuring the headquarters building at the Johnson Space Center, turning streets into rivers of slick menace.

It also transformed the procession from St. Bernadette's to the cemetery from a stately ceremony into a ragged retreat. Zack felt a surge of sympathy for the more casual mourners, such as parents from Rachel's school who felt obligated to attend the services but whose empathies would be sorely tested by hot rain blowing directly into their faces.

Not that the ceremony would be underattended. Zack had had no idea how many people would turn up, but St. Bernadette's had been jammed. Not with just local friends, but workers from JSC and people Megan had worked with over the years: editors, producers, even a few characters who had been *subjects* of various profiles and interviews. Zack was not the type to judge the success or failure of a funeral by the number of attendees, but . . . there it was.

Of course, the shocking and public nature of her death contributed. The headline had made every news outlet. *"Moonbound Astronaut's Wife*

Dies in Florida Car Crash." The story had a media throw-weight equal to the overdose death of some Hollywood actress/model/whatever. Megan herself would have approved of the perfect storm of tragedy and notoriety.

None of which was much comfort to Zack, to Rachel, or to Megan's parents.

James Doyle, Megan's father, was a thick, ruddy man of seventy who looked like a career cop with a history of alcohol abuse, but was, in fact, a retired insurance salesman with a history of alcohol abuse. He had summed it up for Zack: "No matter how bad things are going, they can always get worse."

Zack's own parents were not present, though the circumstances—Dad's increasing frailty, Mom's lack of comprehension—were not happy, either.

Now James Doyle sat across from Zack in the limo thoughtfully provided by the funeral home. He was vainly trying to comfort Megan's mother, Diane, a slim, vital woman of Scottish descent in her midsixties, clearly the one Megan took after.

In the seat ahead sat Megan's brother, Scott; his wife; and their seven-year-old son. Their grief was either overwhelmingly numbing or under control. But thank God they were here. The challenge of having to face them, to comfort them and be comforted, had allowed Zack to compartmentalize his own grief and put it aside.

For the moment. He had yet to break down over the loss of lover and wife.

Or his loss of the Moon. He would have traded that adventure, every glorious moment of it, to have Megan back.

As the car rolled down the Gulf Freeway toward Forest Park Cemetery, Zack thought about the casket in the hearse ahead of them.

Megan was inside. Megan with the deep brown eyes and that wicked smile. The athletic yet feminine build. The slim legs that still, after eighteen years of intimacy, had the magic to stir him. The walk that had caught his eye at Berkeley.

The throaty laugh and perfectly pitched voice that, he realized after many years, was the single trait he found most attractive in her.

All stilled and silenced. *Boxed for shipping.*

At the hospital, he had forced himself to look on her battered body. Not as horrible as he feared—the only visible damage a bruise on the right side of her face. But Zack could not believe it was Megan . . . the collection of bone, muscle, and blood on the gurney was too still to be his often-jittery, constantly mobile wife.

Enough. Time to act like an astronaut—don't look back, look at the problem directly in front of you.

Which was Rachel. She had escaped serious physical injury in the crash, but the shock and trauma would be with her forever.

In the first hours afterward, she had acted irrationally, speaking only to demand her Slate and, when Zack failed to produce it (the unit was still in the wreckage of the car, wherever that was), sinking into a sullen stupor that stretched over three days. She went through the motions of her precrash life—she ate, she dressed, she continued to experiment with makeup. There was nothing robotic about it, nothing overt enough to trigger a diagnosis of depression. She was merely . . . subdued. When addressed, she would respond, but usually with a single word.

At least, that was Zack's perspective. How reliable were his judgments?

Zack could not make words come out of his mouth. *Take a breath.* He had to be strong not only for Rachel, but for Megan's parents, who sat across from them, their faces furrowed with concern. He patted his daughter's hand and tried to be calm and businesslike. "Have you got your poem?"

Rachel's eyes widened in apparent horror. Emotion! Zack wanted to cheer. "Oh my God, I think I left it home!"

Before Zack could react, Rachel's face reset to cold and stoic. Her voice, however, was rich with teenage condescension. "Do you *honestly* think I'd screw this up?"

By the time the cortege reached the grave site, the wind and rain had stopped. The cemetery was bathed in a gauzy sunlight that Zack found both peaceful and unusual.

As the casket was being wrestled into place, another car arrived from a different direction.

For an instant, Zack hoped it would be Harley Drake. Harley had been badly injured in the accident, likely crippled, alive but still unconscious. Zack wanted Harley to wake up and be well, because he was his friend—and because he wanted to know what happened.

But out of the car stepped chief astronaut Shane Weldon and Zack's newly former *Destiny-5* crewmates: Tea Nowinski, Geoff Lyle, and Mark Koskinen.

And Zack's replacement, Travis Buell. The new *Destiny-5* commander— Zack's backup these past two years—was a slight, almost scholarly-looking man of forty. Crew trainers used to joke that Zack looked like an Army helicopter pilot, while Buell seemed more professorial. And Zack had been willing to accept the observation. Buell seemed to live in the realm of ideas rather than physical action. In Buell's eyes you could see the light of true belief, whether in the biblical Jehovah, the perfection of the United States of America, or the necessity of making a manually controlled landing at Shackleton as opposed to one flown by computer. These all happened to be issues he and Zack had sparred over for two years. Even at this distance, in these circumstances, Zack could see the righteous fire in the man.

A step behind the *Destiny* crew came Taj Radhakrishnan, dapper in a London Fog while the astronauts wore hideous yellow plastic raincoats over NASA flight suits. Tea broke from the others and went directly to Zack. "Sorry we're late," she said. "They almost waved us off." Of course . . . the storm that marred Megan's funeral would affect air travel in the area, especially for small NASA jets coming into nearby Ellington Field.

They had not seen each other since the press conference. Now Tea wrapped her surprisingly muscular arms around him. "God, Zack, I am so sorry."

On her best days, Tea Nowinski was the astronaut equivalent of a movie star—blond, blue-eyed, terrific figure—the all-American girl. Half the astronauts in the office thought that she and Zack were having an affair. Not that the idea hadn't crossed his mind. They were indeed attracted to each other. But there were several reasons why the relationship remained professional and platonic. For one, the intimacy required of *Destiny* crews destroyed any vestige of romance. As Harley Drake used to say, "Once you've seen your buddy use the toilet on the ceiling, you never look at him the same again." That went double for any male astronaut lusting after a female colleague.

For another, Tea had a history of passionate, troubled involvements with men, including a recent fling with an Air Force weather officer she had met at the Cape. Watching her dial through an unusually broad range of emotions—from pure joy to hysterical fury—thanks to some petty error on the part of Major Right Now was another disincentive.

And, truly, chasing other women was simply not in Zack's personal tool kit, crowded out by genuine affection for his family and the sheer overwhelming, all-consuming responsibility for the first crewed lunar landing of the twenty-first century.

At this moment, Tea was simply a mess . . . runny nose, blotchy skin, streaming tears. "Hey," Zack said, knowing how forced he sounded, "doesn't this violate your quarantine?" The *Destiny-5* crew should have been locked down, isolated from stray germs.

Instead of snapping a profane reply—her normal response to any facetious question—Tea simply blinked back more tears and knelt to embrace Rachel, who was several steps behind Zack, flanked by James and Diane. Zack noted that although Rachel's expression remained blank, her posture snapped rigid. Was that caused by annoyance at being hugged by a relative stranger?

Or annoyance at being hugged by Tea Nowinski? Zack had neither the time nor energy to ponder the matter. Weldon and Koskinen arrived to escort Tea into the crowd while Taj touched a silent hand to Zack's shoulder.

They had shared an amazingly intense experience—two years of training in Houston, Russia, Japan, followed by six months on the space station. Always cordial, always able to work together, but never close. They had shared no personal conversations, rarely socialized . . . until the mission was over. When they saw each other now, there were smiles, jokes, exchanges of family pictures. It was as if the worse the relations between their nations, the better they got along.

Zack and Rachel took their assigned places.

The mourners remained largely silent through the brief graveside prayer by Father Tony, a young Irish-born priest who had come to St. Bernadette's near the space center because he was a spaceflight fanatic. The poor man surely never expected to be presiding at a ceremony quite like this. He was heartfelt, and mercifully brief.

Then Rachel, finally showing some emotion, blinking back tears and swallowing hard, stepped forward. "This was my mom's favorite poem," she announced. "It's by Sara Teasdale."

The mere sound of her voice triggered audible sobbing from some of the attendees. Rachel unfolded her text and, clearly and more grown-up than Zack had ever heard her—dear God, she sounded exactly like Megan, proclaimed:

> *Perhaps if death is kind, and there can be returning,*
> *We will come back to earth some fragrant night,*
> *And take these lanes to find the sea, and bending,*
> *Breathe the same honeysuckle, low and white—*

She stopped and lowered her head—or so it seemed to Zack, who could barely see through his own tears.

> *We will come down at night to these resounding beaches,*
> *And the long, gentle thunder of the sea,*
> *Here for a single hour in the wide starlight,*
> *We shall be happy, for the dead are free.*

Megan's family took a separate car to the Meyer house, where they would help serve as hosts for the wake and reception.

Weldon joined Zack and Rachel in the limo. To Zack's relief—what in God's name were they supposed to say to each other?—Rachel submerged herself in her Slate, leaving Zack to make a first attempt to reboot his former life. "Thanks for letting them come," he said, "they" being the *Destiny-5* astronauts.

"I couldn't have stopped them."

Well, yes, he could have. But Zack appreciated the sentiment. "What's the latest on Harley?"

"He's better than he was."

Even in his grief, Zack was still attuned to the NASA voice, equal parts condescension and denial. "Will he walk again?"

"Doubtful."

Zack felt ill. For someone as physically active as Harley, to face forty, fifty years in a wheelchair? On crutches? Dependent? Impotent? Death might have been more merciful.

Weldon had lapsed into minimal responses. Zack knew that the chief astronaut still felt guilt about the timing and content of their conversation the night of Megan's death, when Zack—having overseen the horrific business of consigning his wife's body to be shipped back to Houston—found Weldon in the hospital waiting room.

"Well," Zack had said, "I'm not in great shape for a flight to the Moon, am I?"

Of course, they both knew that Zack was off *Destiny-5* the moment Scott Shawler delivered the news. "God, Zack. If we were talking about a sixty-day delay, that would be one thing. But you and I know we aren't." A phone call had interrupted the conversation at that point. Zack and Weldon had not been in contact since.

Now Zack knew who his replacement was, not that there had been much doubt. "So you went for Buell."

"He was the backup."

"Well," Zack said, forcing a smile, "it will silence a few of your critics." A vocal minority within the space blogging community had been outraged at the selection of a non–test pilot as commander of the first lunar landing mission of the twenty-first century—forget the fact that landing *Venture* was nothing like any kind of flying, even helicopter flying. And that it would be mostly, if not entirely, automatic.

"You'll get another chance, Zack. Deke's rules still apply." Deke Slayton had been in charge of astronaut crew selections during Gemini and Apollo fifty years earlier, and his style still shaped the way the office was managed. "If you're assigned to a mission and get knocked out by an act of God, you get the next opening." Slayton had come up with the ruling for reasons of his own—he had been scheduled to make the second orbital Mercury flight, the one after John Glenn's, when a medical condition grounded him for a decade. "Just let me know when you're ready."

"If I ever am." Fortunately, as a NASA civil servant, Zack would not have to find a different line of work. There were sixty astronauts in the agency, but only a dozen actually assigned to flight crews. Others filled administrative or support jobs or worked elsewhere in the government. If Zack never stepped inside a simulator again, he would be kept busy. Indeed, before this past week he had wondered about his career after the lunar mission—he'd thought it might be useful to join the team studying new lunar samples for future manufacturing.

Postaccident, it still sounded like a good option, especially as Zack began confronting the practical challenges of life after Megan. He was now a single parent to a tween daughter. He would be solely responsible for her upbringing, for meals, for advice about boys and clothes and periods.

"You don't think so today. Six months from now, you might feel differently. The opportunity will be there."

My first proposed name was "Jurdu." It was from one of the Aboriginal languages and means "Big Sister." But some overly sensitive idiots argued that it was (a) sexist and (b) inaccurate and (c) just because I discovered the frakking thing, who was I to name it?

This moronic dispute consumed weeks. By then people were calling X2016 K1 "Keanu," and that was okay with me. It sounds Aboriginal, and hey, starts with a K like its catalog number.

KEANU DISCOVERER COLIN EDGELY, COMMENT POSTED AT NEOMISSION.COM

KEANU STAY

Even before the switch from the Moon to Keanu, the *Destiny-7* flight plan showed Yvonne as the lead EVA astronaut, meaning that the first steps on the NEO would be made by an African American woman. To NASA's woefully third-rate public affairs apparatus, this was a major public relations boost. Zack knew better—he doubted that one in a thousand Americans could name a single member of the *Destiny-7* crew, much less care which member of what ethnic group took the first crunchy footsteps. But the timeline had been ripped apart and rearranged in so many other ways, he was happy to let this original sequence stand.

Besides, it gave Zack the second steps. Tired as he was, and painfully aware of the stress he would be facing, he still wanted to go outside and stand on the surface. It was a lifelong dream—and he was damned if he would let a minor matter like lack of sleep get in the way.

The same timeline required the crew to rest for six hours. Looking at *Brahma*'s orbit and public announcements, Houston warned the crew that it might issue an early wake-up, but in any case they would have four hours to change out of their suits, eat, make use of the tiny camp toilet, and catch some sleep, either sprawled on the cabin floor (Tea and Pogo) or swinging in hammocks (Yvonne and Zack).

The microscopic gravity made the hammocks almost redundant. With a mask and earplugs (Pogo and Tea would be on watch), Zack felt as though he were floating inside the space station, or in the *Destiny* cabin on the climb uphill.

He was awakened by Tea's voice. "Houston's got imagery of *Brahma*. Take this." She handed him a cup of coffee.

Pogo was already on his feet, on the radio at the forward station as Zack joined him: "—We're seeing it now. And our steely commander is on the case, too."

The image wasn't much better than the one Zack and Pogo had seen from *Destiny*—it still showed the cylindrical *Brahma* half in blinding sunlight, half in shadow. But the resolution was better. "They did a good job processing this," Zack said.

"Your tax dollars at work."

What was clear was a tube mounted on the side of the Coalition spacecraft. "How long do you think that is?" Tea asked over his shoulder. "Five meters?" *Brahma* was twenty meters long; this object appeared to run a quarter its length.

"It isn't the length that worries me," Zack said. "It's the purpose."

Tea grinned. "So you're telling me size doesn't matter?"

"Looks like a Stinger launcher," Pogo said, not hiding his exasperation at Tea's playfulness.

"Houston, *Destiny* on Channel B," Zack said, using the encrypted link. "We're looking and wondering—is this some kind of space bazooka?" The idea was ridiculous, until you remembered that an early Soviet space station had carried an honest-to-God cannon in case of attack by American killer satellites.

While they waited for Houston's answer, Yvonne asked, "Would they actually shoot at us?"

"Shit, yes!" Pogo said. It was a reflexive answer, but, to be fair, in his life he *had* been the target of Coalition weapons.

Yvonne didn't seem to care. "With the whole world watching?"

"Buell claimed the good parts of the Moon with the whole world watching," Pogo insisted. "Besides, they'll claim we shot first—or make it look like an accident."

The radio crackled. Zack held up a hand for silence, grateful for the interruption in the argument. "*Destiny*, Houston on Channel B. The team here has looked at the *Brahma* device, and it seems to be a modification of a Russian Z25 MPAD, a man-portable anti-aircraft device."

"Ah, Houston," Zack said, "any thoughts on what to expect here?"

The crew was silent through the entire eight-second lag. "*Destiny*, stand by."

Tea erupted. "*Stand by?* That's the best they can do?"

"There's not a hell of a lot we *can* do, is there?" Yvonne said.

"It would be nice to know what they expect." Zack said. "Has anyone been in direct contact with their mission control? It's not as though the number's unlisted." Tea laughed at that. "Is the Coalition talking about having a 'defensive system' on *Brahma*? What did they say their deep-space EVA was for?"

"To attach an experiment package," Yvonne said.

"*Destiny*, Houston on Channel B. We're still . . . working the situation." Zack could hear the frustration in the capcom's voice. "Working the situation" meant that it was being discussed all the way to NASA HQ in Washington, undoubtedly with the Pentagon and White House.

Which meant there might never be an answer. Or if it came, it would be late—or wrong.

Zack made up his mind. He muted the radio and said to Yvonne, "Can you get me a direct link to *Brahma*?"

She smiled. "You mean, 'open hailing frequencies, Lieutenant Uhura'?"

Zack laughed out loud. He might have misjudged Yvonne. "Exactly."

She immediately started tapping indicators on the left display, calling up communications options. "Line of sight would be best, but I can work it through their system, I think." *Brahma*'s frequencies were as accessible as their Bangalore-based control center, if you bothered to search.

Pogo turned to Zack. "Why are we doing this?"

"Timing is everything, Colonel. I can't wait for Houston, so I'm going to 'work the situation' from right here."

Before the pilot could protest, Yvonne said, "Got 'em."

Zack took the headset. "*Destiny-7* for *Brahma* . . . Zack Stewart for Taj."

Pogo couldn't look at him. He clearly wanted to stomp off in anger, but there was nowhere to go. Tea noted this, and placed a hand on his arm.

"Hello, *Venture!*" Taj's voice boomed in their headsets. "Congratulations on your landing!"

"Watch that last step—it's a doozy."

"So we saw." Of course! *Brahma* had been able to monitor *Venture's* bouncy landing.

"Seriously, whatever training you did for low-gravity touchdown, it's not enough."

"We'll be vigilant."

"When are you dropping by?" It killed him to sound like a suburban dad making a playdate, but he had to keep this casual. No doubt Taj was under the same pressure.

"We expect to land on the next rev. You should be able to see us."

"We're standing by to offer any assistance." That was probably as close as he could get to saying, *We're not armed!* "Still offering that cup of sugar."

"We look forward to shaking hands in a few hours."

Zack knew he needed to prolong the contact. "It will be good to see you again. The last time was . . . two years ago."

Taj hesitated, causing Zack to wonder if his *Brahma* crewmates were listening, reacting. Then: "This could be a new start for everyone. Take care, my good friend."

The moment the link was broken, Pogo said, "You didn't ask him about the Stinger!"

"It's an open loop, for God's sake! He wouldn't tell me, and even asking would give away the fact that we can see it . . . whatever it is."

"Noted," Pogo said.

"Keanu's only a NEO, but it ought to be large enough for all of us," Zack said.

"Besides," Yvonne added, "it's moving out of range in a few weeks. Why fight over something that's not even going to be here?"

Zack stepped away from the console toward the airlock, where Tea was assembling the pieces of his surface suit. "Now I know why Weldon gave you my mission," she said.

Yes, Zack thought, but did not say: *Because I am the kind of astronaut who will do anything for the mission, even expose my private grief.*

All astronauts are created equal. Some are more equal than others.

DEKE SLAYTON

SEVENTY-THREE DAYS EARLIER

There were historic buildings on the campus of the NASA Johnson Space Center. Building 30 held mission control; Building 9 the *Destiny* and *Venture* simulators. Building 2 was the tall headquarters building.

And 4-South was where the astronauts had their offices, on the top floor. Where Zack had worked for a decade.

But by accepting a transfer to management status and an assignment to the planetary sciences group, Zack found it easier to make the physical move across the quad to the unremarkable Building 24.

He kept current on aircraft, logging his mandatory forty hours a year, much of it acquired while strapped into an ancient WB-57 flying high-altitude loops to acquire imagery of Keanu.

He also made sure to attend the weekly Monday morning "pilots' meeting" in 4-South to hear the often raucous, sometimes serious, occasionally tedious presentations on technical developments with *Destiny* and *Venture* . . . on the political fallout from Travis Buell's popular and controversial "claim" of the Moon, made all the more interesting by Buell's physical presence.

And to hear the assignments to new missions, including that of Tea Nowinski as commander of *Destiny-7*.

But his days were spent in a nondescript office on the second floor of Building 24. It was early on the morning of June 9; Rachel had had a sleepover at the Meyers', so Zack was in his office at seven A.M. when Harley Drake—another early-to-work type—rolled in and closed the door. "Seen the news?"

"Narrow it down a little for me. Are we talking budgets, politics, women, or Keanu?" Harley had taken the loss of his mobility—and his flying and astronaut careers—better than Zack would have, throwing himself into a new career as a space scientist. He was enrolled in a master's program at Rice, and had established himself as the hardest-working member of the Keanu Group . . . all without losing any of his bawdy irreverence, sometimes shocking the more genteel, academic types in Building 24.

"*Brahma*'s going to Keanu."

The Coalition was scheduled to send its first mission beyond Earth orbit—to the Moon—three months hence. Since *Brahma* would be landing at Shackleton Crater, there was some chance—and outright concern—that *Brahma*'s stay would overlap with Tea's crew on *Destiny-7*.

"Shackleton *and* Keanu?"

"No, fuckhead. They aren't made of fuel and consumables. They are going to forget the Moon and land on Keanu during closest approach."

"That's only two months from now. How the hell can they get a project like that together?"

"Turns out they've been kicking it around for a year, but, really, dude, the spacecraft doesn't have to be changed; it's all guidance and traj."

Zack immediately began to consider the operational challenges of landing on Keanu . . . low gravity, the possibility that rocket exhaust would turn ice and snow into steam—

"I don't get this," Harley said. "The idea that *Brahma* is going to fly to Keanu is huge news—and *I'm* the one breaking it to you? That's not the Zack Stewart I knew."

In spite of his two-year fog—hell, call it depression—Zack was honest enough to recognize the truth of Harley's statement. Besides, his own body confirmed it: He blushed. "All right," he said. "What would you do if you were Zack Stewart?"

"You mean, aside from asking myself why I'm not still in bed with

Nowinski at this hour?" That was another bull's-eye for Harley Drake . . . in the past six months, Zack's relationship with Tea had taken a sharp left turn from supportive family friend and fellow astronaut to . . . well, girl-friend.

With Tea assigned as commander of the upcoming *Destiny-7* mission, America's third visit to Shackleton Station, they had tried to keep the relationship quiet. Obviously they had failed.

"Yes," Zack said, electing not to deny or confirm. "Aside from that."

"I'd be knocking on Shane Weldon's door."

Zack was on his feet before Harley finished the sentence.

Shane Weldon's tour as chief of the astronaut office had ended a year after he made the painful but inevitable decision to replace Zack with Travis Buell. Buell's subsequent behavior on the first landing had contributed to Weldon's change of job—NASA management was equally split between those who blamed Weldon for putting a hothead like Buell in such a visible position and those who thought him a managerial genius and patriot.

Moving him to mission operations made both sides happy. It was a promotion that put Weldon on a path to be head of the Johnson Space Center some day, and it also got him out of day-to-day personnel decisions.

Or so it said on the job description. In truth, Weldon, like the true bureaucratic master he was becoming, never let go of reins he once held. It was said in Building 4-South that not one of the new chief astronaut's crew selections was final until Shane Weldon signed off.

Powerful or not, Weldon's office was strictly government issue, part of a suite surrounding a central reception area occupied by three assistants, one of whom, the ancient Kerrie Kyle, nodded Zack to a couch. "Shane's usually in by now." Workdays at JSC ran from eight to four, if not earlier. Weldon's absence was unusual enough that when he did show up—fifteen minutes later—Zack had to tease him. "Sleeping in these days?"

"Nice to see you, too," Weldon said. "Come in."

Zack followed him into his office, which was dominated by pictures and models of aircraft and spacecraft Weldon had flown—and a huge astronomical image of Keanu so new that it was resting on a chair. "You can move that," Weldon said, realizing it was where a guest would sit.

"It's fine where it is," Zack said.

Weldon had been on his way to his seat. Instead he remained standing while opening his laptop. "Out with it."

Zack felt like a ten-year-old selling chocolate bars for a school project. "Well, this might be above my pay grade, but if it's true that *Brahma* is heading for a landing on Keanu, I think we ought to divert *Destiny-7* there, too." An old Michigan phrase came to him. "It's time for Operation Welcome Wagon."

"Why do you care if we beat them? I have some vague memory that you might have disapproved of Buell's little speech at Shackleton."

"I don't *care* who gets there first. But I think we'll be kicking ourselves years from now if we pass up a chance to go there *at all*. How many monster NEOs will ever be in reach?"

Now Weldon sat, fingers drumming on the desk. "We've never simulated a landing on a NEO."

"Look, are we a space program or not? *Destiny* is the vehicle that's supposed to open up the solar system. It's already been to the Moon twice. It was designed for missions to Mars and—I seem to recall—Near-Earth Objects. The guidance teams will have a challenge with a short deadline, but this would be just the kind of grenade they'd dive on."

"Is there some takeaway from this mission? Some cool science?"

"For God's sake, Shane! This won't be flags and footprints! We're creaming our jeans because we found a few tons of ice on the Moon—Keanu's *covered* with the stuff. It'll be like taking a trip to the birth of the solar system!" He noticed that Weldon was actually typing on his laptop. "Are you writing this down?"

"It's good phraseology. Not that I expected anything less from you."

"So you're considering it."

"Way ahead of you. Did Kerrie say why I was late?" Zack shook his head. "I was in a double-secret meeting with Gabe Jones and the entire eighth floor: HQ and the White House want us to send *Destiny-7* to Keanu, and beat the Coalition there."

He turned his computer so Zack could see the cover of the Power-point presentation. "You bastard!" But there was no anger in it. "Why didn't you tell me to shut up?"

"I'm going to have to sell this thing to a bunch of very skeptical division heads. For every one who's eager to embrace the challenge, there will be two who think it's too dangerous or just too much fucking work. I need to show the same enthusiasm you just did."

"Then send me."

"I might do that. I need to double-team this—"

"Fuck your *briefings*, Shane." Zack leaned on the desk. "Send me *to Keanu*. Put me *on the crew*. I'm the center's expert on the subject. I'm qualified on *Destiny* and *Venture*."

Weldon stared, his face neutral, giving away nothing. "Seven has a crew."

"For a lunar mission. It needs a Keanu expert."

"Which happens to be Zack Stewart."

"Look around the astronaut office and tell me who else even comes close." Zack didn't wait for a correction. "Besides, I'm current on hours and classes."

"No question."

"But you're still reluctant."

"True." Now Weldon looked directly at him. "Really, Zack . . . you lost Megan two years ago, but you've been wandering in the wilderness a little. *Are* you ready . . . mentally?"

"I wouldn't be here." At that moment, Zack realized he needed this mission—this new goal—more than anything in the past two years. If Weldon said no, he was going to walk out of the office and out of NASA.

"I appreciate the enthusiasm, Zack, but—"

Now Zack got to his feet. "Fuck it, Shane. You owe me the spot. Deke's Rules."

Weldon blinked. "No doubt. Of course, Deke's Rules may not carry a lot of weight on the ninth floor or at HQ—"

"Okay, then, look at your crew matrix. You've got Tea, Yvonne Hall, Oliver McCabe and Pogo Downey. Hall is capable, strong, great on EVA, but loaded with Daddy issues. Call her a 'possible.'

"Downey is the best ops guy in the office. And for going into a strange environment on short notice, nobody better.

"McCabe is smart but green and so totally focused on lunar regolith that he's a fucking bore on the subject. You're already planning to unload him." Weldon's face gave nothing away.

"Tea . . . who knows her better than the boyfriend? She'd be a great commander, for a lunar mission. You know and I know how programmed she gets: As commander of a Keanu mission—again, on the shortest notice possible—she is going to drive the training teams batshit with questions and more questions and you don't have time for that. She's on the team, but not as commander.

"I'm the guy. I know both spacecraft well enough to be backup to Tea for *Destiny* and Pogo for *Venture*. I've got as much EVA time as Yvonne. And there is no one at the center, much less the office, who is more familiar with Keanu than me.

"Your predecessor and the ninth floor and HQ thought I was capable enough to be trusted with the first lunar landing of the twenty-first century. Are you going to sit here and tell me I can't handle this?"

"There's still a looming question," Weldon said, apparently agreeing with Zack's impassioned points. "Your family situation. What will Rachel think?"

Since his conversation with Harley, Zack had not devoted much thought to Rachel . . . he needed no special insight to predict what she would think, and say. "She'll like the idea for a week, then she'll hate it. How will that be different from any other astronaut family? She'll deal. It's my decision. My goal. My mission."

Weldon stared for five seconds. Then he offered his hand. "Congratulations, Commander Stewart. *Destiny-7* is yours."

Zack could only nod. He had had magical moments in his life—

telling Megan that he was in love with her, not knowing whether she felt the same . . . the birth of Rachel . . . the call from NASA asking him if he was still interested in becoming an astronaut—

"Know what your real challenge is going to be?"

Zack could think of many sudden, terrifying challenges. The training. Rachel. "What?"

"Telling your girlfriend that you snaked her command."

KEANU STAY

"Thank God we've got the airlock," Pogo said, his face red from the tor-turous business of getting Zack's and Yvonne's suits ready for the EVA, a job that involved swapping out the torsos, gloves, and boots. The only surprise in the comment was that it came from Col. Patrick Downey, USAF, normally a hairshirt stoic on matters of space and livability. Zack, Yvonne, and Tea had spent two hours grunting and cursing as they executed the maneuvers necessary to eat, clean up, use the toilet, and get Zack and Yvonne suited for the first steps onto Keanu's surface. Items had to be removed from lockers, used, then replaced—or the debris stashed in a different locker. "This is like a clown car," Pogo snapped, clearly at his limit. "And what the fuck is this? Yvonne?"

He had a silvery box in his hand labeled *HALL PPK*, Personal Preference Kit, the collection of college banners, family photos, commemorative stamps, and other memorabilia astronauts were allowed to carry on flights—as long as they didn't exceed a kilogram or two of mass.

"I hope that isn't filled with good-luck coins or doodads," Tea said, teasing. Early astronauts had gotten into trouble for sneaking memorabilia aboard their vehicles.

"It's all within limits," Yvonne replied, clearly stung.

"What it is, is in the wrong locker," Zack said, taking it from Patrick and handing it to Yvonne. "20-B is where the PPKs go."

He slid between Patrick and Yvonne and entered the airlock. The chamber was almost as big as the cabin itself. On the day—hopefully a week from now—when Zack and his crew climbed into *Venture* to launch off Keanu's surface, it would be left behind, along with the rest of the descent stage of the vehicle. But right now it was serving as a dressing room, where Tea waited, holding Zack's helmet for the final stage of his suiting. "Oooo, Commander Stewart," she purred in a fairly good imitation of some movie sex kitten, "I'd much rather be undressing you . . ."

"We've still got time to add 'first boff on Keanu' to the resume."

"Optimist," Tea said, resuming her normal voice, "but thanks for asking." She was about to lower the helmet past his ears when she hesitated.

"What is it?" Zack was normally not a nitpicker or worrier, but this was not a normal situation.

She leaned forward and kissed him gently. "For luck." Then the helmet descended, dampening the humming rattle of *Venture's* ambient noise. Tea clicked the base of the helmet into the neck ring, and Zack was now suited up, breathing from its tanks.

In his headset, he heard Pogo say, "Zack, check this out!"

"What is it?"

"*Brahma's* coming in."

Without being told, Tea disconnected Zack's helmet and helped him remove it. "Remind me—"

"—That you've already used a few minutes of air, yeah, yeah."

At the command console, Pogo had turned one of the exterior cameras north and zoomed out.

The image showed black sky over the fuzzy white edge of Vesuvius Vent . . . and a bright star. "Looks like an airliner on approach," the pilot said.

"They're feeding it live," Tea said, calling up the worldwide broadcast from the flight deck of the Coalition craft . . . it showed the snowy surface as seen from an altitude of fifteen hundred meters, according to the updating figures.

"Should we be at general quarters or something?" Pogo said. He had not forgotten the missile launcher.

"Yeah, stand by to repel boarders." Zack was confident there would be no "action"; even if there was, he didn't have a lot of options for counterattack. "Houston, we're holding on EVA prep until *Brahma* is safely down."

Five seconds later, Houston acknowledged. "We copy, *Venture*. Wait until the debris settles."

The bright star resolved into what looked like a beer can with legs, with a fin on one side. *Brahma* was actually stopped in midair, hovering.

"Taj is taking his time," Tea said, paying attention to the commentary on Coalition TV.

"He's not flying it, is he?" Pogo said.

"Don't worry, Colonel—people will still remember you did it first," Yvonne said. Pogo shot her a look that could have burned holes in her forehead.

"Coming down—!" Tea reported.

Like the *Venture* lander, *Brahma*'s engines burned clear; there was no plume of flame, just a brightness at the base of the vehicle and wisps of vapor being blown off the snowy surface. "It looks like *2001*," Yvonne said.

"Like what?" Patrick said, almost snarling.

"The *movie*," Tea said. Zack could see the point . . . there was indeed a resemblance to the big round commercial Moon shuttle touching down at Clavius Base in the Kubrick-Clarke film.

"Fifty meters now, I think," Pogo said.

Then *Brahma* disappeared in a cloud of white.

"What the hell was that?" Yvonne said.

Zack slapped her on the forearm of her suit. "Shut up and watch!"

Through the mist—like the lifting fog on a coastal morning—Zack could see *Brahma* bouncing just as he imagined *Venture* had . . . but only a few meters.

The damn spacecraft actually rotated, allowing the *Destiny* astronauts to see a line reaching from the missile tube on *Brahma*'s side into the ground. The giant six-story vehicle shuddered like a breaching whale . . . then gently settled.

Zack laughed out loud. "I don't believe it! They harpooned it!" Seeing that none of his crew understood, he said, "They fired an anchor from that tube. It wasn't a missile launcher, it was a tool to keep them from bouncing the way we did."

"You mean, they winched themselves in?" Tea said, clearly stunned. Of the four of them, she was the only one with sailing experience.

"Bingo," Zack said. "Just like a sailing ship."

"Well," said Pogo, turning to Zack. "I guess you're not the only Hornblower reader around here."

The crew of spacecraft *Brahma* prepares for its historic exploration of Near-Earth Object Keanu. Data continue to be received via Deep Space Network at Byalalu near Bangalore.

It may be recalled that the *Brahma* spacecraft was launched from European Space Agency's Kourou Space Centre on 18 August 2019.

INDIAN SPACE RESEARCH ORGANIZATION PRESS RELEASE, 22 AUGUST 2019

"Yes, I'm standing by."

Lucas Munaretto was growing tired of using that phrase. In the four days since *Brahma* had launched from Kourou, it was almost the only thing he had been able to say on the air-to-ground link.

The problem was Bangalore mission control, where even the simplest question triggered a series of lengthy consultations. Lucas had noticed this hesitancy during the months of mission simulations but had written it off as the learning process (Bangalore had never controlled a mission this complex). Besides, Taj's international crew had frequently been too slow to act.

But now, as Lucas struggled with a pressure regulator on Natalia Yorkina's EVA suit, he realized that no one on the ground team, not even lead flight director Vikram Nayar, seemed willing to exercise any authority. With the eyes of the world on them, with a crew of four newly landed on Keanu, they were like actors who froze the moment the lights went up.

From his tour on the International Space Station, Lucas knew that NASA did not operate that way. Its communicators were either astronauts or training team members who worked in tandem with shift flight directors. Routine decisions got made instantly. Emergencies obviously required some consultation, but even then the voice on the line would be brisk, professional, informed.

But that reflected the difference in approach: Bangalore had based its style on the Russian method, in which cosmonauts' actions were strictly controlled from the ground. NASA was more flexible, operating on the attitude that a properly trained astronaut was capable of responding to any situation.

Bangalore apparently had little faith in its crew. A shame, since it included the World's Greatest Astronaut.

Lucas Munaretto loved the title, which had descended on him several years ago, during his one and only space mission, the first by a Brazilian astronaut to the International Space Station.

During an EVA, Lucas's partner, a Japanese astronaut, had briefly become disconnected from the station exterior. EVA astronauts were tethered by at least two different lines, but one of those perfect storms struck, where a latch failed at the same time the Japanese engineer was relocating his backup line to a new position on the S6 truss and failing to catch it on first try. That simple motion—normally damped by connection to the massive station—caused the man to keep turning and begin floating away from the truss.

Without apparent concern, and in full view of TV viewers on Earth, Lucas had simply launched himself at his comrade, who had almost floated out of reach, grabbing the errant spacewalker's feet and slowly but steadily pulling him back to safety.

The emergency lasted only a few seconds. Indeed, later analysis discounted the real threat, noting that there were no "rates"—no tumbling or even much motion—on the disconnected astronaut, who was also reachable by the station's remote manipulator arm.

Nevertheless, the legend had already taken flight, unhindered by Lucas's dark-haired good looks, smile, and fluency in four languages, or by his reputation as a daring rescue helicopter pilot, or by his sister Isobel, a former Victoria's Secret model.

The notoriety had obviously helped Lucas win a coveted spot on the *Brahma* crew. Brazil's financial contributions to Coalition space efforts theoretically earned it the right to have a representative on the first big mission, but the Agencia Espacial Brasileira had no astronaut corps, only a pair of pilots who had been hired over the past decade and sent through the training programs in Houston, Moscow, Cologne, and Tsukuba. By 2017, Lucas Munaretto was the only one still qualified, and he faced competition from members of the Russian cosmonaut team and India's vyomanauts, not to mention qualified applicants from the European Space Agency and Japan, and even a disgruntled former NASA astronaut.

He had made the cut, of course, and entered training with a vyomanaut commander and two Russians with wildly varying degrees of experience. Dennis Chertok was fifty and had flown in space five times, all to the International Space Station, one of them as a mission specialist in America's long-gone space shuttle. He knew everything about hardware, operations, and especially EVAs, having logged eighty hours in space walks. Even Taj, notoriously sensitive to slights and perks, had deferred to Dennis for much of the training, right up to the time when his obsessive-compulsiveness became overwhelming.

Natalia Yorkina had never flown a mission of any kind. She had been selected, Lucas suspected, to have a woman on the crew. Dark-eyed, often nervous and giggly, Natalia had not impressed him at first, either. But she turned out to be ferociously competent, eager to learn, and relentlessly hardworking, like an automaton.

Then there was Taj himself, the most stolid, phlegmatic human Lucas had ever met, more like a retired accountant or grim-faced Swiss banker than a test pilot. His greatest virtue was patience . . . which was turning out to be a good thing, given Bangalore's slowness.

The only time Taj lit up with anything like emotion was when learning of some American outrage. Then a smile would begin to form, an eyebrow would rise, and he would rub his hands together in anticipation.

Lucas was grateful to know that his vyomanaut commander had feelings, but as for him, he hated the amped-up rivalry between the Coalition and the United States. True, the U.S. relationship with Russia had blown hot and cold for the past twenty years, and, yes, the Americans had bullied India on a number of issues.

But Brazil's disputes with the Big Brother to the north were largely limited to energy matters. Even those tended to consist of public huffing and puffing.

All of this—the lack of response from Bangalore, the petty gamesmanship, and the fact that the very capable American crew was already headed to the surface—made Lucas want to scream with rage and impatience:

Let's go! Glory awaits!

Big Dumb Object: n., from science fiction, a term originated by critic Roz Kaveney, writing in *Foundation*, the British journal (1981), to describe large, extraterrestrial planetoids, spacecraft, or structures. See Ringworld, Dyson sphere, etc.　　　SCIFIPEDIA, ACCESSED AUGUST 2019

With *Brahma* safely down, Zack actually felt impatient, eager to go outside. Within an hour, he and Yvonne were suited, on oxygen, and waiting for the pressure in the *Venture* airlock to bleed down to zero. Although he was linked to Yvonne, to Pogo and Tea, and to Houston and the world beyond, Zack felt cocooned. It was to be expected, of course, since the suit, which weighed almost a hundred kilograms on earth—more than a naked Zack—was like a man-sized spacecraft.

But it was also the moment. Through his adrenaline-soaked fatigue, he had become mentally untethered. And why not? He was no longer on Earth, he had lost his wife, he was so disconnected from his daughter he had a difficult time imagining her face and voice—

He was like that ancient aquatic beast that found itself spending more time in the open shallows than in the water. He was embarking on an adventure, leaving his old comfortable world completely behind, exploring the Biggest and Dumbest Big Dumb Object in human history—

"Go for egress," Tea said.

Yvonne cranked the hatch open. The light of the Keanu morning was brilliant, not only because of the unfiltered Sun, but the snowy landscape, too. If the sky hadn't been completely black, Zack could have been convinced he was home on the Upper Peninsula, taking a winter walk.

Yvonne was first onto the grill-like platform extending out from the airlock hatch. She turned around, grasping the railings of the ladder. "How am I doing?"

Zack was a step behind her, peering down at *Venture*'s feet at the surface. It looked like recently melted snow and ice cooling over rock. Trickier than the nasty lunar terrain at Shackleton, perhaps, but not dangerous. He gave a clumsy thumbs-up. "It's a nice day. Let's take a stroll."

Yvonne carefully negotiated the six steps down to the surface. The ladder reached only to within a meter of the ground—an easy step on the Moon, many times easier in Keanu's gravity. Picturing Yvonne in near free fall, he cautioned her: "Take it slow, kiddo. It's more like swimming than walking."

"Got it." She was already breathing hard. And when had he started using the word *kiddo*?

With her hands firmly on the railing, Yvonne kicked off and slid oh-so-slowly to the ground. "Okay!" she said, clearly pleased. "Hello, Keanu! May you be as happy to see us as we are to see you!"

Not bad, Zack thought. Yvonne edged away from the lander. "How's traction?" he asked.

"Not great," she said, but quickly corrected herself, "but workable. Sliding works better than stepping."

"Cross-country skiing," Zack said, making his own descent to the pad. They actually had two sets of ski poles available in the equipment bay. Might be wise to break them out early. "Wish you could all be here," he said, stepping off the pad. Yvonne had been too kind . . . in spite of the ankle weights and the cleats on his EVA boots, he almost fell right on his back. Fortunately he didn't, sparing himself and NASA an eternal YouTube moment.

The flight plan called for them to spend twenty minutes doing a "walkaround," getting a feel for the surface—which was crunchy, making Zack happy that he weighed probably five kilograms—and learning how to move.

Apparently determined to break the mold of the taciturn space explorer, Yvonne chattered incessantly about the light, the surface, the view.

Happy to let Yvonne carry the burden of commentary, Zack shuffled as close to the lip of Vesuvius as he dared. It turned out to be only seventy meters away—from the windows of *Venture* it had seemed much farther. It was another reminder that Keanu was *small*.

"Yvonne," Zack said, "let's press to step two." Step two in the flight plan was to deploy the experiment package mounted in a small bay in *Venture*'s side, next to a larger one holding the folded rover.

"Give me a minute, boss," Yvonne said.

Turning, Zack could see that she was still heading toward the lip of Vesuvius. Well, who could blame her?

Suddenly he felt a jolt, losing his footing like some cartoon character. When he stabilized, he could still sense the sickening, wavelike rumbling of an earthquake. "*Venture*, can you feel that?"

"Yeah!" Tea said. "I think it's Vesuvius—!"

Not good. "Yvonne," he radioed, "get back here now!"

Too late. He could see her directly in front of him—no more than ten meters distant—but beyond her bloomed an expanding cloud of white.

"Oh God—!" Yvonne screamed.

The blast of superheated steam blew the *Destiny* astronaut off her feet, launching her into the sky in the general direction of the *Brahma* landing site.

As she flew over Zack, she was cartwheeling.

This is *Destiny* mission control at eighty-one hours, twenty minutes mission elapsed time. The communications team here is troubleshooting an apparent problem with the *Venture* lander's Ku-band antenna, which has caused a temporary loss of video coverage of the historic EVA by astronauts Hall and Stewart. We are in voice contact with the crew and all is proceeding according to flight plan. Video coverage is expected to resume shortly.

NASA PUBLIC AFFAIRS COMMENTATOR SCOTT SHAWLER,
MOMENTS AFTER YVONNE HALL'S ACCIDENT

"Okay, it's calmed down . . ." Shane Weldon's voice was strained in Harley's headset. "What is your team thinking?"

"We're only getting macro data." The moment Yvonne Hall had been blown off the surface of Keanu, Harley Drake had wheeled himself out of the Home Team and next door to the family holding room, with its limited audio and video feed. Not limited enough, apparently: Patrick Downey's wife, Linda, and two tween children were huddled in a corner, flanked by a priest as well as their CACO.

Meanwhile, Rachel Stewart sat, stunned, in the company of her friend Amy Meyer. Rachel stood as Harley approached. "Zack hadn't gotten the package set up yet," he told Weldon, through his headset.

"So you've got fuck-all."

"I'm on it," he said, making reassuring gestures to Rachel. "What about Hall?" Yvonne Hall had no family members in the room, but her father was Gabriel Jones, head of the Johnson Space Center. The relationship wasn't secret—hundreds at JSC knew of it. But neither the director nor his astronaut daughter talked about it or acted as if they had more than a passing acquaintance. Harley could only imagine what was going through Jones's mind. . . .

"She hit the ground pretty close to *Brahma*. They're still getting data from her suit. Zack's on his way."

"That's good." He mouthed *Yvonne's okay* to Rachel and gave her a thumbs-up as he clicked off.

"What, she's okay?" Rachel said, clearly not believing him.

"Sorry, I should have said *alive*. I'm more worried about you."

Rachel shot a glance at her friend, who was sobbing. "Well, I'm freaking out." Her manner contradicted her words; she looked nervous, but in control.

Harley touched her hand. "If you're not a little freaked out, you don't understand the situation."

"Tell me again why my father thought this would be a good idea?"

"Maybe when I come back." Over the past year, he and Rachel had become pals of a sort, bonded by their mutual tragedy—and by, of all things, a shared fascination with Keanu. (Rachel had liked the extrasolar NEO right up to the day her father was assigned to explore it.) "Weldon is demanding that I explain the structure of the universe . . ."

"Yeah, you better go back. Feel free to fix this."

"On it." Harley was not your standard CACO—he had another hat to wear for *Destiny-7*. He had declined the assignment when Zack first asked. ("Christ, don't you remember the last time I was your CACO?") But *Rachel* had insisted . . . and it was Rachel who made it possible.

He pivoted his chair and rolled back to the Home Team.

Having a T1 thoracic spinal cord injury, which was what Harley Drake had experienced for the past two years, sucked in a broad-spectrum way. To begin with, there was the pain and general humiliation. Then there was the horror of lost sexual functioning . . . loss of bowel control . . . giving up flying . . . having to learn to deal with a chair.

But the thing that sucked most for Harley on this day was feeling nailed to one spot. Yes, he was digitally ept, Bluetoothed, and eager to multitask, but he missed being able to stand, to move around, to talk with his hands. He was like the Sundance Kid from that old Western—"I'm better when I move."

Maybe that was why he was so slow to realize what was obvious from the Keanu data.

He returned to the din of the Home Team room, with its conference table covered with laptops and hard copies, resuming the messy business of wrangling seven verbal, loud, entitled specialists. They ranged from seventy-five-year-old Wade Williams, a popular astronomy writer (one of JSC Director Jones's idols, which was the only reason Harley tolerated the arrogant, half-deaf shithead), to thirty-two-year-old Sasha Blaine, a brilliant new Ph.D. from Yale noted as much for her startling figure as for her impressive IQ. There were also other contributors available on Skype . . . hell, Harley felt more like a drill instructor than a project leader. "All right, people! Goddammit!"

That outburst didn't shut them up, but it reduced the decibel level so that Harley could be heard. It was probably fortunate that his mobility *was* limited, or he might have smacked someone.

"This isn't a fucking seminar. We're working critical, real-time mission support, and next door we've got a mission manager who really wants an answer to the question—what is going on with Keanu?"

"Does he want the *right* answer or *an* answer?" Williams said in a Georgia drawl. Glenn Creel, Williams's snarky little buddy on the team—the guy was a television writer, for Christ's sake—actually gave him a high five.

"Okay, Wade," Harley said, reaching for patience and not really attaining it. "Do we have *any* kind of answer? Anything that might keep the crew from further danger?" No one offered. "Then let's review the bidding," Harley said.

"We've had four eruptions on Keanu since *Destiny-Venture* made its orbital insertion burn. What do we know about them? Sasha?"

Sasha Blaine, the tall, nervous red-haired woman from Yale, was undisciplined but had at least demonstrated the ability to understand the team's priorities. "Each venting took place at a different location on Keanu, each with varying duration and apparent force—"

"What about the frequency?" Williams said. "Time between events— increasing, decreasing?"

"Counting down to the destruction of Washington, D.C.?" That was Williams again.

Blaine simply took the question seriously, then dismissed it. "The gaps were two hours, one hour thirty-five minutes, one hour fifty-one minutes. No obvious pattern."

"Wait!" That was Lily Valdez, a professor from Irvine. "Are we seeing increased angular momentum?"

The Home Team chatter died in silence. "Anybody?" Harley said. This was not his area.

"Yes," Sasha Blaine said. "Prior to the, uh, recent events, Keanu had a very slow rotation, on the order of sixty days—"

"—Which was out of family for NEOs," Williams said.

"—Not that there is much of a family for extrasolar NEOs," Harley said, unable to resist. He nodded at Blaine. "Setting aside what we had . . . what we do we have?"

"It looks as though its new period will be twenty hours."

"Something less than a day."

There was something troubling about all these numbers, but Harley was damned if he could see what, especially with Williams in full honk. "I'm more worried about these eruptions," the writer was saying. "They've all been in the same hemisphere, so that's one data point. Is there any other correlation?"

"I don't know if we have enough information to suggest a pattern," Harley said. "We noted only a dozen ventings over the past two years—"

"—and now we've got four in the past few hours," Williams said, unnecessarily.

"Four *so far*," said Creel.

Harley's head hurt. He was missing something obvious—all of them were.

Just then Sasha Blaine said, "We're getting data from DSN," and Harley's headset chirped. He turned away from the eruption of chatter around the table to hear: "Harley, Shane. Two of the guys on *Brahma* went EVA and reached Yvonne. She's alive with a suit leak. They're taking her back to *Venture*."

"Could be worse," Harley said. He knew that this was Weldon's way of asking for an answer. "Wait one, Shane—" He lowered the headset and said, "What now?"

This time the Home Team room fell into silence. Everyone present, or on-screen, looked directly at Harley. "What?"

"Look at this." Sasha Blaine turned her laptop screen toward him.

Until this moment, Harley had convinced himself that the events on Keanu would have some geological explanation—indeed, the likely trigger for the increased eruptions was tidal stress caused by the NEO's close encounter with Earth. It might even explain the change in the object's rotation.

But no longer. Harley looked at the figures for Keanu's trajectory and said, "This sucker's in orbit now, isn't it?"

"Correct," Williams said. "Today's eruptions were much more powerful than any seen earlier . . . strong enough to act like rocket burns."

As Harley let that info-bomb detonate inside his brain, he heard Weldon: "We're all waiting, Home Team. Do you have something? Anything?"

Harley looked at the faces around him, especially Sasha Blaine, who gestured as if to say, *What are you waiting for?*

"Okay, flight. New data shows that Keanu is not a Near-Earth Object. It just burned into orbit, perigee 470,000 clicks, apogee five hundred, inclination seventy-eight degrees, new period circa twenty hours."

"What does that mean, Harley?"

"It means that Keanu is an autonomous, powered vehicle of some kind. Until we come up with a better word, I'd call it a starship."

"Where is she?" Zack said. "Someone speak!"

He had a general idea . . . he had seen Yvonne flying away from him, away from Vesuvius Vent toward *Brahma*. But the combination of short horizon, residual vapor, undulating ground, and restricted helmet vision made it impossible for him to know where she had landed.

Or, for that matter, *if*. The gravity on Keanu was so low that a human could reach escape velocity by running. The eruption that had caught Yvonne might have been strong enough to launch her into orbit.

Assuming, or hoping, that that hadn't happened, Zack turned his back on Vesuvius and, keeping the *Venture* lander to his left, began hopping, sliding, and shuffling in the same direction Yvonne had flown.

There were voices on the control loop—Tea and Pogo as well as the capcom—but no information.

"Quiet down, everybody!" Zack snapped, using what Rachel would have called his grown-up voice. "Yvonne, do you read?"

He waited, afraid he would hear more screaming, but just as afraid he would hear nothing. "Yvonne . . ."

Then he heard harsh breathing, the sound of a mouth literally on a microphone. And a moan. "Copy. Zack?" Yvonne, alive!

"Can you tell me where you are?" *And please don't say halfway around Keanu.*

"Ah . . ." She was clearly in pain. "Down, somewhere." Another moan.

She was probably shifting to look at her surroundings. "Beyond *Brahma*. I can see the top of it."

"Then I can reach you in a few minutes." He tried to pick up the pace and fell flat.

Aboard *Venture*, Tea heard him. "Zack, what's up?"

He managed to push himself upright. Fortunately his suit was so rugged that he had few worries of damaging it. "Me, again. Yvonne," he called, "are you hurt?"

"Feel like I fell off a building." She was trying for astronaut cool but sounded terrible. In fact, she sounded as though she might be going into shock.

"I'm almost there," Zack said, hoping that was true; the silvery stub of *Brahma* was now only half-visible above the horizon. "Tea, I need Pogo—"

"He's already in the lock, about to depress."

"Is Houston in the loop?"

"Listening," Tea said. "They're talking to me and Pogo on B."

"Okay." Shuffle, slide. It was like cross-country skiing, but with no time to enjoy the scenery, which reminded him of the long-lost Arctic ice cap and its jagged, untouched mounds of snow. But all under a black sky and the huge blue sphere of the Earth.

To his right—was that a wisp? Vapor! Outgassing from Yvonne's backpack, or possibly a leak. "Yvonne, I've got you in sight!"

Within moments he could see her, sprawled on her back facing away from him, one leg bent horribly. As Zack approached, he noticed the first sign of real color he had seen on the surface of Keanu . . . a bloodred mist rising from Yvonne's injured leg and quickly freezing.

"Tell Pogo to pick it up!" he said.

Yvonne Hall was having a dream.

It had started out so beautifully, stepping down to the surface of Keanu. She felt snug, secure, strong in her suit . . . true, the surface had been icy and treacherous. But after a few steps, she had learned to move without feeling as if she would fall over.

She had managed to raise her head enough to see Earth in the black sky and wonder just how many of the invisible billions there were watching her steps here.

Then the dream had gone into nightmare territory. So strange! She had felt nothing beyond a sense that the snow beneath her feet had melted.

Her faceplate went white, and she felt herself lifted.

Twenty-two years ago, just before her parents split up, the family had taken a last-chance vacation in Mexico, where Yvonne had allowed herself to be strapped into a parachute harness, then hauled into the air behind a speedboat. After a moment of terror, she had enjoyed the feeling of nothing beneath her feet—

This experience started just like that, but within seconds had gone bad, bad, bad, as she tumbled through the fog and steam.

She could see the ground turning crazily, ten or more meters below. And through her confusion, she wondered, *How long before I smash?* and *Oh my God did I fuck up?* and *I'm sorry!*

But all through that long arc she felt nothing! The suit protected her from the steam, isolated her from temperatures, kept her alive—as long as it held.

She descended slowly—and here the experience was exactly like dropping to that beach in Mexico—but was unable to turn herself at all. She fell like a doll thrown onto the snow and rock, face first.

She tried to raise her arms, too late. Her nose smashed into her faceplate. Her leg bent under her so viciously she could feel cartilage tear and bones break.

As she slid to a stop, she tasted blood and blinked tears.

But she was alive. What about her suit? If it tore she would hear hissing, start feeling cold—but only for a few minutes.

She realized the only sound was her own harsh breathing. Okay, that was good.

Someone was calling her. Zack!

Then she did hear a small hiss. She could feel a chill.

Her suit *had* been breached! In pain, she rolled over . . . she could not feel her left leg.

No wonder. It was bent in a way that couldn't possibly be good. And just above the knee there was a mist of pink.

Okay, okay. Training. When in doubt— What the hell did astronauts tell themselves again?

She fumbled for the equipment bag on her chest. She was getting colder, breathing faster. How long? Where was Zack? Goddammit, why wasn't he here?

A bungee cord. There. Fumbling, she managed to get it—*fuck, only halfway!*

She rolled again. *God, that hurt.*

Zack: "Yvonne, can you tell me where you are?"

Got it! Around the leg. Pull it. Tight. Tight! Seal it. "Uh, down."

That was all she could do.

Time passed. Might have been seconds, might have been ten minutes. She began to think about Tea and Pogo, and the nasty little secret within her personal kit, the Item that actually filled the container—

She felt herself being lifted. "I've got you." Zack! Zack had found her!

"Careful!" she begged. Or, at least, that was what she thought she said.

She realized he was carrying her! Of course, though human-sized, she probably only weighed a couple of kilograms—

They both fell over. "Shit! Sorry!" Zack again. Yvonne couldn't feel her leg anymore.

She was picked up again, but this time it wasn't just Zack; someone else helped. Another astronaut, not Pogo Downey. The suit was blue, not white—

From *Brahma*, veteran cosmonaut Dennis Chertok and Brazilian Lucas Munaretto, the handsome, self-styled World's Greatest Astronaut. "Okay, we've got some help here," Zack told her. "You'll be back in *Venture* in a few minutes."

She still felt dreamy.

The only thing she kept telling herself, over and over again, was, *Don't mention your PPK.*

"You've got to be kidding me." Just two hours after the eruption and rescue of Yvonne Hall, Zack Stewart stared at the bland panel of the *Venture* workstation. Shane Weldon had just told him something he could not believe. Rather, something he could not accept.

Dennis and Lucas had helped Zack carry Yvonne back to *Venture*, meeting Pogo on the way. Since Dennis was a medical doctor, Zack allowed him into his spacecraft to attend to the injured astronaut. The impact on consumables was negligible, for now. "You two play nicely, okay?" he told Pogo and Lucas.

"Maybe we'll try to get to step one of the checklist," Pogo said.

"Both checklists," Lucas added.

"If you can, but stay very close to the lander." He feared another eruption.

Wedging three suited spacewalkers into the airlock had been tricky, especially with one of them immobilized. But it had worked. Still wearing his suit, sans helmet, Zack had wormed his way into the main cabin, leaving Tea to assist Dennis with Yvonne.

He grabbed a headset, where he heard Pogo patiently updating Houston on the situation.

"Zack is online," he announced. Without waiting, he delivered a brief update on Yvonne: alive, badly injured, being attended to by Russian doctor-cosmonaut.

All Weldon could say was, "Copy." Which surprised Zack, until he heard, "Channel B."

Switching over to the encrypted link, he expected a torrent of questions from his flight director, not just about Yvonne's physical condition but also her mental state. But Weldon had another surprise. "We've got news from the Home Team. It appears you didn't land on a NEO."

Shane Weldon had a dry, deadly sense of humor. No doubt it had come in handy in bars and the grab-ass sessions that were mission operations meetings, but right now it just bugged Zack. "What the fuck are you talking about?"

Weldon got serious. "Home Team analyzed the eruptions, which affected Keanu's traj. It's now in orbit around Earth. Short version, you landed on a spacecraft."

Zack's mind quickly cycled through a whole set of images triggered by that word. *Star Wars. Star Trek.* All kinds of weird metallic beasts from books and movies and comics, none of them resembling this stark but peaceful snowy landscape.

None of them anything he expected to encounter in his own life. "Good to know," he said, sounding far more casual and flippant than he felt. "This wasn't in the mission plans."

"Copy that. We're all in uncharted waters."

"What do you want us to do?" He knew what *he* wanted to do . . . but *Venture* didn't belong to him.

Then Weldon uttered more words Zack never expected to hear from Houston. "Knock on the door. See if anyone's home."

Again, Weldon didn't wait for a response, speaking right through the lag. "You *can* say no. There's a lot of sentiment here for packing up and coming home. Flight rules require a mission abort if a crew member becomes incapacitated.

"Our recommendation is, if she's dying, you come back. If she's stable, exploration takes priority . . ." The rest of the message, if anything, was lost in a wash of static.

"Wait one."

Zack turned in time to see Yvonne—out of her suit now, wearing her suit undergarment with the legging cut away—being carried into the cabin by Tea. "Good timing," Tea said. "How about a hand?"

Together the two of them easily lifted Yvonne up to a hammock. Zack got a look at the leg, and it was not pretty: a combination of bad break and exposure to vacuum . . . the worst frostbite imaginable.

She was conscious, at least. And she gamely offered a thumbs-up. Zack patted her shoulder, then slipped back into the airlock, where a tired-looking Dennis was leaning against the curving wall of the chamber. "What's the prognosis?"

"She's alive, but her leg—she will probably lose it."

"So she should be returned to Earth."

Dennis smiled and spread his hands. "Yes, by all means, lift off at the first opportunity. Just be sure to let me out before you do. . . ."

"Come on, Dennis!" Though they had never flown a mission together, Zack had trained with the doctor-cosmonaut in years past. He was well aware that Dennis was fatalistic even by Russian standards.

"A day will not make her condition worse. You should consult with Houston. Or have me come back tomorrow for a house call."

"Is there something you could do *here* and now?"

Dennis considered this. "I could set her broken bones. I could also trim the damaged tissue . . ." Without waiting for a request from Zack, the cosmonaut began undoing his suit. "It might take some time."

"I'll tell Taj."

Zack returned to the cabin, almost colliding with Tea, who had just finished attaching medical leads all over Yvonne. "Anytime you want to catch me up on whatever the fuck is going on . . ."

"Watch and learn." Finding that the communications problem had cleared up, he got back on the line to Weldon, relaying Dennis's diagnosis and the emergency treatment to come. "Assuming medical gives a go," Weldon said, "you're confirmed for one sortie, into the vent."

"What length?" On the two *Venture* lunar missions, astronauts had demonstrated the ability to do overnight and even three-day sorties using the rover. It was a vital tool in the box; it was impossible to cover much territory—to literally get more than a couple of kilometers away from your landing site—to do any worthwhile science or engineering, then pack up and return, all in the standard eight-hour limit for suits.

"Overnight. Meanwhile, we'll start working ascent trajectories for tomorrow."

So now he was going to be camping out overnight on an alien starship! The fun never stopped. "So, to recap, with an injured crew member and a rival vehicle next door, with no sims or specific prep, we're supposed to explore an alien starship."

"Good summary."

Zack turned to Tea, who was hearing this for the first time. "You're second in command. Any objections?"

Tea blinked. "You're not asking me, you're telling me." Zack could only nod. "Besides," she said. "*Brahma*'s going in, right?"

Zack picked up the headset. "Houston, *Venture*. We're go for First Contact."

While Zack was dealing with Yvonne's situation and the larger issues, Pogo Downey had followed Lucas back to the *Brahma* lander. "Your guy's giving up his time to help us. Consider it payback."

It was also a chance to get a close-up look at the Coalition craft and its "harpoon." Zack's conclusion turned out to be right: The thing wasn't a weapon, at least not in any way Pogo could see. It actually gave *Brahma* an anchor to the slippery, low-gravity surface.

Pogo had conflicted views about Zack Stewart. The man was smart, that was clear. He knew science and engineering. He knew systems and procedures. Unlike just about everyone else, he knew the history of same, the how and the why some systems had evolved.

Even better, he was smart in a smart way; he knew his strengths and his weaknesses. He never pretended to be a pilot, unlike a few other civilian science types in the astronaut office, who started dropping terms like *shithot* and *ops tempo* into conversations that previously featured *latte* and *Chardonnay*.

He worked hard and led by example. He'd get his hands dirty, and when he played Mr. Goodwrench (an increasingly vital role on space missions), he was good with tools.

He liked science, but kept it in its place. And he had a glib way of making even the most idiotic experiments—the kinds astronauts usually described as "looking at stars, pissing in jars"—seem relevant.

Which got to another point: Zack was savvy, too. He had built effective, long-term relationships with science and medical folks—though that was to be expected for an astronaut from what Pogo called the "pencil-necked geek" world.

But to have made friends with the puppet masters in mission ops, the flight controllers? That took skills worthy of a K Street lobbyist, the kind Pogo had watched in horror during a tour at the Pentagon.

Stewart even seemed to have administrative folks on his side—the secretaries and IT types. Of course, tragic widowerhood didn't hurt with the gals.

But, shit, he had to have had something going for him, for NASA to have given him command of the first lunar landing of the twenty-first century.

And yet . . .

Pogo had known quite a few special operators, Navy SEALs and Air Force pararescue guys, who had a cold-eyed ability to jump into icy water or fly a mountain pass on a moonless night, to cap an insurgent with a sniper rifle or slit one's throat with a knife—and never question the order or worry about the consequences.

With a few drinks in him, he would gladly include himself in that particular club.

He wondered if Zack Stewart was ruthless enough to kill someone, or even more challenging, to order a man to his death.

The EVA ops around *Brahma* were basic: opening up bays in the descent stage and pulling out boxes. After fifteen minutes, Pogo was bored.

He was also distracted by the conversations between Zack and Taj, who had wisely decided to switch to a common frequency and dispense with relays through their respective mission controls. The first thing Pogo picked up was that Taj was dealing with a problem in its command-and-control system. It was all he could do to keep from telling *Venture*—"Hey, even the Indian guy has to call Bangalore for computer help!"—but he restrained himself.

Especially since the next thing he learned was that the eruptions on Keanu were actually some kind of braking rockets . . . somehow making jokes at Taj's expense seemed too trivial.

As a kid Pogo Downey had always thought UFOs were alien space-ships, that the government was hiding something. He'd largely put those suspicions aside by the time he entered the Air Force Academy, where he'd learned new and better ways to distrust governments. But he still believed that humankind was not alone in the universe. So to be standing on an alien artifact . . . well, it wasn't *entirely* unexpected.

It was actually pretty cool.

By the time Natalia Yorkina, the second Russian on the *Brahma* crew, joined her teammate Lucas on the surface, it was obvious that Pogo was a third wheel. "Heading back. Good luck," he told the Coalition team.

"We will all need luck," Natalia said.

When Pogo reached *Venture*, Zack was back on the surface, already pre-paring to deploy the rover. "Getting a *Buzz*" was what the training teams had called it.

For years NASA had been in the stupid habit of bestowing individual names on pieces of equipment. The agency had even held a goddamn contest to name the rover that would be used on the third lunar landing, and "Buzz" had been the winner . . . after the second man to step on its surface.

Well, wherever he was, Buzz Aldrin was laughing, because while rovers *Neil* and *Gene* had been relegated to traverses on the nasty, asbestos-like lunar soil, rover *Buzz* was the first on an entirely new world.

Or starship. Let's not forget that.

The *Venture* lander stood eighteen meters high and, with the low sun angle, cast a shadow three times that long. In that shadow, Zack pulled the lanyard that opened an entire fifth of *Venture*'s landing stage . . . *Buzz* slid out, tilted, then began to unfold itself.

During training on Earth, the deployment process had been fairly noisy, reminding Pogo of the rattling grind of an old roller coaster pulling its cars to the top of the loop.

But here, in the snowy vacuum, there was no noise. With a strange sort of majesty, *Buzz*'s wheels dropped into place, the cabin inflated to its full size, and the gold Mylar antenna unfurled. In no more than a hundred and twenty seconds, the spidery vehicle was ready for action. "It looks bigger here," Pogo said. In the bays at Huntsville, surrounded by various models of lander and rover mockups, *Buzz* had looked a little sad and puny. Not on Keanu, though.

"Big enough." Zack seemed distracted, which was understandable. Already tasked with a challenging spaceflight, he had watched his mission transformed into something out of legend: the first exploration of an alien artifact.

How could anyone prepare for that?

Pogo joined him in transferring additional equipment from the *Venture* lockers to *Buzz*'s frame: additional oxygen tanks, the scientific package, new cameras, cabling. The work progressed in stops and starts. One tank simply would not come out of the bay. "It's like it fucking grew!" Pogo snapped, only dimly aware that he had just cursed on an open communications link.

Here he saw Zack Stewart in all his stoic glory. Without a word he jumped ahead on the unstow checklist and opened the adjoining bay, patiently handing the gear stored there to Pogo until it was empty.

Then he took a screwdriver and poked a hole in the adjoining wall. He used a pliers to peel open the leaves of the wall. "Is that a good idea?" Pogo hadn't considered such a maneuver. It reminded him too much of working in his home garage. . . .

"This isn't a load-bearing piece," Zack answered, going back to the screwdriver, which he jammed into the opening to free the jammed tank. "Besides, when we leave, this all stays behind."

Pogo couldn't decide which was more surprising, the fact that the tank was freed in this manner or that those were the only words Zack Stewart uttered in half an hour.

Buzz had a bubblelike pressurized cabin large enough to hold four astronauts packed so closely they might have to take turns breathing. With two, it approached comfort. For now, however, there was no need for

Zack or Patrick to depressurize the cabin: *Buzz* could be driven from out-side, too. (It was a battery-powered electric vehicle not much more com-plicated than a golf cart.)

Or, as Zack quickly demonstrated, it could be pushed and pulled on the snow toward Vesuvius.

Within minutes, the two were standing at crater's edge. "How are you holding up, chief?" Pogo asked. He was concerned about Zack's silence during the work with *Buzz*.

"Just scouting the terrain. Check it out." Zack picked up a chunk of ice and launched it into the vent. "Can't just drop it . . . it might take ten minutes to hit."

From this distance, Vesuvius Vent reminded Pogo of Meteor Cra-ter in Arizona, a substantial hole in the ground at least a click across and almost a couple of hundred meters deep. He had visited it for lunar geol-ogy training. But the Arizona crater was rocky while Vesuvius Vent was largely whitish, covered with impossibly ancient ice and snow, except where the heat of the venting had exposed the surface.

Zack began "giving the suite," doing a geological survey of the scene. "If that eruption had been volcanic, those bare spots would be black."

"It would have rolled some of these boulders, too," Patrick said. He was damned if he'd let Zack dominate the survey. Why waste five hun-dred hours of geological training?

"So it really wasn't an eruption, just a venting. Steam."

"Heat down below."

"Some deposits and layering."

"A long time ago, though."

As they spoke, Zack and Pogo crab-walked their way along the rim, away from *Venture* and *Brahma*. "Too bad the floor is shadowed," Zack said.

"If it *is* a floor, and not a bottomless pit."

"If it's a pit, it can only be a hundred kilometers deep."

Pogo saw something below, and stopped so suddenly he almost lost his footing. He raised his sun visor to be sure. "Zack," he said, "take a look."

Zack joined him, both men looking down into the shadowy depths. "*Venture*," Zack said, "are you getting imagery?"

"Not with you jiggling around," Tea said. Helmet cams were great tools, but had the disadvantage of reacting to every twitch and jolt an astronaut made.

"Okay, we'll try," Zack said. "Call this anomaly one."

"We can't make it out—"

"It looks like a ramp," Patrick said. "Directly at one o'clock, one third of the way up from the floor." Indeed, from this angle he and Zack could see the vent floor . . . a relatively smooth, snowy surface . . . and what could only be a ramp hewn out of the vent wall.

"I make it ten meters wide," Zack said. "But that's only a guess."

"It looks wide enough to drive a rover down."

"Greetings!" From their voices on the radio, Pogo had heard Lucas and Natalia approaching. Now they appeared, Lucas literally towing a pile of equipment and supplies on a sled! "Cool! Somebody back in Bangalore was thinking ahead," Pogo told them.

"This looks like a Russian innovation to me," Zack said.

Now there were four spacewalkers gathered at the rim. Zack pointed out the ramp. Patrick heard Natalia gasp. "Amazing . . ." she said.

Lucas sighed. "Too bad it doesn't reach to the top."

"It's a long way away," Zack said. "We'd have to drive a couple of hours just to get to the other side."

Which reminded Pogo: "What are we doing with *Buzz*, anyway? There's no easy way down to the bottom of this thing."

Zack turned in his cumbersome suit, his gold sun visor raised . . . Pogo could see him smiling. "Everybody grab one wheel."

Without understanding, Pogo simply followed orders, reaching for the rover. "Now what?" he said.

"Lift," Zack ordered. *Buzz* weighed three hundred kilograms on Earth; on Keanu it could have been raised by a single human. It was only the sheer size of the rover that made it helpful to use four pairs of hands. "Now," Zack said, "to the rim. Right there, the steep spot . . ."

Only then did Pogo realize that Zack planned to literally throw *Buzz* the rover off the rim. "On my mark," Zack said.

Pogo wasn't the only doubter. "Zack, are you sure about this?" Natalia asked.

"Yes. We need to explore Vesuvius, and the rover has the tools. No more questions. One, two, three—!"

Propelled perhaps three meters laterally, off the rim of the vent, *Buzz* floated down, down, down, kicking off one outcropping and starting a slow tumble, but still remained upright. The astronauts could see the rover bounce twice, then, just like *Venture* during its landing, settle onto the snow and ice.

"I don't fucking believe it," Pogo said.

"How do we get down?" Lucas asked.

"We've got no choice but to follow," Zack said. He walked Pogo toward the rim—then pushed him over.

Pogo had logged two hundred parachute jumps back at the Air Force Academy. He was no stranger to the momentary terror of a great leap, though the impromptu, unequipped nature of this push caused him to tense.

The crazy maneuver confirmed one thing: Zack Stewart was the right choice to lead a mission like this.

CAPCOM: *Venture*, Houston. Yvonne, the center director is standing by.

VENTURE (HALL): You mean my dad.

CAPCOM: Yes, your father, Dr. Jones.

VENTURE (HALL): Does he have something official or, ah, medical to discuss?

CAPCOM: That's negative. He wants to speak . . . father to daughter.

DIRECTOR (JONES): I just want to know how you're doing.

VENTURE (HALL): I've already told the docs. They're watching my condition.

DIRECTOR (JONES): We all are . . .

VENTURE (HALL): So much for privacy.

DIRECTOR (JONES): If you want to call this . . . call everything off, we'll pull you out of there.

VENTURE (HALL): That sounds more like JSC director than father.

DIRECTOR (JONES): I'm sorry.

VENTURE (HALL): Well, Mr. Director, tell my father that I'm enthusiastic about completing my mission.

DESTINY-7 AIR-TO-GROUND TRANSCRIPT (NO DISTRIBUTION)

Yvonne removed the headset. *Four hundred thousand clicks from Earth, and I still can't get away from this man.*

She felt sick. She wanted to go home. But she would be double damned if she would make Gabriel Jones's life any simpler or easier.

Flight surgeons report that *Destiny* astronaut Yvonne Hall's condition is stable following an incident that took place during her historic EVA. An unexpected eruption from the Keanu feature known as Vesuvius Vent is believed to have caused a fall and subsequent damage to Hall's suit. She was safely retrieved by *Destiny* commander Zachary Stewart and Coalition cosmonauts Munaretto and Chertok, and is now resting comfortably aboard *Destiny*. Further updates will be issued as warranted. Coverage of the second EVA by Stewart and *Destiny* astronaut Patrick Downey resumes shortly.   NASA PUBLIC AFFAIRS, AUGUST 22, 2019

The assault on Vesuvius Vent, which began with the bombardment of rover *Buzz*, followed by the parachute-free free fall of Col. Patrick "Pogo" Downey, USAF, continued with the free-fall landing of Dr. Zachary Stewart, then the sled of equipment provided by the Coalition of Space-Faring Nations.

Cosmonauts Lucas "World's Greatest Astronaut" Munaretto of Brazil's AEB (Agencia Espacial Brasileira) and Natalia Yorkina of the Russian Federal Space Agency followed more sedately; they had come equipped with rappelling gear and chose to leave anchor lines at the top before sliding down.

Watching the process made Zack impatient and confirmed his original judgment. Lucas, in particular, kept bouncing in the low gravity, literally hanging in midair for seconds at a time at the end of his rope, until regaining contact with the surface, and traction.

Natalia proved to be either an experienced climber or a natural low-gravity operator.

No matter, Zack was happy to have the rope option.

It was one thing to take a literal giant leap to the bottom of Vesuvius . . . it was quite another to do so with no obvious way back up. His last order to Tea was to get together with Taj and do a detailed survey of the Vesuvius slopes, in hopes of finding a road to the top.

While he waited, and while he still had communications with *Venture*, he was able to check his messages, which could be read on a tiny LED inside his helmet, about six words at a time.

There was a text from Rachel: HEARD YOU TAKE STEPS BUT COVERED MY EYES. BE CAREFUL AND COME HOME! LUV U.

He started to laugh. Even though it was easy, as the father of a teenage girl, to be distracted by the laziness, sloppiness, and occasional snotty attitude, Rachel was inescapably his child.

And Megan's.

He did not want to unwrap the Megan memory box just yet. It would be too distracting. *Focus on your environment!*

He was standing in the bottom of a giant pit as wide as Minute Maid Stadium, just out of the cold shadow that darkened two-thirds of the surface here.

The surface itself was more rock than snow. It was nowhere near flat, either, but rather gently rolling, like the surface of a frozen ocean.

He was tired, his hands ached from the struggle against EVA gloves, yet he felt buoyant, alive, elated. Zack extended this private moment long enough to piss in his diaper. He comforted himself with the knowledge that he was continuing an astronaut tradition that went back to Alan Shepard on the first *Mercury* . . . and Buzz Aldrin during the first walk on the Moon.

Now it was time to dig more deeply into Keanu. The only moment in his life that compared was his first date as a licensed driver.

In fact, he could see several clefts in the shadowed walls of the vent. He couldn't wait to start. He was delayed only by a mandated rest break (something he had learned to appreciate during his space station EVAs). Lucas and Natalia were busy unloading the sled, while Pogo was unspooling fiber-optic cable from *Buzz*. That line would provide real-time communications to Tea and *Venture*—aside from the habitability module on

Buzz, which allowed for extended EVA, the cable was the only clear advantage the NASA team had over the Coalition so far.

Constant, real-time communication between *Venture* and Houston had its drawbacks. There wasn't an astronaut alive who enjoyed having his every syllable broadcast in real time to millions. But it also allowed Rachel to see what her father was doing—and even send him the odd text.

Zack wondered if she sent messages to Tea, too. They had developed their own independent friendship since that very tricky moment nine months back, when Zack had first introduced his fellow astronaut to his daughter . . . as his girlfriend.

It was his own birthday, and he had continued the Stewart family tradition of selecting a favorite restaurant—this year a new California cuisine place on El Dorado. Rachel was present, of course, and so were the Meyers . . . By prearrangement, Tea had arrived ten minutes late. Zack had allowed her to kiss him, then introduced her as his date.

All Rachel had said, then, was "Gee, I wondered who the extra chair was for."

That night she had been more pointed. "I think she's fine, okay? But, God, you could have told me in private!" Well, no . . . they had been fighting so much over so many trivial matters that season that Zack had simply been afraid to have a conversation with his daughter.

Things had gone better, with Tea spending more and more time at the Stewart house, and even going shopping with Rachel.

The only crisis had come when Zack took Tea's spot as *Destiny-7* commander. She had become . . . just another astronaut. Ever since the crew suited up at the Cape prior to launch, there had been no shared looks between them, no secret touches, very damn few private words. Yes, this mission was all-consuming, but did it have to destroy any vestige of human emotion? Was that what real spaceflight did?

More troublesome was the possibility that the mission just exposed Zack's lack of true feelings for Tea . . . or hers for him—

"Zack, look what we got here!"

It was Lucas. The Brazilian astronaut—who had spent so much time in Houston over the past decade that he seemed more American than Zack—had unpacked a portable aperture-radar unit from the Coalition's sled and was panning it, like a twentieth-century video camera, around the bases of the vent.

Zack and Pogo shuffled toward the Coalition team. "What have you got?"

Lucas handed him the radar gun, but Zack saw only a confused image that reminded him of a prenatal sonogram—more evidence that the Coalition team was better equipped and trained for exploring Keanu. "An opening," Lucas said. "A big one."

Pogo took the radar gun. He seemed to have a better idea of what it showed. "He's right. Sucker's ten meters wide, at least, and at least half that high. You could drive a semi through it." As he handed the gun back to Lucas, he added, "Did I say straight edges?"

Keanu maneuvered. And there was a ramplike structure inside this vent. And now what seemed to be a portal with straight edges . . .

Zack could feel his heart rate climbing. "Let's get rolling, then."

They pressed forward like Arctic explorers . . . or so Zack imagined. Pogo led the way on foot, followed by Lucas pulling the sled, Natalia playing out the fiber-optic cable, and Zack driving *Buzz* at the rear. It was his job to keep Tea and Houston informed of their progress. The exchanges were curt and to the point. "Fifty meters from the cleft." "Copy, fifty."

"Notice anything about the surface?" Pogo said.

Immediately behind Pogo, Lucas tried to halt but fell on his face, a victim of a high center of gravity. The others helped him up; no damage, thank God. It was a real concern, since, from his perch on the front of rover *Buzz*, Zack could see that there was less snow beneath their boots and wheels.

More amazingly, there was also none of the expected gray, lunarlike soil. What they were walking on, what stretched before them to the cleft, was a flat, cracked, and weathered surface that reminded Zack of an ancient Roman roadway.

"*Venture* and Houston," he said, trying to hold his helmet cam steady. "Are you getting this?"

Houston only copied, but Tea said, "Jeez, all you need is a welcome mat." When she added, "Be careful, baby," he smiled like a teenager with his first crush; maybe she did still like him.

They pressed forward, the cleft now clearly visible as an opening. "Not only do we have some kind of pavement below us," Pogo said, "there's obvious machining on the opening."

Zack could see it, too: scarring and scraping that looked too regular to have been made by hand tools. And there was something else—

"Anyone *feeling* any different?" he asked.

"You mean, other than extremely nervous?" Lucas said, violating every unwritten rule concerning astronaut demeanor.

"I'm getting better traction on my boots," Natalia said. "And sled feels heavier!" Zack had noticed that under stress, Natalia's otherwise-excellent English began to shed its articles.

That confirmed Zack's perceptions. "The rover's not sliding as much."

"Could gravity be increasing?" Lucas asked.

"Could it be that we're on firmer footing rather than sliding on ice?" Pogo snapped.

"Houston and *Venture*, we offer that as food for thought," Zack said, short-circuiting a pointless debate. "We are inside the cleft now."

They had all moved from sunlight to darkness. "Lights going on," Zack said. Rover *Buzz* had been designed to operate in lunar night, so it had a set of honest-to-God headlights.

"We have portables," Natalia said, bending to the sled. "Give us a moment."

As she and Lucas went to work removing several lights and stands, Pogo returned to the rover. "What do you think?" he said. "Leave the rover here, or take it into the cave?"

"We need equipment, we might need shelter. As long as there's room for it, I say drive on."

Houston concurred. Then Pogo said, "I'm having comm problems. Going to Channel B."

His voice sounded different in Zack's earphones. "What do you think of the Coalition bringing portable lights, rappelling gear, and a sled?"

Zack had been wondering the same thing. "They had some idea they were going spelunking."

"I wonder what else they know that we don't?"

"Lucas says he's nervous."

"Let's hope the lights are the only tool we actually need."

After a pair of lights was set up, all four explorers took a meal and rest break. Elapsed EVA time was two hours, not in itself a problem. Typical station EVAs ran seven to eight hours. But here the astronauts were working in gravity, slight but nevertheless real. And not one of them had really rested for today's expanded activities. Zack, in fact, had already spent an hour on the surface dealing with Yvonne's injury.

And who knew when any of them would be able to stand down. At the moment, the into-Keanu EVA looked open-ended.

Realizing that dragging the sled across the "pavement" would be difficult, Zack offered to move the Coalition's gear to the racks on rover *Buzz*. "Canny," Pogo said. "We move more easily, and we get to see what else they're carrying."

If that was Pogo's goal, he was disappointed. The Coalition gear consisted of half a dozen unmarked containers, although Natalia donned a set of microfocals that attached to her helmet. "For geological study," she said, volunteering an explanation without being asked.

With the exit lights growing smaller behind them, now relying on *Buzz*'s headlamps, the explorers probed deeper into the cleft. Zack walked point, in Pogo's phrase, while his fellow astronaut drove *Buzz*, and the Coalition partners flanked him.

"Comm is getting ratty," Pogo said. This time he wasn't kidding. The standard VHF signals wouldn't travel far through Keanu's rock, and even the Coalition's cable was suffering dropouts. It was obvious from the spool that they were almost out of cable, too.

"How deep is this thing?" Zack asked.

Lucas aimed the radar gun. "Maybe a hundred meters to go."

"Then what?" Pogo said, not bothering to hide his irritation.

"Ah, it's very confusing."

"How confusing can it be? It's a hole or it's a wall."

Natalia came to Lucas's rescue. "It looks like a junction. Branches."

That possibility was as terrifying as it was exciting. "Houston, *Venture*, Zack. We might be coming to a fork in the road at the same time we go dark."

This time both Houston and *Venture* had the same firm reaction. Weldon said, "You're closing in on three hours elapsed EVA time. Hold at the junction."

Bangalore and Taj were even more insistent with the Coalition pair.

There had been no further change in the environment, aside from a general sense that he was getting heavier. (How heavy, ultimately? If they reached the equivalent of Earth gravity, they would barely be able to move; the EVA suits weighed more than a human being. Rover *Buzz* wouldn't move far, either. Its suspension had been engineered for lunar gravity.)

The same "paving stones" lined the floor of the cleft. The walls and ceiling had the same scraped look. How long ago had this been carved? Zack wondered. Ten thousand years ago? About the same time human beings were figuring out how to cultivate crops?

A hundred thousand? When humans were barely out of Africa?

A million? When there were no recognizable human beings on Earth?

Maybe ten million—maybe longer!

He could hear Lucas and Natalia patiently debating their situation with Taj in *Brahma*, and Nayar at Bangalore. "How can we stop here? What have we learned?" Lucas said. The young Brazilian clearly had not absorbed the astronaut rule book, either about admitting fear or having open debates with mission control.

But Zack was glad he was along. Every group needed someone who would say what the others secretly thought.

More troubling, it appeared that Natalia's EVA suit was overheating, a common problem with the Russian-built unit. So far it was likely to be an inconvenience rather than a disaster for the EVA.

Zack motioned Pogo forward, almost beyond the range of *Buzz*'s lamps.

"Houston, *Venture*, Zack. How do I read?"

"I've got you," Tea said. A few seconds later, there was a static burp, presumably Houston.

"Tea, what would you be doing if you were here?"

"Call me chicken. I might camp out in the rover."

"I hear you, but I'm too wound up to get any real rest," Zack said. "While our friends are catching up on news from home, I think we're going to recon this junction."

Pogo was so excited he trotted ahead of Zack. "Take it easy, cowboy."

"Come on, Zack! I mean, look at the situation: Keanu slows down and goes into orbit. It's got a big old entryway at the logical landing site. Doesn't it all add up to them wanting us to say hello?"

Zack had known Pogo for almost a decade—knew him to be religious, a straight arrow . . . and also, in spite of his physical chops and manly skills, a bit of a geek. The Air Force jock had read far more sci-fi than Zack, who gave up quickly on movies and books when presented with space battles that looked like aerial engagements from World War II. "I'll give you this," he said, huffing and puffing. "It's what we signed up to do."

They were deep into the junction now, a terminus of sorts where the main shaft ended, and at least four passages branched off at different angles. Pogo suddenly disappeared around the right one, leaving Zack alone and, except for his helmet light, in the dark.

"Pogo, you can't get ahead of me like that—"

Zack found him a few meters into the next passage, frozen in what struck Zack as an awkward posture, his head tilted back as far as it would go in the suit. "Okay," Zack said, catching his partner and tapping him on the shoulder.

Pogo only said, "Look up there."

Directly in front of them stood a marker of some kind, a stone plate embedded in the wall of the passage several feet above eye level.

All Zack could say was, "Oh."

The plate showed a gauzy helix of some kind, monochrome, at least as far as they could tell by their helmet lights. "If you move your head, it changes," Pogo said. Zack did better than that . . . he actually stepped to one side.

The helix seemed to expand. "It's 3-D," he said. He raised his hand, hoping to see it pass through the image, if that was what it was. But he couldn't reach it.

"It looks like a model of a galaxy," Pogo said.

This was Zack's area of expertise, and he knew that current galactic models were less helical and more spherical. But they had changed once in his lifetime; no reason to assume they wouldn't change again. Besides—

"Is that a marker of some kind?" If you accepted the idea that the 3-D image showed a galaxy, a bright dot was placed halfway between the end of one spiral arm and the fuzzy center.

"Maybe it's their version of the *Voyager* record." One of the first deep-space probes back in the 1970s had carried a laser disc filled with music, art, samples of what passed for human culture . . . just on the slim chance some alien intelligence might pick it up.

An alien intelligence that also possessed a laser disc player, which would put them far ahead of anyone on Earth. Zack knew all about the challenges of creating any sort of message that would last hundreds or thousands of years . . . it wasn't just content, it was delivery system. "Maybe they're telling us where they came from," Zack said.

"Who, exactly, is 'they'?"

They heard voices on the radio—Lucas and Natalia were trying to catch up. "We're in the right passage," Zack told them, just as flickering shadows alerted him to their arrival.

They stopped and stared. "Welcome to the next sign," Pogo said.

Lucas sounded annoyed. "What sign?"

Zack explained, "He just means, the next bit of evidence that we are encountering an alien life-form."

"Ah, evidence of life-form," Lucas said. "Not the life-form itself."

"Not yet," Pogo said.

"What do you see?" Zack asked the new arrivals.

"It almost looks like DNA helix," Natalia said.

Now that Zack stood back, he recognized Natalia's suggestion as a possibility. He had grown up with DNA models that consisted of tiny colored balls arranged in a double helix . . . but suppose a more advanced view was more complex and chaotic? Might a DNA model resemble a galaxy?

"Nah," Pogo said. "A galaxy makes more sense."

"To us, maybe," Zack said. "But if it's DNA, it might be a way of saying, 'If this is you, come on in.'" He suddenly wished for direct, real-time communication with Houston and the Home Team. *Wait until they see this—*

As Natalia carefully recorded images from every possible angle, Lucas jumped, trying to touch the marker. Top heavy, in low gravity, he really only waved at it, but one thing startled Zack.

He thought he heard a faint scrape as Lucas's boots reconnected with the pavement. *Sound?* Impossible!

He stomped his own boots on the pavement. All he learned was that it made his feet hurt. "Did anyone hear anything?"

"Why would we be able to hear?" Pogo said.

"Because we have a trace atmosphere," Natalia said. She was holding a small instrument that reminded Zack of a light meter—a portable barometer! "Still some way to go before it gets as dense as that of Mars, but measurable."

"Composition?"

"This only shows me pressure."

"Could it be from the rover?" Rover *Buzz*'s pressurized module would leak some of its air; other pieces of equipment, such as the fuel cells, inevitably emitted gas, too.

"Not unless your rover has a serious leak," Natalia said. "Even then, I

think this space is too large." She was being kind. A moment's rough cal-
culation proved to Zack that there was no way the rover's outgassing—
or a dozen rovers' outgassings—would account for a pressure reading of
any kind.

"Hey," Pogo was saying. "Do you see anything strange on the plate?"

He had moved from spot to spot, experiencing the changing views possible from different angles and heights. "Our marker has been damaged."

Zack looked closely. The plate behind the 3-D projection appeared
to have been partially eaten away, as if splashed with acid. The edges of
the damaged area were unexpectedly regular, however. "That's strange.
Someone's been naughty here."

"Maybe we aren't the first to find this sign," Natalia said.

"You mean we're looking at *two* alien races?" That was Patrick. "This
is getting even cooler!"

"Are we sure we're even dealing with *one*?" Lucas turned away from
the marker, as if it made him nervous.

"Let's let the experts decide and decipher," Zack said, not especially
eager to give up the lead role—but not wishing to have his team waste
time debating when there was clearly more exploration to be done. "It
would help if they could see this."

It took half an hour to restring the cable and bring the camera to the
site of the marker. As the startling images traveled at light speed along
the cable, back to *Brahma* and *Venture*, and then, two seconds later, to
Houston, Bangalore, and the world, Pogo gestured at the high ceiling—
higher than a basketball hoop—and broad passage.

"Whoever or whatever they are, they're big suckers."

Tea Nowinski's father had an expression that, unfortunately, perfectly described his daughter's job during the EVA into Vesuvius Vent. Forced to serve as the link between Zack and Patrick and mission control, she was "the meat in the sandwich." Squashed, covered in mustard, not a pleasant place to be.

In fact, she also had to serve the same role for Dennis Chertok and his commander aboard *Brahma*. For the past four hours, all she had done was flip switches to change frequencies on the radio, back and forth from the direct link to Zack and Patrick, and at times Lucas and Natalia, then another channel to Houston (formerly Weldon, now the Stay-2 shift director Josh Kennedy), then a third channel to Taj in *Brahma*.

All the while watching the startling imagery that flickered on the small screen on *Venture*'s control panel: the view from the bottom of Vesuvius Vent; the pavement; the cleft; the dark, forbidding passage.

The *marker*.

Maybe it was better that she was so busy, or she would have been paralyzed at the implications . . . that she and Yvonne and Dennis and *Venture* and Taj and *Brahma* were sitting not on the icy/rocky surface of a Near-Earth Object, but on the hull of a giant interstellar spacecraft.

And possibly a few kilometers—or meters!—from its crew!

She was only able to hear fragments of the reaction in Houston, the automatic use of the stoic word *copy* to acknowledge the latest bombshell, broken by Kennedy's occasional honest blurt of "Wow" or "Oh man."

What was going on with the Home Team? For that matter, what was her father thinking, back home in Woodland Hills?

What was really going through Zack's mind a kilometer from here?

She wanted to be dealing with those matters, not feeding Yvonne Hall and checking her dressing, or searching out bandages and medical gear and food and water for Chertok, all the while struggling with the question of what the cosmonaut was seeing, and whether he should see it.

Her immediate goal now, at EVA plus four hours, was to get Dennis out of *Venture*.

Yvonne rested in a hammock stretched across the rear of the *Venture* cabin at nose height. There was another set of attach points even higher up—it was where Yvonne was originally supposed to sleep. (*Venture*'s main cabin was taller—four meters in height—than it was wide, a design necessitated by its dual use as a vehicle capable of lifting off a planetary surface. In lunar gravity, there was no danger in falling out of a hammock eight feet off the ground.) But that would have put her out of reach. Even so, Dennis had had to stand on a stool to perform his basic surgery.

"I have done all I can do," Dennis announced. "She will be stable for at least a day. In this gravity, possibly more. But my professional recommendation is that you return her to Earth at first opportunity." He smiled to show that he was aware of the political and operational challenges of that decision.

"I'll tell Houston."

He indicated the airlock. "I will need some help suiting up."

"Get started and I'll be right with you." As the cosmonaut slipped through the hatch into the next chamber, Tea climbed the stool to have a look at Yvonne. "How're you feeling?"

"About like you'd expect."

Tea had conflicting views of her fellow astronaut. She had known Yvonne for a decade—had actually served as the astronaut in charge of training Yvonne's group of candidates, so she had seen the young engineer's baby steps into the program. She had proved to be middle-of-the-pack in most regards . . . she lacked the operational strengths of some of her colleagues—those who had come to NASA from military units—and sometimes let her temper show.

But it turned out that she possessed astounding physical skills and a long-distance runner's stamina (Yvonne ran marathons) as well as terrific eye-hand coordination that made her everyone's choice for both remote manipulator work and EVAs, those being the two primary skill sets needed for station and lunar missions.

She wasn't just a jock, either; Yvonne turned out to be uncommonly levelheaded about the social aspects of being an astronaut, unlike a few of her fellow candidates, who fell into the usual trap of thinking they were the space world's equivalent of rock stars.

Tea had, of course, known that Yvonne was Gabriel Jones's daughter from a failed first marriage. Growing up in and around NASA had probably cured Yvonne of any illusions about the special nature of astronauts. At the time Yvonne joined the office, her father was actually in Washington at HQ, deputy associate administrator for exploration, one of the folks charged with developing and managing missions to the Moon . . . and to Near-Earth Objects. Jones's appointment as JSC director had no immediate effect on Yvonne's career. There was also some sniping about who got assigned to a flight crew—by anyone who didn't get assigned; any reason would do.

(Tea could only imagine what snarky comments were zipping around Building 4-South when her lover, Zack Stewart, was not only placed on her crew, but given her command!)

Destiny-7 had originally been Tea's mission, and she had not only approved Yvonne's assignment, she had asked for her.

And now, having seen Yvonne's accident, having had to deal with its aftermath, she wondered if she'd made the right choice.

Yvonne had made no obvious mistake, it was true—but she had demonstrated one fatal flaw:

She was *unlucky*.

"Can I get you anything?" Tea hoped Yvonne could drink on her own . . . "Do you want your father back on the line?"

"God, no." The injured astronaut shifted in the hammock, moaned. "Just get me my PPK," she said.

Tea wondered briefly why Yvonne wanted to share the hammock with a big silver briefcase, but if it made her happy—and quiet—she was all for it. "Coming right up."

"Shut up, Jason. The only thing we've learned from dealing with aliens is that they can't be trusted."

"So you're suggesting we can only fight them."

"Well, we could *surrender*, which is obviously your preference. But I like mine better."

EXTRACT FROM *STARSHIP "KILROY WAS HERE,"*
A SCI-FI NOVEL BY WADE WILLIAMS (1999)

"So this is the famous Vault."

Harley Drake rolled his chair through the doorway. He had been summoned out of the Home Team by Weldon, who introduced him to a tall, gangly, almost goofy-looking man of forty in a short-sleeved white shirt and several badges. "Brent Bynum," Weldon said, "National Security Staff, our White House liaison." Bynum said nothing, offering only a slight nod of the head.

Weldon led this short parade to the back side of Building 30, to a door that said *ELECTRICAL*.

And proved to lead to a spacious closet with a pair of ancient mainframes stacked floor to ceiling, and just enough room to reach another door . . . that led to a conference room beyond.

Weldon flipped on the lights. "We're getting a lot of use out of it this month."

Harley was surprised at how cool the room was, as if it had superstrength air-conditioning. "Is this little exercise going to be worth my time? Because you may have noticed that we have a crew wandering around loose on an alien spaceship."

"It won't take long, and yes." As Harley wheeled up to a polished conference table, Bynum opened a safe—aside from table and chairs and a blank HD television screen, the only furnishing in the room. He took out a blank sheet of letter paper and slid it to Harley, with a pen. "Please sign this." They were the first words the White House man had uttered.

"Nice to meet you, too." Harley scribbled his name without hesitation.

Bynum continued: "Now, print these words above: 'I understand the penalties associated with unauthorized disclosure of this information.'"

Harley carefully printed the sentence, but now he smirked. "How long do you think this information is going to remain secret?"

Bynum merely blinked as he collected the paper. "I'm sure some of it is on the Web even as we speak." Then he stepped back and, as far as Harley was concerned, faded into the wallpaper.

Weldon pulled an aged manila folder from the safe. Harley couldn't wait to flip it open—how often does anyone see any document that is so ridiculously secret? The folder was smudged, ancient—it even smelled of mildew—and contained a solid two inches of documents, many of them tabbed.

The cover page was priceless—an original typed sheet from someone called "Lt. A. G. Cumming" working for something called "Project Grudge," part of the Technical Intelligence Division at Wright-Patterson Air Force Base. Dated January 4, 1948—six months after the first widespread flying saucer reports, from what Harley recalled—and originally classed as "Secret," it bore half a dozen strikeouts and upgrade marks.

It was also labeled *Copy 1 of 5 copies.* Who got the other four? he wondered.

Beneath the cover was a two-page memo summarizing what was known about flying saucers and suggesting that a "protocol" be developed in case some sort of extraterrestrial beings—here called "Foreign/Non-Human Entities"—happened to show up, alive.

On the sound assumption that whatever this Lieutenant Cummings had proposed in 1948 was likely to be revised, expanded, and eventually contradicted by the newest documents in the file, Harley flipped ahead several pages. "I was hoping for the secrets to the Roswell crash. Until today I was skeptical about the idea that we had alien bodies at Hangar 18. . . ."

"The whole Roswell–alien body thing was made up in the 1970s."

"So you've read this."

"No," Weldon said. "I'm not cleared for it." Which surprised Harley. "But I was interested in UFOs as a kid."

Harley quickly worked through the pages, seeing little more than a series of cover pages recounting each new name of the organization that succeeded the Technical Intelligence Division, ultimately becoming the Air Intelligence Center—at which point the "protocol" was transferred to "joint control" between the Air Staff, the CIA, the National Reconnaissance Office, and the State Department. (At one point in the early 1980s, some low-level Air Staff officer—clearly not worried about potential damage to his career—had dubbed the protocol "Have Atom".)

"Don't fucking *read* it, Harley. Skim. The world is waiting for me."

"I'll try not to move my lips."

The content kept expanding, but the principles did not: Non-Human Entities should be treated as potentially hostile, like the crew of a captured Soviet or Red Chinese aircraft or vessel in the absence of a formal declaration of war.

Any landing or crash site should be sealed off and treated as a radiation leak. A team of pre-identified experts—Harley was amused to note that linguists were high on the list—would be activated and brought to Wright-Patterson and designated "The 48 Committee." Decisions should be made at the presidential level, with input from his national security adviser and the secretary of state. Financial support would come from the intelligence community black budget; support personnel would be Air Force. All information would be treated as highly secret.

But there was nothing mysterious about the document, nothing worth classifying . . . except for the fact that it proved that the U.S. government had taken the possibility of extraterrestrial life seriously as early as 1948.

Harley Drake had grown up with the idea, of course. Every other cartoon he had watched as a kid, most comic books, a good number of books and movies . . . all assumed that there was intelligent life elsewhere in the universe, often hostile life.

Even at ten he had not expected to find a giant alien spaceship parked over Washington, D.C., but he had been waiting for the day some backyard astronomer would announce that he'd picked up an extraterrestrial radio signal.

The closest he'd come was the day he first heard about Keanu. So the events of the past few hours didn't require a major paradigm shift; it was like hearing the results of a blood test. "Okay, I've got the idea, Shane. Mr. Bynum. There's a whole set of plans for dealing with E.T., assuming we run into one on Keanu."

"You didn't read the last page very closely, which was the one thing I was cleared for: It says that the 48 Committee will designate a point of contact and team leader, reporting directly to them.

"That team leader is *you*, Harley. You are now planet Earth's general in charge of First Contact, and that's how you're going to be introduced if I ever have to talk about this in public."

His first impulse was to tell Weldon to piss off . . . and to take Bynum with him. He wasn't that happy trying to wrangle the great minds of the Home Team; he surely didn't need to face reporters or deal with the White House.

But the second impulse was to remember the aviator's creed: Never turn down a combat assignment.

"Okay," he said.

"This changes very little, of course. Your primary job is making your experts available to mission control. . . ."

But Harley had ceased to pay attention to Weldon or Bynum or the political challenges of the Alien Protocol. He had just realized what was disturbing about Keanu's newly increased rotation.

"Shane, we're going to lose contact with *Venture*."

Weldon was an agile thinker, but fatigue, pressure, and setting combined to make him blink and say, "What?"

Harley quickly recapped the information from the Home Team, noting that *Venture* and *Brahma* had landed close to the western limb of Keanu, as observed from Houston. "Keanu is rotating, and sometime in the next hour, two at most, Vesuvius Vent and those two spacecraft are going to be out of direct line of communication."

"And this might last ten hours?" That was an eternity in mission operations.

"Yeah, best guess—" Weldon was already on his feet and heading for the door, leaving Harley alone in the Vault with the White House security man.

"I think that means we're done," Harley said, wheeling himself out.

The President of the Russian Federal Space Agency sends his congratulations to cosmonauts Chertok and Yorkina for their heroism in
rescuing American astronaut Hall, and for their continuing participation
in mission *Brahma* under command of ISRO's T. Radhakrishnan. The
President notes that today's use of Russian equipment to correct de-
ficiencies in a critical American operation is the sixth such event since
1975, including the recent evacuation of a sick astronaut from the International Space Station in September 2017.

FEDERAL SPACE AGENCY (ROSCOSMOS) PRESS RELEASE, 23 AUGUST 2019

"Zack, check this out."

The beam from Pogo's torch wiggled as it described a circle farther
down the branching passage.

A passage that ended in shimmering brightness. Zack had to blink
several times, clearing the sweat from his eyes, to be sure what he was
seeing. It looked like a wall of ice, something found in an Antarctic
cave . . . but it also reminded him of the northern lights . . . It was gauzy,
somehow insubstantial.

"Stop right there," Zack said.

"Don't worry, I wasn't going anywhere."

"Lucas? Natalia?" Zack knew they had to be behind the American
pair. He just wanted to hear their voices.

"I see it," Lucas said.

"We all see it," Natalia said, sounding snappish. Her suit was probably
still overheating, making her hot and causing her faceplate to fog. "What
is it?"

"Bubbles." "I see texture." "It looks like a curtain." All three of them had instant theories.

"I just hope it isn't one of *them*," Pogo said. Of course, why couldn't the inhabitants of Keanu be shimmering energy beings? The Air Force astronaut continued to surprise Zack with his imagination.

"Let's get some snaps for the folks back home," Zack said, really missing real-time communication with Houston or *Venture*. "Lucas, what does the radar say?"

"Scattered return," the Coalition astronaut said. "It's not a solid surface."

"Is it moving or held in place?" That was Natalia.

"Seems to be attached around the edges."

Lucas's information confirmed Zack's own perceptions. They were looking at some kind of curtain blocking the end of the passage. "I hate to say it, but there's really only one way to find out what this is."

Zack patted the equipment belted to his suit. He had a small geological hammer. Unhooking it, he waved it in front of the curtain. Got no response.

So he chucked it at the shimmering surface, which swallowed it instantly.

"What do you suppose that means?" Pogo said.

"It means a hunk of metal could pass through. Which means—"

"Copy that, Commander." Pogo skipped forward, but Zack followed and caught him.

"Commander's prerogative. If I don't come back, you're in charge."

Without further discussion, or hesitation, Zack headed right toward the curtain, which shimmered and glittered, but did not move.

He stopped a meter away. For an instant he thought the curtain might be nothing more than an image, some kind of 3-D projection. Slowly, he reached out until his gloved fingertips disappeared into it. The gloves prevented him from feeling texture or temperature . . . but there was a kind of resistance, like pressing against a pillow, or, more likely, an energy field.

"Zack, let us put a line on you." Pogo was right behind him.

"You don't have a line. Come on," he said, feeling impatient, "where's your sense of adventure?"

"Patrick is right," Natalia said. "You can't be reckless!"

"I'm simply going to see if this is permeable. I'll keep talking. If I lose comm, give me one minute, then come and get me."

He stepped forward, right into the curtain . . . and was immediately bathed in light and drowned in bubbles that literally flowed across the surface of his suit and helmet. "It's as if I'm taking a bubble bath, but they have substance. They're more like transparent ball bearings, maybe."

No answer. He counted. "Step three, step four." The bubbly bearings did not resist him. He was able to step just as freely as he had in the outer passage.

"Six, seven . . ." On the eighth step he was through the bubble curtain—

—Into another passage much like the one he had just left, just as broad, high, and dark!

The beam from Zack's helmet light simply vanished, as if dying in a vast open space. He turned right and left. Another marker sat on the wall to his right. Unlike the one outside the curtain, this marker looked untouched.

Maybe it was new.

He took one more step and felt himself slip. He did not fall, but what he saw then almost staggered him.

He was standing in a pool of water. The snow that had accumulated on his boots and legs from the excursion across the surface of Keanu was *melting*.

There was air pressure on this side of the curtain. The temperature was above the melting point of water.

Which meant that the bubble-beaded curtain was actually some kind of airlock.

"Can we go in?"

Looking up from her phone, Amy Meyer peered past Rachel into the auditorium, where several dozen reporters with computers and camera operators were bombarding Gabriel Jones, Shane Weldon, and Harley Drake with shouts. It didn't appear to be going well.

"Why would you want to do that?"

"Never mind," Amy said, possibly remembering that Rachel's mother had died on the way to a press conference. "Hey," she said, "just in case." She pulled something from her shorts pocket . . . opening her hand, she revealed a brownish cigarette.

"I can't believe you brought a joint here!"

"Fine, I'll go flush it—"

"No!" Rachel said, wrapping her hand around Amy's. "We just might need it."

Rachel had her back to the door, which kept opening and closing every few seconds. She and Amy had escaped from the family holding cell to go in search of food and had been swept here by the crowd.

But they didn't have to stay, and they wouldn't. Rachel had a headache; she felt sick to her stomach.

Nevertheless, getting this far had been useful. From what she'd heard through the open door and being talked about in the hallway, Rachel knew that her father was alive, but now completely out of touch inside the NEO. And that he and Patrick Downey had been in their suits for something like five hours, with no end in sight, and that the doctors didn't see any problem with that, even though Rachel remembered her father coming home from five hours of spacewalk training in the big pool with his hands so bruised the fingernails were black, and with giant welts on his neck.

She didn't expect to be able to talk to him, not during the EVA . . . but what she really hated was not being able to *hear* him. She thought of her Slate and how really useless it was sometimes.

"Rachel!" It was Jillianne Dwight, the *Destiny-7* crew secretary, striding toward her with a frown on her face. "You're not supposed to be out here!"

Rachel didn't know Jillianne very well—her father had been on the crew for only a couple of months—but she liked her.

Until today. The moment Rachel's name broke through the general din, several reporters turned and made eye contact. "You're the daughter!"

Rachel turned to Jillianne. "Happy now?"

Before anyone could ask a question—at least, a question that Rachel understood—Jillianne and Amy formed a human shield around her and marched her down the hall and out a back door.

Jillianne said, "I need to get you back to the family room."

"I'm not going back to the family room."

"Well, you can't be out here. They'll eat you alive."

Rachel thought. "Let me talk to Tea."

Jillianne considered this. "Fine. But phones off."

Rachel and Amy were happy to comply. They were fine as long as no one decided to search Amy's pockets.

The atmosphere inside mission control was completely different from that outside—serene, silent. The only sound was the familiar hiss of static.

On the screen, Rachel and Amy could see the top half of Yvonne Hall in her hammock. The rest of the view was Tea Nowinski, who kept bobbing up and down, clearly making some adjustment on the panel above the camera. When her face came into view, Rachel was horrified at the way she looked, with her hair ratted atop her head. Rachel knew ten times as much about makeup and clothing as Tea did. . . . One of the fun things about her relationship with Dad's girlfriend was teaching her.

Of course, at the moment, Tea had other things to worry about.

Flight director Josh Kennedy spotted them and did a double take. He seemed about to drop his headset and approach them when—

"Okay, Houston, we've got a link again . . . holy cow!"

The big screen cut from the *Venture* interior view (which remained in a small picture-within-picture) to a dark exterior showing three astronauts, one NASA and two Coalition, with some kind of silver screen behind them. "Looks like they're on television," Amy said.

"They *are* on television," Rachel said. Amy was starting to become annoying.

The Coalition pair was literally working on the camera, their helmets looming in front of the lens. The chatter on the air-to-ground was the Russian and Portuguese equivalents of phrases like *Got it* and *Okay*.

"What's that shiny thing?" Rachel asked out loud.

Kennedy turned toward her. Once he registered the appalling fact that she was Zack's daughter, watching this amazing feed live, he leaped into action, taking Rachel by the arm and trying to get her out of mission control. "We're thinking it's the outer door of an airlock."

That was not what Rachel needed to hear. Her father had somehow fallen into a sci-fi movie . . . she wanted it to end. *Come home!* "Where's my father?"

"Uh, he went through the airlock," Kennedy said. Then, to the others in the room, "Anybody seen Harley Drake?"

Then Kennedy's eyes went wide. Rachel turned to look at the screen. Amy and Jillianne grabbed her hands as everyone in mission control inhaled at the same time.

On the screen was a hand, then a waving arm. Her father's. "Houston, Pogo," Downey said. "Looks like Zack wants us to follow him."

JSC DIRECTOR JONES: I can take three questions—

QUESTION: Given Hall's accident, shouldn't you be bringing the astronauts home?

JONES: Flight surgeons are monitoring her condition, which is stable. Yvonne herself has said that this vital exploration must continue.

QUESTION: Is there any worry that the Coalition craft contributed to the explosion?

JONES: The event on Keanu was a natural event . . . the only surprise was the actual timing.

QUESTION: What if there are further surprises?

JONES: The mission continues, of course. As we like to say, failure is not an option.

QUESTION: Are you worried about your daughter?

JONES: I'm worried about everyone in that crew!

PRESS BRIEFING ON NASA SELECT TV AND WEB

It took less than ten minutes for the other three to pass through the membrane, as Zack now called it. "One at a time," Pogo had told his Coalition friends, "with me first."

Now, completely disconnected from the camera and link they had managed to rig on the other side of the membrane, in contact only with themselves, the four moved swiftly across the rocky surface of a chamber that reminded Pogo Downey of Kartchner Caverns, the giant cave he'd visited while a college student in Arizona—huge, dark, unknowable.

Mindful of the one major limitation on all this activity—air and water supplies in their suits—he asked, "What's the hurry?"

"I just . . . need to see this," Zack said. He actually sounded out of breath. Was it exertion? Or excitement?

"What are these shapes?" Natalia said.

Pogo realized that over the thirty-or-forty-meter traverse from the membrane he'd seen shadows in his peripheral vision . . . had assumed they were just visual effects from four bobbing helmet lights hitting boulders or possibly stalagmites.

Idiot. He wasn't in Kartchner Caverns. He was inside Keanu . . . it was strange how the mind kept laying familiar shapes onto alien ones.

Lucas went up to the nearest shape, shining his torch up and down. "It's another marker!"

Indeed, it looked like another spiral galaxy or double helix, but larger and more detailed.

Zack didn't have to ask any of them to take pictures, or do a radar scan. Lucas, Natalia, and Pogo swarmed the marker, recording every possible angle. Lucas had hauled a new camera from the sled, bulkier and less finished-looking than the other instruments. "What's a Zeiss MKK?" Zack said.

At that moment, Pogo noted a wisp of vapor on the leg of the commander's suit. "Boss," he said, suddenly worried, pointing. "Check your pressure."

But Zack didn't seem worried. "This chamber is pressurized. Look at the ground . . ."

Pogo did, and saw a *puddle*. "Zack," he said.

"I think it's water," the commander said quickly. "It appeared to be melt from my boots. Yours, too, I'm guessing."

Natalia disagreed. "There's more here than we were carrying."

Then Lucas said, "I hear something."

And Pogo realized he had been hearing it, too. "Is that the wind?"

"What the hell is going on?" Natalia said. She sounded nervous. Pogo couldn't blame her. Puddles of liquid? Air pressure? Wind? Some of those conditions could exist on the surface of Mars, so it wasn't unthinkable.

But on a NEO—*inside* a NEO?

"Let's press on," Zack said. "Time is our enemy."

All four began to shuffle forward again, individually stopping to take images. Natalia was taking soil samples, scooping or scraping from the ground or the base of the markers (they'd passed half a dozen of them by now, each one clearly a cousin to the others, but all slightly different.) She held each one up to her microfocals before bagging it. Given the obvious fogging in her faceplate, she had to be getting frustrated.

"Hold up," Zack said.

Pogo and the others had already stopped, because all of them could see the same thing now.

Whether it was the combined illumination from their helmet lamps or some other source, the walls of the chamber were now barely visible . . . enough that the astronauts could see that they were covered with cell-like hexagonal structures of varying size, ranging from two meters wide to multiples of that, more or less symmetrical.

"Looks like a beehive," Zack said.

"I wonder where the bees might be." Natalia again, still sounding unnerved. Given the unholy uncertainties they were facing and the nagging problems with her suit, Pogo sympathized.

But that kind of unease could be contagious. They'd already seen more evidence of alien life than any humans in history—cumulatively. Who knew what lay ahead—what was right around the next corner?

"Zack," Natalia said, "what is our plan? Walk until we reach consumable limits, then turn back?"

"Essentially."

"Yeah," Pogo said. "Too bad this is such a short stay—and there's no chance for a follow-up."

"I really wish we had a better view," Zack said. "More light."

"Let me," Lucas said. To Natalia, he said, "Do you have any idea of the oxygen content here?"

"Substantial, over a quarter," she said, "but it's raw data."

"But it's not pure oxygen."

"No."

To Pogo's surprise, the World's Greatest Astronaut skipped a few meters ahead and raised a fat pistol in his gloved hand.

Where the hell had he found a flare gun? Of course—in the *Brahma*'s survival kit! There was one advantage of having your Earth return craft double as your lander. "Is it okay?" Lucas asked.

"Might as well," Zack said. "We can't see much without it."

The Brazilian astronaut fired the flare, which corkscrewed in the low gravity, reaching high into the chamber before igniting.

"Holy shit!"

Pogo couldn't help himself. Not only was the chamber so big that its far reaches could not be seen, but the Beehive itself had opened. The floor spread right and left with no walls, honey-combed or not.

Stranger yet, the collection of markers had been replaced by different structures—actually, they looked to Pogo more like growths. They were tall, fragile-appearing things that in some cases stood ten or fifteen meters high. "Corals," Pogo said. He had dived the Great Barrier Reef.

"Not quite," Natalia said, going closer and examining the nearest growth with her focals. "Corals have a jagged, irregular structure . . . these look spherical."

"Like the filling in the membrane?" Zack said.

"Apparently."

"Too bad Houston can't see this. They'd freak."

"*I'm* freaking," Zack said. "It was bad enough to realize that Keanu was a vehicle, not a natural object. I frankly don't know how to handle alien artifacts *and* landscapes."

"And the rest of us do?" Pogo said.

Even Natalia laughed. "Your openmindedness makes you the perfect choice to lead us, Dr. Stewart."

"We have two hours of consumables before we have to turn back," Pogo said. "We can camp out in *Buzz* and upload everything we've found. Then we would have input from Houston before we came back."

"That's my big worry," Zack said. "I don't know Yvonne's condition. We might get back in touch and be told the mission is over, we're going home.

"This might be the only chance we get—and I don't want to miss something important, because no human may ever be here again."

"Relax. We're doing everything we can." Pogo was getting impatient with Zack's expressions of doubt. Sure, they were justified. But a commander can't afford to appear indecisive or weak.

Of course, a good soldier doesn't question or undermine his commander, either. Both of them were no doubt getting tired. The suits were ridiculously easy to wear and work in, but they were still heavy and confining.

And even though gravity here was light, being on your feet for hours—

"I have a theory," Lucas said. Pogo realized that the other three had been clustered at the base of a coral tower.

"Please share."

"These corals might be building blocks."

"Building blocks of what?" Pogo said.

"Of life! What else?" Natalia said.

"Oh, hell, I don't know. Maybe they're building blocks of a new car or a piece of cheesecake! Goddammit, people—"

"Calm down, Pogo."

He really was feeling impatient. "I just don't think it's a smart idea to be putting everything in familiar boxes. . . ."

Lucas spoke up. "Of course, we will leave the analysis to the experts on Earth."

"Absolutely," Zack said. "It's just human nature. And now I have an entirely new image to confuse the matter: These corals look like fractal structures—"

"Yes," Lucas said, either warming to the idea or simply playing along, "Mandelbrot sets!"

Pogo noticed that Natalia had not only gone silent . . . she had stopped working her way around the coral and was frantically trying to reattach one of her scanners to the front of her suit.

Shit, he thought, *she's gone blind.* As he got closer, he saw that her visor was completely fogged over. "Boss, we've got a problem here!"

"Don't," Natalia said. The astronaut code: death before dishonor.

"Shut up. You're overheating. You can't continue to function in that suit."

Zack and Lucas came up. Zack took in the situation quickly. "Okay, Lucas," he said. "The EVA is officially over. You guide her back to the membrane. Wait on this side of it. Pogo and I will be right behind you."

Lucas didn't argue. He was probably as exhausted and overwhelmed as Pogo.

The Coalition team turned and started back the way they had come. Pogo realized now that they had not only walked into a huge chamber . . . they had come down a gentle slope—

"Pogo," Zack said. "Is it my imagination, or are *we* seeing better?"

Pogo had just noticed that himself. He looked away from Lucas and Natalia toward the center of the chamber.

The view forward was brighter. "It's like dawn. . . ."

It was indeed. As the four of them watched in openmouthed wonder, high above them on the "ceiling," a dozen long mobile shapes lit up, strong enough to brighten the chamber like a summer sunrise.

Pogo put his hand on Zack's shoulder. "And the Lord said, 'Let there be a light in the firmaments.'"

It bordered on blasphemy. But given the circumstances, Zack could not argue.

Her PPK still clutched to her chest, Yvonne listened to Tea's side of two and sometimes three conversations. One was the open channel with Houston, the other the encrypted one. Then there was the link to *Brahma* and cosmonaut Dennis Chertok, her savior, who had now returned to the Coalition craft.

There was even a fourth . . . Tea's regular call every minute or so for "Zack, Pogo, from *Venture*, do you read?" That conversation was one-sided, and increasingly pointless. Yvonne wondered if Zack and Patrick, and Lucas and Natalia, were even still alive, because as far as she could tell, Keanu was a hostile environment.

She wanted off.

From the encrypted comm, she knew that the planners in Houston were preparing *Venture* for a departure—"R plus ten hours," R being the moment the explorers returned.

That was one scenario, she knew, the one assuming her condition didn't worsen. It allowed the crew to have some kind of rest before managing a liftoff from another planet, and a life-or-death rendezvous with the *Destiny* mother ship.

There was an R plus six, and even an R plus two. Knowing how difficult a rendezvous would be—and, frankly, remembering that the shorter the gap, the worse her health—Yvonne was hoping the choice would be R plus ten.

That would bring the *Destiny-Venture* crew back to Earth within three days . . . carrying samples from this NEO starship-or-whatever-the-fuck-it-was. They could be astronaut heroes.

And Yvonne could forget about what was in her PPK.

Given the effects of the tranquilizer Dennis had given her, she wasn't sure she really believed it, anyway. A bomb—an honest-to-God suitcase nuke, the kind she'd heard about in spy movies.

It had happened eight days before launch, the day the crew was to move into the trailer at Johnson Space Center where they would be kept in medical isolation, and would start sleep-shifting to accommodate lift-off at a ridiculous hour.

Yvonne had just parked her car and was pulling her travel bag out of the trunk when her cell phone rang. There was a text asking her to stop by Building 30 on her way to the trailer.

She had walked into a hallway to find her father waiting for her.

Gabriel Jones had divorced his wife, Camille, when their daughter Yvonne was thirteen years old. The young space scientist had been caught having not one but two extramarital affairs, one with a fellow researcher, the other with the producer of a Discovery Channel series in which he had starred. "He just found a more exciting life."

Or so the former Camille Hall told her daughter. Watching her father from afar—there was financial support, but damned little additional contact over the years—Yvonne concluded that her mother's bitterness was justified:

Gabriel Jones had let fame and power go to his head.

Worse yet, he lacked real human feelings. "Oh, he can turn on the tears like a faucet," Mom would say. "But it's all show: nothing inside."

Which he had proved conclusively on that occasion. Yvonne stared in stunned silence as her father, the head of the Johnson Space Center, showed her a suitcase and told her it contained a small nuclear device known as the W-54C, with a yield of 2 kilotons and a blast radius of a kilometer. It was to be detonated if the *Venture* landing on Keanu proved to be dangerous to Earth. "We're talking some kind of contamination."

"Glad to hear you've got this all thought out. 'Some kind of contamination.' Christ."

"Don't swear." That was typical of Gabriel Jones, too. He was like one of those Baptists who was against sex because it was too close to dancing. . . . "It will be thought-out. You will have a set of orders. This is only a last resort."

"Not so good for me, though, is it, Daddy?"

He had stared at the floor. Typical; she could not remember ever meeting his gaze. "Two things. The circumstances that would cause you to use this are so horrendous that death would be preferable. Imagine you were on an airplane plunging toward the ground—"

"God, you really are a cold, sick son of a bitch!" Before he could protest, she said, "Why me? If anything should be the commander's job, this is it! Or it should be Downey. He'll follow orders."

"Downey is dogged and he's capable and does what he's told, but he also has a streak of . . . well, he might be *too* quick to pull the trigger.

"Tea's out because she's involved with Stewart. Her judgment will be colored by that."

"I guess that's why Zack doesn't have the package, either."

Here her father looked uncomfortable. "Stewart is brilliant and flexible, all the things we want in a mission commander. But, as you said, he's involved with one of his crew.

"He's also too convinced of his own intelligence. No matter what scenario we could come up with, all of our war-gaming showed that Zack would keep trying to the bitter end and beyond! He would be too slow to realize—"

"—That the patient was terminal?"

Gabriel Jones smiled tightly. "Exactly." Then he said the worst thing anyone had ever said to Yvonne: "You're your father's daughter."

She had walked away at that point.

But she had allowed the device to be stowed in her PPK.

And now, her leg shattered, her career destroyed, with very little knowledge of what was happening to Zack and Pogo and the others inside Keanu . . . Yvonne Hall swung in a hammock, cradling it.

Praying she would not have to use it.

Remember these from Hynek and others?

Close Encounter of the First Kind—sighting of an alien vehicle.

Close Encounter of the Second Kind—physical evidence of an alien vehicle.

Close Encounter of the Third Kind—contact with alien beings.

Close Encounter of the Fourth Kind—abduction of human by alien beings.

Close Encounter of the Fifth Kind—two-way contact between humans and alien beings.

Close Encounter of the Sixth Kind—death of humans caused by alien beings.

So where are we now? Close Encounter 5.5?

POSTER ALMAZ AT KEANU.COM, AUGUST 22, 2019

"What do you think? Are they some kind of plasma? Or just the thirtieth-century alien equivalent of neon lightbulbs?" Zack was looking up at the ceiling, at the items he could not help calling *glowworms*.

"Got to be plasma," Pogo said.

The last twenty minutes had stretched and twisted to the point where time had no meaning. The strange glowworms had crawled into what seemed to be semipermanent positions on the ceiling, several hundred meters over what appeared to be the chamber "floor."

As they moved, the environment continued to change radically. The light brightened, giving Zack and his team a better view of their surroundings: the walls of the Beehive, the forest of corals, and the vast distance across. In fact, the other side of the chamber could not be seen.

It started to rain, too. Not a gentle, midwestern summer sprinkle, like those Zack knew from childhood . . . this was windblown and gusting, like a tropical storm.

Like the rain that fell during Megan's funeral. The four of them could only stand there, sprays of water spattering their suits and helmets. "At least now the outside of my helmet looks like the inside," Natalia said.

There was no immediate danger; astronauts trained for EVAs wearing these same suits in huge water tanks. The danger would come when they took these suits into the frigid, two-hundred-degrees-below-zero environment beyond the membrane.

Worry about that later. Meanwhile, the experience of hearing rain rattling on the helmet—well, Zack would have found that unnerving.

Except that by now *everything* was unnerving. The very ground began to rattle and shake. The coral structures began to crumble. "Is like earthquake," Natalia said.

"It's more like being on a ship at sea," Zack said. He'd experienced both: Earthquakes were sharp jolts that struck without warning, but swells at sea built . . . you could actually feel them approaching.

And these Keanu waves endured for a minute or more. "I feel heavier," Lucas announced.

"Me, too," Pogo said.

"Well, we're getting a sort of sunrise," Zack said. "Maybe the artificial gravity machine is coming online, too."

"I hope the standard setting isn't equivalent to Jupiter," Natalia said. Zack had been kidding, as usual, but Natalia's statement was sobering; the size of the passageways already suggested that the Keanu-standard life-forms were larger than humans, which suggested more massive creatures suited to . . . well, 2.5 times Earth gravity, for example.

He surely didn't want to walk in three or four times Earth gravity.

Now that he thought of it, he doubted they could get far, even if Keanu developed gravity equal to Earth's surface, where each suit weighed more than the astronaut.

And how the hell would they get out of Vesuvius? Those ramps would need to reach pretty close to the top. . . .

But he *was* feeling heavier. He took a few tentative steps. Goddamn it, this was the end. "Everybody, grab your stuff. We're pulling out."

"No!" That was Lucas, but Natalia and even Pogo uttered similar protests at the same instant.

"We're in uncharted territory, people! Our mission is to get back alive. I'm worried about—"

He stopped, no longer sure of what he was saying. His eye was drawn to the strange landscape of Keanu's interior. It was a giant cave, of course, but lit by squiggly yellow shapes that hovered over a green, purple, and pink countryside, if one stretched the definition of countryside to include "vegetation" that looked more like structures found on a coral reef. And you accepted a sky that was reminiscent of a giant sports arena. (The chamber's upper reaches—its ceiling—were lost in mist and shadow.)

And windblown rain. There was a strong breeze blowing from Zack's left, the direction of the membrane. If it had been the other way around, he'd have been worried about a leak.

Wait . . . Something was moving out there. "Uh, does anyone—?"

"We see it, too!" said Lucas.

What looked like a scaled-up version of the bubble bearings in the membrane—only three meters wide and high—was rolling across the ground toward them, changing directions to avoid the corals, sloshing and spilling fluid, leaving a trail of moisture that was visible even on the moist soil.

"Any thoughts?" Zack said. "Is this the Keanu version of a tumbleweed? No means of locomotion." The rolling bubble seemed to be blowing in the wind.

"What if it's alive?" Pogo said.

"Then get ready for First Contact," Lucas said.

"We are not prepared for anything like that!" Natalia said. She was on the verge of panic.

"Everybody hold position. Act like professionals."

The rolling bubble turned toward them. Now Zack could see that it was opaque with dark shapes, like curdled milk. Pogo backed away, out of Zack's limited peripheral vision, saying, "It's fighting the wind, Zack!"

"So it is." All he could think to do was raise the camera. Running wasn't an option.

Another astronaut rule was, when in doubt, do nothing. You'll only make it worse.

Closer and closer . . . "It is coming right at us," Lucas said.

"Give it room! Everybody back away!" Zack said. Commanders got the goodies on missions—the first steps. They should also get first shot at the bad stuff. "Let me be the target."

Natalia and Lucas scuttled off to the right, putting a crumbling coral tower between them and the rolling bubble.

Which was now less than fifty meters away.

"I sure hope this thing is friendly," Pogo said.

"Let's make the assumption for now. . . ."

The argument ceased, because the bubble sloshed to a halt . . . ejected an object almost the same size. The bubble then dissolved into a whitish puddle on the ground.

The ejected item looked like a sow bug, but only for a moment, as it came to a stop, then unfolded itself.

And stood up. Zack tried to remain calm and scientific. Bilateral symmetry, check. It had two legs and two arms as well as two sets of different types of appendages around its middle. It looked heavier and thicker where the middle pairs attached.

A head of sorts, check. But nothing resembling a face or a nose or eyes . . . just various openings, one of them ringed with cilia that seemed to flex rhythmically . . . breathing?

But was it animal or machine? At this distance, in this light, it was difficult to tell . . . the creature's skin was shiny, but was it wet metal, or slime? It appeared to be a harness of some kind, dripping with fluid the same color as the dissolved bubble.

"Looks like it's standing guard," Natalia said. Which was true: As soon as it unfolded to full height—half again as tall as any human—the creature seemed to freeze in position.

"Maybe it's a sentry," Zack said. He hated having to anthropomorphize his Keanu experience, but it was the only way to make sense of things. Besides, the builders, owners, or inhabitants might have stationed someone to check passports here at the entry to the NEO's interior.

For a moment Zack was face-to-face with the creature. Twenty-five meters of distance, and at least one of height separated them, not to mention however many eons of evolution. But it seemed to Zack that the Sentry was taking his measure—

"Rain seems to be stopping," Lucas said. Zack had been concentrating so totally on the Sentry that he'd stopped paying attention. But yes, the windblown gusts had stopped . . . the entire chamber glowed with a sheen of moisture that reflected the golden light from the glowworms.

Then the Sentry moved.

Its major left-side appendages rose suddenly to its head. Zack had begun to form an image of the Sentry as the Tin Man from Oz . . . stolid, rusted to immobility . . . now trying to salute.

Look at what's here, not what you remember!

Then the creature took a step . . . and staggered.

"It looks like it's hurt!" Natalia said.

"Everybody stay back!" Zack said. The Sentry began to flail, like a man in extreme pain.

He could see its chest heave. *Okay, it's organic, not a machine.*

Then the Sentry abruptly turned toward Pogo Downey, who, inexplicably, was walking forward.

The being snapped out a hand, as if trying to reach Pogo—

Swaddled in his suit, Zack could not feel what happened next, but he saw a flash. Lucas had taken an image with that damned Zeiss unit! And in the low light, the autoflash had triggered!

With frightening speed, the Sentry turned toward Pogo, and swung one of its middle arms out and across, like a samurai swordsman.

Pogo's helmet detached, and with it Pogo's head, blood spurting from the neck ring of the EVA suit. With three swift moves, the Sentry clove the torso from top to bottom, separating one arm and leg, then the other, finishing its disassembly of Col. Patrick "Pogo" Downey, USAF, with a reverse horizontal slash.

Natalia screamed. Lucas shouted.

Zack was frozen, confused, horrified. All he saw was Pogo's body, a quartered bloody mess on the ground.

Then he breathed again. He grabbed Lucas and Natalia and herded them back toward the membrane. "Go, go, go!" He wanted as much space between them and the Sentry as he could get, as quickly as it could be gotten.

But Natalia's visor fogged over, obscuring her view forward. She fell twice in her first ten steps, with Zack and Lucas frantically trying to right her again.

The falls allowed Zack a glance back at the Sentry, who was in pursuit, but more deliberately. "It looks stunned," he said.

It seemed to Zack that the giant being was losing mobility . . . its arms and hands were roaming over its torso, as if suffering from either heat or pain.

The third time she fell, Natalia was the one who looked back. "I think it's dying. . . ."

The impulse to flight was momentarily suspended. Zack and Lucas turned. The three watched as the Sentry began to jerk and heave, as if racked by seizures. Vapor rose from its body, as if the creature were burning up from within.

Then, abruptly, the Sentry collapsed . . . and within seconds ceased to spasm.

"What the hell?" Lucas said, clumsily crossing himself.

"I saw an animal being gassed in Leningrad once," Natalia said. "That's what it looked like."

A thought occurred to Zack: "Do you suppose the environment killed it?"

"Wasn't it designed for this environment?" Lucas said, sounding almost offended at the idea. "Didn't it live here?"

"We don't know *anything*," Natalia said. She was collapsed, almost immobile. Zack wondered what it was like inside her suit.

He barely had time to curse Lucas—and mourn Pogo.

It was clear that Natalia would not be able to move with any speed. Zack realized he would have to help her with every step . . . and every moment they remained in the Beehive they were vulnerable.

"Lucas, get to the rover. Tell Houston and Bangalore what's happened. Recharge your suit, get food and water, then come back. We'll be following!"

He wished he could have given the Brazilian astronaut better orders, but he had nothing left, just a firm idea that information on today's events needed to get out—someone needed to survive.

If he and Natalia managed to survive as well, there might be time then to think about Pogo . . . recovering his remains.

Lucas didn't argue, which meant that the seriousness of the situation was apparent even to him. Zack watched him go back up the slope, into the heart of the Beehive.

"Come on, we've got to move, too," he told Natalia.

Gamely, she got to her feet. "I'm stable," she said.

"Fine," he said, "but take my arm, too." And so they set off, like lovers strolling through a park . . . and about as fast.

And not very far. Within a few meters, Natalia essentially sat down. "I can't."

"No problem," Zack told her, lying only slightly. "We'll just wait until Lucas returns." He checked his own consumables: still two hours, plenty of time to observe, if not act.

The environment in the chamber continued to change. The "weather" had grown calmer; the rain had stopped, even though a gentle wind continued to blow now . . . detectable in the cloud of particles that wafted past Zack's faceplate.

The corals had completely collapsed everywhere. If Zack's eyes could be trusted—and what could be trusted at a time like this?—they were being transformed somehow. Zack focused on one area where an older pile of pinkish debris was being replaced by greenish shapes that expanded and stretched.

That *grew*. That was the word. The corals were growing into vegetation of some kind.

Or possibly quasi machines like the Sentry.

Zack wanted to put more distance between himself and whatever was happening in this chamber. In fact, he would have been completely satisfied to be watching these events through a TV camera while safe aboard *Venture*.

Or better yet, back in Houston. He had been frightened before; now he was terrified. It wasn't just the shocks and the violence . . . it was knowing he was out of his depth, so far beyond a comfort zone that he could no longer remember what it was like to operate normally.

He turned back to the Beehive, hoping for a last glimpse of Lucas, but the World's Greatest Astronaut had likely let fear fuel his retreat, because he was long gone.

Zack had nothing else to do but look at the Beehive. Now he could see that some of the cells here had changed, too. Formerly open, smaller ones and at least two jumbo units were now sealed, covered with some kind of translucent film that swelled.

That almost breathed—

"This is stupid," Natalia announced, hauling herself to her feet.

She was already up, if unsteady, and heading back into the chamber before Zack could reach her. "Movement adds heat, kiddo. Don't run off," he told her. He peered into her helmet . . . it was so fogged over he could barely make out a face. "How is it in there?"

"Hot and wet. Feel like I'm drowning." That sounded terrifying. Learning to live and work in suits, under pressure, without succumbing to claustrophobia was one of an astronaut's biggest challenges. And that was when the suit was operating properly.

If Natalia felt as though she were drowning, she probably was. And Zack could do nothing to help—

"I'm going to try something," Natalia said. She raised her arms, hands touching the sides of the neck ring where her helmet was attached, and *unlocked it.*

"Hey, Natalia, that's not a good idea—!"

Too late. The cosmonaut raised the bulky helmet off her head, revealing a wet face and the reddest complexion Zack had ever seen on a human being.

How long would it take for her to die? Would she turn blue from lack of oxygen? Or would she freeze . . . or begin twitching and shuddering like the Sentry?

None of those things happened. She opened her eyes then, looked directly at Zack, smiled, and inhaled.

She was racked with a coughing spasm. "You tried it. Now put the helmet back on," Zack said. She'd lost precious minutes of oxygen, but she hadn't killed herself.

But the coughing stopped. And Natalia said, "I'm okay."

Zack was surprised that he could hear her words, slightly muffled by his own helmet. And surprised that she was still alive, in no more distress than when sealed up in the suit.

"It's oxygen," she said. "I saw it on my spectrometer. Ratio is high, maybe thirty percent . . . but pressure is still low here." She took a deep breath again. "Feels like being on a mountain top. Dry. Lots of smells I can't identify."

"Don't get too comfortable," he said. He was happy to know that Keanu's environment was less immediately hostile than open space—at least if you steered clear of things like the Sentry. "Think alien organisms."

"This place was a hundred degrees below zero a few hours back. There shouldn't be anything alive."

"And look at it now." She was edging back into the chamber, toward the dead Sentry, and Pogo.

"Where are you going?" Because Zack was still using radio inside his helmet, and she was not, she barely understood him. He repeated himself, shouting.

Then she nodded, understanding him. And said, "I always wanted to do an alien autopsy."

Zack did not follow. He considered his own consumables, the likelihood that Lucas would take longer than expected to return . . . and the fact that Natalia seemed just fine.

And without her helmet, he could not easily hear her.

Was it responsible? At the moment only Natalia was exposed to the Keanu environment—and by extension, *Brahma*. The *Venture* was still safe, and so were Tea and Yvonne.

Idiot: Whatever contaminants you would breathe with helmet off are already coating the exterior of your suit! Besides, the gravity was still increasing . . . Zack was finding it hard to move.

Not that he was eager to go far. He could see Natalia slowly circling the dead Sentry, occasionally raising her camera, then shifting to her spectrometer.

But Zack was intrigued by what he was seeing in the Beehive cells. They were continuing to swell and discolor. At moments he thought he could see shapes inside several of them.

That was disturbing: the color of the cells was exactly like that of the bubble that had disgorged the Sentry.

God, what if there was some link between the Beehive and the Sentry? Zack was torn between an immediate desire to head directly toward Natalia . . . and a horrid fascination for what was happening here.

Shit. His suit was hampering his ability to get close enough to see.

With one last glance at Natalia, happily performing her alien autopsy, he embraced the decision he had actually made moments earlier.

If the environment within Keanu was changing to suit humans—an idea that was now inescapable—then logic said it would not harm him. It certainly wasn't harming Natalia.

He stopped the airflow inside his suit, saving it for the return trip through the membrane, then cracked the neck seal of his helmet.

He was immediately struck by the smell of Keanu, a combination of wet soil and fragrances he could not identify, but which were not unpleasant. Something was growing here—with a hell of an accelerated incubation period.

He took in a deep breath. Actually found it invigorating. "Hey," he called to Natalia. "You were right."

Startled by the sound of his voice, she looked up. "I still feel good."

"See anything interesting? Is it man or machine?"

"Both, I think . . ." She stopped, staring past Zack in a way he didn't like.

"Do you see something, Natalia?"

"Yes." He could barely hear her. "The Beehive."

There was no escaping it. He turned.

Several of the smaller cells in the Beehive were now transparent . . . and the shapes within them could be clearly seen. Zack saw a rise nearby that would allow him to get closer, and he began scrabbling up the slope.

Within moments he was incredibly close—he could have reached into the nearest cell if he'd wanted.

Not that he wanted to touch anything. The shapes inside were large, greenish-brown sacs, pulsing, as if alive.

Natalia joined him. "What do you think they are?"

"Well, it looks as though we've been watching life evolve," Zack said, "only a few billion times faster than we'd expect."

"Evolve into what?"

"Whatever it's supposed to be."

"What could that be? Not more Sentries, I hope. Wait—" Natalia was pointing into a different cell, where the "evolution" of one sac seemed close to completion. "My God, do you know what it looks like?"

"Yes," Zack said. The sac now looked like a cellophane-wrapped human body.

"I don't like this!" Natalia announced.

Zack was torn between a similar emotion, and a sense of wonder so powerful it was almost sexual. This was why he'd studied stars and planets . . . why he'd become an astronaut.

To learn the secrets of the universe . . . to see new marvels.

The Russian astronaut backed away, crawling down the slope away from the cells. "Natalia . . ." Zack heard his own voice quaver. Almost every part of his being was ordering him to run! Hide!

Zack looked back at the human-shaped sac . . . two legs, a torso, two arms, a head. It was shorter and smaller than the Sentry. It was Zack's size.

The hands had a thumb and four fingers.

The shape literally writhed, its hands clawing at the translucent material covering its "face." Zack had to suppress the impulse to help it. . . .

He needn't have worried. Suddenly the "face" was clear.

It was not only a humanlike face, it was a face he recognized.

Zack Stewart had seen more impossible sights in the past eight hours than most humans saw in a lifetime. Hell, more evidence of alien life than any humans had seen all through history.

But what he saw in that Beehive cell was so unexpected and impossible that by contrast the wonders of Keanu's interior were a strip mall in Houston.

The face he saw clearly now, brown eyes opening, mouth gasping, was that of his dead wife, Megan.

Part Three
"SOME FRAGRANT NIGHT"

"Someone's emerging!"

Harley Drake looked up as Sasha Blaine shrieked. "Calm down," he told her, trying to make sense of the image on the screen that showed a suited *Brahma* crew member on the camera side of the membrane. Intelligence and outside-the-box thinking were sometimes a piss-poor substitute for operational cool. "Which one is that?"

More subdued, Blaine settled back into her chair. "No stripes on the suit, so it's got to be Lucas."

"He must be talking to *Brahma*." Harley reached for his headset and within seconds was plugged into the cacophony of voices—Lucas and Taj and Vikram, the Bangalore flight director, Tea and Kennedy, all were talking over each other. So much for coolheaded mission control ops. . . .

Meanwhile, all around him, the Home Team swelled in numbers. (During the dead time with no link from the astronauts, several had wandered off in search of food. For all Harley knew, some had simply gone home; there was no penalty for early withdrawal.) With each arrival, the chatter inside the room rose geometrically.

Which was why Harley barely heard the words, "Pogo is dead!"

"Everybody shut up!"

The room went quiet, and everyone was able to hear Josh Kennedy's voice. "Break, break, Lucas: Say again."

Finally the link was silent, except for the vague hiss and crackle of the basic wave. "I repeat, Pogo Downey is dead."

Another beat of silence, and then the questions exploded from both mission controls. Harley eventually realized that Something Big and Mobile had shown itself inside Keanu, and that someone—it was unclear who—had shot at it, and Pogo had been cut down.

The other members of the Home Team were plugged in now, too, listening but unable to speak. Their faces showed their disbelief and horror at not only what had happened, but how fast.

Though he had a scientific bent, Harley Drake had only a dim sense of the painstaking and tedious accretion of data points that most often led to big breakthroughs. Even in space ops, things happened slowly.

Today was different. First the news that Keanu was likely artificial. Then the stunning series of jabs—the ramps and passages, the membrane.

Now a regular goddamn torrent of new marvels was gushing over them. These alien markers. The huge inner chamber. "Sounds like Burroughs' Hollow Earth," said Williams, to annoying titters from around the table.

Air pressure inside this chamber? Variable gravity? A source of illumination?

Fractal corals. Water. Wind. Weather.

And, oh yes, some kind of hostile entity.

Images of the environment began appearing as thumbnails arrayed around the main picture on the big screen.

But Harley couldn't appreciate them. He kept thinking about Patrick Downey—good old Pogo—dead! "Home Team for Josh," he said into his mike, hating to interrupt the ops, but not hearing the information he needed.

It took Kennedy a moment, but he said, "Josh for Harley: Speak."

"I hope this is still encrypted."

There was a long beat. "Wait, yes," the flight director said. "*Our* feed is. Don't know about Bangalore."

"No matter. Somebody's got to get to Linda Downey immediately."

"Shit, yes. On it. Thanks!" On another screen, this one showing the live feed from inside mission control, Harley could see Kennedy tapping the incoming capcom, Mr. America Travis Buell, on the shoulder and pointing him out the door—

To tell Linda Downey she was now a widow.

Harley suddenly remembered his own role as CACO: Rachel Stewart would need reassurance, too. "I'm going to the family room," he announced to the Home Team, as if anyone cared. All were too busy oohing, ahhing, and otherwise babbling over the wonders and horrors from Keanu.

Before Harley could disconnect his headset, he heard: "Harls, Shane."

"Don't you sleep?" On a normal space mission, even one to deep space, mission control teams were required to go home and rest up between shifts. Shane Weldon should have been home for dinner three hours back, in bed by now. But then Harley should have left the Home Team, too.

"Based on what I've seen today, I may never sleep again."

"I hear you—"

"There's a shitstorm headed your way now, Harls. Our White House friend Bynum has lit up the board. We're simultaneously embargoing all transmissions—"

"Shane, I've got to get to Rachel."

"Got it. Just a heads-up. Call me if you start to drown."

The Home Team was closer to the family room than mission control. Still, given Buell's head start, he shouldn't have arrived just when Harley did.

Harley knew the veteran astronaut; he was usually conscientious. "What the fuck is taking you so long! It won't be fun, but this is your new job—"

"I know, Harley!" Every astronaut knew. Back in the 1960s, Ted Freeman had been killed in a Saturday morning T-38 crash . . . and a reporter reached the widow with the news before NASA did. Nobody wanted that to happen again. Buell waved his cell phone. "They just told me Jones is coming. . . ."

"What, so he can drown her in tears? Get in there and do what you were told."

To his credit, Buell opened the door immediately, though the suddenness of the gesture and the clearly troubled look on his face was a blatant warning to everyone inside: Bad news was coming. "Ah, Linda, I have to talk to you."

Downey's wife slowly rose to her feet, reaching for one of her children as she did. Harley was right behind Buell, projecting a calmer manner, he hoped. "Rachel, step outside with me. Everybody else, too."

Rachel and her friend Amy shot out of the room as if jet-propelled, so fast they almost collided with Gabriel Jones and one of his staffers as they arrived.

"Sorry, folks!" Harley used his chair to block the door, allowing the other friends and family to exit around him.

"Harley—" Jones had his best fatherly face on.

But Harley exited the room and closed the door behind him. "It's being handled."

He turned to Rachel. "Your dad is fine."

Of course, to the others—friends and family of Patrick Downey—Harley might just as well have shouted, "Your man isn't!"

Harley was anticipating another blast of questions; instead, he saw shock, disbelief, fading hope. "Ladies and gentlemen," Jones said, having to settle for breaking the news to someone other than the widow, "there has been an accident on Keanu. Colonel Downey has been lost."

Harley shook his head. There was never a good place to hear news like that, but some places were better: to learn in a hallway that your brother, father, next-door neighbor was just killed in some freak space accident. . . .

As the sobs began to swell around him, he rolled to Rachel, who was huddled with her friend. "Outside," he told them.

The moment they exited the building, into the humid Houston evening, Harley told Rachel about the membrane, the markers, the Beehive, the entity that had apparently attacked and killed Patrick Downey.

"So you don't really know my father is okay!" Rachel was oscillating between hysterical anger and plain old hysteria.

"Word from Lucas was that your father and Natalia are still safe and sound."

"But they're inside! That's where something just killed Mr. Downey!"

"Come on, Rach—you know your father. He wouldn't have stayed if it were still dangerous." Even as he said it, Harley knew that was a mistake. "Anyway, his suit's going to run out of oxygen soon. He and Natalia will be back in sight before you know it."

Rachel was hugging Amy. It was clear she really *wanted* to believe Harley.

She just didn't.

Zack Stewart had little time to ponder the mind-blowing impossibility of seeing his wife's likeness inside a Near-Earth Object two years after her death in Florida. At least three other Beehive cells around "Megan" were active, too, each one extruding another human-shaped object. To the extent he could see faces, he recognized no one else. Which made him doubt his instant conclusion that he was looking at Megan.

What the hell, he could be suffering from shortage of oxygen, or too much. Either one would likely result in hallucinations, and suggested that the smart, immediate move was to put his helmet on and get the hell out of this chamber.

"Bozhe moi!"

From his time on the ISS, Zack knew a lot of Russian: "My God!" Natalia was farther along the face of the Beehive. From Zack's point of view, she was a funny-looking creature in the thick suit topped by her smallish head in its skull-hugging communications cap. At the moment, with her face to her hands, she looked even odder.

Zack half-jogged, half-slid toward her. "What is it?"

She pointed at one of the other swollen pods. "Zack, I know that one!"

"What do you mean?" He didn't want to influence Natalia by telling her what he thought he'd seen.

"It's my coach. Konstantin Alexandrovich! He taught me to ski and shoot!" Zack remembered that Natalia had been an Olympics contender in the biathlon as a college student.

"It's just an illusion." He was trying to convince himself at least as much as he was trying to convince her. "Your brain is superimposing familiar images on alien structures."

"He was not familiar! Konstantin died in January. I haven't seen him in ten years." Natalia uttered a worried whimper, like a dreamer in mid-nightmare, and backed away.

Left alone, Zack forced himself to be analytical and scientific. This pod thing was indeed human-shaped, just like the Megan-thing. And, yes, clearly possessing a face. Obviously a human male. Closed eyes, nose, mouth.

Some of the thin film covering the face suddenly split open, exposing a "mouth" that displayed what any reasonable observer would call teeth. And a couple of them looked shiny, like steel.

Like old Russian dental work—

"Zaacck!"

Hearing his name, Zack turned. Natalia was a few meters away, sitting on the ground, eyes closed, hugging herself. "What is it?"

"What?" she said, looking startled.

"You just called me."

"I did not."

"Then—"

Zack had no need to complete the question. He could see the Megan-thing less than a dozen meters away . . . still lying on its side in its Beehive cell, but using its hands—and they were clearly hands now—to claw away the brownish covering.

Revealing a pink face underneath, skin as pure as a newborn baby's.

And those brown eyes, open wide again, blinking in confusion and terror.

And a mouth, white teeth, tongue.

The Megan-thing coughed and wheezed, less like an asthmatic trying to catch its breath. More like a newborn after the first slap.

Now it—she—looked at him. "Zack," she said. The voice was *Megan's*.

Zack disconnected his gloves, dropped them, and began clawing at the second skin that still bound the thing to the cell.

She was warm to the touch. Although her hair was cropped, even in her writhing struggles she looked and felt . . . familiar.

Zack pulled her free. Gently in the low gravity, both of them settled to the slimy mud of Keanu, the Megan-thing still largely covered in her second skin, essentially in Zack's suited lap.

Then the Megan-thing began to thrash like a panicked drowner . . . and scream.

"How are you doing, *Venture*?"

"I'm maintaining, Houston," Tea Nowinski said, on fifth thought. Her first through fourth thoughts had been *How the fuck do you think I'm doing?* In actual fact, she had been trying to use the bathroom, a procedure dreaded by all space travelers, with good reason. But with Yvonne sedated, in dreamland, and the comm links quiet, Tea had figured she had fifteen minutes to uncover the noxious little chamber behind the curtain—

She had almost completed this mission-critical task when Houston called.

The *Venture* cabin, in spite of its oddball height, now seemed cramped and crowded to Tea. That might have been due to Yvonne's hammock, which would normally have been stowed this time of day. The radio hissed and crackled constantly. There were pumps and motors.

It was far from comfortable, though it was obviously more comfortable—not to mention a lot safer—than being in rover *Buzz*, or in an EVA suit.

Nevertheless, Tea was growing restless. Yet it was a violation of the astronaut code to let your emotions show, unless they were just forced giddiness at the wonders of weightlessness. And Jasmine Trieu, the new capcom, was just too nice to be the recipient of much nastiness.

It was now ninety-four hours mission elapsed time, EVA plus nine of the *Destiny-7* mission to Keanu, and Tea was beginning to get a bad feeling about things.

That, of course, was the half-joking way astronauts dealt with the threat of death in space. It went all the way back to test piloting. Cheating death.

Tea had grown up in the United States at the turn of the twenty-first century knowing that throughout human history, people faced death frequently and inescapably. They died in foxholes, they drowned when ships sank, they were struck by cars, they were lined up and shot, they burned to death in fires, they choked in mine cave-ins. . . .

But, like most first-world citizens, she had managed to reach the age of forty without ever having been in serious fear for her life.

Setting aside the fact that launching on a rocket and making a flight into space dramatically increased one's chances of dying—the current probability of a fatality was between one in fifty and one in twenty—Tea's most memorable near-death experience had been in an airliner landing in Minneapolis during a summer storm. A sudden crosswind had tipped the 737 forty degrees right, then a similar amount the other direction . . . twice . . . before the pilot applied power and aborted the takeoff. Had the wing hit the ground, the aircraft would likely have cartwheeled across the runway, disintegrating on the tarmac and likely slamming into the terminal, impaling fragile humans on jagged metal or crushing them.

It hadn't. The moment of stark terror had lasted perhaps five seconds.

Of course, the insidious nature of death on space missions was that it either got you almost instantly—*Challenger, Columbia, Soyuz 11*—or not at all. The truth was, near-disasters like *Apollo 13*, with its five-day nail-biter of a loop around the Moon with three astronauts huddled in the lunar module "lifeboat," or the 1997 collision between an uncrewed supply vehicle and the *Mir* space station, had given flight controllers and crews the confidence to feel that, given time, they could salvage any situation.

Tea hoped she was in one of those situations now. But just because no astronauts had died some hideous slow death until now didn't mean it couldn't happen.

Look at where they were—parked on the exterior of some kind of gigantic alien spacecraft. One crew member was already dead! Another one had been seriously injured.

Two more were . . . where? Alien captives? Dead?

One of the missing was a man she had come to love. Poor Zack! So sweet, so smart, so handsome! He had turned out to be the most stable relationship Tea had had since grade school. Until the past two months, when her *Destiny-7* mission turned into his, she had looked forward to taking the next step with him, to get married. It was time; Megan's death was two years past. Zack wouldn't forget her, and Tea didn't want that. The tragedy had shaped him, made him somehow more human, less the brilliant super-astronaut.

Besides, Zack's astronaut career had seemed to be over. And with two lunar landings, one as commander, behind her, Tea would have no reason to risk another rocket ride, either.

But now? Lucas was recharging his suit from rover *Buzz* supplies, but where were Zack and Natalia? Tea could read consumables status; they were at or beyond the redlines for their suits.

And what *had* happened to Pogo? One hour he was here in *Venture*, his big, goofy self . . . the next he was some kind of space-age statistic! A snap of the finger—gone!

Killed by something inside Keanu.

It was suddenly okay that Houston had interrupted her private moment. Tea needed to know what was going on. "So, what did I miss?"

Jasmine seemed relieved to have her talking. "Josh is asking Lucas if he can drive *Buzz* through the membrane."

"Why would he do that? Zack and Natalia need to be out of there!" Too much frank emotion, but if the flight director was talking to *Brahma*, it would be overlooked.

"Believe that's what's driving the drive-through option," the capcom said. "If they can't come to recharging, we take it to them."

"If that's the only option, then I like it better."

"Flight wants you to talk to Home Team."

For one moment—God, she was getting tired!—Tea wasn't sure what or who the Home Team was. "Sure, put Harley on."

"Harley is out of pocket at the moment. The next voice you hear will be Dr. Sasha Blaine."

Tea had some vague picture in mind—Blaine was another bright young woman, much like capcom Jasmine Trieu, in fact. Smart, sure, pretty, but socially awkward. Too wide-eyed. "Copy. Hello, Sasha. Please catch me up."

"I hardly know where to start," Blaine said, then disproved her statement by quickly recounting the latest thoughts on Keanu's artificiality and on the markers. "We're torn about what message or messages they carry."

"They might just be signage. *Close Before Striking* kind of stuff."

"That's high on the list. They also seem to be transmitting a set of beeps and clicks."

"What band?"

"Several, from high to low. Something we detected, obviously."

There was more, none of it particularly informed. Rather, Sasha Blaine just seemed to be giving Tea the latest notions and gossip . . . which was not typical NASA policy with crews in flight.

She wondered why. What was Houston hiding from her?

As soon as Sasha Blaine clicked off, flight director Josh Kennedy was on the line. "Tea, Josh. You should get some sleep."

"Knowing it and doing it, not so easy."

"Take a sleeping pill."

"Hard to play nurse that way."

"We're monitoring Yvonne. And Dennis is preparing to come back when you wake up."

Here it came: "What's the plan, Josh?"

"*Brahma* has agreed to another tag-team EVA. You and Taj. Rescue and retrieval."

She felt sick. Oh God, no! But she forced herself to sound calm, she hoped. "It's usually one or the other."

"The mission is to rescue Zack and Natalia, retrieve Pogo's body. While you grab a couple of hours sack time, we'll upload a timeline and map."

Tea realized she had been crouching. She straightened up, looked around the cabin. Uncomfortable, yes. Time to go out for a walk.

In her mind, however, this would be rescue only. Pogo was beyond her ability to help.

Her priority was Zack.

The Megan-thing was still thrashing.

Zack Stewart held on to it for what seemed like minutes. He knew it was probably a few seconds. "Natalia!" he called, his voice little more than a croak.

Natalia pulled herself away from her own private horror show and rushed to Zack. "What is it?"

"I don't—" Zack couldn't answer; he didn't know what this thing was, and it was taking all his strength to keep it—her—from tearing both of them apart. "Just . . . grab hold!"

Natalia hesitated for several seconds. Then she grabbed the Megan-thing's legs. But one of them slipped free and a foot smacked Natalia's face. "Shit!" She was bleeding, but regained control.

Zack had a death grip on the creature's upper half, pinning its arms to the torso and trying to keep clear of the head, which jerked so violently he half-expected to see it snap off.

Then, as suddenly as if a switch had been thrown, the Megan-thing went limp. Natalia felt it, too. With blood covering her face, making her look like a flesh-eater from a horror movie, she said, "Can I let go?"

Exhausted, Zack nodded, relaxing his own grip on the Megan-thing.

It was resting against the wall below its cell, legs out, arms open as if in welcome.

Then it opened its eyes. "Took you," it said, still wheezing, "long enough."

"Jesus!" Zack couldn't help it. Natalia let out a screech, too.

The Megan-thing whispered, "Don't shout."

"Sorry." *Sorry?* What the hell was this? He was treating this creature like a human being! "Uh," he said, struggling to find the right tone—the beheading of Pogo Downey still fresh in his memory—"who or what are you?"

"My name is Megan Doyle Stewart."

That was impossible, of course. Megan Stewart was two years dead, buried in a muddy grave south of Houston.

This was . . . some construct, some machine, some . . . thing.

Zack glanced over at Natalia. Still bloody-mouthed, she was on her feet, walking away from them. Zack wanted to shout at her, *Stay here!* But not with this creature identifying herself as his late wife.

All right, he thought. *Take a breath. Play the cards you're dealt.* This thing claimed to be Megan. Nothing to lose by acting as if it were. "Shouldn't you be asking, 'Where am I?' And maybe a few hundred other questions."

"Yes." She closed her eyes briefly. In their years together, Zack had nursed Megan through several cases of the flu. That was what she looked like now: weak, pale, with flashes of life. She seemed to gather herself. "But . . . I already know where I am. I'm inside Keanu." She smiled then.

Zack couldn't believe he was having a conversation like this. He liked to believe he possessed above-average mental flexibility. He was willing, possibly eager—likely too eager at times—to think outside the box. But this situation . . . "Would you answer a question for me?"

The Megan-thing actually smiled, then nodded.

"Do you know this? 'Perhaps if death is kind, and there can be returning—'"

"Yes, yes, Sara Teasdale, my favorite poem, which ends, 'we shall be happy, for the dead are free,' which strikes me as pretty goddamn funny at the moment. You used it at my funeral, right?"

She seemed to draw energy from the idea—no wonder, since it suddenly seemed to Zack that somehow his wife had cheated death. "Who was there? Who cried?"

Her familiarity with the poem and questions about the funeral confirmed Zack's decision moments earlier: He would have to operate on the wildly improbable assumption that he was, indeed, face-to-face with his formerly dead wife.

ISRO mission *Brahma* continues to stir mixed emotions in the population, from eager pride to surly indifference. Pride in the role of vyomanaut T. Radhakrishnan is obvious. The indifference is also understandable. In a nation of one billion souls, most of them still living in poverty, what is to be gained from an expensive space mission?

But if the past thirty years have taught our nation anything, it is the value of information. We have invested in *Brahma*'s mission for that reason.

COLUMNIST KULDIP SANGVHI AT E-PAPER *VIJAYA TAMATAKA*, 23 AUGUST 2019

Natalia heard Zack call her name but did not respond. She did not want to see what he was doing with the creature from the cell. She wanted to get out of this chamber, back to *Brahma*.

She wanted to return to Earth and never think about Keanu again.

It was unprofessional, she knew. She had worked so hard to become a cosmonaut, one of the few women ever to fly for Holy Mother Russia, and had always believed that she wanted to explore the solar system, work and live on the Moon, visit Mars.

And she had made it to this place, to the interior of a Near-Earth Object, where against all rational expectation, the environment was suitable for life.

It was, in fact, almost comfortable. Though there was still a warm mist in the air, the wind had died. Bizarre plants seemed to spill out of the ground, blossom, die, and then be replaced by something entirely different.

Of course, this was not exploration . . . it had turned into a nightmare.

Knowing she would need it—hoping it would be soon—Natalia went in search of her helmet.

She had left it at the base of the Beehive wall, not far from the cell where "Konstantin" had been writhing. As Natalia bent to pick up the helmet, she heard a voice, in Russian and in agony, scream, *"Help me!"*

Natalia couldn't help looking. And there, outside a cell, dripping with ichor and shivering like a naked man at the North Pole, was the very image of Konstantin Alexandrovich Fedoseyev, world champion cross-country biathlete, a man she had trained with from the ages of fourteen to twenty.

She stepped closer, though not too close. The Konstantin-thing was twitching and writhing . . . but also trying, pathetically, to take steps.

Now she could see its face . . . pink-skinned, bright-eyed, complete with the signs that it was growing a mustache.

Even spasming, it reached out to her—and called her name!

"Stay away!"

"Natalia!" it said. "I'm alive!"

"Stop using my name!"

The creature lunged at her, but was still so unsteady it fell at her feet. Natalia stepped back. This was strangely familiar . . . like that terrible night during training in Osterland, when her coach and friend—Konstantin some twenty years ago—assaulted her.

If this "Konstantin" got too close, would he have the same smell of stale liquor on his breath? "I said, stay away!"

The Konstantin-thing rose to its knees and continued to whimper. Largely covered in a second skin, it was nevertheless the perfect replica of the coach as he must have been in his later years. Jowly, pot-bellied . . . the shape of his penis and dangling testicles visible through the covering.

She would not look at it. She would certainly not meet this thing's eyes. Her aunt Karolina, a villager from the woods near Kaluga, had given her a tool for such situations.

She crossed herself as best she could in the suit.

Then she raised her hand to "Konstantin," index finger and little finger extended. *"Stay back!"*

Instead it lurched at her, clutching her ankle.

She hit the creature in the head with her helmet. But its hand still held her booted leg.

So she hit it again. Now she was free.

Then she hit it a third time, a fourth.

The Konstantin-thing stopped twitching and lay still at her feet. One side of its head was flattened, pulpy.

Had she killed it?

She hoped so.

With one last look around, she examined her helmet for damage . . . found none except squashed fragments of second skin.

She wiped those off, then put the helmet on again.

I am moved to post the words to the Navy Hymn, suitably updated:

Lord, guard and guide the men who fly
Through the great spaces of the sky
Be with the travelers in the air,
In darkening storms or sunlight fair;
Oh, hear us when we lift our prayer,
For those in peril in the air.

POSTER UK BEN AT NEOMISSION.COM

Very appropriate! Well done!   POSTER JERMAINE, SAME SITE

Nice sentiment, but Pogo Downey would be spinning in his grave if he knew you'd used the Navy Hymn.   POSTER JSC GUY, SAME SITE

Lucas Munaretto had hated to leave Zack and Natalia behind, especially with Downey dead. But orders were orders, and he had seen the wisdom in sending one member of the team back through the membrane.

Not that he wanted to stay in that horrifying environment. He was *happy* to say good-bye to Keanu and its little red glowworms and chaotic weather and murderous machine. He just wanted Zack and Natalia to come with him.

Reaching rover *Buzz* and the link, he had told Bangalore and Houston everything he had seen, then followed their orders to enter the rover, eat, rest, and recharge his suit.

Exhausted, he had essentially passed out, waking two hours later with sore muscles in a sitting position, the suit cold and ill-fitting. It was only static-distorted shouting from the earphones of his headset that penetrated his fog.

"We've been calling you for half an hour!"

"I had my headset off."

"Leave it on." He tried to remember who the communications operator was in Bangalore. One of the crew training team—Sergei? Nair?—he couldn't tell. A familiar voice was supposed to be comforting to a flight crew member.

"Who is this, please?"

"Vikram." Shit, the flight director himself. "Can you function?"

Lucas had trained on the NASA rover only once, during a crew exchange in Houston. Whereas he knew every instrument and metal seam in the *Brahma* cabin—knew the sounds and smells—rover *Buzz* was an alien environment, a squat cylinder eight feet high, and not much wider or deeper. It was cramped, and because in addition to forgetting to turn on the radio, he had also neglected the interior lights, it was quite dark.

"I'm ready to go," he told Vikram, reaching for his helmet and his gloves. He was almost afraid to ask what Bangalore had in mind—

Then the rover *rocked*. "Jesus!" It was the second most terrifying moment of this day—and one of the top two in Lucas's life. Had the thing that killed Downey come after him?

"Say again, Lucas."

A light swept through the rover interior, and Lucas relaxed. He pressed his face up to the window embedded in the rear hatch . . . saw two astronauts, one in a Coalition suit, one in a NASA model. "Zack and Natalia are here!"

"Double check that," Vikram said, the exasperation audible in his voice, even across the time lag . . . and distance of 440,000 kilometers.

The speakers inside rover *Buzz* crackled, and even as he heard Bangalore in his headset, he now heard Tea Nowinski's voice in the cabin. "Lucas, it's Tea and Taj. Are you in suit?"

Twenty minutes later, he was completely suited up and outside rover *Buzz*, listening to Taj. "Dennis has moved over to *Venture* to keep an eye on Yvonne."

Taj had brought another sled from *Brahma*—empty. "You didn't have time to put anything in it?" Lucas joked.

"Didn't you get briefed?" Tea said, sounding irritated. "This is to let us haul bodies out of there." She grabbed the tether and began hauling it toward the membrane, less than a hundred meters away.

Lucas had no answer for that, which seemed to further annoy Tea. "They're an hour past the extreme limit of their consumables."

"In normal circumstances, yes." As Taj and Lucas hurried to keep up with Tea, Lucas told the others as much as he could about the wind and glowworms.

Taj seemed confused. "You're saying there's a *breathable atmosphere* through this curtain?"

"All I know is that it's not vacuum." Lucas turned to Tea, seeking an ally on the side of optimism, however brief and foolish. "Do we know how the suits will operate under pressure, with some oxygen in the environment?"

"Yes," Tea said. "They will operate exactly the way they would in vacuum. Unless Zack and Natalia opened their suits and breathed, they are almost surely dead."

"What if they sat down . . . rested . . . slowed the rate of consumption?"

"They've run those calculations, too," Taj said.

"They can't be very precise—"

"They *aren't*," Tea said, clearly wanting to end this line of discussion. "That's why we're still calling this a rescue and retrieval mission."

They had reached the membrane. "We just walk through this?" Taj said, clearly doubtful.

"It's about ten meters deep . . . maybe less," Lucas said.

"Can't you fucking remember?" Tea again.

Lucas was appalled, not just by her obvious anger. He was embarrassed to know that their words were being recorded, even if they wouldn't be heard for hours yet. "The boundaries are compressible. It seemed thinner the second time I went through."

Tea was examining the seam where the membrane attached to the rocky walls. "Are we being heard?" Lucas asked.

"Only in both mission controls," Taj said. "Both sides agreed on a blackout."

"A first for everything—"

Tea shut up as the membrane bulged.

Someone was emerging! Taj hauled Tea away from the seam. "Stand back, everyone!"

It was Natalia, stumbling forward.

Lucas caught her. She was clearly happy to see them, so happy she was almost incoherent, speaking half in Russian about *vorvolaka*.

"Calm down!" Taj said.

"I'm *really* glad they can't hear this at home on television," Tea said, grabbing Natalia by her shoulders and turning her face-on. "Natalia, where's Zack?"

"I left him—"

"You *what*?"

"Wait, Tea." It was Taj, who had been reading the oxygen levels on Natalia's suit. "We've got to get her to the rover. She's almost out of gas."

"Fuck! Fine!" Tea joined Taj, each taking Natalia by the arm and half-escorting, half-hauling her back to the rover.

"Zack was okay when I left him," Natalia said, quickly explaining that both astronauts had removed their helmets and breathed the atmosphere of Keanu.

On hearing this, Tea seemed to relax. "Okay. What else is going on in there? What is *vorvolaka*?"

"A word my grandmother would use. Is like 'ghost' or 'undead.'"

Even though she had calmed down considerably since finding them, Natalia was almost hysterical, and her English was the first casualty. Lucas had a difficult time understanding her.

"Wait, wait, wait," Tea said, clearly impatient with the cosmonaut's Old World imagery. "You're not making sense."

They were at the rover now. "It is very hard to believe," Natalia said. Then she patted her helmet camera. "But I will show you."

Taj pulled a linking cord out of his chest pack. "You'll not only show us, you'll be showing Houston and Bangalore."

My name is Rachel Stewart. I am eleven years old. I live on Chestnut Drive in Clear Lake City. My father is a NASA astronaut. My mother is driving me crazy with her camera.

UNPUBLISHED TEXT FROM RACHEL STEWART, SIXTH-GRADE ASSIGNMENT,
ST. BERNADETTE'S SCHOOL

"What about Rachel?" To Zack, it was as if "Megan" wouldn't allow herself to say, *Was Rachel killed with me?* or *Was she badly injured?*

"She was shaken up. She went through a very traumatic period. Lost her mother, all of that. But from the accident? A bump on her head and some cuts."

"Tell me about her!"

So for ten minutes, he did—suitably sanitized. This was not the time or place to complain about Rachel's inability to be the perfect dutiful daughter.

"And she's in mission control?"

"She was a few hours ago."

"I want to see her."

Zack hesitated. "As soon as we can figure out how to get us in touch—"

Then she stood and began rubbing off the second skin, revealing some other layer of shinier material underneath. Stranger and stranger.

"What about Harley?"

Zack had to tell her about Harley's injuries. "It wasn't his fault," she said. "It was just . . . all messed up."

"Well, he still feels guilty. But I'm going to guess that getting absolution from the person he killed might make him feel better." She actually shot him a perfect Megan look—*Ha-ha*—as she stood and began to rub off the flaky outer husk, leaving the tougher layer beneath.

"Do you feel different?"

"Yes and no. Physically, mentally, I feel pretty much the way I did before I got killed—which, by the way, is a phrase I'm really never going to get used to.

"I'm breathing. I have a heartbeat. What's different is my outfit." She nodded at him. "I bet it's more comfortable than that suit." She was picking at her second skin.

"You're going to be naked if you keep that up."

"I'm not so sure about that." She had done her legs and arms. "Help me with my back."

The outer layer of the second skin was more fragile than Zack had thought. "Is this drying out and flaking off?"

"God, I hope so."

Zack stood back then, looking away in some bizarre and unnecessary attempt at politeness. The moment allowed him to think again about larger issues. "So what do we call this event?" he said. "A resurrection?"

"I guess. I mean, not in the I-saw-Jesus sense. But I never was as religious as you."

He had no immediate comment. Megan noted his silence. "You still don't believe this, do you?"

"Put yourself in my place: Would you?"

"Hell, no!"

"As long as we understand each other."

"The moment I have some definitive explanation for my current state, I'll pass it on."

Zack nodded. "Do you remember *anything* after the accident?"

She pressed a hand to her mouth. "Yes. I'd have to say I was dreaming. Long, crazy dreams that . . . actually, I do remember, sort of. I was floating or flying or just aware." Then she forced a smile. "What I remember most, though, is being in that car with Rachel and Harley. Not, bam, an hour ago. But it feels like . . . it all happened yesterday."

She rocked her head from side to side. "I'm digging the repair job on my neck. I'm guessing it was broken."

"Among other things," Zack said, barely able to utter the sentence. "How did you know you were on Keanu?"

"I just knew, the same way I opened my eyes and spoke English."

"But you knew English before."

"Fine. Come up with a better analogy. I just knew I was on Keanu, that I'd been killed and brought back." She frowned, clearly searching for a way to describe it. "Think of it like a role in a play—I'm an actor who just knows her lines."

"What else do you know? You knew you were on Keanu. Is there anybody else here? I mean, who did this to you?"

"When I ask myself that question, I hear or feel or download one word: Architects."

"That's all? Just Architects?"

"That's the word in my head." She was nearly naked now, sitting knees together, arms around them, swaths of the underlayer second skin still clinging to her.

"Is there something I can do for you . . . ?"

"You could start by calling me Megan. You were never much for using my name, did you ever realize that? But given the circumstances . . ."

He realized that she was correct. He'd almost never called her by her name. Rachel was often *Rachel*, yes. But Megan had always been *honey* or *baby*—

"Megan," he said, "Mrs. Stewart . . ."

"Now you're just being silly."

"Megan . . ."

"Yes, Zachary." That was what she'd called him most of the time.

"Nothing, just trying it on again." He couldn't help smiling. Even if this encounter turned out to be some insidious alien monkey trap, Zack was going to enjoy it to the extent he could.

"Oh." She frowned. "Hey, I don't suppose you have anything to eat."

Zack was able to pry an energy stick out of his helmet stash. "There are only a couple of bites left."

"Men, never thinking about food." But she happily devoured it. "Remember that restaurant we went to in Los Angeles? Barsac?"

Another memory only he or Megan would know. "Yeah. Most money I've ever paid for a meal. But a good one."

She waggled the last bite. "This is better. . . ."

"Well, you haven't eaten in over two years. Talk about sharpening your appetite." She laughed so hard she actually shuddered. "You must be cold."

"Not really. The breeze is warm, kind of like Santa Anas." She clapped her hands together, as if cleaning them off, another familiar Megan gesture. "*You're* the one who must be uncomfortable. Take off that suit." She saw the immediate look of confusion and reluctance on his face. "What now?"

"I'm not sure—about you or anything right now. Not hitting on all six. For example, I haven't thought about my EVA partner for thirty minutes."

"Where do you think he is?"

"She. Natalia Yorkina, one of the *Brahma* crew. And I just don't know." In fact, he'd tried calling Natalia on radio, and gotten nothing but static. For the first time in his astronaut career, Zack literally had no idea what action to take.

"Nothing?"

"Comm isn't great in here."

"Maybe she's just exploring."

Zack just shook his head. *Set that matter aside. Again, look at the situation you are in. Consider "Megan's" suggestion about your suit.* He wasn't going back to the surface any time soon. Why damage the suit, or waste energy hauling himself around in it? He reached for the first release—

"You also have that look on your face. That I'm-cooking-up-a-plan look."

"I want to get you out of here. And I want to find Natalia."

"What about the others?"

The others! Zack had been so focused on Megan, he'd forgotten about the other cells. "How many are there? Are you in some kind of contact with them?"

Megan held up her hand. "I don't know, I don't know. I just . . . woke up. But I hear . . ." She cocked her head—again, a familiar gesture—then suddenly took off toward the center of the Beehive.

"What?" Zack said, struggling to unzip and lever himself out of the suit. "What did you hear?" But Megan didn't answer.

The extraction took almost ten minutes, a mark that would have been a record under ideal circumstances. By the time Zack had propped the suit against the nearest wall and hung the Snoopy cap around his neck, Megan was calling, "Over here!"

He found her quickly . . . cradling a girl-thing in her arms. "She was just . . ." She made soothing sounds that seemed to have no effect.

"Who is she?"

"How the hell should I know? She's a girl, okay?"

Zack looked at the cluttered wall. There were more than he remembered. He could count two dozen now, most of them inert. But three were clearly active: one for Megan, one had probably belonged to the Konstantin-thing, one to this girl-thing.

A fourth cell also appeared to be active—at least Zack could detect a humanoid figure through the translucent wall.

It was shorter than him, not a child . . . in fact, it appeared to be an elderly woman lying on her side. Unlike the other figures, she was in a fetal crouch . . . osteoporosis?

But whereas the Konstantin-thing and Megan-thing had moved, this one lay frozen and still.

"What are you looking at?" Megan said, her voice sounding tired.

"Another one of whatever you are. But interrupted, I think."

"You need to see what's over to your right."

"Oh, shit," Zack said.

It was the Konstantin-thing, the one Natalia had been observing . . . obviously it had somehow gotten free. Just as obviously, someone or something had clubbed it to death.

"Who was he?" Megan said.

"Don't *you* know?"

"No! Weren't you listening? I'm getting jumbled images and occasional words. . . ."

"Sorry. This was a . . . a person from Natalia's life."

Zack shifted himself around, a move much easier now that he was out of the suit and clad in the long john–like undergarment. Had Natalia done this? Had she simply freaked out, or had the Konstantin-thing attacked her?

Suddenly even less certain of his judgment, he glanced at Megan, who was looking past him. "Company's coming," she said.

Four space-suited figures, three *Brahma*, one NASA, were headed their way.

Zack reached for his Snoopy cap.

"—for Zack, I think we can see you. Wave or something. Put your goddamn ears on!"

Uh-oh. *Tea.*

"There," Natalia said. In the strange low light of the Beehive, three human
shapes—two adult-sized and one that was half their height—stood just
out of easy reach. Tea was so shocked she almost stopped in her tracks.
One was likely Zack—but who were these other figures? Especially the
little one?

"Are those your *vorvolakas*?"

It reminded Tea of movies where explorers penetrated uncharted
lands like central Africa or the Amazon jungle . . . the natives going about
their inexplicable business.

"Don't go near them!" Taj ordered. "Stay on mission!"

Tea agreed. She wanted to know Zack was safe.

The traverse through the membrane should have been the fulfillment
of a lifelong dream for Tea. The goal of every female astronaut, every one
of them a *Star Trek* fan, was "to boldly go where no man has gone
before . . ."

Here she was, and she could already hear her father saying, "How's
that working for you?"

Not so well, Dad.

How could it work as exploration? Pogo was dead. Zack was over-
due. Nothing she knew about Keanu twenty-four hours ago seemed to fit
anymore.

There was awe and mystery—did that phrase come from another

sci-fi television show?—in the Beehive and the bizarre environment. But there was also the risk of swift death—

Lucas suddenly peeled away from them. "Lucas, dammit," Taj said. "Get back here!"

"I see . . ." It was all the Brazilian astronaut said, possibly all the English he had at the moment.

As Tea, Taj, and Natalia watched, Lucas ran up to the trio.

"Oh God," Natalia said.

And he knelt to the smaller one. The little creature clapped its hands together and launched itself at Lucas. Tea started to move toward them, but now Taj stopped her. "I think he knows that one."

Sure enough, Lucas and the tiny being were hugging, a ludicrous sight. "Lucas," Taj said, sounding like a flight controller worried about a missing aircraft.

"Camilla!" Lucas shouted into their headphones. "My niece! Is my niece!"

He was carrying a creature toward them that looked to Tea like a little girl.

A little *human* girl.

And she spoke, chirping away in a language that could have been Spanish or Portuguese. "Anyone know what she's saying?" Taj asked.

Lucas stood the girl on the ground. "She says I am the world's greatest uncle!"

So now their party numbered five as they crossed the last hundred meters to Zack and his companion. "Camilla" and Lucas chattered away, with Lucas trying to keep Taj and Tea involved. Apparently Camilla had been diagnosed with leukemia at a young age, and had died eighteen months ago while Lucas was off training in Bangalore.

Tea tried to understand why there were creatures inside Keanu that not only were humanoid, but seemed to be copies or reconstructions of people who had been part of their lives on Earth . . .

Tea did not have a religion. Her father had been as open an atheist as common sense would allow, and Tea had generally felt the same. But for the first time in her life, she felt she might have missed something.

Answers to the larger questions of life and death would be most welcome now as they emerged from the Beehive.

And there was Zack Stewart—standing around without his helmet, like an astronaut relaxing after an EVA training session.

As they closed the last fifty meters, trying not to be distracted by the panorama beyond, Tea saw him pick up his Snoopy cap and give an awkward wave. "Here we are!"

We?

Tea's relief at seeing and hearing Zack immediately gave way to near-panic . . . someone who looked a lot like a dirty, nearly naked Megan Stewart was standing with him.

"Hey, Tea!"

In her life, Tea had fantasized about meeting an alien, but never ever had she expected the E.T. to recognize her and say her name!

The reunion was noisy, chaotic, and brief. "No, I've been breathing Keanu's air for almost two hours now," Zack said, as Taj kept insisting that he get back into his suit again.

He did allow Tea to recharge his backpack from hers, giving him two hours of consumables for the trip back through the membrane. "Thank you," he said, finally looking into her eyes—granted, through her faceplate.

Tea wanted to say, *How come you're not screaming? How can you stand this?* But in the circumstances, the best she could offer was, "What can I do?"

"You wouldn't happen to have a very large extra spacecraft in your pocket, would you?" Zack shook his head. "We need the rover."

"Copy that, but . . ." Tea looked at the relatively benign terrain, then back up the slope toward the Beehive and the passage beyond.

Zack was doing the same thing. "It should fit."

"Speaking of fits, isn't that what Houston's going to throw if we drive the rover in here?"

"No doubt, but I have to tell you . . . the one thing I'm really enjoying about this mission is that we don't have mission control hounding us every minute."

This was the Zack Stewart she had grown to admire, and love: smart, confident, direct.

"I'll take Taj and we'll go get *Buzz*."

All through this, Megan Stewart stood with arms crossed. Tea wasn't convinced it *was* Megan Stewart, but if so, what the hell was going through *her* mind?

The Johnson Space Center cafeteria had been hard-hit by the extra-large mission control staff and the press contingent. Soups and sandwiches were gone; entire display cases, normally filled with pie and cake, were empty. Nevertheless, Rachel and Amy were able to grab several snack bars, bags of M&M's, and sodas. "God, they only have Cheetos," Amy said. "I want SunChips."

"You'll take Cheetos and like them, young lady," Rachel said. Both started giggling, then suppressed it as the Latina cashier shot them a glance.

"God, be careful!" Amy said.

"They know me," Rachel said, with more hope than certainty. "They just don't get many fabulous girls here."

That started them giggling again, until Amy's phone sang to her. She grabbed it as Rachel led her to a table as far from the cashier as possible.

As they sat, Rachel said, "I thought you had it off."

"Just turned it on a minute ago." Amy had already fallen into that dead-eyed zone of the distracted. Knowing there would be no significant conversation for the next several minutes, Rachel turned her Slate back on.

She had never seen its screen so full. Her personal inbox was jammed, her Facebook was overloaded, and her newsfeed updated every couple of seconds.

story was about Keanu, *Destiny*, the accident involv-
Yvonne Hall, and the NASA cover-ups of everything! "God, thing on my screen is blinking."

"Mine, too," Amy said.

Rachel turned to her personal messages. She felt the need to connect with her friends about more important things than this stupid mission her father was on.

"*Luvng your escape!*" one friend wrote.

"*420@JSC! Wicked!*" said another.

Rachel turned to Amy. "I thought you said you had it off until a minute ago."

"Okay, I had it on silent."

"Amy!" Rachel grabbed her friend's phone. Not only was it transmitting their words, the camera was on, too. "You had it on the whole time!" She clicked it off.

"Look, it's nothing. You remember Tracy wanted to come. I just let her listen!"

"She did more than *listen*. I think she put us on the Web!"

"So what? Half the planet is on the Web. It doesn't mean anything."

"Amy, God . . ." Rachel struggled for words. Sometimes Amy could be so shallow. "People are searching for *JSC* and *Keanu* and probably my name, too. So a lot of people know exactly what we've been doing and saying." She got a sick feeling. "I think some of these headlines came from your phone." She held her phone and its news feed up to Amy's face.

"They shouldn't be covering stuff up."

"Yeah, fine. But, you know, what's also bad is that everyone knows we were *blazing*!"

"Rachel, with all the crazy shit that's going on here, I still don't think anyone *cares*!"

Rachel suddenly saw a person who might care. "Quiet," she told Amy, and nodded toward the main entrance, where Jillianne Dwight had just entered with a uniformed member of the JSC security team. "Leave your stuff."

"But I'm still hungry—"

Rachel yanked Amy to her feet and practically dragged her toward the side exit. There were still dozens of people in the cafeteria. Maybe they wouldn't be spotted—

They emerged into the muggy JSC night on the wrong side of the building. Darkness was good, however. And not a single person was visible. "Where are we?" Amy said.

"If we keep going, we'll be in the astronaut building. My dad used to have an office on the fourth floor."

"Could we?"

"No, it's locked." Rachel walked as fast as she could without breaking into a sprint. Her plan was to go all the way around the astronaut building, then back to mission control. Fortunately, the grounds at JSC were easy to navigate . . . nothing but concrete walkways and a few flower beds. Her father had told her it was designed like a college campus because if NASA ever got closed down, that was what the center would become.

Whatever. She only wanted to be sure she and Amy didn't get caught. "Do you still have the pot?"

"Yes, of course! Oh, shit—"

Rachel looked for a place to throw it. "Around this corner—"

They made the turn and ran straight into three men, two JSC cops and a blond man in a short-sleeved white shirt. Rachel tightened her grip on Amy's upper arm, as if to say, *Ignore them and keep going.*

"Rachel Stewart!" It was the blond man.

"What?" Rachel remembered him. Bynum, the guy from Washington.

"We've been looking for you."

"Okay," she said. "You found us."

He turned to the guards. "Take their phones."

For the next several hours—possibly as many as ten—the *Venture* crew will be in a communications blackout created by the new rotation of Near-Earth Object Keanu. The same orbital mechanics affect the crew of *Brahma*. Mission control continues to be in contact with the *Destiny* spacecraft, however, and it is possible that at certain times telemetry and voice may be relayed. We will, of course, continue to post whatever data we receive as we receive it.

NASA PUBLIC AFFAIRS, AUGUST 23, 2019

Tea and Taj had been gone only half an hour when Zack noticed that his charges were beginning to yawn. "Oh my God," Megan said.

She was so immediately unsteady that Zack got worried. "Are you feeling faint?"

"No, just . . . tired." She sank to the ground where she was. The girl slid close to Megan. In moments, both were, to Zack's eyes, sound asleep. "That was very strange," Natalia said.

"Have you ever seen a baby fall asleep?" Zack said gently, afraid he might wake them, and just as afraid he might provoke Natalia. "They go and go and go for hours, then they're like little machines when you switch them off." Just saying it reminded him again of Rachel. What was he going to tell her? How was he going to explain this?

"Well," Lucas said, "they *are* only a day old."

"I think we need a fire." Without further discussion, Zack left Lucas to keep watch, then began to forage in the immediate vicinity. Natalia joined him—more, it seemed to Zack, to avoid being anywhere near the revived pair than because she wanted to help. "Why do you need a fire, anyway?" Natalia said. "It's warm enough in here."

"At the moment," Zack said. "But we don't know what it's going to be like when the glowworms go dark—"

"—Assuming they do go dark."

"Whether they do or not, fire gives light, it helps with cooking, and it provides protection."

"You think a flaming torch is going to help you fight off that thing that killed Pogo?"

"No. But it might be a hell of a distraction. And there's a scientific question to be explored, Dr. Yorkina."

"The ability of the human mind to focus on the irrelevant during times of stress?"

Zack laughed. "Okay, a second scientific question, which is, can we actually build a fire inside Keanu? We've got oxygen, but do we have tinder?"

He stopped and waved at the new growth: spindly, leafy structures that resembled trees. At the moment they reminded him of the pathetic potted sticks that dotted the raw real estate development he had lived in at age seven.

Natalia forgot her own miseries and fears long enough to play along. "Well, even if these are wood, or something resembling cellulose, it will all be green. I can't imagine it will burn easily."

"There's another reason I need a quest for fire," he told her. "Frankly, it gives me something to do while they sleep and the rover gets here." He stripped some of the leafy material off one of the new growths. It felt dry, but not flimsy. It also had substance.

Within minutes he had an armful. "So," he said, as casually as he could, "what happened between you and Konstantin? Was he—?"

"It was not *he*, it was *it*. And I killed it." She admitted her action as casually as if saying she had crossed the street.

"Mind telling me why? Did it attack you?"

"I was afraid it would."

Zack could only nod. What were his options? Arrest her? She wasn't even a member of his crew. "And then you ran."

"I was in a panic." Only now did she look at him. "I still am."

"I guess we all are," he said. "What about Megan and Camilla. Are they *its*?"

"Yes."

"But you're not afraid of them."

"I will be cautious around them, but no . . . not like Konstantin."

"Why not?"

"Because the human Konstantin was a brute! Any replica of him was certain to be just as dangerous. Were you afraid of your wife when she was alive? Should we be in fear of that little girl? I don't think so." She stood, arms filled with vegetation. "We should get back now."

Zack had no better alternative.

"I gave them water and food," Lucas said, as soon as Zack and Natalia returned.

"Good thinking," Zack said, kneeling to arrange his collection of Keanu kindling in the classic Boy Scout fire stack.

At any other time, Lucas would have smiled. Now he just looked embarrassed. "Even if that stuff will burn, how are you going to ignite it?"

"Well, we know there's oxygen here, or none of us would be breathing."

"Are you *sure* about them?" Natalia said, nodding at the sleeping undead. "That they're breathing like us?"

Zack chose to ignore the comment, shredding the leafy stalks as best he could, creating a pile of lighter material that would, he hoped, be more receptive to flame. Then he stood up. "Now, all we need is a spark."

"Don't Young Pioneers rub two sticks together?" Natalia said.

Lucas chose to be supportive. "We could try to get sparks off a couple of rocks, maybe. . . ." He presented Zack with a pair of likely candidates.

Zack thanked him and took one of the rocks. "First, though—" He pulled his backpack over to the protofire and opened a valve. "A little extra O_2 flow . . ."

Then he pulled the geological hammer from the bag on his suit. With the hammer in one hand and the rock in the other, he knelt and held them just over the kindling, in the stream of fresh oxygen flowing from his backpack.

Once, twice. "I'm not seeing a spark," Natalia said.

"Your observation is noted," Zack said, really wishing she would go away. The two hits had been unsatisfactory. For the first time since conceiving this procedure forty minutes ago, he began to doubt it would work.

"Let me," Lucas said. He took the hammer and rock from Zack's hands, got into position, and swiftly chipped a chunk of the rock away so cleanly it gave off visible sparks.

Three more swift chips, and a spark ignited the kindling.

Lucas immediately bent down to adjust the O_2 flow as the leafy Keanu vegetation proved that it would burn, at least for now.

He sat back, looking surprised and still smug.

Zack wanted to hug him. "You are officially the World's Greatest Astronaut."

Did I think I was discovering an alien spacecraft? Are you *insane*? I don't believe in UFOs or close encounters or anal probes. No. I just thought I'd found something big and new . . . ice and rock from deep space. Christ, what a stupid question.

COLIN EDGELY ON *TODAY*, NINE NETWORK, SYDNEY, 23 AUGUST 2019

"Something's going on up there," Brent Bynum told Harley, Shane Weldon, and Gabriel Jones.

They were gathered in the Vault again, along with a half dozen other staffers and horse-holders. There was no preliminary chat, other than several quick expressions of sympathy to Jones on his daughter's health. The director had simply said, with uncharacteristic understatement, "She's stable and the mission is proceeding."

The lack of sentiment allowed Weldon, in perfect Weldon style, to say, in answer to Bynum, "No shit, Sherlock."

He smiled sideways at Harley, who did not return the smile. While he had no fears about annoying Bynum, he also knew that a meeting ran better, which is to say faster, when the guy who called it was happy.

Bynum could not be happy, of course. None of them could. The realization that the *Venture* crew was out of direct contact with Earth and mission control for any period of time would have been a major problem in a normal mission; given the tragic and bizarre information that had already reached Houston, it was a disaster.

The only thing to do was to work it through. So Harley said, "Can you, ah, clarify that for us?"

"Yes. Excuse me." Bynum bowed his head and clasped his hands for a moment, as if previewing his remarks. Harley wondered, given the incredible circumstances, what information could possibly be sensitive enough to justify such caution. "*Brahma* is not affected by the loss of signal."

Weldon reacted first. "That's impossible!"

"That was our position, too," Bynum said, "given the rotation of Keanu and other factors."

"What are you telling us?" Weldon said. "You can't punch a radio signal through a NEO."

"Correct. *Brahma* is sending a signal *around* Keanu."

Now Harley found the energy to speak. "And just how in the hell did they manage that?"

Bynum turned toward him. The man was impressively calm and low-key. "This will be easier if I start with the image."

On cue, one of his assistants enabled the screen at the end of the table . . . which showed a white rectangular shape trailed by a small white blob. "This is a long-distance image of *Brahma* taken yesterday from Hawaii. I believe it's about thirteen hours before *Destiny* landed, but I'm assured that figure is irrelevant."

Harley knew the Air Force had a satellite surveillance station in Hawaii equipped with telescopes that peered up at satellites. He also knew that it was impossible to get much of an image on a bird even at geosynchronous orbit, thirty-six thousand kilometers up. This would have been at ten times the distance. "They must have had some impressive upgrades at Maui," he said.

"Who cares?" Harley snapped. "They dropped a satellite?"

"Correct," Bynum said. "A microsat designed to loiter in—what do you call it?—a super-high Earth orbit—"

"That makes sense," Weldon said. "It just hangs there on the far side of Keanu. *Brahma* can pop signals to it. Signals get relayed to Bangalore."

"It looks bigger than a microsat," one of the staffers said.

"That's due to the sun and imaging," Bynum said. "It's apparently only a meter across."

"Makes it hard to hit the horns," said another man in the room. "Horns" were the antennae on the satellite itself.

Weldon was completely taken with the concept. "The satellite is only a couple of kilometers from events on Keanu. What's trickier is getting that signal to Bangalore."

This time a different staffer joined in. "Why worry about getting the signal to one spot on Earth? Just aim it toward commercial comsats in geo."

Harley was already tired of this space ops chat. "People, we're losing focus here! Forget how they did it." He turned to Bynum. "The point is, they have comm that we don't. And you guys intercepted it, and I bet you cracked whatever encryption they put on it."

"Correct," Bynum said.

"Now we're getting somewhere. What have they learned? What have they said?"

For the first time Bynum looked uncomfortable. "Some very strange things. Apparently there are people inside Keanu."

That bit of news silenced the Vault. "Did you say *people*? Not aliens? Not extraterrestrial life-forms?"

"No. People. Human beings . . ." Bynum trailed off and merely looked uncomfortable.

"Well," Weldon said, "that explains where all this space zombie crap is coming from. Bangalore leaks."

"Which means that the rest of the world is somehow cleared for Bangalore's data," Harley said. "Just not NASA. The people who could use it."

"Bangalore has released nothing," Bynum said. "The only information out there is rumor and fantasy."

Gabriel Jones cleared his throat. "But we all know, Mr. Bynum, that in circumstances like this, where there's smoke . . ." To Harley Jones, he looked exhausted. Well, all of them did—except Bynum, whose shirt seemed to be starched. Did anyone still do that anymore?

"Zombies? That's a pretty strange flavor of smoke. It doesn't even make sense. Zombies are mindless flesh-eaters, not people." Weldon pushed his chair back from the table. He was about to walk out.

"It would be helpful if we had the raw intel," Harley said to Bynum.

"Not just your summary. Assuming anybody wants my Great Minds to go to work on this."

Bynum blinked. His body language tipped Harley to his answer, which was, "You aren't cleared for the raw intel." As the others in the Vault immediately protested, Bynum held up his hands. "I'm not cleared for it, either! Sorry. Maybe Dr. Jones can make a request. I'm just the messenger."

Now Weldon was on his feet. "Well, Mr. Bynum, you know what happens to messengers." And he walked out.

Obviously hoping to forestall a mass exodus, Jones said, "This situation may resolve itself before any other action takes place. Where are we in our loss of signal?"

"Six hours yet," Harley said. The number caused audible groans around the Vault.

"Then I suggest we all use this time to take stock, recharge, and be ready, because when we have comm again, we'll have to hit the ground running."

Harley marveled again at the way a string of empty words could motivate a group of human beings. Jones had told them nothing, yet the team in the Vault—Weldon excepted because of absence, and Harley because of habitual pessimism—rose with something like enthusiasm, ready to go forth and do battle.

Harley had to get his Home Team up to speed. When communication was reestablished with *Venture*, they were going to have to provide answers. And right now they barely understood the questions.

As he left the Vault, however, there was a JSC security guard waiting for him. "Mr. Drake? Are you responsible for Rachel Stewart?"

Keanu is a starship: how did the word get out? Impossible to say, though some day some Ph.D. in media will be able to reconstruct it. At the moment, the primary suspects are sources within the Bangalore and NASA mission control centers. All it would take is one text message. HUFFINGTON POST NEWS WATCH, AUGUST 23, 2019

The fire sputtered and never reached the roaring stage, no matter how much leafy stuff they piled on it. But it gave them a bit of light, as well as a bizarre shadow against the Beehive wall . . . which turned out to be rover *Buzz* on approach.

All five of the astronauts were going without helmets now. "This troubles me," Taj said. "We're exposing ourselves to this environment."

"What choice do we really have?" Zack said. "If we had to rely on our consumables, we'd be back on the surface by now. Besides, it doesn't matter what our bodies are exposed to. Our suits are totally contaminated. *Venture* has tools for dealing with lunar dust, not Keanu's organisms."

"This does nothing to cheer me." Taj shuffled off, taking his Zeiss camera.

Tea and Zack pulled a few food items from the rover. The vehicle also gave each of the astronauts a bit of privacy. "Thank God," Zack said. "My diaper is beginning to chafe."

"So sexy," Tea said.

But there was nothing in the way of clothing or blankets. "The rover wasn't designed for camping," Tea said.

As the newly undead continued to sleep, Zack ordered Natalia and Tea into the vehicle for a rest. "We're going to need our energy for recon."

Taj was back in earshot by now. "What recon?"

"We've got a whole new world here. We ought to take a look while we can."

"Zack, Keanu's in orbit now. Let the next crew do it. They'll have the proper equipment."

"NASA can't mount another visit for at least a year, and I don't think the Coalition can, either."

"What difference does a year make? This thing has been traveling for ten thousand times that!"

"It hasn't been alive, like this," Lucas said. He raised his arm toward the landscape, now looking more like an Amazonian rain forest . . . except that the "trees" were no more than a few meters tall. All of it bathed in the near-twilight cast by the strange little glowworms. "It's like . . . the Garden of Eden."

Taj grunted. "Which makes us what? The Serpent?"

"Hardly," Zack said. "The environment seems optimized for humans."

"For a while, at least," Taj said. "It clearly wasn't optimized for the Sentry." He nodded at the sleepers. "I wonder if our . . . newly alive could eat anything that's growing in here."

"Speaking of them," Lucas said, "what do we do with them? No matter what kind of exploring we do, we have to leave in a day or so!"

Zack had been worrying about this. "Well, *Venture* has room for one passenger. And Camilla is only half the weight penalty of a full-grown human—"

"Are you insane? You can't be thinking about taking these two back to Earth!"

"You bet I'm thinking about it—"

"Just because one of them looks and sounds like your wife? Zack, you're too tired to be making these decisions!"

Zack was very tired, but he'd been in similar states of exhaustion several times in his life. He believed it helped him think more clearly. He took Taj by the arm and turned him toward the sleepers. "For the record, I'm not at all sure who or what that person is. But all the evidence tells me it's my dead wife, somehow restored to life by some pretty goddamned advanced technology. So, allowing for that, what do I do? Leave her?"

"For the next mission, yes."

"How is she supposed to survive? She and the girl?" Zack pointed back to the Beehive. "Or the rest of them."

"I think my commander believes Keanu will provide," Lucas said.

Taj was usually a serene individual—Zack had never seen him truly angry. But at that moment the vyomanaut shot his Brazilian crew member a look of such loathing that Zack got to his feet, afraid that he had to prevent a fistfight. "I am trying to protect my mission and my crew!"

"We both are," Zack said, using a voice he had perfected in refereeing fights between Megan and Rachel. "This situation is unusual—"

But Lucas wasn't ready to give up. "You both keep looking at this like it's a malfunction in a sim! This world is sending us a message! It welcomed us! It has changed its environment to suit humans! It has revived and rebuilt the dead! And even if *one* of them were someone we knew, it would be significant. Three makes it mind-blowing, possibly biblical!"

Zack was happy to hear Lucas say it—it saved him from doing so.

"Ah, yes, this could be God's work. But tell me, my friend, how does a Catholic explain this?" Taj said. "As I recall, you believe that eventually humans will be raised up body and soul after Jesus returns."

"Yes."

"Jesus has not returned."

"Not that we know of," Lucas said. He smiled. "We haven't quite finished exploring Keanu."

"You guys are loud," Tea said, joining them.

"Couldn't sleep?" Zack said.

"And miss all the excitement?" She brought a drink box from inside the rover and offered it to Zack. She had drinks for Lucas and Taj, too. "Hydration?"

"Sorry," Lucas said.

"Don't be. No one should be sleeping when there's a whole dang planet to explore." Tea caught herself and nodded toward the two bodies around the fire. "Except for them."

"You should be part of this debate," Taj said. "I'd wake up Natalia if she didn't need the sleep. We're trying to understand what we face. Our Brazilian friend cites Jesus as a possibility."

Never much of a Lucas fan—certainly not a player in his World's Greatest Astronaut game—Tea couldn't help being sarcastic. "As in 'Jesus, take the wheel?'" she said, singing a phrase from an old country song. "Is he driving the Chariots of God?" She turned to Zack. "Am I remembering that right?"

"Chariots of the Gods, plural," Taj said, sneering. "And that was a popular explanation for the Pyramids, how they'd been built by alien visitors. Not really applicable here."

Lucas refused to be baited. "I'm not suggesting anything like that. But given what I've seen today, how can any of us rule *anything* out?"

"But surely this violates your beliefs," Taj said.

"Catholics don't believe that after death they will simply regain their bodies. That never made sense. Which body? The one that was filled with cancer and killed you? The body that was torn apart in a plane crash? After death, we will be *transfigured*. We will become something new." He stood up, and pointed to Megan and Camilla. "Very possibly we will become like them. Which suggests to me that if you didn't believe in God, now would be an excellent time to consider it." He smiled his beautiful smile.

Zack could tell Taj was holding something back. "Come on, Taj . . . everything is on the table here."

"There is, in my tradition, a version of what might be happening here. The Vedas, our sacred Sanskrit texts, mention the akashic records—a library of all human experience. What if that exists? What if the universe is nothing more than a giant akashic record . . . and these aliens somehow access it."

"And you think *my* religion is crazy," Lucas said. He got up and headed for the rover.

As they watched him go, Taj shrugged. "Saying it isn't the same as believing it. And even if he's convinced himself, at least he has a strategy: He will treat these things as transfigured humans. It's more than I have."

Tea knelt by Zack. "Talk to me, because I'm worse off than Taj here . . . I'm totally lost."

Zack looked at the two sleepers. "Speaking to them as if they are revived humans is fine. But when it comes to actions? I'm still not sure this isn't some kind of ruse."

"So they're artificial."

"It would make sense. But why would anyone make duplicates of specific humans—"

"To make us trust them."

Zack pointed to the sleeping Megan. "I would trust that creature more if it didn't claim to be my wife."

Tea touched his hand, the only physical contact they'd had since she had buttoned him into his suit.

"Zack," Taj said, "we still haven't agreed on a plan."

Zack stood and stretched. "I don't know yet. For the moment, I want to see about Pogo. Whatever we do, I don't just want him . . . left over there."

Tea stood, too. "What do you say, Taj? This sounds like a job for you and me."

She didn't give Taj the chance to argue.

"Are these girls under arrest?"

Harley had followed the guard to the ground floor of Building 1, where he found Rachel, her friend Amy, and a very distraught Jillianne Dwight, all kept company by a nervous official in a blue jacket. His contractor badge identified him as *BURNETT, TOBY*. He appeared to be about thirty.

"No, but they were in a restricted area—"

"Where were you?" Harley said to Rachel.

"The cafeteria."

"Actually," Burnett said, "they ran from the cafeteria. I suspect they were trying to get into Building Four-South." Burnett's tone suggested that this was some kind of temple. Well, Harley knew, to most of the starstruck JSC employees, the astronaut office was the holy of holies.

Not to Harley, however. "Her father's an astronaut. She's probably been in that building more than you have, Toby." He wasn't going to give Mr. Burnett time to argue. "Give them their phones."

"No, Mr. Drake, I don't think we can do that."

Harley had never quarreled with JSC's private security guys. But he was beyond patience now. "Think again, Toby. Unless you can hold up a document showing that these young women—minors—waived the right to personal possessions by entering this facility—at the invitation of the director, by the way, not on their initiative—you're on thin ice. Actually, you're on no ice at all. I don't care what seems to be going on here, this is a civilian center. You can't hold their phones, and you can't hold them. So get over yourself and let them go."

But Burnett wasn't bending. "Mr. Bynum said to hold them." Harley sighed. He knew Burnett's type: impressed by power and authority, but also smug in his own.

Here was an opening. "Brent Bynum?" Burnett nodded. "Is Mr. Bynum employed by Wackenhut, which would make him one of your supervisors?"

"No, sir."

"He's not with NASA, or certainly not with the Johnson Space Center, either, is he?"

Burnett considered this. "I don't believe so."

"In fact, Mr. Bynum, with whom I've had several meetings already today, works for the White House. Which means he has zero authority to be ordering you around—especially zero authority to be ordering you to detain people and confiscate property."

Burnett considered this for a moment. Then he reached into his desk and pulled out Amy's cell phone and Rachel's Slate. "Thank you, Toby," Harley said, knowing it was time to let the man down easily. "I will see what I can do about keeping these young ladies where they can be found."

Moments later the four of them were out in the muggy night, heading in the general direction of mission control. "Thank you," Rachel said. Amy said nothing; she was already firing up her phone and going glassy-eyed.

As they reached the entrance to Building 30, then entered, Harley quickly updated Rachel on the loss of signal from the *Venture* crew. "We aren't going to know anything about your dad until tomorrow." He looked up at Jillianne Dwight, who had been notably silent until now. "Can you drive them home?"

"Love to. But . . . I'm parked behind Building Two."

"We'll wait right here."

As Jillianne headed out, Amy announced that she needed to use the bathroom. Harley pointed her down the hall, then turned to Rachel . . . who suddenly looked like she'd had the shock of a lifetime.

"Something wrong?"

She held up the Slate. The headlines on the screen said, *"Humans Alive in Keanu." "Crew Finds Undead." "Most Shocking Discovery in History." "Space Angels!"*

"May I?" Harley took the unit and tabbed his way through half a dozen sites, all of them blaring the same general stories: A *Destiny* astronaut had been killed (true). *Destiny* and *Brahma* crews had discovered alien civilization (truish).

They had also discovered *living humans* inside Keanu—at least one of them identified as a deceased Russian. "What the fuck?" Harley was usually careful about cursing in front of young people, but his guard was down.

"You don't know anything about this?" Rachel said.

"Hell, no!"

"What do you think?"

"My first response, and my hundredth . . . garbage. Batshit crazy time. I mean, *maybe* the crew found a humanoid body—"

He shut up as Amy rejoined them. Rachel said, "Can't we just go back to the family room?"

"No, you're going home for the moment. To Amy's."

"Harley, come on—!"

Jillianne returned at that point. "Okay, girls, I'm parked illegally. . . ." She dangled her keys. It occurred to Harley that she might be eager to get back to her husband or whatever, too.

Rachel was in a semicrouch, her face filled with disdain. Harley decided, not for the first time, that he would not want to trade places with Zack Stewart—at least not when it came to being the father of a teenage girl. "Rachel, your father is the best person in the world to be handling this situation. Trust him. I do. The moment anything happens, the moment we have any news, I'll be in touch. I'll get you right back over here."

Rachel hesitated, then reached out for her Slate. But Harley held it away. "Let me keep it for a moment. It's better than mine. I'll give it back to you tomorrow."

Rachel stared, horrified. "Don't worry, I won't troll through your pictures." She still wasn't convinced, so he leaned close. "They took mine."

Once she realized she was helping Harley in a conspiracy, Rachel gave up the argument. Even though Amy was pouting, she allowed them both to be led off by Jillianne.

Harley had not shown Rachel the last image that appeared on her Slate.

It was a dark, unclear picture of a woman who, except for short hair, looked exactly like Megan Stewart.

Tea found Patrick Downey's remains just where Zack had told her, less than two hundred meters deeper into Keanu, and in exactly the same horrific condition: flat on his back, headless, sliced from neck to toe, still more or less contained inside his blood-spattered EVA suit. She noted that pieces of Pogo's helmet had been gathered into a small pile. Small comfort.

Zack had confessed, "I had nothing to cover him with." And Tea had nothing, either. Human decency suggested that she should cover him with earth (a term that seemed increasingly inappropriate), but although "trees" had risen, there was nothing like loose soil here . . .

"Any suggestions?"

Taj was with her but completely distracted by the environment. "We cremate our dead," he said.

"Yeah, well, Zack might have been able to light that one fire . . . I don't think we're equipped for a funeral pyre."

"I wasn't suggesting that. I'm more worried about how we get him back."

Tea had not allowed herself to think that far into the future—a realization that alarmed her, since her whole career was based on her ability to project, plan, prepare. But Taj's point was logical: Don't leave your dead on the battlefield. "Then we'll need a plastic bag."

"There might be something inside the rover. An equipment bag, perhaps. Shit!" Taj batted at something around his head . . . an insect or bird, Tea couldn't tell, but it was just large enough to be an annoyance.

Tea took several swipes at the creature and nailed it on the fly. She bent to examine the carcass. "Now, that is weird." She stood up. "It has edges. Looks like a flying Lego."

"I don't care about the bug!"

"Come on, Taj, try to relax—"

The vyomanaut turned on her. "I might tell *you* to get serious! Do you realize the danger we face?"

"Yeah, well, we all knew the job was dangerous when we took it . . ." She needed to keep busy; during almost every waking moment of her previous spaceflights, she had had switches to throw, experiments to operate, toilets to fix, food to prepare. So far, the Keanu mission was way too light on operational activities. She began collecting big "leaves" to cover Pogo's remains.

"Tea! This is not a joking matter! It's not just our lives—all of Earth is at risk!"

There was no way out of this. Taj was squatting, head turning right and left, as if he expected to be attacked by a wild animal at any moment. Tea knew she would have to engage him . . . the last thing she wanted to do. "Okay, how?"

"These creatures we've found. Think of what they represent."

"You mean, beyond that old 'advanced technology that's indistinguishable from magic'?"

"It's *extremely* advanced technology! And it isn't benign, it's aimed at us. If, in addition to traveling from one star to another, the Keanu entities can generate creatures from our lives . . . Tea, there's no weapon on Earth that can touch them."

"Fine, conceded. Whoever built this place and runs it is completely out of our league. But I still don't see the threat. What could we possibly have that they want? Resources? Water? Plutonium?" She opened her hand to the dynamic environment around them. "They can cook up a whole jungle in an afternoon! They could probably snag a comet and turn it into anything they need, metal, cellulose, fuck, I don't know . . . magic beans."

Taj had closed his eyes. He was rocking gently on his haunches. "I don't assume hostility. Indifference is just as bad. Keanu's magic might harm us in the same way a human foot crushes an anthill. That is my fear . . . that anything could emerge from this place."

"Or any*one*." Tea had not thought of it until this moment, but who- or whatever built Keanu had somehow crafted "undead" from the lives of Zack, Lucas, and Natalia, but not from Taj's or hers.

Not yet, anyway. Was that still to come? Or had the window closed?

Taj got up and stretched. His movement drew Tea's eye, forcing her to look beyond him deeper into Keanu's interior.

Where she saw a structure. At first it looked like a geological formation—a literal pile of rocks, possibly sandstone—hidden in the foliage. But the more she stared at it, the more it looked artificial. The term *human-made* came to mind, but she suppressed it. Still, in its tapering lines, it could have been an Egyptian pyramid or a Mayan temple—

Goddamn Keanu twilight. She spread a last covering of leaves over Pogo's remains, then immediately started walking toward the structure. "What's the matter?" Taj asked.

"At your one o'clock, about half a click out."

"Dammit," Taj said. "I suppose we have to check that out."

"Unless you've got something better to do."

It proved surprisingly difficult to reach the structure, which Taj immediately began calling the Temple. "I wish we had the science gear with us," he said. "We might be able to see what it's made of. . . ."

"Shit, Taj, we'll *be* there in another ten minutes." This Taj—hypercautious, stodgy, reliant on instruments—was easier to take than the paranoid version on display forty-five minutes earlier. But only slightly.

On approach, the Temple turned out to be larger than Tea had originally judged, and much farther away. For the first time she felt misgivings about her impulsive approach . . . maybe Taj was right. This structure looked old and weathered, but the *Destiny* and *Brahma* explorers would have noticed something *this* big. Zack had originally reported that the interior of Keanu—prior to "sunrise" when the glowworms illuminated—was bare rock. He had not mentioned a three-story ziggurat within five kilometers. And he wasn't the type to let it slip his mind. . . .

"Why don't we hold up right here?" Tea said, as they reached the edge of the clearing surrounding the Temple.

"I concur," Taj said. His thoughts must have paralleled hers, because he moved left along the boundary of the clearing, eyes fixed on the ground.

"How new does it look to you?" Tea said.

Taj picked up a handful of stalks that reminded Tea of reeds . . . if reeds happened to be the color of blood. "They appear to have been chopped off."

"So this clearing is . . . new?" Tea was relieved, though that implied other dangers.

"As new as everything else, I think."

Now Taj regarded the Temple itself. "It is more rectangular than pyramidical," he said.

"Is that a good or bad thing?"

It sounded like a joke to Taj, and he showed his irritation again. "It's just an observation. Feel free to add your own."

Architecture was not one of Tea's specialties. She could tell a skyscraper from a bungalow, sure. She might go so far as to say she could tell Federal style from Art Deco, and she had vague memories of hearing the term *Bauhaus*. "Taj, to me it just looks like a fucking pile of sand-colored bricks."

"The same. But resembling a cube. Given the proportions of the gates and ramps . . ."

"Don't start reading more than you should."

"I was just wondering . . . a human building that height would have three or four levels. How many does our Temple have?"

"I guess that's one of the things we'll have to find out, won't we?"

They continued around the perimeter, with Tea growing increasingly agitated. "I don't see any doors or windows."

"Neither do I." Taj offered one of his rare smiles. "We must be careful about anthropomorphizing the structure. We call it a temple and look for temple-like openings. It might just be a solid pile of rocks, like a giant cairn or grave marker."

"Don't try to cheer me up, okay?" Taj had identified Tea's biggest concern. Like all of them, she kept slapping familiar names on what she was seeing—ramps, trees, temples—without any real knowledge of what these objects were.

That seemed like a great way to get yourself in trouble. But then—

"What do you think?" Tea said. "Could that be the entrance?"

Embedded in the surface of the Temple that faced away from the Beehive was the biggest, most complex marker they had yet seen. Below that was an opening.

"Yes. And it seems to have the same proportions as the membrane passage," Taj said, raising his camera.

"What do you think? Shall I see if anyone's home?" Tea said.

"Let me."

"Actually, no. My idea. My risk. Besides, you're *Brahma* commander. . . . I'm slightly more expendable than you." Before he could argue, Tea was several steps away, heading directly for the big marker and the door.

"Do *not* go inside!"

"Not planning to!" she called, picking her way carefully across the surface, which was nowhere near smooth. It was ridged and tufted, like a Kansas wheat field after harvest. Anthropomorphizing again, Tea thought it looked as though some machine or entity had cleared this area—hastily?

She stopped about ten meters from the opening and clicked off several images. "I don't see a door," she called to Taj. "None of those magic beads, either."

"Can you see inside?"

"Nope. It's all shadows." But she did feel something strange . . . a tugging at the camera. She loosened her grip, and the unit almost flew out of her hand. "Whoa! I think there's a big magnet in there!"

"Come back here now!"

Taj didn't have to tell her twice. She clutched the camera to the front of her EVA long johns, turned, and hopped quickly over the ruts back to where she started.

She realized that the feet of her undergarment were going to be filthy, which was all going to wind up back inside the boots of her EVA suit. Bad protocol there.

"Did you feel that?" she asked Taj. "It was as if the camera was being pulled out of my hands."

"I felt nothing." He gestured at the camera. "I hope that effect didn't erase the images."

Tea hadn't thought of that. Maybe that was the reason for the Temple's magnetism.

Or not. How could she have any real idea? Nothing here was as it should be!

Taj was saying, "We'd better get back. However we're going to deal with Keanu, it's got to be easier as a team."

"We're calling them *Revenants*," said Sasha Blaine, as the footage of an
impossibly alive Megan Stewart froze on the screen.

Harley Drake raised his head and tried to reconnect with the chaos
in the Home Team.

He had been thinking about Pogo Downey. He had lost colleagues
and close friends before—a buddy who hit the ground in an F-22 during test pilot school, and another who was shot down by a SAM over
Yemen. Those were just close friends; other second-tier acquaintances
had died, too.

And, of course, there was Megan Stewart.

So he was quite familiar with the sensations experienced on hearing
the news, the ashen looks on faces, the constant headshaking and confusion, and the rituals.

Except for those associated with death in space. He had joined NASA
too late for the horrors of *Columbia*, when seven astronauts had been
killed as their orbiter broke into pieces, burned up, then scattered itself

across Texas and Louisiana thanks to an undetected breach in its thermal protection system.

Pogo's death would be the top story on every news site around the world. What was it they said about Lincoln? "Now he belongs to the ages."

Now Patrick Downey belonged to the Web pages.

All of them knew flying in space was risky—that you had, in essence, a one-in-fifty chance of being killed. You were actually far safer working in a coal mine for twenty-five years, or serving consecutive combat tours.

But knowing that didn't make it easier. A friend was suddenly gone. Bad, but worse yet—killed by some unknown entity.

That was the true horror. . . . What in God's name was running around loose inside Keanu that was capable of killing a man?

And wanting to?

There were reports that this thing, the Sentry, had died, too. Which was another problem. Better to have captured it, interrogated or studied it.

Harley was afraid for his friends on the mission. "Sorry," he said, "what the hell does that mean?"

"*Revenant* is a French word," Wade Williams said, winding up for another giant info-dump, "meaning a visible ghost or an animated corpse!"

But before he could take another breath, after which he would be unstoppable short of violence, Steven Matulka, one of the more socialized members of the Home Team, a generation younger than Williams, slapped his hand on the table. "For God's sake, Wade!"

In the immediate silence, Harley noted the shocked look on Wade's face—Matulka was a protégé of the older writer; this might have been the first time in a twenty-year relationship that the younger man had spoken up—and several bowed headshakes around the room. Sasha Blaine had her hand over her eyes.

"Speaking of rope in the family of the hanged man?" Harley said, offering a nod of thanks to Matulka. "Don't worry, I'm not that sensitive."

"It's not that accurate, anyway," Matulka said, with a by-your-leave gesture to Harley. "Megan Stewart's earthly remains are here in Texas, so *corpse* is the wrong word.

"*Ghost* doesn't apply, either. According to the data we've received, those beings are corporeal. Flesh and blood."

"I'll give you flesh," said Williams, unwilling to cede the stage for long. "Don't know about blood!" It wasn't as witty as he'd hoped. The room was silent again.

"I'll give you *this*," Harley said. "*Revenant* sounds better than *zombie*. So, fine, use it. But you seem to be grabbing the shovel by the wrong end here. You've managed to come up with useful names for all these new things—"

"It's a hard habit to break," Blaine said. "If you name something, you own it."

"Fine. Let's consider Keanu and the membrane and the Sentry and the Revenants as proprietary. Publish your papers and claim priority. At what point do you start giving me, and by extension, the folks in there"—he aimed a thumb in the direction of mission control—"and the White House and the world some goddamn concrete data? Everything you've *named* could be a potential threat to our existence! Keanu maneuvers and seems to be inhabited. Fine, but by what? Is your Sentry a machine or a life-form? Either way, how can we communicate with it—or things like it—so no one else gets killed? What about the environment? Why is it changing so fast? How long does that go on? And there's the big one. How the hell can there be people inside that thing? Formerly dead people the crew knows. That may be the freakiest question in human history.

"You've got some facts. Start giving me explanations that fit, or you might as well go home."

Within moments, the dozen members of the team had broken into smaller groups . . . except for Williams, who was left by himself, busy pushing his glasses back up his nose.

Which gave Harley a terrible, wonderful idea. If there was one thing he hated more than having to answer reporters, it was having nothing to say!

Why not send members of the Home Team out to brief the world, one by one?

Better yet, why not send Wade Williams out there . . . he could soothe or baffle the press as needed, with the added bonus that work inside the Home Team would go faster and be more productive.

And Harley could worry about Rachel Stewart.

CROCKETT: So you've heard about what's going on with the *Destiny* mission.

BOONE: You mean the alien stuff?

CROCKETT: Don't you think it's cool that our astronauts may have discovered intelligent life on another world?

BOONE: I'd be more impressed if they discovered intelligent life on this one. (WAH-WAH SFX)

CROCKETT: Seriously . . . there's also this rumor going around that they've discovered souls . . . that these aliens are smart enough to bring dead people back to life.

BOONE: All I can say is, if they revive my uncle Eduardo, I'm not giving the money back.

KPRC RADIO "ALL-AMERICAN" GUYS, AUGUST 23, 2019

She was late again. She was supposed to be meeting with a producer, but something had gone wrong—goddamn Houston traffic, maybe—and she was half an hour behind schedule.

And then she didn't have her Slate! How the hell was she supposed to make her pitch without it?

And where were her pants? What was she thinking, going out naked from the waist down?

It made Megan Stewart feel cold.

She shifted on her bed. Ouch. That didn't feel right—

She opened her eyes. Why was she in the backyard? And where was Rachel—?

Then she sat up and began to tremble. The dream was already returning to the place dreams go. Here was the reality . . . she had been sleeping in the open air next to a rock, said air and rock being part of the environment of the Near-Earth Object Keanu.

Another figure lay next to her . . . the girl Camilla. Across from her, her husband, Zack. Beyond him, the white cylindrical vehicle known as rover *Buzz*.

It was morning, at least as far as her biological clock was concerned.

Oh, yes, she was alive again after being dead for the past two years. She had been resurrected somehow, on another planet.

Among other sensations—rather far down the list, but still worth noting—her throat hurt. For that matter, she ached everywhere.

"Hey," Zack said, waking up and trying to stretch in his EVA underwear—never a flattering look. "Good morning."

"You don't look very comfortable."

"You don't, either." That much was obvious as Zack slowly rose to his feet. "How did you sleep?"

"What was it I used to say? 'Like the dead.' Now I know what that means."

He got that cautious look on his face, one she had learned to recognize. "So what does it mean?"

"Well, I misspoke. I'm alive, right?"

"But you must remember . . ."

"Being dead?" How did she answer that? She wasn't entirely sure herself. She had fragmentary memories of the accident. Her frustration with the weather, with Rachel, with Harley's attitude. The truck suddenly filling the view. She hadn't had time to feel fear. Just a moment of—surprise. "Some of it. It's like the dream you can't quite bring back. I know part of me was floating. Flying, actually."

"Or just disembodied."

"I like my word better. But, fine. And I was bombarded with images and memories and . . . stuff."

"No visits with dead relatives? No Uncle Marty or Nana Becky?"

"Yes and no." She really didn't want to be debriefed—she was hungry and needed to urinate, not necessarily in that order. But, like therapy, this was helping her remember. "I knew they were out there. That everyone was out there, if I would only reach out."

"Only the deceased?"

"No! Every*one*. Every*thing*. People, animals, rivers, even planets! The Sun! I was . . . connected. Which is why disembodied is the wrong word, so there. Your fire's out," she told Zack, pointing to the pathetic pile of coals. "And I'm going to find . . ."

Zack pointed directly away from the rover, which was at his back. "There are some tall trees that way."

"You're such a dang Boy Scout."

Like any human, from time to time, Megan had wondered about her own death. Would it be some long, slow fade-out with cancer or pneumonia— or perhaps worst of all, dementia? Or a violent lurch from this world to the next?

The real issue had always been, *Would you want to know it was coming?* She had had mixed feelings about that. The long, slow fade-out, dying in bed in the fullness of years, great-grandchildren gathered around . . . knowing you were slipping away, feeling, if not exactly eager, then at least accepting of the inevitable . . . that had its attractions.

Well, now she had some hard data. She knew that a person didn't just switch off. That old line about not knowing what hit you? Total bullshit. She felt the impact of her face on the window of the car. The sounds! Metal. The snap of bone—her neck? God! It made her sick to think about it.

Camilla was up now, too, chattering in Portuguese. Lucas and Natalia must have heard her, because they suddenly appeared from the rover with water and food.

As the two *Brahma* astronauts tended to their charge, Megan asked again about Rachel. "You have to tell me everything, baby. If you ever want to hear about the Architects, that is."

So, as they ate what appeared to be oatmeal from a bag and sipped orange juice from drink boxes, Zack spoke about Rachel, her struggles after Megan's death . . . her smile, the joy he took in rediscovering his favorite movies with her . . . her moodiness . . . her refusal to play the piano; it all bubbled out of him almost too easily, without censorship or structure. "I can't believe you did that."

"What?"

"You let her give up the piano! I'd have screamed at her to stick with it."

"You mean, screamed more." Zack smiled. Megan liked that. It meant that he was relaxing. "So, what happened to my video?"

"Oh, it was aired on GoogleSpace, won a posthumous Peabody, and is now required viewing for every spouse in the space program."

"Good!" She picked up the camera from its spot atop Zack's discarded space suit and handed it to him. "Make sure you record the sequel."

Zack aimed the camera at her. "Any time you're ready . . . why not tell the world about the Architects?"

She realized that she did know something about them—as if she'd learned it in her sleep. "Well, they're millions of years older than we are . . . the human race, I mean. Even their sense of time is totally different. A day for them is like a whole week for us."

"Compared to the Architects, we're mayflies?"

"Something like that."

He thought. "They're powerful enough to raise the dead."

"So it would seem, but don't ask me how." She nodded to Camilla. "Maybe she'll know. Maybe each of us has a different piece of the puzzle."

"Where are they from? How far away? How did Keanu get here?"

"I don't know where they're from—obviously a star system at least ten light-years away, maybe more. But that's just me, Megan, doing the math. As for Keanu, all I can say is they don't have any faster-than-light warp drive. The Keanu trip took thousands of years."

"What do the Architects look like?"

Megan tried to picture them, but failed. But—"*Post-organic* is the phrase or image that comes into my head. They used to have bodies, but over time, as they made genetic improvements, they became more and more like machines."

It was like reading a book. Every one of Zack's questions triggered some kind of response—either an image and a set of terms, or a blank page. "Something happened a few tens of thousands of years ago and they realized they needed to devolve, to be organic again. Which is what they were looking for with Keanu. They found other races, including the . . . the Sentries. But none of them seems to have worked out." She could feel herself getting excited, speaking too fast, as always.

"'Worked out' how?"

"I don't know. I just get images of other beings and a feeling of failure." In fact, it made her uncomfortable. "You asked about the resurrectees. Keanu isn't just a ship or a transport, it's also a space probe. It gathers data wherever it goes. It gathered us as soon as it came within range. . . ."

"Two years ago?" She was nodding. "So it has some kind of . . . soul catcher. Which means humans do have souls and consciousness does go on after death . . ."

"You're getting ahead of yourself," Megan said, holding up her hand. "I have to stop."

"Is something wrong?"

She had a terrific headache. "I think I may have overdone it," she said, forcing a smile. "Not enough bandwidth."

It was a good moment to break: Taj and Tea were returning, and after scattered greetings, the talk turned to the discovery of the Temple. Taj held up his camera. "Let me find the footage and I'll play it for you."

Zack turned to Megan. "Do you know anything about a Temple?"

Her headache had subsided the instant she stopped trying to answer questions. "Not sure. The word *temple* doesn't mean anything to me—"

She stopped in midsentence because she saw Tea Nowinski shuffling past Zack and sliding her hand across his shoulder. She might as well have kissed him, because that brief tell was enough to convince Megan that her former husband and Tea were lovers.

Zack knew Megan had seen it. The instant Tea was around the rover and momentarily out of sight and earshot, he came to her. "I'm sorry."

Megan was surprised at how annoyed she was at the thought of Zack and Tea together. "Feel free to tell me this didn't start until after I was dead."

"You know me better than that."

Fortunately the burst of jealousy was as short-lived as it was bizarre. She had been dead, right? Was this second chance at life—thank you to the Almighty or these Architects or some combination of the two—a *real* second chance?

Was she still married? Her Mormon friend Robin had believed that she and her husband were "sealed for eternity" . . . right up to the time they got divorced. By her own much looser standards, Megan had no claim on Zack, legal or moral.

She had to ask herself, was she still in love with him? But she would also have to ask, what difference did that make? What possible life could they share? What could she expect from her own, under the circumstances?

Was Zack convinced he had discovered the real Megan Doyle Stewart? His actions and words gave that impression, though Megan felt he wasn't fully committed to the idea. (For that matter, was *she* sure? How would she know?)

One thing Megan felt with great certainty was that she was still a mother. "Zack," she said. "I want to talk to Rachel."

Zack got that worried look on his face, one she had come to know. "Wish we both could, but we don't have real-time communication here."

Taj said, "I can do it."

Zack seemed surprised. "You can do what? We're in LOS for hours yet."

"I can communicate with Earth in real time as soon as I can get close enough to punch a signal through the membrane." He held up the Zeiss unit. "This will transmit to *Brahma* and then to a relay satellite."

Zack considered this. "Being able to do it doesn't mean it's a good idea—"

Megan knew that voice; Zack was about to dig in. "Look," she said, "I realize you aren't quite ready to accept me. Fine. So let's put it in terms everyone can understand.

"Unless I talk to my daughter, I'm not telling you another damn thing."

... The *Destiny* flight director is the operations agent for the NASA Launch Package Manager and Mission Manager. He or she is a member of the board responsible for assuring that the mission-specific operations document meets the defined requirements, and that associated operational risks have been adequately addressed. He or she is also responsible for arranging necessary Mission Operations Directorate expertise and support. . . .

FLIGHT DIRECTOR TASKS, JSC MOD, JANUARY 2019, REV. G (EXCERPT)

"If her father says it's okay, then it's okay." Josh Kennedy delivered his judgment, then turned away.

After returning Rachel to the family room, Harley had headed directly for mission control. Wanting to avoid any immediate contact with the great minds of the Home Team, he made sure to go around the building, rolling up to Josh Kennedy, who was preparing to hand flight director duties to the Stay-3 leader, Lee Shimora. "Got a sec?" Harley had said.

Kennedy looked at Shimora, then back to Harley. "Do you see any activity here? We're just warming chairs until we get data."

Harley showed him Rachel's Slate. "Someone's got data."

That gesture triggered an energetic response from Kennedy and Shimora. Both men began e-mailing and phoning their counterparts in Bangalore.

Within half an hour, prodded by Harley's disclosure of the *Brahma*-dropped relay satellite, Bangalore mission control managed to acknowledge that they (a) did indeed have a relay satellite and (b) would be willing to bring Houston into the communications loop. "Generous of them," Harley said acidly, "given that they leaked everything to the planet, anyway."

To the surprise of the Houston team, Bangalore was in the process of reestablishing contact with Taj and his crew inside Keanu. Bangalore leader Vikram Nayar—who apparently never slept or left the center—claimed that Bangalore had not had contact for the last six hours, that this was a new and welcome resumption. "Whatever," Shimora snapped, "their default setting is lies and bullshit. Nayar hates us. As long as they'll give us comm, I don't care if they claim to have seen the Easter Bunny." He was even younger than Kennedy, who often struck Harley as an undergraduate, but considerably more worldly.

Most of the immediate take from the session was data and imagery. "They're gonna go apeshit back in your cave, Harls," Shimora said.

"I'm going a little ape-like myself here."

The team at the Keanu end of the link was Taj and Zack . . . to Harley's horror, neither one in pressure suit. They had apparently taken up position just inside the so-called membrane, feeding communications through its cable up to *Brahma*, thence to satellite, Bangalore, and Houston.

There was a third person with them, too.

Even knowing about the so-called resurrected ones—what the Home Team called *Revenants*—and having seen the initial image of Megan Stewart, Harley was still stunned senseless at seeing her "alive," hearing her voice.

She had even waved at them. Had called out for Harley by name!

In spite of the confusion—Taj was talking to Nayar in Bangalore while Zack was trying to get word directly to Houston—Megan had made a public request: "Harley Drake, get my daughter on the line!"

Shimora said, "That's way up the list of terrible fucking ideas." He pointed to the screen. "We don't know who or what that is!"

But Kennedy stepped in. "Josh for Zack," he said, "this is your call."

After five seconds, all three could see Zack nodding, his verbal assent following: "Do it!"

Harley rolled out to fetch Rachel for the strangest conversation any human being had ever had.

He had returned Rachel to the family room, now almost empty, since Pogo Downey's family had departed, and other relatives and friends had dispersed rather than ride out the long silence from *Destiny*.

With the flexibility of youth, Amy was asleep across three folding chairs when Harley arrived. Rachel looked up from a new Slate—obviously Amy's—when the door opened.

The girl acted as though she wanted to run. "Fuck you, Harley, you better not be here to tell me bad news."

He grabbed her hand and pulled her close. "Far from it, kiddo. You saw that picture of your mom?"

"This won't be HD quality," Kennedy said. "Don't freak out if we lose contact, either. Comm is ratty in the extreme."

"As if I care," Rachel snapped. Her face held a perfect mix of fury and terror. She looked over at Harley, who could only nod with a reassurance he most certainly didn't feel. "Will she be able to see me?"

Kennedy pointed to one of the cameras that gave the public a live feed of mission control. "We've linked that camera to Bangalore."

Rachel put on the headset, and walked toward the screen. "And there'll be a lag," Kennedy said.

But no one cared, because the screen came alive.

The camera angle on Megan was looking up, too close and definitely low-def, but still Harley could see the moment when mother recognized daughter. Signal quality be damned, the woman's eyes went wide and her hand suddenly covered her mouth. Then: "Daddy was right," the voice from the screen said. "You got bigger."

Rachel's eyes filled with tears. Harley knew what the girl was thinking . . . the last words she'd exchanged with her mother were angry ones. "Oh my God, Mommy!" She could barely get the words out.

At that moment, Harley's lingering doubts about this "Megan" vanished. *Let the girl be the judge. If she believes this is her mother, then so be it.*

"It's all right, sweetie. The circle of life."

"You always said that was crap, Mom. You said life was harsh."

"I'm better informed now."

The picture fuzzed out for several seconds. Rachel could only stare with teary eyes. When contact resumed, she cleared her throat and said, "Did you see angels?"

"Only now."

Harley couldn't decide which effect was more annoying, the lag or the occasional glitches in video or audio. Rachel, however, seemed not to be bothered. "How did this happen?"

"I really don't know, sweetie. I mean, I assume there's some big old purpose, but no one has explained it. One moment I was with you in Florida . . . you know. Then I was here looking at Daddy."

"God, how's Daddy?"

"See for yourself." The camera jiggled and panned to one side. Harley and Rachel could see Zack Stewart, a bit scraggly looking, but smiling and waving. Then the camera shifted back to Megan.

"What's going to happen?" Rachel said. "Are you coming home?"

The lag stretched on to double its normal length before Megan said, "No. For one thing, there's no room."

Rachel shook her head in disbelief, and suddenly Harley realized that this conversation might indeed have been a bad idea. It was one thing to see your lost mother . . . that one last look was what every sad song in history asked for.

It was quite another level of horror to lose her a second time. "But . . . you can't *stay* there!"

Another long lag. This time "Megan" seemed to be talking to Zack or someone off camera. Then, strangely, she seemed to pull away, as if that someone had hold of her. "Listen, Rachel . . . I don't really know the purpose to this, to my being back. But I can tell you this, my darling daughter . . . I think you're going to get a message. I don't know what or when. Just . . . don't be scared, okay?"

Confused and hurt, Rachel looked at Harley. "What is she talking about?"

"I don't think any of us know, Rach." He felt stupid, but wasn't going to compound the stupidity by giving uninformed advice.

Rachel turned to face her mother. "I'll try. I won't be scared."

Another lag; this one ended with a smile. "You won't know what I'm talking about until it happens."

The picture jiggled, as if the camera operator had to change position. Off-screen voices could be heard . . . Spanish? No, Harley realized: Portuguese. Lucas.

Zack appeared in the frame. "We've got to break off. Uh, we're doing fine, under the circumstances." He waved.

Then the screen went to snow. Harley rolled as close to Rachel as he could, acutely aware that she might just collapse. He signaled Kennedy to join him.

But the girl surprised him. She swiftly wiped her eyes and shook her head. "Well, that was pretty weird."

Harley took her hand. "Why don't you stick with me for a while?"

"That would be great."

To Kennedy, Harley said, "I'm taking her to the Home Team."

Q: How did you learn you had been selected as an astronaut?

HALL: Oh, wow. You know how it goes . . . if you get a call from the HR guy, you didn't make it, but if it's the chief astronaut, good news? Well, I was actually *at* Houston, at JSC, for a meeting on the *Saturn* launcher when I ran into the HR guy. And he got this weird look on his face and said, "I need to talk to you." And I went, "Oh, crap." Then he said, "No, wait, not me, exactly—" So then I knew. It was kind of typical . . . I was always around NASA all my life.

ASTRONAUT YVONNE HALL, *DESTINY-7* PREFLIGHT INTERVIEW

"Don't touch that!"

Dennis Chertok literally jumped so high that he bumped his head on the sloping wall of the *Venture* cabin. Keanu gravity at work. Yvonne had awakened and seen the cosmonaut busy opening cupboards on the rear bulkhead. Her shout startled him. He rubbed his head. "That's a fine way to talk."

Emerging from the druggy sleep of several hours, she reacted without thinking, just feeling that somehow this wasn't right. "What the hell are you doing here?"

"I'm your attending physician." He was wearing his Coalition undergarment along with, strangely, a pair of half-glasses that made the cosmonaut look very much like some old country doctor on a house call.

"I thought you'd left!" Attuned as she was—as they all were—to the steady drone of fans and pumps, she also realized she and Dennis were alone in the cabin. "Where's Tea?"

"EVA," Chertok said. "She and Taj went into the vent with the others."

"And she let you babysit me?"

"Both mission controls approved." He inclined his head toward the communications panel at the front of the cabin. A computer screen was showing nothing but snow, though Yvonne could hear static and occasional voices on the comm. "Feel free to confirm."

"No, thanks." She reached for a handle, trying to get herself out of the hammock.

"Careful."

"A fall won't actually hurt in this gravity." Nevertheless, just raising her head made her feel queasy . . . and low gravity or not, her bandaged leg felt leaden. "What did you do to me?"

"Set your broken tibia, removed vacuum-damaged tissue."

"Well, thank you. But I feel like shit."

"You are rather badly injured." She barely knew Dennis Chertok, having shared a single training session with him years back. She knew his reputation, of course: he was the Tape Monkey, the Mr. Goodwrench, the Cosmonaut Handy Man, the five-time space veteran who could repair a malfunctioning toilet with a cardboard tube and a paper clip, or reprogram a computer with one typing hand tied behind him.

All this, and a medical doctor, too. Through her fog, glancing down at her thickly bandaged leg, Yvonne wondered just what improvisations Dennis had developed to deal with her injuries. "I feel as though I should eat something."

Dennis gestured toward the cupboards he had just been warned off. "That's what I was looking for. Food."

"Check the left side. My stuff is in the third row."

The cabinets contained not only food, but the medical kit, clothing, supplies, any gear not directly related to operational tasks like EVA.

"First let me help you down—"

"I'm fine!" That came out louder than she intended.

Dennis simply turned away. That was one of the great things about Russians, Yvonne realized. They were happy to let you dig your own grave. Over his shoulder, he said, "What sounds tasty?"

"A sandwich." Astronauts chose their own meals and on her ISS tour, Yvonne had learned that her favorite was a ham and cheese sandwich smothered in mustard and pickle. Living in zero or near zero-g made you crave sharp flavors.

As the cosmonaut rummaged in the juice boxes and shrink-wrapped trays, Yvonne continued her extraction, a process complicated by the bulky PPK case that shared the hammock.

Eventually, with no obvious grace, she managed to get her legs headed out and down, leaving the PPK behind. The deck, which looked a long way down, proved to be a gentle half-step.

"So, what's the latest?"

"There is bad news. Patrick Downey is dead." Now Yvonne knew she was too drugged to function, because she somehow absorbed that shocking piece of information without question, or tears. She knew that space-flight was incredibly dangerous. She had clear memories of the loss of *Columbia* and its crew when she was a freshman at Rice. Given where they were, what had already happened to her, somehow the news seemed inevitable. "Tell me how."

Dennis handed her a sandwich, then helped himself to an entire turkey dinner as he calmly told her a science fiction story . . . at least, that was the only way to take it. The bizarre environment inside Keanu, the changing structures, the glowworms, the atmosphere.

And, of course, the growing things. "Wait a minute . . . Zack's *dead wife*?"

"So it would seem. Natalia's dead coach. A dead child Lucas knew."

"What does it mean?"

Dennis did not look up. Only now did Yvonne see how shaken he was. "This is . . . beyond my understanding. Alien spacecraft, yes. But to find these . . . back-from-the-dead people. It is disturbing." He aimed a plastic fork toward the communications panel. "The lack of communication makes it much, much worse. My imagination . . ."

He stood at that point, stepped to the forward bulkhead, and looked out the window.

"You're freaking me out, Dennis."

"Then I've succeeded." He was looking at her now, and at the interior of the cabin. "It's too bad you don't carry any weapons."

"Maybe you should bring something over from *Brahma*."

He looked over his glasses. "Don't tell me you believed that nonsense."

"Our two organizations haven't exactly been getting along."

"Even during the cold war, when your country and mine had thousands of missiles pointed at each other, we still had agreements about keeping activities peaceful in space."

She chose not to argue. "When do we find out what's going on? I can't believe they've all been gone this long." In Yvonne's world, EVAs lasted eight hours, maybe a little more. Not twenty-plus.

"I have no idea. We get bursts of contact through *Brahma*, but that's all. Last message was two hours ago, from Taj. I know *he's* alive, at least." Dinner tray in hand, he suddenly seemed lost. "Where do you store—?"

"Let me." Reflexively returning to her familiar dutiful astronaut role—though never the dutiful daughter—Yvonne took the tray. Then she realized . . . it was from Pogo Downey's locker.

"Yvonne, is something wrong?"

She couldn't speak. She could only wave the empty tray.

Dennis guessed her objection. "Yvonne, he is gone. He will never eat any of those meals. You might as well blame me for breathing his air."

"I know." She knew, but that cold truth was still unbearable. Pogo was gone! The big, bluff, sometimes goofy pilot, the man she'd trained with for two years . . . she'd been to barbecues at his house, even Christmas with his family last year.

Killed by some alien!

Dennis left her alone in the forward cabin. By the time she had wiped her eyes and taken a deep breath, he had returned.

"Now, what is this item?"

He was holding the silver case of her PPK. Even though she knew he could not possibly harm it, much less set it off, she still hated seeing it in strange hands. "Personal gear," she said, forcing a smile. "It's where I keep my first day covers and vodka." Russian cosmonauts were notorious for sneaking booze aboard space missions.

Dennis smiled back, though Yvonne sensed that he was unconvinced. "We may have to break out the vodka, for medicinal purposes."

"Not just yet." She took the case and wedged it into another cabinet. Then she looked at her watch. "How many hours left before we regain comm?"

"Houston won't be in touch for four hours yet."

"I should clean up." She smiled, still feeling shaky and uncertain. "That leaves me three more hours."

"I know one thing we should do," Dennis said. "Keep the doors locked."

"She says she saw a man!"

"What the hell does that mean?"

Zack ended the TV link between Megan and Rachel because mother and daughter were both getting upset—Megan was sitting off to one side, face in her hands, Tea's arm around her shoulders—and because Lucas had rushed up with Camilla in hand. The girl's expression was one of giddy excitement, while Lucas was frantic. "Just that! She says there was a man beyond the rover a few minutes ago."

"Where? What was she doing?"

"I let her go to the bathroom, all right?" Lucas added embarrassment to his confusion. "We were both maybe fifty meters that way." He was pointing in the general direction of the Beehive, and the membrane beyond.

"What exactly did she see?" Zack knelt in front of Camilla and assumed his best fatherly manner, willing a smile to his face. "Please ask her to tell me."

Lucas translated. "'I saw a man with no clothes on.'"

No clothes argued against this mystery "man" being cosmonaut Chertok. "Anything else? Was he carrying anything?" He gestured with his hands.

Camilla shook her head. Nothing. Now she was getting frightened by all the adult emotion. Zack gently patted her head and let her be.

"Thoughts? Taj?"

The Indian commander had been staring off into the forest, hoping to see what the girl had seen. "Well," he said, "you three—Keanu brought back someone for each of you." He pointed to Tea, then himself. "What about us?"

"Maybe we aren't worthy," Tea said, joking.

Zack said, "Well, maybe you are now."

"Oh, great; more hungry mouths to feed."

In Zack's professional judgment, the situation was close to spinning out of control. Granted, he was completely exhausted—in that state it was easy to feel overwhelmed.

But here he was . . . here *they* were . . . five space travelers and a pair of reborn humans, with limited food and resources . . . with limited communication . . . all this while trapped in an environment that changed according to rules they could not know, at the direction of entities known only as the Architects.

Looking at it in summary, well, hell, he should have gone into a fetal crouch hours ago. "Natalia!" The Russian woman had been working on her space suit backpack, which lay half-opened. "Do you have any ideas?"

"About what?"

Zack barely suppressed a blistering reply. He had to remember that English was still Natalia's second language. She would likely not know how infuriating her answer sounded. "About this new creature, or anything of interest. The Architects. The Temple."

Natalia only shrugged. She opened her mouth to speak, but said nothing, as if changing her mind in midthought. Given Zack's suspicions about her actions regarding the Konstantin-thing, it wasn't likely she would have much to say that was useful, anyway.

Besides, Lucas was approaching, with further information from Camilla. "There's one more thing: Camilla says the man had red hair."

"Oh, shit," Tea said, making the same intuitive leap Zack made. "Pogo."

"Does that make sense?" Zack asked. "You're suggesting that Pogo's been revived."

"Zack, it makes as much sense as anything I've seen in the last six hours. Come on."

In my Father's house there are many mansions. If not, I would have told
you: because I go to prepare a place for you. JOHN 14:2

It was a single word, even a sound, repeated several times in various
forms, as if being tried out via air-to-ground radio.

Pogo.

Patrick Downey's call sign had been hung on him during his first
operational tour flying F-35s. During gunnery training at Nellis he had
somehow managed to get ahead of one of his own missiles.

Which then took him for a target. Fortunately, the missile was inert.
By frantically deploying chaff and other countermeasures, Second Lieutenant Downey had been able to avoid being shot down by something
he'd launched. He even earned praise from his instructor for "getting
ahead of the syllabus," which didn't call for countermeasure instruction
for another two weeks.

That night in the O-Club, Shawn Beckman said to Patrick, in front of
half a dozen other pilots, "Dude, you are your own worst enemy."

And Jeff Zajac, another pilot, just happened to say, "Yeah, like that
old comic strip. 'We have met the enemy, and he is us.' What the hell was
it called?"

A third pilot, Rickie Bell, said "*Pogo*," and a call sign was born.

The rule with call signs was, if you don't like what's suggested, don't
worry; something worse will follow. Bell wound up hearing "Tinker" for
his entire flying career. Beckman earned the relatively neutral "Becker-
wood," but Zajac, after an unfortunate shaving accident that left him with
temporary damage to his face, was henceforth saddled with "Scabber."

In Pogo's mind, it served him right.

But why was he thinking about that? Nellis training was almost twenty years ago.

He'd been dreaming. No more.

Suddenly he had questions. Where? What? How?

He couldn't breathe! Something covered his face! He clawed at it, found that yes, he could see . . . he could suck air into his lungs. God.

But he was in a coffin! Wait, there was light. As he began to thrash, the walls gave. They were like thick plastic.

Then he remembered the Sentry. The big sweep . . . the sickening horror of knowing he had been cut, sliced, vision going red, feeling himself literally fall to pieces: dead.

But no more.

He slid out of the cell.

For the first time in his life—lives—he screamed. It was both terror and joy and there was no chance he could stop it. It was as if his body had to announce itself, or calibrate itself.

He was naked where he wasn't covered in second skin. Yes, he was obviously in Keanu. . . .

But he was alive!

And, from the looks of things . . . the lifeless cells around him, the quiet gray "sky," the lack of wind and sound . . . apparently alone.

Thinking, thinking. Zack and the others . . . were they nearby? God, maybe they'd left. Maybe he'd been "dead" for a long time. Weeks. Months. Centuries.

He stood up, stretching. It felt as though he'd been immobile for a while. But, then, he was in a new body. He twisted, touched his toes, flexed. Aside from a growing hunger, and a nagging headache, he *felt* right.

He looked at his surroundings, from the wall of cells to the surface of the ground, now mossy as opposed to icy rock, to the oddly shaped trees that effectively blocked his view toward Keanu's interior.

As he took tentative steps, he was grateful for the moss . . . it felt soothing on his bare feet, which turned out to be as tender and callus-free as a baby's—or an astronaut's after a six-month stay in space.

He looked back at the cells . . . the three he had seen with Zack, Natalia, and Lucas lay open, dried out, dark. As if the stone had been rolled away from the tomb, to put it in biblical terms. Not that he was making any blasphemous comparisons; his resurrection was not *that* Resurrection, though, given the events of the past day, he was feeling more secure in his belief in the latter.

His cell was still oozing, pieces of its walls and sheaths of second skin hanging off it. *Afterbirth* was the word that came to mind. Well, technically, afterdeath.

Only now did he notice that there were at least two other open cells, too . . . not as weepy and moist as his own.

At least two someone elses had been reborn.

Pogo wondered where they had gone, and when. And who they were?

But he was racked with questions . . . no doubt contributing to the throbbing in his temples. For example, if he returned to the site of his "death," what would he find? His torn body? The remains of his EVA suit?

Why did he care? Because he felt the clear urge to have that suit and the helmet. He *needed* them—

Don't panic, Pogo.

He was an operational sort, trained to look at the mission, then take the necessary steps. Given the goal of returning to *Venture*, then the first step would be . . . search for his suit.

If he found other revived beings, he would deal with them. If, miraculously, Zack and the other astronauts remained here, so much the better. He had a message to share, with them, with the people of Earth.

Time to move. To find something to eat.

And for his head to stop hurting.

Pogo Downey headed into the woods.

Within five minutes, they had reached the place where Tea and Taj had left Pogo's remains. Zack was, momentarily, struck again by how little of Keanu he had seen. It was likely less than a couple of square kilometers . . . while the chamber proper was at least fifty times larger.

And this chamber was only a fraction of Keanu's interior volume. Was the rest of the NEO solid, or were there other similar chambers, each with its own glowworms, its own environment? With other Temples and Sentries?

"Over here!" Tea had run ahead of him. She and Taj had come with Zack, to act as guides.

"You didn't bury him."

"With what?" Taj said, over her shoulder. "The closest thing we have to a shovel is a space pen."

She stopped suddenly. Zack joined her, kneeling at the spot, gently lifting giant leaves and uncovering the rendered remains of the late Pogo Downey, essentially three big pieces of former human somewhat wrapped in blood-soaked shreds of an EVA undergarment. "Is this the way you left it?"

"No! He was still . . . in the suit!" Tea said. Then, "And I left his helmet right there, too. It was the grave marker—"

"Was this stain here?" Zack pointed to a discoloration that surrounded the body . . . it was dark, not exactly the color of blood, though it was difficult to tell in this light.

"No," Tea said. "It was all dirt before. What do you think it means?"

"No idea." He saw something else, too—the foliage had been disturbed. "I think there's also a trail here," he said. Rising, he followed it deeper into the brush.

He didn't have to go far, maybe twenty meters. "Found it!"

Tea and Taj were only a few steps behind. They stopped when they saw what lay at Zack's feet. "Oh, there it is."

The white EVA suit and its bulky backpack lay in a clearing like a fallen soldier. It bore the clear signs of severe damage: three huge gashes across its front, one of them so deep it effectively tore the garment in half.

Zack touched the jagged tears, the multilayered fabric thick in his fingers. It took a lot of strength to just slice through a suit like this.

"This," Tea said. "is extremely fucking bizarre."

"Okay," Zack said, "if Pogo's body is still here . . . who's that red-haired naked guy?"

"Is it possible that what Camilla saw was an entirely different revived being?" Taj said.

"It has to be!" Tea said. "It's not the same at all! Megan and Camilla's bodies weren't *here*!"

"Right and right," Zack said. "But it's logical that there might be some commonality between these revivals." He indicated the discarded suit. "I mean, look at the evidence."

Taj wiggled an index finger, reminding Zack of a college professor. "I think this entire world consists of molecular machines or whatever you want to call them. Everything that enters this environment is nothing but fuel or materials to be reassembled, if needed. Everything that you see can become anything its designers want."

Tea allowed herself to join in the speculation. "Even the ice and snow on the surface . . ." She looked alarmed. "Have we ingested anything?"

"Food and water have come from our supplies," Zack said, not liking the obvious conclusion—that they were all infected. "But we have been breathing the air for over a dozen hours."

"Shit."

Tea started to walk away. Zack followed, gently taking her arm. "Hey, hey, hey, stick with me. I'm sorry . . . you know me, always happy to take an unpleasant idea and play with it. We don't know anything yet. Even if we are somehow contaminated, we don't know if it's bad."

"Yes," Taj said, "look at it this way: It might mean we can never die."

"Good to know," Zack said, "given the grim options we face at the moment."

Tea stared at the two men. "Assholes."

Ten minutes later they were back at the rover.

Given the increasingly uncertain circumstances—and trying not to imagine a revived Patrick "Pogo" Downey shambling around Keanu—Zack sensed that now was the time, as his colleagues in mission control liked to say, to lean forward. To lay out a plan and execute it.

"Okay, everyone, gather round."

Within moments he had them all in a group. Lucas and Camilla, Natalia, Tea, and Taj.

Megan.

"My best guess is that in four hours we'll be back in complete contact with Houston"—he bowed to acknowledge Taj and *Brahma*'s back channel—"and we are likely to receive orders to return to *Venture*. Since we obviously aren't equipped for real exploration or life support, that will be the plan.

"But we aren't leaving anyone behind," he said, realizing that some part of his brain had been working the problem and had made a decision. "*Venture* has room for an adult passenger, so Megan goes with Tea and me with no strain." Pending further data, he was not going to factor this potential ghost Pogo Downey into the equation.

"I'm happy to take Camilla, too, but given that both vehicles were designed to lift off the Moon, there's ample margin in propellant for *Brahma* to launch with fifty extra kilos, too. Consumables like oxygen and water might be an issue, but again, both spacecraft are configured for a crew of four and minimum ten days."

He looked to Taj for confirmation. "We may have more," the vyomanaut said.

"Right now we're on day five. If we lift off later today, we're home on day eight, nine latest. We all may have to, ah, breathe slower, but we should be able to make it." He wasn't entirely joking about that; one of the strategies developed for shortfalls in oxygen supplies was to drug one or more crew members, effectively cutting the rate of oxygen consumption in half.

"First step," Zack said, turning to point. "I give you rover *Buzz*. Pressurized, capable of traversing several hundred meters with three passengers in a shirtsleeve environment." He pointed to Megan. "You will be the driver."

Megan smiled faintly. "I see a problem," Natalia said, looking to Lucas and Taj, as if to say, *You idiots, why do I have to say this!* "Fine, Megan and Camilla drive to bottom of Vesuvius Vent. But, five astronauts, five EVA suits. How do our three passengers get from the rover to the spacecraft?"

The mind under stress was a wonderful tool. Zack was pleased that Natalia asked this, because he hadn't solved that problem . . . until just now. "We do what they planned to do with a damaged shuttle in orbit. You fly up to it and send one EVA astronaut over carrying two extra suits. He goes inside, helps the crew members into them, and tows them to safety.

"So, we park the rover inside the membrane, meaning we have a pressurized environment outside it. Taj and Lucas go back to *Brahma*, then Lucas takes Taj's empty suit, brings it to the membrane, puts Camilla in it and carries her back to *Brahma*. Repeat for Megan to *Venture*."

"It will take time," Natalia said. "Just getting back to the vehicles, up the vent—!"

"That's why we need to get started."

To Zack's surprise—the gesture was as familiar as it was unexpected—Megan raised her hand. "I have a better plan."

The group of eight had not been noisy, not in any way Zack noticed. But he did notice the sudden silence. "First we need to visit the Temple."

"We already did," Tea said quickly.

Megan refused to look at her. "You never got inside, though." She stood and took Camilla by the hand. "We can." Camilla nodded.

Zack glanced at Taj, Lucas, Natalia, Tea, each one responding with surprise or a headshake. "You know that?" he said to Megan. "That you can get in?"

"I wish I could be more specific. But, yes. We can, we should . . . it's *vital*."

"I need more than that," Zack said quietly.

Taj suddenly put a hand to his right ear, where he wore an earpiece. He simply stepped away.

Megan was slowly shaking her head from side to side, eyes closed, as if searching for a lost memory. Then she looked directly into Zack's eyes. "I can't give you more. All I can tell you, darling, is that all your life you wanted to solve mysteries. It's the one thing that drives you, more than love or money or family. Here you have the biggest one in human history, and it only costs you an hour of time, maybe two."

"I'm risking the lives of seven other people."

"Thank you for including us, but we won't leave unless we go to the Temple first." Zack watched as Lucas translated Megan's words for Camilla, who nodded enthusiastically.

Zeiss camera-communicator under his arm, Taj returned, sparing Zack the agony of telling Megan that he would have to leave her . . . "We have a problem," he said. "It seems that Pogo is alive and he has contacted *Venture*."

Tea, Lucas, and Natalia asked different questions with what sounded like one voice. "Where is he?" "How'd he get through the membrane?" "What did he say?"

Taj motioned Zack and the others to follow him behind the rover. "You need to see this."

All five EVA suits had been stored here, three *Brahma* and two *Venture*, leaning against the side of the rover like a row of worn-out football players.

Now there were four. Zack could do the math. "One of the suits is gone. Mine."

Taj nodded. "And Downey is obviously wearing a suit that has a radio operating on *Venture* frequencies. And he is at the floor of Vesuvius Vent."

Lucas said, "Now what do we do?"

Zack tried not to war-game it. *You're a smart guy. A decision like this is like shooting an important basket—think too much and you'll fuck it up.* The loss of his suit didn't affect the plan in any major way. "Two teams," he said. "Taj and Tea, back to *Brahma* and *Venture*, catch up with Pogo and prepare for the suit transfer. Use Yvonne's and Dennis's when you come back.

"The rest of us are taking the rover to the Temple. We will be at the membrane in two hours, answers or not."

He didn't wait for a response or a demurral and avoided looking into either Megan's or Tea's eyes. "Go!"

Now he had a plan. Of course, there was that old saying: No battle plan survives contact with the enemy. Well, hell.

Were the Architects enemies? One way to find out.

Thank you for agreeing to participate in supporting the *Destiny-7* mission. Your signature on this document indicates your acceptance of the security requirements in Tab A. . . .

COVER NOTE TO HOME TEAM MEMO, FORWARDED IN ITS ENTIRETY TO
SKY NEWS BY WADE WILLIAMS, AUGUST 23, 2019

"Sit down and shut the fuck up."

Harley had brought Rachel to the Home Team room for the replay of her conversation with Megan. It had taken a while to get the dozen participants together—several had gone elsewhere to nap or eat.

By the time Williams, Creel, Valdez, and Matulka had been corralled, Harley had lost patience and ordered Sasha Blaine to start the playback.

Which allowed Harley to speak sharply to Wade Williams when he was the last stray to bumble in, making the additional mistake of wondering aloud what was going on.

There was an audible intake of breath around the table at Harley's words, as if he had risen from his wheelchair and slugged the elderly writer-scientist. For perhaps the first time in his seventy-odd years, Williams chose not to speak and searched for a place at the table. But he was so noisy about it that Harley was forced to say, "All right, Sasha. Hit pause."

As, on the screen, Megan Stewart looked out at the group from inside Keanu, Harley addressed Williams. "If you can't figure out what we're doing anymore, Dr. Williams, I suggest you ask Mr. Creel to fill you in, quietly. I understand he's familiar with the task.

"You were all eager to sign up for this job. Based on the performance of the majority, I'm guessing you were only thinking how neat it would look on your résumés. It obviously wasn't because you understood the hard work involved. Yes, you may not be eating good, regular meals. Yes, you may be awake for two days straight. And yes, you may have to listen to someone in authority speaking sharply to you."

Rachel had giggled. And in the darkness, Sasha Blaine had given Harley a thumbs-up. "I'm not going to apologize for it. We're doing important work, and the process is likely to be painful. Remember, however, that although Houston may not be a garden spot, it's a damn sight better than being in *Venture*, or running around inside Keanu.

"So here's what I need, and what I'm going to have: complete cooperation, and zero bitching. Anyone who doesn't feel he or she can commit to those two rules, there's the door. Anyone who stays is expected to comply."

The room was silent until Williams raised his hand. "May I speak?"

"Briefly."

"I won't argue your, ah, self-evident points. I would just note that creative work and genuine insights do not occur on schedule or demand."

"Noted," Harley said, "and I'm completely aware of that. I'm only trying to create an environment in which creative work can be accomplished in an optimum manner . . . a flash of genius is no use to us if it doesn't support the mission.

"Which is," he said, feeling the need for a reminder, "to complete the reconnaissance of Keanu and return both crews safely to Earth—"

The door opened again, and this time Harley's anger was genuine rather than strategic. "Goddamn it, how many times do I have to—"

He stopped when he saw that the new arrivals were White House adviser Bynum and Director Jones. Weldon was with them, looking indecently fresh. There were also a couple of the usual trailing horse-holders.

"Sorry for the interruption," Jones said, and immediately stood aside. "Mr. Bynum has some important new information for us." Jones looked as exhausted and grim as Harley had ever seen him.

Bynum cleared his throat. He did not ask for lights, meaning that his

face stayed in darkness, and his words seemed to originate with an invisible speaker.

Perhaps that was the idea.

"Obviously this business of seeing humans allegedly being reborn on
Keanu represents a . . . paradigm shift." Harley wondered who had come
up with that painfully neutral term. Obviously it was a less emotional
choice than *mind-fuck*. "I've just gotten off the phone with the president—"

"What about the pope?" someone said, to more laughter than was
justified. In the dark room, Harley couldn't identify the speaker.

"The president," Bynum said, clearing his throat again, "has officially
classed the entities on Keanu as hostile."

That pronouncement triggered a wider reaction, typified by one loud,
surprisingly female voice, "That's fucked up." Sasha Blaine! Harley was
starting to like this young woman.

Harley chose to let the uproar continue for a few extra seconds before
saying, "People, remember the rules."

He addressed Bynum but caught Weldon's eye. "Mr. Bynum, what
exactly does this mean?"

"That none of the entities will be allowed to leave Keanu's interior,
much less enter either the *Venture* or *Brahma* vehicles."

"Which means this isn't just our president, but the leaders of the Coalition nations."

Jones finally spoke up. "They judged the, uh, Revenants to be hostile
from the very beginning."

Bynum persisted. "This decision also means that returning crews will
be quarantined. Preparations are being made for secure containment of
the *Venture* interior, for example. Meanwhile, regarding current mission
operations, a recall is being sent to the crew as soon as full radio contact
is restored—and deadly force is authorized."

"You mean *kill* them?" This time it was Lily Valdez who spoke.

But it was Rachel Stewart who stood up, clearly visible in the light
from the screen, and a surprising vision to Bynum, Jones, and Weldon.
"How can you say that? That's my mother up there!"

Bynum sputtered, unable to deal with a question from an unexpected source. Gabriel Jones said, tiredly, "We're not going to attack these things. We just want our people back, safe and sound. But, Rachel, honey, there's no way that creature is actually your mother. . . ."

"She knows things only my mother would know!"

Harley reached for the girl and gently pulled her close. "It's okay," he told her. "We're going to make the best of this."

"What this decision means," Bynum said, "is that whatever actions you recommend, treat the Keanu situation as a public health threat. Minimize contact. Resist it. Disengage." He moved slightly, allowing Harley to see his face . . . Bynum seemed to have aged a decade overnight.

Jones waved Bynum and the others to the door, but Weldon lagged behind. "Harls, a moment."

Harley didn't want to leave Rachel, who was shaking with rage. All he could do was hand her off to Sasha.

Outside, in the hallway, as Bynum, Jones, and the others kept a polite distance, Harley launched the first salvo. "Didn't you guys just tell me I was in charge of this?"

"Not quite," Weldon said. "You are the head of the committee, meaning that you are the one we turn to for answers. What this order does is shape your guidance to the Home Team. In other words, don't waste time trying to unscrew the inscrutable. Concentrate on safety and security."

"What a lot of fucking bullshit."

"You want out?"

"I don't quit in the middle of a job." He knew Weldon wouldn't have allowed that in any case. "But I want you to know, since none of your other little friends seems to get this, that the smart way to play this is to assume those people up there are who they say they are."

"Those people. These Revenants?"

"Call them whatever you want, Shane. They are living, breathing proof that the universe is a shitload weirder than we know, and there are creatures out there who can operate its machinery better than we can. Which should be no fucking surprise, really. So why do you want to poke them with a stick? It's only going to backfire."

Weldon closed his eyes. Harley knew the man didn't disagree. But Weldon's greatest professional strength happened also to be his biggest personal weakness: He did whatever those above him asked, and usually better than they could have imagined. "What do you want me to do, Harls? This is the White House and the Pentagon at work."

"Remember one of those little sayings you mentioned when I was an ASCAN?" Weldon, as a senior flight director, had been on the panel that interviewed Harley when he first applied to become an astronaut candidate. "'We're looking for people who understand the importance of making decisions they can't take back.'" Harley pointed down the hall, at the group waiting impatiently for Weldon.

"I'm going back to wrangle the geniuses, and I'll keep your guidance in mind. But when you get back to mission control, don't let them make a decision we can't take back."

Although communication between Bangalore and Korolev mission control centers and the *Brahma* spacecraft is temporarily unavailable, all signs indicate that the mission is proceeding as planned. It is believed that *Brahma* crew member Natalia Yorkina, citizen of Russia, was the first to enter the Keanu interior and has performed the bulk of the scientific survey.　　　　ITAR-TASS REPORT, 23 AUGUST 2019

"I'm going out," Dennis said.

"You've got to be kidding me."

"You heard the message." The cosmonaut was already in motion, heading toward the *Venture* airlock and his EVA suit.

Yvonne couldn't have stopped him. Even in low gravity, the pain and swelling in her leg made movement difficult. "Dennis, the man is dead!"

"It's better for all of us that he is met—out there." He tapped the nearest bulkhead. "Not in here."

Yvonne had spent a terrifying half hour. The only thing she could compare it to was being flung across the surface of Keanu yesterday—frightening as that had been, it had lasted only a few minutes.

Her life on Keanu had now become a long nightmare from which there was no awakening. . . .

It had begun with a radio call, "*Venture, Venture*, come in." At first Yvonne had been happy, believing she was back in direct contact with Zack and Tea.

But the moment she answered—"This is *Venture*. Hey, welcome back!"—she heard a voice that gave her chills.

"This is Downey and I need assistance."

She had looked at Dennis at that moment. The Russian cosmonaut's eyes, normally sleepy-looking even in midday, went wide with alarm. He had torn the headset off her, silencing the exchange. "Don't answer!"

"Okay," she had said, "that will be good for two minutes. Then what?" She held her hand out. Dennis returned the headset.

"We should call Bangalore."

"You do that. But I'm not taking orders from them."

"We can't deal with this alone!"

"Houston will be over the horizon in two hours. Maybe I can stall him until then—"

But the voice from Vesuvius Vent returned. "*Venture*, Downey. Do you copy?"

"How the fuck can this be happening?" Yvonne said. "Didn't you say he was dead?"

"Yes. There was no doubt. I saw the footage of the body. There was much discussion while you were unconscious."

"But here he is."

"As with Zachary's wife and the others. Yes, apparently Downey is restored."

"Okay, then what? Do I help the guy? He's one of the crew."

"You don't know what he is, what any of them are. Bad enough that our friends are dealing with them . . . we cannot let one of these creatures reach our ships."

"Well, we're locked in here. What about *Brahma*?"

"It's not just access I worry about. It's also potential damage. Suppose this being is hostile."

"He can't hurt us in here."

Then Dennis had decided. "No, I have to meet him."

Now he had his suit open—on the *Brahma* suits, the backpack was the dorsal side, and opened, giving access. Dennis had his feet in the legs of his suit and was wriggling his arms into the arms and gloves. In spite of the tension, Yvonne had to admire the man's skill at this procedure. Of course, he had been doing it for twenty-five years. Had helped design the suit, in fact.

"What about me? Have you looked at my leg lately?"

She had, and she didn't at all like what she saw . . . the dark signs of blood poisoning.

"My absence will have no immediate effect on your condition."

"But there's a chance I could be incapacitated. And if you somehow wind up incapacitated, both vehicles are untended, and I think that's a bad idea."

By now Dennis had his head through the neck ring into his bubble helmet and was sealing his backpack. He had to shout to be heard. "It is a worse idea to do nothing."

He began opening cabinets inside the airlock. "What are you looking for?"

"A tool."

Yvonne wasn't buying it. "You mean a weapon."

"Fine. A weapon."

"So that's your big plan? Knock him on the head? Either you'll crack his helmet and kill him, or you won't do anything. Seems like a waste of time."

"I'd rather face that decision with a weapon than not have one if I need it."

Yvonne considered this. No point wishing for Houston to come on the line and tell her what to do. She was on her own . . . and she agreed in principle that this "Downey" creature should not be allowed into *Venture*—not yet.

"Okay, the utensils we use are all plastic. Flashlights, pens, all of that stuff is lightweight."

"I remember." That was right, Dennis had lived on the International Space Station for almost a year. He knew what kind of gear you'd find in a NASA space cabin.

"The toolbox outside, though. There should be a torque wrench."

Dennis considered this. Through the faceplate of his helmet, already fogging with each exhalation, he smiled. "Thank you. You should seal this and evacuate the chamber. Keep it that way."

As Yvonne returned to the main cabin, dogging the hatch behind her, she felt dizzy and afraid.

As she entered the commands to bleed air from the *Venture* lock, allowing Dennis to exit, her eye caught the silver case holding the Item. "What the hell are you looking at?"

Q: What is the one thing you do better than anything?

DOWNEY: Well . . . break things and kill people, I guess.

ASTRONAUT CANDIDATE INTERVIEW WITH LT. COL. PATRICK DOWNEY, USAF,

MAY 11, 2011

Right up to the time he found himself staring up the vertical side of Vesuvius Vent, the Revenant formerly known as Pogo Downey had a warm memory of the radical maneuver Zack had chosen to get people and machines to the bottom. *Yeah, just throw everything overboard.* The assumption was that astronauts could be hauled up by rope—and the rover abandoned.

That made sense, as long as you had a fellow astronaut at the top of the slope with a line.

At the moment, Pogo was alone . . . and searching in the darkness for the ramp Zack had suggested as a backup return route.

It had been easier to see in glowworm light. When he emerged from the passage between the membrane and the vent floor, he found that the glowworms had shut down! There was no light but the beams from his helmet lamps . . . and faint starlight.

Making matters more challenging, he was cramping. EVA suits were not tailored to individual astronauts, but they came in three sizes: Pogo had worn large while Zack Stewart used medium.

He had also not been able to perform any system checks.

The critical driver now was oxygen. There was less than ninety minutes left in his tanks. If he'd had time and been alone, he would have recharged them at the rover . . . but he had been able to slip into the camp for only a few moments.

"Pogo, do you read me?" Chertok's voice had a strange, distant sound. Probably bounced all the way to Earth, then to Keanu.

But at least someone had answered.

Downey's response was, "Five by," a callback to flight tests of three generations earlier. *Five by five. Clear.* "Where are you?"

"On Vesuvius rim."

Downey looked up the cliff face in the general direction of *Brahma.* "I don't see you. Too dark." *And those Brahma suits are blue.*

Another lag. The signal was definitely being routed, probably through Bangalore. Which meant that everyone knew what had happened to Patrick Downey.

During his trek through the membrane, down the long passage and then across the floor of the vent, Pogo had made major changes in his plans.

At first, realizing he was alive again, he had wanted to get back in touch with Zack and the others. But three events had convinced him that was a bad idea: The first was finding the body of another Revenant, a sign that Pogo's former colleagues were prepared to be violent.

Second was the sight of Zack and the other crew members in complete disarray, suits discarded, in the company of other humans, among them two members of the untrustworthy Coalition crew.

Third was finding his own body . . . seeing his own bloodied face frozen in final agony—

He needed an advantage. High ground. Leverage.

He was also determined to contact Linda and the kids.

Surely they had been told of the earlier accident—strange to think of the words, his earlier death. The thought of their pain and uncertainty triggered blinding tears.

All he wanted in life was to be able to take that away, to make it better, to hold them again. *No, it was all a mistake. I'm alive!*

He could reach his family—and gain needed leverage—only by going outside the chamber and back to *Venture.*

So he had stolen a suit and helmet.

All during this time he had been bombarded with strange pseudomemories. Images of structures and landscapes somewhere deeper inside Keanu. One was dark, glowing, burned. Another was filled with greenish fog and strange floating shapes. There was a recurring image of a large, multilimbed creature dressed in garments that were a kind of shiny armor.

He knew their names. Garudas Scaptors. Architects. The fact that there were several factions of Architects, each with its own agenda.

And the stupid Sentry, which wasn't a Sentry at all, but simply another life-form. If it had a more accurate name, it would be *candidate*. For what, Pogo didn't know.

There was so much more . . . concepts that lurked at the borders of memory, like lessons in computer science studied twenty years back: the idea that entities, organic or not, had a greater footprint in the universe than suggested by visual borders or physical limits, that they left quantum "wakes" or "clouds" that could be detected—and manipulated—years after death or destruction.

The dizzying confusion of it, the lack of words to fit concepts, his frustration with his own inability to understand how, why—it made him physically ill. Yet as he reached the rim of Vesuvius—spotting Dennis, who had switched on his helmet lights—he suddenly knew what his mission was.

Not just to go home, to return to Linda and Daniel and Kerry.

To punish the Architects for their cruel and ill-planned contact with the human race.

Then go home.

As he passed through the Beehive, he had flung rocks at as many cells as he could. The destruction was minimal, but likely significant.

"Where's the ramp from your twenty?" he radioed to Dennis. As he waited, he looked at the rocks and ice around him. His hands felt empty. What he needed was a stick, something to steady himself. Deep in the shadows, under a cleft, were several items that, in a terrestrial cave, would have been called stalactites.

Pogo wondered briefly if it was possible for a human to break ice that had been hardened for ten thousand years. The answer was yes—

"To my left, your right . . . two hundred meters."

Downey was in motion before Dennis finished telling him, slipping and sliding, bracing against the vent wall with one free hand, the other using the ice shard as a cane.

He felt faint—probably stressing the suit's oxygen flow, which was not designed for cross-country hikes—and the momentary lightness reminded him all too much of the circumstances of his own death. Just how had that happened? Clearly Lucas had spooked the Sentry, but what kind of creature responded to a simple flash of light with a killing blow?

Unless that creature was so strong and fast that it was merely intending to grab and hold him—

There was the ramp, its terminus littered with small rocks mixed with snow. Clearly no one had tried to use it in centuries or longer.

But he could pick his way across the rubble, using his "cane." And once he got past the debris at the base, the ramp proved to be relatively clean, though strangely broad. You could have driven two rovers up this thing, side by side.

A good thing, too. The low gravity meant little traction. Every other step resulted in a skid . . . and though he knew, intellectually, that he could survive a fall, he had no wish to return to the vent floor and start the climb again.

He was running out of time.

A bobbing light played across the irregular vent walls. Dennis making rendezvous. "I see you."

"Copy that."

Downey reached the rim before Dennis arrived. He stopped, catching his breath, wheezing a bit. He could see *Brahma* off to his right, a six-story silver skyscraper that seemed ridiculously close . . . and *Venture* beyond, squat, lit like a Halloween pumpkin.

"Downey." Dennis stopped several meters away. "Welcome back."

The lag was driving Pogo crazy—even though the EVA suits effectively masked physical gestures that accompanied speech, it was annoying to see the Russian raise his hand in greeting . . . and have the words trail by seconds.

Maybe that explained what happened next. In silence, the cosmonaut reached out to him with his right hand . . . but there was something in his left! And Dennis was raising that hand—

Downey blocked it with his cane. The movement was exaggerated by low gravity—Chertok spun.

And the icy tip pierced Chertok's suit.

The Russian stared at the gash in the thick blue fabric and a quick spew of bloody droplets that quickly froze, becoming red sleet.

Only then did Downey hear the man say, "Take my hand."

So it hadn't been a mistake! Dennis Chertok was drawing him close to hit him, likely to smash his helmet.

Now it was Dennis Chertok whose air and life were hissing out of a hole in his suit. He dropped the tool and frantically reached for his chest—obviously he couldn't see exactly where he'd been cut.

Did he have a patch? One hand pawed at a pocket on the left leg of the suit.

His faceplate fogged over, then frosted. Words in Russian. Downey heard what he knew to be a curse, followed by a single word: *Spaseniye.* Help.

Then a strangled hiss. Chertok fell over, face down in the snow of Keanu. No movement. He was dead.

Pogo dropped his ice spear and picked up the tool. Better.

Pogo had no memory of the next few minutes. It was as if he had teleported, à la *Star Trek*, from the rim of the crater to a place midway between the two vehicles, approaching *Venture* from its back side.

He hadn't meant to hurt Dennis Chertok. Well, maybe he had wanted to punish him for meeting him with a weapon. Surely the Russian must have known what would happen. Did the man have no understanding of what Downey had endured?

But dead? No. Of all people, Downey knew what *that* felt like. The sudden, permanent, inescapable disconnect. Of course, whereas Downey had been dismembered, literally seeing if not really feeling his body being torn apart, Chertok had frozen and suffocated . . . it must have been like drowning.

Downey had always heard that drowners felt peace at the end. He rather hoped the same was true for cosmonauts exposed to vacuum. . . .

Still, it shouldn't have happened. He was too quick to react, too uncontrolled.

But it was done. "Yvonne, Pogo. I've got a problem."

At least the lag was gone—Downey could communicate directly with *Venture* through line of sight. "No shit, you stupid bastard. I saw what you did."

"Then you know it was an accident." As he talked, Downey realized he couldn't just stand on the surface of Keanu debating Yvonne Hall. He continued to approach the lander.

"What do you want?"

"What the hell do you think? I want to come aboard! I can't stay out here."

Another half dozen steps closer. "Where are Zack and Tea?"

"No idea. Still in Keanu."

"How do I know you didn't hurt them?"

"Why don't you ask them?"

"I would if I could."

"Well, they were fine last time I saw them." That was the truth . . . Downey had no reason to lie. "Come on, Yvonne, it's me. We're friends."

"We're *crewmates*. A whole different deal. Especially when it's past tense." For the first time since returning to life, Pogo Downey felt a flash of real anger. Stupid bitch—she really had no understanding of the loyalty one member of a crew owed another. Especially during a mission. What was it the Russian trainers told cosmonauts? "Learn to work together, because if one of you screws up, all of you get blamed." That was the reality.

"Well, I'm returning to *Venture*."

"I can't let you in."

"You can't stop me."

There was another long silence. This time it was broken by a familiar crackle in Downey's headset. "*Venture*, Houston. *Venture*, Houston, do you copy?"

As quickly as he could, he said, "Houston, Downey on EVA. Do you copy?"

Houston's response would have taken eight seconds, but Downey would never know, since Yvonne immediately radioed, "Downey is on the surface and attacked Chertok. I consider him a threat."

Then she switched to Channel B, making it impossible for him to hear. "Downey for Houston, how me?"

Another long lag. Finally a different capcom: "Ah, welcome back, Pogo. Stand by."

Shit.

For a moment he paused, looking to his right at the taller *Brahma* lander . . . it was unoccupied. Taking that over—it would be another Horatio Hornblower maneuver, just like the gravity gauge. Only now they would be "cutting out" an enemy vessel. Well, not they . . . just Pogo Downey.

Then what? Claim it for the United States and NASA? Repel boarders? Launch it and leave Taj and his crew stranded?

The display in his helmet had just flipped to yellow. He had half an hour of oxygen left. Getting aboard *Brahma* would allow him to keep breathing, but he'd be trapped. It was unlikely he could recharge his suit's tanks from those on *Brahma*—hell, he'd spend an hour just trying to make the radios work.

No, *Venture* had to be his target.

"Downey for *Venture* through Houston. I'm at the ladder."

No answer. No answer!

Although NASA's *Destiny-7* mission has had its share of setbacks, including the loss of a crew member, the agency is reporting that communications should resume shortly and that the astronauts will soon complete their EVA and return to the *Venture* lander. The crew of three is expected to splash down in the Pacific sometime Sunday.

Meanwhile, an insurgent armed with a handheld missile launcher brought down an American helicopter in northern Pakistan today. . . .

LEAD TEXT, *CBS CABLE NEWS*, AUGUST 23, 2019

"We've got AOS," Josh Kennedy said.

Harley knew it before the worn-out flight director said it, because all around him, at the twenty consoles, blank or safe-mode screens had suddenly lit up with data, live feed from *Venture*.

Knowing acquisition of signal was imminent, Harley had left the Home Team room, leaving one order behind: Jillianne Dwight was to take Rachel and her friend Amy home. Rachel was exhausted, for one thing. For another, the outcome of the whole Keanu adventure was still in doubt. Harley ordered Jillianne to deliver Amy to her parents, then put Rachel to bed and get hold of the information flow. (He had given the girl back her Slate. It was hers, after all, and with revelations flooding the data devices in the Home Team, Harley no longer needed it.)

Now he watched as Shane Weldon walked into mission control hours after his team—lead for the mission, scheduled originally to handle ascent from Keanu and rendezvous with *Destiny*—should have been on duty. Although he loomed over Josh Kennedy, Weldon let the junior flight director reestablish contact, which he did, first, by nodding to Jasmine Trieu, his capcom. "Make the call."

"*Venture*, Houston, acquiring you at Stay plus twenty-six hours, eighteen minutes."

Within seconds, Harley and the others were horrified to hear a very shaky, obviously rattled Yvonne Hall. "Houston, *Venture*, we've got a serious problem."

The next ten minutes were completely panicked, though an outside observer would never have known. The default setting in mission control was cool, calm, collected. Smart decisions required smooth hands and lowered voices. But from experience, Harley saw the signs of confusion . . . the furtive glances between Kennedy, Weldon, and Trieu. And then between Weldon and Jones and Bynum, who had just arrived.

The tension was also evident in the way several controllers in the back row pushed their chairs together and conferred quietly.

Eventually they all got the update: Yvonne was out of her mind with fear, trapped in *Venture*, and Patrick Downey was trying to get inside.

Dennis Chertok was dead, apparently killed by Downey. (That explained why Trieu's fellow capcom, Travis Buell, was so busy. He was talking to Bangalore.)

And there was no immediate word from the five explorers inside Keanu—or information about the three Revenants.

Four Revenants, if one included Pogo Downey. For a moment, Harley was genuinely glad that he was not responsible for unfucking this clusterfuck, to quote one of his early flight instructors. Yet . . . he wasn't sure he trusted Jones and Bynum to find the best solution.

"What do I do?" Yvonne had gone to the encrypted channel and was talking to Jasmine Trieu—another woman's voice, which Harley hoped Yvonne would find soothing.

Meanwhile, Buell was apparently talking to Pogo Downey. Harley rolled toward the capcom console . . . more out of morbid curiosity than any operational need—the same reason he had left the Home Team and come to mission control at this particular moment.

But after a cursory confirmation, Buell was not saying anything to Downey. And it didn't appear that Downey was being verbal.

He was active, however. Yvonne had turned on both of *Venture*'s exterior cameras. The forward view showed nothing, but the anterior had Downey coming up the ladder, a horror-movie version of Armstrong's first steps on the Moon . . . in reverse.

There was an in-cabin view, too, locked off and aimed at the forward console. As Harley and the entire team watched, Yvonne Hall briefly appeared, hopping on one foot and trying to steady herself. In Keanu gravity, that meant keeping herself from bouncing toward the ceiling.

"What is she doing?" Harley said.

Buell had been watching more carefully, it seemed. "Trying to find something to jam the hatch."

"Doesn't it lock?"

"Not by design." And why should spacecraft hatches lock? The most likely result would be an EVA crew member trapped outside thanks to a loose washer in an otherwise "foolproof" system. True, there had been locks for the main hatch of the early space shuttle, back when NASA had been forced to fly several commercial or foreign "astronauts" who had not been thoroughly vetted concerning their mental stability under duress.

Jasmine Trieu was handling this matter, however. "Okay, Yvonne, keep this in mind: As long as the inner hatch isn't sealed, the outer hatch can't be opened."

Harley realized he should have thought of that. It was better than a padlock.

"Copy that," Yvonne responded. "But that leaves me at risk if he pokes a hole in the chamber!"

Trieu conferred with Josh Kennedy. "Can you put on your suit?"

Harley knew what that answer would be: No, it was torn. Sure enough, the only thing Jasmine Trieu could tell Yvonne now was, "Stand by."

Meanwhile, Harley became aware that Bynum, Jones, and Shane Weldon were having what passed for a violent argument—at least, what passed for one in the reading room–like silence of mission control. Harley couldn't wheel himself closer without announcing that he was eavesdropping, but by turning his head, he could hear Bynum's mention of "dire circumstances in a worst-case scenario" should the "Item be enabled," followed by Weldon's calmer "don't think we're there yet."

Gabriel Jones reacted strangely, jabbing a finger in Bynum's chest and saying, "You are way ahead of yourself!" Then he walked out of mission control.

After a moment, Bynum and Weldon hurried after him, leaving Harley and anyone who witnessed the outburst baffled. Granted, the situation on Keanu—unusual by definition—was unprecedented and unpredictable. There were no back pages in a flight data file dealing with "crazed astronaut tries to break into lander."

But to leave in the middle? What the hell was wrong with Gabriel Jones?

And what the hell was this "Item"?

This is *Destiny* mission control. Keanu's rotation now allows direct line-of-contact communication between Houston and the *Venture* vehicle on the surface. Telemetry is being received here; astronaut Yvonne Hall is in a rest period. We expect to regain contact with the EVA team momentarily, at which point live transmissions will be resumed.

NASA PUBLIC AFFAIRS COMMENTATOR SCOTT SHAWLER, AUGUST 23, 2019

At the first blow, the entire cabin rang like a church bell. "Stop that!" Yvonne said, feeling in equal parts frightened, ill, and, especially, foolish, since no one, least of all Downey, could hear her.

She had done as Trieu instructed, leaving the hatch between the *Venture* main cabin and its airlock open, essentially locking the outer hatch. (An interlock inside the hatch froze the outer latch mechanism unless the inner one was closed.)

But Downey had climbed the ladder and, after a fruitless session of tugging on the door, had actually struck it with something hard.

She finally got on the radio again. "That won't work."

"What choice do I have?" he said, after a lag. "I can't stay out here."

"Let's talk, Pogo. Talk to mission control, too." She had been able to see him through the hatch port, but now light streamed through. Where had he gone?

"Sorry, I don't have time for that."

"What do you want?"

"I just want to go home."

"You and me both!" Yvonne said. Then the other channel lit up. "Yvonne, Houston. The director is online."

Her father? "Copy that." What else was she supposed to do? Coo, *Oooh, Daddy?*

"First, I just want you to know we're doing everything we can here."

She wanted to scream. That wasn't a father talking, that was a man with his head up his butt—wondering what the rest of the world would say. "Too bad the decisions have to be made up here, by me."

"We're confident—" he said, then paused and started over: "*I'm* confident in you."

To do what? Figure out how to stop Downey, or blow myself up? "Thanks for that," she said, knowing the sarcasm would likely not be noticed through the radio connection.

"How are you feeling? How is the leg?"

Oh, yeah, her leg: the one she would almost certainly lose if she managed to survive this. "Leg is stable," she said.

As she talked and waited for a response from her father, she hopped from window to screen to window, searching for Downey. Still nothing. "The situation is . . . critical, Yvonne."

Fuck him. "Just what exactly are you trying to tell me, Daddy? Why can't I just let Downey in . . . maybe I can talk sense to him."

Was that him? A shadow around to the left—

"Negative, Yvonne. All our data shows that astronaut Patrick Downey died six hours ago. The person you see cannot be given access to *Venture.*"

True, the person running around out there sounded like Pogo Downey, but he was wearing Zack Stewart's suit.

"Which is where this all started," she said. "I can hold him off, maybe until his air runs out, but it would really be helpful if you guys could do something from there." Was there some kind of remote-control switch the EVA support guys had, something that would disable an astronaut's backpack? Until a few hours ago, Yvonne would have been horrified at the thought of it . . . now it didn't seem so undesirable.

"You are the best option," her father finally said.

"So we're back where we started." She had lost the shadow . . . damn, she hated this.

"Not quite. Every minute he remains outside he's one minute closer to his redline."

"That's all you've got to say to me?" She wasn't sure what she wanted. . . . An apology for twenty-odd years of neglect? An even better apology for putting her in this horrific situation?

"We—" he said, then had to correct himself again. "I am proud of you."

Which only convinced her. Things would have to be a lot worse, as in bugfuck crazy Pogo Downey about to stab her, before she would blow up the Item.

Before she would make her father's life any easier.

Then she saw Downey again, back on the surface at the rear of the lander, heading for the front. He had something in his hand . . . the same weapon she had told Dennis to take.

"I want to come inside. You have something I need."

"You ain't coming in here." There he was . . . right outside the forward windows, looking up at her.

She knew she sounded more confident than she felt—*thank you, NASA, for sending me on speaking tours*—but it was all surface. She realized this situation was much, much worse than being flung across the surface of Keanu.

Five meters lower, eight meters away, Downey looked up at her. For a moment their eyes met through the multiple layers of glass.

Houston had heard some or all of this. Now Jasmine Trieu was saying, "Tell him to wait until Zack gets back."

Which she did.

Downey was already in motion. "Zack won't be here for hours. That's assuming he ever gets here. No, it's you and me."

What was he doing? Picking up a rock?

"Last chance."

"Pogo, come on, be real."

"Are you going to open the hatch?"

"I can't." There it was.

As she watched, the space-suited figure clumsily hurled a rock the size of a bowling ball directly at the forward windows.

Downey's aim was terrible, but *Venture* was a big target. The rock hit with a shuddering thud and bounced off.

"Stop that!"

"I've got lots of rocks, Yvonne." And he bent to pick up another one.

Shit, shit, shit. "Houston, what the fuck do I do now? He's throwing rocks at me!"

"*Venture*, Houston, ah, we don't think he can really damage the vehicle. . . ."

A second thud, this one almost a direct hit on one of the windows.

Yvonne knew spacecraft and structures. She knew that, yes, a vehicle like *Venture* was actually a thin aluminum shell that could be punctured with a screwdriver. But when pressurized to ten pounds a square inch, it was harder than any rock Downey could throw at it.

Still, that second shot had come close to a window . . . and Yvonne could see a ghostly crack.

The multipaned windows were vulnerable. The same air pressure that bolstered the thin metal skin would cause a seriously cracked window to blow out.

She grabbed the metal case and opened it. "Okay, Downey, you want to play rough. *I'm arming the Item*, you dumb bastard."

Three seconds later, her answer was another thump from another rock, followed by Jasmine Trieu's frantic, "Negative, *Venture*! You are not authorized for that step!"

But she was already deeply into the process. She had opened the case, removed the false front, and entered the first set of codes. She felt stupid, slow, and numb . . . the drugs doing their work.

She was not planning to die. This was just a contingency move, to allow Houston to come up with an answer.

The countdown started from ten minutes. *Be cool*, she told herself. *You can stop it at any time.*

She picked up the Item and stepped toward the front windows. "Can you see this? It's a bomb, and it's armed!" There was no sign of Downey, no word on the radio.

Then Yvonne heard a different sound, not the thump of rock against the rugged cabin wall, or the more frightening crack of impact on the window. This was a more distant clang.

An alarm sounded on the control panel, two indicators suddenly red.

Fuel tanks! Downey had managed to poke a hole in one of them, and it was big enough to create a cloud of freezing vapor: Yvonne could see it from the left front window.

"Pogo," she radioed, knowing she sounded tired and pathetic. "What the hell are you doing? This fucks all of us. . . ."

Houston was on the line, Jasmine Trieu sounding strained. "*Venture*, we show a drop in hydrogen tank two—"

"I know," Yvonne snapped. "Pogo!" she shouted.

It took almost ten seconds. "I'm at the hatch," he said. "Put your stupid bomb in the lock, button yourself up, and open the outer door. And I'm counting, too. Up to ten, when I put a hole in another tank. One, two . . ."

She considered her options. "Houston, can you hear this?" Goddamn time lag. The clock on the Item showed 6:30 and counting. "What do I do?"

Gabriel Jones was back on the link. "Yvonne, it's your father again . . . we are talking to Downey. He's not responding. But I want to say again, don't do anything—"

Then the whole damn lander shook. Pogo must have really blown that second tank.

The entire left side of the console, all the systems related to ascent engine and propellants, was red red red. There was not going to be a lift-off, no rendezvous with *Destiny*, no return to Earth. Pogo had fucked her completely. Zack, Tea, all of them were going to die here.

Slumped against the bulkhead, she reached into her suit and grabbed the key on her neck chain. Three minutes, now less. She could shut it down. . . .

"Yvonne, talk to me—"

Another clang. Downey was determined to wreck *Venture*! Maybe if she tried a different approach . . . She got to her feet and stepped to the window. "Pogo, let's talk this over. I'll . . . I'll shut off the timer."

There he was, out front, arm raised. He launched what looked like a snowball right at the window.

Direct hit.

The last thing Yvonne Hall saw was the crack in the outer pane suddenly mirrored by a deeper one in the inner pane. Part of the window blew out, beginning the swift, permanent, fatal venting of *Venture*'s atmosphere—

Two meters behind her, the timer on the Item reached zero.

In pain, exhausted, infuriated, Pogo Downey saw the puff of air and the spewing of Plexiglas fragments. This was the coup de grâce—already hobbled by two plumes from punctured tanks, the *Venture* was like a wounded bull in the arena.

Yvonne would not survive this. But the vacuum inside the *Venture* would allow the outer hatch to unseal, allowing Downey access to the Item, giving him a weapon.

No. Between one step and the next, Downey saw the entire lander expand and fragment.

As brains, bone, blood, and whatever it was the Architects had used to rebuild him vaporized, he had a fraction of a second to realize he was dying for the second time.

On the screen in mission control, Harley saw Yvonne at the forward station. He was not wearing a headset, so he could not hear the exchanges, which were clearly fraught: Prime capcom Jasmine Trieu had tears in her eyes while the secondary communicator, Travis Buell, was throwing his hands in the air.

And Gabriel Jones, in headset, was seated between them, pounding on the desktop.

Harley had seen the intense knot of controllers around the lander consoles, specifically the propellant team, and knew there was some kind of problem.

As if they needed more problems. Where were Zack and Tea? Communications were reestablished, but no one seemed to be calling them.

Then the screen went to snow.

And all the *Venture* consoles went white, as the constant flow of temperatures, pressures, and other indicators ceased to make sense, or just ceased all together.

"*Venture*, Houston," Jasmine Trieu was saying. She repeated it.

Gabriel Jones slumped. Shane Weldon put his arm around him and said, "Get Bangalore on the line." Then he shouted, to no one in particular, "Do we have a telescopic view?"

It only took a few seconds, but some clever operator in a back room called up a long-range view of Keanu from some Earth-based telescope.

The screen now showed a silvery crescent . . . and an expanding cloud in the upper portion, roughly the area where *Venture* and *Brahma* had landed.

"I take it that's not another eruption," Brent Bynum said.

Harley Drake realized that they had lost *Venture*, and with it any chance of bringing his friend Zack Stewart and his crew—Revenants or not—home again.

Part Four
"IN THE WIDE STARLIGHT"

"Did you feel that?"

Tea and Taj had reached the membrane and were about to drive through when something strange happened. "I saw it," Taj said. "The inner surface of the membrane—"

"Yeah, it fluttered," Tea said. "But I felt some kind of ripple or vibration. Not a quake, I don't think."

"It's hard to tell from here."

"Then we get out."

Normally the procedures to egress from rover *Buzz* would have taken fifteen minutes, most of them to allow pressure to drop so the hatch could be opened. But Tea and Taj had simply not bothered to close the hatch. Indeed, they had driven from the campsite to the membrane without donning their suits.

"Do you smell something funny?" Taj asked.

"No," she said. "But I'm surprised my senses are working at all." This wasn't quite the truth; her eyes had definitely noted the rippling of the membrane. And even swathed in the increasingly dirty, sweaty EVA undergarment, she had definitely felt a tingling akin to the forerunner of a thunderstorm on a midwestern summer day.

And since she was running through the sensory spectrum, Tea motioned for Taj to freeze. "I hear something," she said, though she could not have described it.

"More wind?" Taj said. "I think I hear it, too."

Tea held out her hands. "It's not much. I can't really feel it." She noticed that the vyomanaut had the Zeiss in his hands, dutifully recording
images. "What's your magic radio telling you?"

Taj shook his head and showed her the instrument panel on its
back, which had a signal indicator just like that on Tea's cell phone. "No
bars."

"Why is that?"

"I don't know. I never had more than one deeper into Keanu. We're
closer now, so it should be better."

"Unless there's suddenly a bunch of rock in the way." Tea's mind had
instantly fixed on a horrible concept. "Do you think maybe there's been
a landslide out there?" All through the journey into the junction, she had
had to remind herself that although it looked like a West Virginia coal
mine, the passage was larger and had remained open for likely thousands
of years.

Still, the idea of being trapped . . .

"I think we need suits now."

Twenty minutes later, Tea and Taj had donned, sealed, and tested their
suits . . . and penetrated the Keanu side of the membrane.

Now they were emerging into the junction. "Still no bars?" Tea asked.

"Zero."

Never one to hope that bad news got better with delay, Tea plunged
into the gauzy curtain without hesitation, praying that she would not find
it blocked with tons of fallen Keanu granite.

She didn't. Not that what she found was much better. "Oh fuck."

There was no longer ice on the other side. The entire junction was
filled with fog generated by puddles of water that were cooling and
refreezing. . . . "*Venture*, Tea. *Venture*, Tea for Yvonne . . ."

She listened and heard no response, no change in the steady background hiss. "I'm open to suggestions," she said to Taj.

"Volcanism?" Taj said. "An eruption of some kind?"

"Could be." She ventured several steps away from the membrane, but not too far. "We knew Keanu wasn't inert, so I suppose it's possible. I don't much like what that could mean for the vehicles."

"That's what we get for naming the vent Vesuvius."

Tea couldn't help laughing. "And you say *I* trivialize the experience of spaceflight."

"I can no longer suppress my natural gallows humor."

"Well, hell no. Given the circumstances." During this exchange both explorers had put twenty meters between themselves and the membrane. "Problem," Tea said. "If this heat was the result of a volcanic event out in the vent itself . . . where's our camera and the cable?" Tea cursed herself for not asking the question earlier, but she had simply missed it; the items were gone, picked cleanly and taken away.

"Pyroclastic venting—"

"—Would have blown them sideways, yes. Though I've got to tell you, Taj, I don't think you get a lot of pyroclastic pressure when you're in a vacuum. Even so, I would think we'd see cut cable or a camera smashed against a wall."

"Here's something else," Taj said. "Listen."

The dominant sound in Tea's earphones was her own near-panicked breathing. But, yes, there was a click-click-clicking sound, at the rate of almost one per second. "What is it?"

"Geiger counter. It's on my chest pack."

"Did it do that when we came through here earlier?"

"No."

"So now there's radiation?"

"Low-level, and very inconsistent. The rate rises and falls every few steps."

Tea considered this. "Heat, overpressure, radiation. Call me a pessimist, but it's as if someone set off a nuke."

Taj stopped in his tracks and turned toward her. "I think so, too."

"The Architects have their own anti-missile system?"

"That would be rather less startling than most of what we've seen."

Tea saw no point in going farther. "I'm not getting anything from *Venture*."

"No response from *Brahma*."

"If there's serious damage to either vehicle, we are in a world of shit."

Now Taj laughed out loud, a harsh, unfriendly sound. "We have been in a world of shit since we landed here!" He seemed more hunched over than usual. "Houston and Bangalore will be working the problem."

"You guys have a rescue vehicle anywhere close to launch?"

"Let's not get ahead of ourselves."

"Good point," Tea said. "But since we can't go forward, I suggest that in the great explorer tradition, we go back where we came from."

They made a quick return through both membranes to the Keanu interior and rover *Buzz*. Once they had opened their suits and removed helmets and gloves, Tea insisted that Taj share water and food. "We need it, and God only knows when we'll have it again."

"I was thinking of the others."

"There's not enough for everyone, no matter what we do. We're going to have to find some sort of nourishment here." Tea had not really considered the possibility until she heard herself say it. The thought frightened and depressed her. It was bad enough to consider the many ways you could die on a spaceflight—getting blown up or depressurized merely the top of the list. She hadn't thought to add starvation.

She continued to remove her suit, then started in on the crusty undergarment.

"What are you doing?"

"Stripping." It was clear Taj had no idea why. "So I can run better, Taj. We have no other way to contact Zack, so we're doing it old-school." She smiled. "They can't be far, maybe a couple of clicks. I know they're headed for the Temple. I can get there in twenty minutes."

"So fast?"

"I ran the eight hundred in high school and college."

"What should I do?"

"I'd keep working the radios. Come to think of it, let me see that dealie." She gestured for Taj's magic Zeiss radio/camera. "You know, we've got the rover as well as our suits. We should be able to talk to the vehicles and mission control without this."

"Yes," Taj said. "What is the point of your observation?"

"Let me take this thing."

She expected an argument, but all the vyomanaut said was, "Be sure to bring it back."

"Cross my heart."

"Any other suggestions for me while you're gone?" Taj's English grew wobbly with fatigue, but he still managed to do sarcasm.

"Yeah, given what's happened, make sure somebody doesn't come along and tirejack the rover."

Destiny-7 EVA manager Mariah Nelson and her team have worked TIRELESSLY to support suited crew ops on Keanu. Her conclusion is that all astronauts should have expired at least four hours prior to end of Stay-2. That they have not, at last report, indicates that we are breaking new ground. Please share ANY THOUGHTS AND INFORMA-TION with Mariah.

NASA MISSION OPERATIONS DIRECTORATE, STAY-2 SHIFT STATUS,
AUGUST 23, 2019

"Do you see it yet?"

Zachary Stewart's ragtag team of five—there was no other phrase in his increasingly tired mind—had covered several hundred yards of Keanu real estate, heading deeper into the interior. They should have been closing in on the Temple.

"No," Megan said. She had taken the lead, causing Zack to wonder if she was following some memory—or just being Megan, the woman who loved maps and happily gave directions. "If what Tea and Taj said was right, we probably still have a hundred meters to cover."

Zack regretted not having Taj, or especially Tea, with him, at least to serve as cavalry scout. For that matter, he was also wishing he hadn't left the helmets and suits behind at the campsite, even though they were nothing more than dead weight. Taj had been able to punch through the rock and membrane with his Zeiss radio, but even with Houston theoretically reachable, Zack would still have to be able to get a signal to *Venture*, and he couldn't do that until he returned to the other side of the membrane.

No, he had put together the best plan for the circumstances. And dealing with both Megan and Tea was beyond him right now. They would all be back at the membrane soon enough. . . .

For an instant, the glowworms went dark, as if they'd had their plugs pulled.

Natalia stopped. "What was that?"

"The beginning of night?" Lucas said.

Zack wasn't sure the momentary shadow meant anything, until a gentle breeze started up and began to gust.

More from habit than any other impulse, he looked at Megan, who was standing still, facing away from him, eyes closed and head down.

Camilla was in the same posture.

"Megan," he said.

Megan literally shuddered, then opened her eyes. "Oh, fuck."

The wind had continued to rise. The dense foliage all around them waved. It was like being on the leading edge of a tropical storm, the kind that blew through Houston every few years.

The air even began to smell different . . . moist, thick.

"What's going on?" he asked.

"Something bad happened."

"What?"

"On the surface." Megan was pressing her fingers to her temples, as if trying to tune in a poor signal. Then she abruptly dropped her hands and looked at him, wide-eyed. "Did you have a bomb?"

"What are you talking about?"

"It's so damn weird . . . like, like you just picked up an old family album and remembered some uncle." She pointed to the glowworms, then at the waving, windblown trees. "The light faded for a moment, and then I knew that something had gone boom. Something *you* brought."

Camilla started clutching at Lucas, talking to him in Portuguese.

"And she knows, too?" Zack said.

Lucas held the girl, listening briefly, then said, "Yes, something bad happened. She's very afraid."

Zack turned to Megan. "I didn't bring a bomb." Even as he said it, he could easily imagine two possibilities: One, *Brahma* had a weapon. Two, *Venture* did, too . . . but the commander never knew.

There was a sound from somewhere nearby, a deep, guttural noise. *Like a giant clearing his throat,* Zack thought.

The others heard it, too. "Zack, what do we do?" Natalia asked.

"For the moment, record it," he said, wondering at the sad sound of his own voice. He looked at Lucas, who had his camera out. Then at Megan. "Unless we should run. . . ."

Megan looked as numb as Zack felt. She could only shrug as, with no warning, two giant watery globes appeared from the woods.

They stopped, dissolved, and disgorged a Sentry each. The beings looked identical in size and coloring. The only difference was in their vest belts; one of them looked worn and used, the other straight from the box.

Like dogs after a bath, the Sentry pair shivered and shed the enveloping goo, splashing it on the five humans. Zack was horrified, both by the potential contamination and by the taste, which reminded him of polluted seawater.

Now he had to act. "Everybody back!"

He took Megan by the arm. To his surprise, she fought him! Camilla did the same with Lucas.

Zack started to say, "Let's get out of here—" But before he could finish the order, the nearest Sentry snapped out a limb and reached directly for Megan. Zack feared that, like Pogo, she would be sliced up.

But the Sentry pulled her close, then rolled into a giant three-meter-tall ball, enveloping her.

The other Sentry did the same with Camilla. Natalia and Lucas were unable to react any more effectively than Zack.

The Sentries then rolled off, deeper into Keanu.

Zack stared after them, stunned to immobility, hearing Lucas say, "I think they're headed for the Temple."

Approximately twenty-eight hours after landing on Keanu, one hundred twenty hours after launch from Kourou, Bangalore Space Centre lost contact with spacecraft *Brahma*. The cause of the problem is not known at present. Further information will be made available in due course.   ISRO PRESS RELEASE, 23 AUGUST 2019

"Tell me you didn't put a nuke on this mission."

Harley Drake rolled up to Brent Bynum. The White House representative was standing behind Shane Weldon and Josh Kennedy, who were asking every member of the flight control team, one by one, what data they had last recorded prior to loss of contact—and what, if anything, they were seeing now.

"This isn't the place to discuss those issues," Bynum said. "We need to go to the Vault." He picked up his Slate—which had been vibrating nonstop ever since the most recent "event" on Keanu—and headed for the door.

"Fuck the Vault," Harley said. "I've made my last visit to that place."

Weldon pushed back his chair. "So, Harley, is that the status report from Home Team?"

"No. But I can probably give you a tentative report, along the lines of 'We got nothing.'"

"What makes you think there was a nuke on board?"

"I know you guys. A couple of hours ago you were telling me to class the 'entities' as 'hostile.' Then you start talking about some 'Item.'" Harley jerked a thumb toward the screen, which was still showing a ground-based telescopic view of Keanu and a scattering debris cloud. "Then there's that."

Bynum looked beaten down. "I still don't think we should talk here."

"Every person in this room has a need to know," Harley said. "If you can't trust them . . . well," he said, shaking his head, "you really can't be *more* fucked than you are now, can you?"

Before Bynum could answer, Weldon stood up. "Harley is correct. NASA, the White House, the Department of Defense, and Homeland Security authorized the placement of a small nuclear device aboard *Venture*. Although no orders were given for its use, it is likely that it was detonated and caused the loss of the vehicle."

"And *Brahma*," said capcom Travis Buell. "The guys in Bangalore don't know what hit them."

"I wonder what's on the news," Jasmine Trieu said. Red-eyed, she was sitting next to Buell, having finally been ordered to stop calling for *Venture* to answer.

Bynum held up his Slate. "It's every bit as bad as you could imagine. . . ."

"They're reporting loss of both vehicles?" Harley said. Bynum nodded. "What do they give as a cause?"

"So far, unexplained venting. Natural causes."

"Well, they're going to figure it out soon enough."

Bynum opened his hands. "Sure. But they're not going to learn it from me."

"Brent," Harley said, "we aren't learning much from you and we're all here together."

Weldon stood. "There isn't much point to assigning blame. The Item was triggered—why, by whom, we don't know, though Yvonne Hall was the one with the codes."

"And a crazed Revenant banging on her door." That comment came from Jasmine Trieu.

"We still have two crew members unaccounted for," Weldon said.

"Two plus three from *Brahma*, plus the Revenants," Harley said. "Or is there something else you guys are keeping from me?"

"No," Bynum said. "That number is correct."

"Then we've got to keep trying to raise them," Harley said. He rolled toward Buell. "*Brahma* had that relay sat. Is it still alive?"

Before Buell could respond—and his posture told Harley the answer was likely negative—one of the other controllers in the front row suddenly shot to his feet.

"I got something!" he said. He was a young man of Indian ancestry, but Texan in voice. "I've got *Destiny*."

"How the hell did it survive?" Buell asked.

"It was on the other side of Keanu when the bomb went off," Trieu said. "And, am I right? Shock waves don't propagate in vacuum?"

"It was several hundred kilometers away," Weldon said. "Even on Earth, it wouldn't have sustained much actual damage. I was worried about its electronics, though. Keanu must have shielded it. . . ."

With that news, the group—Bynum included—reacted like hangover victims given a dose of vitamin E.

"Okay, everyone," Weldon said. "Let's see what kind of shape our bird is in. At least we've still got *something* out there we can use."

He turned to Harley, who was already in motion. "I'll see what the great minds can do with this."

Harley knew that his Home Team was getting the feed from mission control. They knew what he knew. There was no reason for him to trundle right in there.

Or so he told himself. He really needed a moment to think. He wanted to strangle Brent Bynum—not in a personal sense, since the man was clearly just a messenger—but just to strike a blow against what his father would have called "institutional fuckheadedness," the kind of arrogant blindness that believed you could put a nuke on a risky mission, then be surprised when it went off.

It was dawn in Houston, the air already thick, the buzzing and flapping of bugs and birds already audible, the sky to the east thick with rosy clouds. *Red sky at morning, sailor take warning.*

Harley flinched. Wade Williams was lurking in the shadows, sitting on a concrete bench, a bottle in his hand. "I'm afraid I don't have any orange juice, but . . ." He had a six-pack at his feet and offered a bottle to Harley.

Who took it. *What the hell,* he thought, twisting off the top. "How'd you manage to get this in here?"

"I may be a pompous ass—don't argue with me—"

"Oh, I wasn't." But he smiled to take the edge off the remark.

"I know what I am and how I come across. All I can say is, I come from a long line of pompous asses. It's what happens when you're smarter than most people you meet, and louder, and unable to keep from making that clear." He smiled and took a sip. "Anyway, I have a few fans squirreled away at JSC."

"Cheers to your fans," Harley said, taking a drink, and only then looking at the bottle: near beer. "O'Doul's? Damn, Wade, I thought we were going to commemorate the serious shit we were in by getting loaded!"

"Not since 2012 for me, unfortunately." He got a faraway look in his eye. "Still, just holding the bottle—the weight of it—helps me think."

"And what are you thinking? I presume you and the team heard—"

"—All of it, the whole sorry mess." The old man rubbed a hand across the stubble on his face. "I'll say this for you, Drake. You and NASA sure know how to pack a thousand years of thrills into a few days."

"It's all kind of hard to believe, isn't it? Last week we were thinking we were just damn lucky to have a chance to do a NEO landing without sending a crew on a nine-month mission, and now . . ."

"You've had First Encounter, Re-Encounter, Close Encounter—"

"—And Stupid, Senseless, What-Else-Can-I-Do-Wrong Encounter. That would be today's."

Williams actually shook with amusement. "I won't ask you to believe that I'm in any way eager to stop living, but my gratitude at my continued existence has been seriously enhanced by this week . . . even allowing for the, uh . . ." He waved his hand at Harley. "What-Else-Can-Go-Wrong aspects?" He chuckled. "I lived through 9/11, but always thought that Pearl Harbor might have been more shocking. With this . . . now I have some idea."

"This," Harley said, "is like living through the week of the Crucifixion . . . or when that big asteroid killed off the dinosaurs."

"True. Either way, it's sort of a privilege to bear witness."

"What was it Mark Twain said? About a man being tarred, feathered, then ridden out of town on a rail?"

"'If not for the honor of the thing, I'd rather walk.' Actually, it was Abraham Lincoln."

"You're the writer." Harley looked at his bottle. "Are you sure this is nonalcoholic?"

"Fatigue and terror do strange things to the mind. Speaking of which," Williams said, shifting to the lecture mode Harley knew so well, and hated, "I've been thinking. Thinking about what those fine folks you gathered have come up with."

"Given that, so far, all I've gotten are some cute names—"

"Oh, we've got a model for your Revenants and such. The idea is, just as there is no true physical separation between your body and the universe—even when your core organism ceases to function, there are still atoms of moisture and skin and exhalation that linger, float off, whatever—the same thing applies to your mind, your soul, your life force. There is also some kind of physical connection between the electrical field that is you, Harley Drake, and the universe.

"Your carrier might be shut off. That is, you die. But the information lingers . . . like cloud computing, it's all around us . . . accessible."

"So our souls are some new kind of matter, is that what you're saying?"

"That's one way to look at it. I mean, hell, the universe is largely made up of dark matter and energy, and we still don't have a terrific handle on what that is or does. Why not some other kind of energy or information? It's probably affected by gravity, too. The cloud of souls travels with the Sun."

"Sounds like the opening line of your next novel."

"Those days are gone, my friend. But the image is elegant, is it not?" He let the contents of the bottle slosh. "Everything that ever lived on Earth—or in the solar system—is still with us, in some fashion. It's all information . . . the folks who built Keanu just know how to access it and repackage it."

"They must have a pretty impressive search engine to pull Zack Stewart's wife out of a library like that."

"We suspect they got some clues or information from the arriving astronauts. We think the, ah, markers help. Scanned them, I think. Then they're retrieved the same way the National Security Agency plucks a single cell phone conversation out of an entire city's signals. Random frequency tracking, amped up a bit."

"Yeah, a bit," Harley said. "Then, of course, there's the whole business of growing new bodies."

"That's just twenty-second-century Earth biotech, don't you think? If we live long enough, we could have new carcasses, too." Williams wheezed, tipped his bottle toward Harley. "We both could certainly use one."

In shadow, another person came around the corner—female, tall, and, from the lingering odor, just off a cigarette. "Oh!" Sasha Blaine said. "There you are."

"Caught," Harley said. "We were about to head back in. . . ."

"Before you do," Sasha said. "I've just had this mad cool idea and you should hear it in case it's more mad than cool."

"Hit me with it." Harley was no longer convinced that the O'Doul's was actually near beer; either that, or in his fatigued, stressed-out state, he was all raw emotion . . . because he suddenly, instantly wanted to hold Sasha Blaine. Gawky, too tall, too jumpy, it didn't matter. He was in love with her . . . and there was a testament to the persistence of human emotions in the face of crisis.

Blaine blinked. "We heard that even though *Venture* and *Brahma* are gone, *Destiny* is still in orbit."

"Yes."

"And that five of the astronauts might still be alive."

"Still good."

"Which doesn't mean much, because without *Venture* and *Brahma*, they're trapped, and nobody has a vehicle that could be prepped and launched on a rescue for at least six months."

"That would sum it up." Harley had been so focused on the horror of this nuke that he had not gotten his head around the real collateral damage . . . the fact that the survivors were *stranded* with no hope of rescue.

Eyes closed, Blaine hugged herself, a set of gestures Harley always associated with brilliant, socially awkward types who were about to tell you something insane. Williams saw it, too, nudging Harley.

"Sasha," Harley said, realizing he would have to drag it out of her. "What's on your mind?"

"Why don't we land *Destiny* on Keanu?"

Tea's run to rendezvous, even though she was barefoot and wearing nothing more than panties and a tank top, was quick and exhilarating. Maybe
part of that was due to her near-naked state. She felt primal. Eve in Eden,
maybe.

The only techie part of the experience was the Zeiss unit slapping at
her back. (She had looped its strap over her chest, bandolier style.)

It was also helpful to find smooth running surfaces inside the chamber. Nothing would kill the runner's high, amplified by danger and novelty, more quickly than bloodied feet.

The danger and novelty were enhanced by the apparent change in
conditions. The interior seemed to be growing dark—it was difficult for
Tea to see the glowworms through the overhanging vegetation, but it
seemed redder and, though this could have been an illusion, briefly black,
switched off or in some kind of Keanu eclipse.

The temperature seemed to be dropping, too, though that could have
been due to her lack of clothing. And the oxygen content was changing—
or was she feeling that because she was running hard while horribly fatigued, dehydrated, and out of shape?

Either way, though Tea wasn't in love with the Keanu environment,
given the unattractive options at the moment, she really wanted it to stay
human-friendly.

After emerging from the Beehive, she made a quick pass through the campsite, where she stopped long enough to reorient herself. There was no high ground that would allow for a broader view . . . the best she could do was plunge back into the jungle on the same path she and Taj had used in returning from the Temple.

As she ran, she felt occasional flutters on her skin. . . . Keanu insects? Or just vegetative debris being blown by what was now a steady wind? None of it stuck to her long enough for her to tell, and she sure wasn't going to stop to conduct a biotic study. Aside from the Zeiss, the only other piece of technical equipment she carried was her watch, and she had already been gone from the membrane for twenty minutes.

There it was, up ahead, the stony top of the Temple, still maybe a mile or more away—

—And here was Zack Stewart, no more than twenty meters in front of her, standing in a clearing with Lucas and Natalia.

"Zack!" She couldn't believe how weak her voice sounded, how tired she felt! She had to stop, panting, watching helplessly as the other three reacted with what appeared to be confusion.

It was Zack who reached her first. "What's wrong? Where's your suit?"

"That's what you've got to ask? 'Where's your suit?'"

In their time together, Zack Stewart had shown Tea that he would see humor any time, under any circumstances.

Until now. "It wasn't what I asked, goddammit!" he snapped. "Why are you *here*? And what the hell is going on?"

She told him about the strange event. "We felt something, too." By then Natalia and Lucas had joined them. All three seemed subdued and lost . . . Tea wanted to ask about the Revenants but knew that she needed to stay on message.

Once she'd told them all about conditions on the other side of the membrane—and the lack of contact with either *Venture* or *Brahma*—she wished she hadn't. Zack accepted the loss of the trip home stoically, the way he accepted most bad news. Well, he'd had practice.

But Natalia sank to the ground, as if to say, *Kill me now*. She was completely spent, emotionally and physically.

Lucas was a different case, flailing between disbelief and open hysteria. "What do you mean, gone? What about Dennis? Did you even try to contact him? Where is Taj?" He seemed incapable of comprehending the situation—even though he was still speaking English, it was as if he were suffering temporary aphasia.

It was understandable, but hardly worthy, in Tea's view, of the world's greatest astronaut. Or any astronaut.

But then Zack told her what had happened to Megan and Camilla, rolled up and swept away by Sentries. And she wanted to join Natalia in an exhausted, Daddy-make-it-go-away crouch. Or start babbling like Lucas.

Zack saw it, too. He slipped his arm around her, offering (and likely taking) comfort while providing actual support.

Then, calmly, rationally, he examined the situation—and the options going forward. "Assume the worst: Both spacecraft are gone. What would you do? Natalia?"

She only shook her head. "Lucas?"

Lucas was still struggling. "Are we sure they're gone?"

Zack turned to Tea, his whole manner pleading for her to give him something. "I think we all go to the membrane."

He actually smiled. God help him, he liked a debate. "That's the logical step. But if both landers are gone, what's the point?"

"Eventually someone from Earth will come after us." Tea turned to Natalia and Lucas. "There's another *Brahma* that could be ready, right?"

Natalia nodded. Lucas was slower to react, and even then, Tea wouldn't have called it a response.

"Come on, Tea, that's bullshit," Zack said. "NASA couldn't have another *Destiny-Venture* ready for launch within six months. A second *Brahma* is at least a year away."

But Tea liked an argument, too. She had been waiting to have one with Zack ever since entering Keanu's environment, and this subject was as good as any. "NASA could push *Destiny-8* forward to maybe a hundred days, darling."

"So we'll be, what, only ninety-five days dead as opposed to a hundred and eighty?"

"This environment might support us. There's air, there's water."

"Which is why I gave us five days. A, we've found no food. B, how long is the environment going to stay 'human-friendly'?"

"Don't be such a pessimist."

Tea saw the expression on Zack's face—the pre-shock to the quake to come. But he suppressed it, smiling, even though it must have almost killed him. "You're right. Let's be positive."

He pointed at Natalia and Lucas. "You two, go with Tea. Grab your suits and stage with Taj and the rover at the membrane."

"Where will you be?" Tea said.

"I'm going after Megan and Camilla."

So there it was. Tea knew Zack well enough to know he was not likely to change his mind. "So you believe that's really Megan."

"I guess I do."

Tea didn't know whether to punch Zack or kiss him. She was impressed by the enduring nature of love—and just as pissed off at him as she could possibly be. "You won't have any way to communicate, no weapons. Even if you . . . free her? Is that the plan? You could make it to the membrane and find us gone!"

She knew he was already thinking a step beyond her. "If what you're saying is true, a few hours or days won't make any difference."

"You'll be going in with no backup."

"Backup hasn't made any difference."

She took him by the shoulders and spoke quietly but firmly. "Listen, Zachary. One of the reasons I fell in love with you was that, you know, forget Lucas here . . . *you* were the World's Greatest Astronaut. If you took a risk, it was informed and reasonable. You knew where the line was, and you never crossed it.

"But this caper—this is nuts. If you don't come with us, you'll *die*."

He put his hands on hers, squeezed them. His voice grew softer, almost dreamlike. "It may have looked calculating, but I've always followed my instincts. And all of them say to go after Megan. If she lives, I'll live. And if she dies . . ."

"You're chasing a fantasy!"

There . . . she had said it. She did not really believe the Revenant was the real Megan Stewart.

"Tea—"

"Zack! Do the math! Alien beings. Big smart spacecraft! The ability to replicate living things. Add them up and what do you fucking know? You've got a familiar face to talk to!"

"That's what these Revenants are, guys. Sorry, Lucas. I mean, if I went to Brazil, I'd learn Portuguese. I'd wear something that looked Brazilian. I'd try to connect . . . Revenants are just their way of doing it."

For a moment, Zack looked cowed. It was the first time Tea had ever seen him in that posture. "She knows things she shouldn't know."

"She isn't Megan," she said, firmly, feeling that she was this close to hauling him back from the edge. "But I'm me and you know that. I love you. Come with me . . . come where you *belong*. . . ."

"Right now I belong here."

Tea Nowinski had a sentimental side. It had hurt her in many relationships and was probably going to do the same now. But not yet.

"This time you're wrong, Zack. Wrong, wrong, wrong. You stay here or go gallivanting after . . . what looks like Megan, you will never see Earth again. *You'll never see your daughter again.* Have you thought about that?"

"That's actually all I'm thinking about."

"Okay, then, what do I tell her? 'Sorry, kid, your father chose not to come back to you because he had to chase—'"

"Stop it." He was cold now, another Zack state she knew. There would be no explanations now, only orders. "You need to get going. All of you."

Well, hell. If Tea looked at it realistically, she and Lucas and Natalia—and Zack and Megan and the others—were already doomed.

In that case, why not spend your final hours doing what you wanted?

"Okay, Zack, do your thing. I hope it works." She gave him what she knew would be the last kiss they shared. "At least you should take Taj's magic radio."

There's a freaky—hell, terrifying—rumor on the Net that the flash on Keanu was caused by a NUKE. Did the U.S. launch something? Has some kind of space war started? Has someone gone INSANE?

POSTER JERMAINE AT NEOMISSION.COM

The U.S. has nothing nuclear that could hit Keanu, so relax. And what would be the point, anyway? POSTER BELLANCA FAN, MOMENTS LATER

"Take all your knowledge about mission operations and set it aside," Harley Drake told Shane Weldon and Josh Kennedy, as Sasha Blaine and Wade Williams looked on. "And I'll have a vodka tonic."

He addressed his second order to a bored-looking young woman wearing an apron and holding an order pad. Above the bar behind her, a muted television was interviewing a Buddhist monk about "alien reincarnation." "Everyone else?"

Harley had finally escaped from the three rooms where he had been forced to spend his last three days. Home Team, Vault, mission control—none of these venues suited this presentation.

He had gone off campus, to the New Outpost, a bar across NASA Parkway from the Johnson Space Center. The original Outpost, a shack in the middle of a parking lot that had more craters than a similar plot of land on the Moon, had been a fixture in the community for decades but had been torn down.

Now there was this slick new hangout, with autographed astronaut photos on the walls, glassed-in memorabilia.

As far as Harley knew, no astronaut ever went into the place. Which was why he'd suggested it this day. There was little chance he would see anyone he worked with.

By now JSC was crawling with reporters—and dozens of staffers whose curiosity and self-importance had overwhelmed their adherence to the privacy code. If a security guard or assistant cook spotted Weldon, Drake, Bynum, and the others huddled in conference, word was going to be on the Web within seconds.

"Besides," Weldon had said, "I need to get outside that gate."

So here they were, Harley setting the tone with his order of an alcoholic drink at lunch, and that was stretching the lunch hour to late morning. Very 1960s, Apollo-era. Weldon unbent enough to order a beer, and so did Sasha Blaine. (Harley was liking this girl more with each new revelation.) Williams, with his years on the wagon, stuck to club soda, and Kennedy ignored the offer.

"So," Harley said, once the waitress had returned to the bar, "are we clear on the proposal?"

Kennedy actually sneered. "You mean, crash-land *Destiny* on the surface of Keanu?"

"It's not really a crash landing," Williams said, his voice at least twice as loud as necessary—or prudent. Harley's expression warned the elderly writer, and he continued more quietly. "That's why Harley said to forget what you know about ops—the closing velocities will be so low that you could think of this as a rendezvous between *Destiny*—"

"—and a spacecraft a million times larger and more massive," Shane Weldon said, sipping from his beer. He turned to Blaine. "Of course, that's just a wild-ass guess. You'll run the figures."

Blaine had her Slate with her. "I'm sure they're good enough for this discussion, but I'll run them, just in case."

"Can we get serious here?" Kennedy was no longer hiding his impatience. He had already glanced at his watch.

"You got somewhere else to be, Josh?" Harley said. "Is there a kids' soccer game on the schedule?" He had judged Kennedy to be one of those precise, ascetic youngish men who worked hard and played, whenever possible, without alcohol, late hours, and unsavory companions. They had been the dominant personality type in mission ops for a generation. It was probably inherent in the job; you couldn't be a boozer or a womanizer and still possess the appropriate seriousness to manage a flight into space.

Or so the mythology had it. Harley agreed that guys who followed rules made better flight directors—as long as that job was defined as . . . following the flight rules.

But in a situation like this, where the rule book was having its pages bent, if not entirely ripped out, NASA needed a riverboat gambler. A buccaneer. A Shane Weldon.

Not an earnest young father. "Since when is my personal life any of your business?"

"It's not," Harley said, "unless it keeps you from doing your job."

Kennedy was bright enough to take the temperature of the room, and right now it was cool toward him. "Sorry. Let's work this through."

Harley said, "The idea is to command *Destiny* to make a burn, to descend in the flattest trajectory possible . . ."

"And just skid across the surface?" Kennedy's voice was now neutral, but it was clear he was still horrified.

"It's largely snow," Weldon said. Kennedy shot him a look that said: *Traitor.* "The impact velocity could be as low as three meters a second."

"Or . . ." Harley said, not wishing to attempt conversions or even division with a vodka tonic aboard.

"Sixty to eighty kilometers an hour," Blaine said, blushing. Was it doing the math so quickly under pressure? Or the beer? Or something else?

The figure sounded good to Harley until Kennedy said, "That speed would still beat the hell out of my Hyundai."

Williams was spoiling for a fight. "Your Hyundai wasn't designed to be blasted into space, then survive thousand-degree heat on a lunar return."

"Don't we both know that those are different kinds of durability? The vibration damping and thermal protection aren't the same as impact resistance, right? I mean, the tiles on the space shuttle could withstand temps of three thousand degrees, but if you dropped a penny on them they would split in two."

Weldon said, "Josh, no one is suggesting that we might not lose an antenna—"

Kennedy had placed his palms on the small table. He would not look directly at anyone. "It's the solar panels I'd be worried about, though, okay, you ought to be able to operate for a few days with only one. But consider trying to maneuver to the right attitude, make burns, and reenter without data from Houston."

"This is where mission ops will shine," Harley said. "You guys will have the departure burns and times precalculated and preloaded to *Destiny*'s onboard computers before we make the landing."

Kennedy was nodding, though not so much in acceptance as impatience. "Yeah, yeah, got that. So we pancake down on the surface and manage not to rip a hole in the side of the vehicle, or scrape off both panels and every antenna." Now he looked up. "You've got four, five people in suits. How the hell do they get on board?"

Harley hadn't given this problem much thought. Because it was not designed for EVA operations, *Destiny* did not possess an airlock the way the *Venture* lander did. Which meant it didn't have easy-open hatches. There was access through the nose—where the Low-Impact Docking System allowed *Destiny* to dock with *Venture*. And there was the side hatch, which was how the crew of four entered the vehicle on the pad and departed from it after landing.

The capsule could be depressurized in an emergency. Its electronics were hardened against exposure to vacuum. But which hatch to open, and how—those procedures weren't in the front part of the training manual, and the surviving *Destiny* astronauts would be exhausted and totally dependent on guidance from the ground.

"That is what you guys need to work on," Harley said, feeling the warmth of the vodka through his entire body. "Which way in is better, through the LIDS or through the side access?"

Kennedy had his own Slate out now and was tapping notes to himself and his team. Nothing made an engineer happier than a tricky engineering problem.

"There are other challenges, too," Weldon said, for Kennedy's benefit, and to keep Harley and his team on track. "We might have five or six people rather than four; how do we protect them against g-forces on re-entry? Water and oxygen and food shouldn't be immediate problems, but I'm just guessing on the oxygen front.

"There's the whole business of sample returns, assuming they're still carrying anything, and how to secure those when we pluck them out of the ocean."

"And how easy is it going to be to get five exhausted astronauts out of *Destiny* when it's bobbing in the Pacific?" Harley disliked many things about the *Destiny* design, had fought wars against all of them a decade past. But his greatest hatred was for the water landing, a relic of the Apollo days. *Destiny* could have been designed to thump down safely on a military range like Edwards, but weight considerations and trade-offs had killed that idea. Now the capsule splashed down off the coast of California, near the Channel Islands, where it would be picked up by a NASA-chartered freighter.

"If I may," Williams said, knowing well that no one would say no, "I just want to say that this kind of rapid response makes me proud and thrilled. It's like watching the rescue of *Apollo 13*. It's NASA at its best." He tipped his club soda to Weldon and Kennedy. "Cheers."

Harley said, "Before we pin on the Congressional Space Medal, what are the next steps?"

"We have to be ready with the landing plan as soon as possible," Kennedy said. "The moment we hear from the crew, we should start counting down to a burn at first opportunity."

"And a data upload based on that," Weldon said. He and Kennedy fired times, phrases, and names back and forth for several minutes, then both stood.

Harley tried to help with the sales pitch. "This isn't as crazy as it sounds. Ten years ago, when we were looking at NEO missions, we were planning to simply fly a *Destiny* right down to a surface."

"Down to the surface of a NEO the size of a football stadium," Kennedy said. "Or maybe a kilometer across. Keanu is a hundred times larger, with real gravity of its own. I'm not saying it's impossible. I am saying it ain't the same deal."

"Whatever, we'll be ready in two hours," Weldon announced. And he tossed down the last of his beer.

Emerging into the Texas afternoon was like entering a broiler. The clouds, threatening rain, managed to dull the glare, but they added to the oppressive thickness of the air. Even with Sasha Blaine pushing his wheels, Harley could feel his energy being drained. "It's amazing," Blaine said.

"The discomfort?"

"No!" she said. "It just all looks so normal! Insane things are happening half a million kilometers away, and all these people are just living their lives!"

It was true. There was a McDonald's a hundred meters down the road, cars still lined up for lunchtime drive-through. Other vehicles, each one sealed and air-conditioned against the tropical Houston summer heat, glided past on NASA One. Harley knew that there were dozens of protesters at JSC's back gate, but not out here.

"Jealous?" Harley said.

Blaine blushed again. "Kind of, yeah. This has been . . . fun. And it just shows me that I'm thirty-two and I have no life. No boyfriend, no hobbies, no pets. I just do calculations and teach and every now and then I slip the leash and come someplace like this."

Harley was in front of his used Dodge Caravan, modified for easy access and equipped with hand controls. "The one benefit, and it may be the only benefit, of being differently mobile is that I don't have to park across the lot."

Formerly mobile Harley Drake, driver of a Mustang, would have added, "And since we don't need to be back at the Home Team for a couple of hours . . ." And likely driven off for an afternoon of sport with Sasha Blaine.

But this was wheelchair Harley, spinal-cord-injury Harley, unable-to-function Harley.

It was also Home Team and Alien Protocol chief Harley Drake.

He used his key to open the side door, then waited for the special lift to extend. "I'll see you back in the center in an hour."

Then Blaine said, "Oh, you've got someplace better to be?" Harley was forced to conclude that she hoped he might have something more distracting in mind.

"Yeah," he said. "Don't worry. I'll tell you all about it when I get back."

I'd hate to die twice. It's so boring.   RICHARD FEYNMAN'S LAST WORDS

Rachel awoke in her own bedroom, confused and not terribly rested. The light was wrong—bright through the shades. Right, it was afternoon . . . she had slept a long time.

But the sound of the house was wrong. The drone of the air conditioner was audible. That was the problem: Rachel could actually hear the machine.

Which meant something was missing.

Over the past two years, she had gotten used to having the house to herself. Her father made it a point to be home whenever she was . . . he had rearranged his work schedule to allow for telecommuting in the afterschool hours, either plopping himself at the kitchen table while Rachel pretended to do schoolwork, or sitting on the sidelines at soccer with his Slate right up to the time Rachel finally told him she hated soccer and was quitting . . . and generally found other things to do between three and six P.M.

But whenever Zack was home, he had music playing . . . country, classical, horrible early nineties pop; it didn't seem to matter, as long as sound filled the house.

As if her father couldn't stand the silence. Back when she had had actual conversations with Zack, as opposed to arguments, Rachel had thought about asking him about the music . . . but, feeling she knew the answer, never did.

And now . . . would she ever?

Her father was . . . somewhere on Keanu, out of touch and, according to everything NASA had been saying, out of oxygen, food, and water . . . somehow in contact with the late Megan Stewart.

Maybe she should have taken the sedative Jillianne Dwight had offered. If it hadn't been so freaking horribly hot outside, she would have sneaked out to the porch and lit up a joint.

As it was, the trip home had been uncomfortable. Amy simply would not shut up about all the weird stuff she'd seen, and how she couldn't wait to tell everyone how she and Rachel had almost gotten arrested by the FBI. The fact that Rachel had had a conversation with a being who seemed to be her dead mother, reincarnated . . . well, that never seemed to strike Amy as all that interesting.

It was a relief to see her go.

Inside the house, Rachel had walked right past the telescope in the living room that Zack had used to first show her Keanu. In the last few months, of course, no telescope had been necessary.

Rachel had wondered what she would see if she used it now. She hadn't been online for twelve hours.

Before she checked her page, she glanced at the news feed.

It was all Keanu: *"Astronauts Out of Contact"* . . . *"Space Crews in Danger"* . . . *"NASA Hiding Zombie Planet"* . . .

Some of it seemed to match what Rachel had seen and heard, and some of it was crazy.

The phrase *zombie planet* made her sick. Keanu-Megan wasn't a zombie. She knew things that only Rachel's real mother would know!

She turned to her page and saw that the counter had maxed out on seven thousand messages. Glancing through the first hundred, she saw about seventy versions of, *So sorry to hear about your father!* The rest said things like, *What'd you expect?*

There were, of course, the stupid smutty messages, too, boys and men from many nations offering to "comfort" her. Rachel had been online since the age of six; there was nothing new or notable in any of this. All it did was remind her of Ethan Landolt and the fact that he had not even *tried* to get in touch with her since the launch.

With brutal efficiency, she clicked through more of the messages. Same, same, same. *Condolence, your fault, send me a naked pic.*

But then her eye saw something that didn't fit the pattern. *This is the beginning of a new age,* it said. *How great for you to be the first to know that we live on after death. You're like the women around Jesus at the Resurrection.*

That really freaked her out, because she had been feeling something like that . . . and felt stupid for entertaining the idea for even a second. She was just a fourteen-year-old Texas girl whose father happened to be an astronaut. There were a hundred astronauts, so how did that make her special? Her mother had died, but there were hundreds of thousands of girls in the United States in the same situation, too.

She took her fingers off the Slate. At that moment, it looked and felt as alien as anything on Keanu. She wanted it out—

There was a gentle knock at the door. Jillianne. "Hungry?"

The NASA secretary had made turkey sandwiches and a salad and encouraged Rachel to drink water. "I'm guessing this is the first home-style food you've had in days."

Rachel had to admit it was.

"How are you feeling?"

"How do you think?" Rachel caught herself in time, making that sound more plaintive than nasty.

"Well, I'm stunned and afraid and overwhelmed, and I'm just looking at this from the outside."

"You work with my dad."

"Yes. I was actually thinking more about . . ." She clearly didn't know how to say *your mother.*

"Yeah. Me, too." And just like that, Rachel began to cry, dissolving into a collapsing, sobbing crouch. It was as if she ceased to function.

Jillianne flew out of her chair and around the table to offer comfort, which only made it worse. Soon both of them were sobbing. Eventually Rachel was able to say, "I just don't know what to do!"

"Neither do I, honey," Jillianne said. "I don't think anybody knows. Look, you've had a series of emotional shocks. You haven't really slept. You might want to reconsider that Xanax."

"No," Rachel said. She got up, found a Kleenex, wiped her eyes, and blew her nose. She thought about that message, about the women around Jesus. Not that she thought much about Jesus Christ, but she found the idea intriguing. "I can't sleep through this. If my dad gets back in touch—"

"You want to be there, I know." Jillianne looked around. "Well, then. I suppose we should go back to the center."

"Yes. But I have a stop I want to make."

"I'm your driver. At your service."

Tea Nowinski was buttoned up in her EVA suit, within sight of the re-arranged floor of Vesuvius Vent, when the tremor hit. There was no doubting it: Even through the thick fabric of the suit, with sound and sensation muffled by the helmet, she was jolted, as if she had missed two steps coming down a stairway.

It only lasted a second, however. The jolt, a moment of vertigo, then all was calm.

Taj was walking behind her. Behind him was rover *Buzz*, with Natalia and Lucas inside. "Good God, don't tell me someone else has a bomb. . . ."

"That felt different," Taj said. He pointed to his feet, then at the brightness ahead of them. "It seemed to come from deep within, not out there."

After assuring herself that the occupants of the rover were okay, she resumed her trek.

She had led Lucas and Natalia back through the Beehive to the mem-brane, with the necessary stop at the campsite to pick up their suits.

Getting herself resuited took twice as long as it should have. She was operating on fumes, of course. She also recognized her own reluctance to go forward . . . emerging to Keanu's exterior meant she would be one step closer to knowing the fate of what was now her vastly reduced team;

would they be able to contact mission control and have some hope of rescue? (On a related note, would Taj ever forgive her for leaving his Zeiss radio/camera with Zack?)

Or were they doomed to death on Keanu? So far, she had to admit, the odds were not good.

At least Lucas and Natalia's suits had proven to be sound. Even if they possessed tools for repairing leaks or valves, they were no longer capable of performing critical repairs with any confidence.

Taj, in fact, had asked, "What's our fallback plan?"

"You mean, we go out there, find nothing left, no communication? Our options will be either to sit down and die, or go back through the membrane."

As they had departed, the return-to-interior option began to look like a poor choice. The wind had grown stronger, the glowworms darker . . . and the vegetation was going through another transition, from "jungle" to something Tea could only describe as "crystal city." Plants were disintegrating and angular structures were forming on the ground.

She had been happy to be inside her suit, tanks recharged and good for a few more hours. She wasn't sure the atmosphere inside Keanu would remain breathable.

Taj must have thought the same, because all he said was, "I don't think we're welcome inside there any longer."

At that moment the five of them felt a second jolt. This one was shorter, if possible, and oddly less jarring, though the rover rocked gently on its suspension for several seconds.

"Everyone still okay?" Tea got a "Fine" from Lucas. "Okay, saddle up!"

She actually began to trot, a ridiculous notion, given the high center of gravity and uncertain footing. But she felt that if she didn't escape from the dark passage soon, she might just . . . sit down and die.

Step, slide, step, slide. Repeat. Taj was doing the same thing. The pair on foot were pulling ahead of the rover.

Finally they emerged into the vent itself . . . and beheld the changes.

"It's mostly bare rock," Taj said.

"The snow and ice melted in the heat, sublimated away," Tea said. She clicked her radio. "*Venture*, Tea. *Venture* for Yvonne." As she kept walking, she repeated the call, listening for a response that never came.

In her earphones, she could hear Taj making similar calls to *Brahma*, with no better results.

Now that they were in the relatively open center of the vent floor, she thought it worth a shot to try contacting mission control directly. If *Venture* was gone, of course, she would be relying on a potential signal relay through *Destiny*. Where was the mother ship, anyway?

"Houston, this is Tea. I'm in Vesuvius Vent with Taj, Lucas, Natalia. Do you copy?"

Nothing. "Taj, I suppose you're missing your radio."

"No response," he said.

It was clear that they needed to get out of the vent. A climb up the rocky sides wasn't impossible—with most of the snow gone, Tea could see potential handholds.

But Zack had talked about a ramp . . . and there it was, curling up the inside of the far wall, a few hundred meters away. She pointed her team toward it.

Ten minutes later, somewhat out of breath, she was at its base, which was rubble-strewn. A suited astronaut on foot could get across it, but a path would have to be cleared for the rover.

"Lucas, Natalia, you two wait here. I don't want you to depress that cabin until we have to. Taj and I will scout up top. We'll come back and help clear this junk." Then her tone changed. "Do Indians have any tradition of granting last requests? You know, if someone is going to die?"

"No more than any other culture. Why? Feeling pessimistic about our chances?"

"Well, somewhat. But I was just curious about how you guys came so prepared."

"What do you mean?"

"Let's see. The relay satellite. A terahertz radio. The set of scientific instruments."

"Tea, *Venture* could just as easily have carried all of those. In fact, I think our guys got some of the ideas from NASA."

"Oh, bullshit, Taj. Christ, the only First Contact tool you left out was the sign reading *Welcome to Earth*."

Taj hesitated. Then he said, "A year ago an observatory in Crimea was looking at Keanu in the high radio frequencies. They saw something anomalous—not just unusual activity, but pulses and patterns that, in their judgment, could not be natural."

"We should have been looking at those things, too."

"Maybe you did, maybe you just happened to miss them. In any case, we were told there was a high probability we would be making contact." They had to stop to let the rover negotiate the last turn. "Well, is that what you wanted to know? That we were ready?"

"Yeah," she said. And then couldn't resist it: "Now I can die happy."

They were halfway up the ramp—with less than two hundred meters to go—when Tea heard a magical sound in her headset. "—on UHF, comm check. *Venture* crew, Houston. Tea, this is Jasmine."

"All right!" Tea said, practically shouting. The next few moments were a comedy of overlapping messages, broken sentences, all complicated by the eight-second round-trip lag. But eventually Houston knew that four were still alive and on the surface, that Zack was alive and yet to be heard from.

More to the point, Tea knew that *Destiny* was still operating in orbit around Keanu, and that the rocket scientists in mission control were seriously considering bringing it to the surface for a possible rescue. "That's assuming *Venture* and *Brahma* are both too damaged for use," Jasmine Trieu said.

"We understand," Tea said. "Can you relay for Taj?"

"We're already doing so," Trieu said, after the lag.

"Then let's get eyeballs on the situation." Tea and Taj continued their ascent, covering the last fifty meters in what seemed like three flying leaps.

The view from the rim was disheartening. "Oh, fuck, Taj, where are they?"

The surface had been blasted clean . . . this small piece of Keanu real estate, which had resembled a glacial valley on Earth, now looked like the Moon, a vista Tea knew as well as any human being.

She had been prepared to find damage. What was killing her was this: Both *Venture* and *Brahma* were *gone*. It was as if both vehicles had simply launched without them.

"Tea, Houston. We did not copy your last." Christ, Houston had heard her despairing comments. *Nice work, Nowinski.*

"Roger, Houston. Taj and I are at the top, noting, uh, some thermal effects of whatever happened." What *were* they telling the people of Earth? "Are you getting imagery?" She had no idea if her helmet cam was working, or if working, capable of punching an image to Houston via *Destiny*.

"A fuzzy landscape," the capcom finally said. "Can't tell much except dark sky and brighter surface."

Tea chose not to answer that directly. Taj had started toward the landing sites halfway around the rim of the vent, so she followed.

She hadn't gone far when she saw a flash of genuine color next to a collection of smallish boulders near the rim.

She signaled Taj to go the private channel. "That looks like a *Brahma* suit." It was a *Brahma*-style EVA suit . . . rather, the top half of it.

Tea heard a long, anguished sigh in her earphones. "Yes, that's Dennis," Taj said. Of course, Taj's identification was unnecessary: Dennis Chertok was the only missing member of his crew. "What was he doing out here?"

Tea bent as close as she could. Not only had the body been fragmented by the blast, but the multilayered fabric and helmet had been fused to the rock. The helmet was still intact, but frosted on the inside, mercifully obscuring Chertok's face. "I have no idea," she said. "All I know is that there seems to be blood on the inside of his faceplate."

Taj indicated the rocks behind the body. "Might be from impact."

Tea straightened and turned away. There was no immediate value in trying to conduct a postmortem. Their goal now was to keep from adding to the body count.

She saw more color now . . . fifty meters away, four gold-colored uprights—well, two uprights, two that had been twisted and knocked over.

Venture's legs. The rest of the twenty-ton, five-story-tall, two-billion-dollar spacecraft, the pride and joy of an entire nation, had simply vanished, along with Yvonne Hall . . . and Patrick Downey?

Taj joined her. He could see the same wreckage. "And over there . . ." he said.

To their left, looking toward the blue-and-white crescent of the rising Earth, was an even more appalling sight: the wreckage of *Brahma.*

Venture had been vaporized by the heat of the detonation, but *Brahma*'s wounds—though equally fatal—were more varied. In the first milliseconds of the blast, the Coalition vehicle had lost two of its legs, then toppled and melted as its fuel tanks exploded.

What remained was a lumpy, half-shattered cylinder lying on its side. It was still recognizable as a vehicle of some kind.

Taj was saying, "Do you suppose we're being exposed to radiation?"

"Yes, and that would be the last of my worries at the moment. I mean, are we likely to live long enough to die from too many rems? Besides, the suits should offer some protection."

Tea had to fight her emotions. She wanted to lie down and cry. Even as she reported the grim news to Houston—and heard Taj telling Bangalore—she fought to keep from simply sobbing.

There'll be plenty of time to lie down later, she thought. *If Houston can't pull off its little miracle with* Destiny.

"Houston for Tea . . . We, ah, confirm loss of both *Venture* and *Brahma.* We got some clear imagery. Stand by."

They were wondering just what the hell to tell her.

"Copy that, Houston . . . Tell you what: Taj and I are going to head south of this site, roughly where Yvonne wound up yesterday. Give us half an hour and see if we can't pick out a runway for you."

"Are you sure you want to do this?" Jillianne Dwight said, as she drove
through the open, silent gates of Forest Park Cemetery.

"I can handle it," Rachel said.

"I know, sweetie. It's just . . . it's been a weird couple of days." She
glanced at the Slate in Rachel's lap. "Are you going to post something?"

Rachel shrugged. "That's why I have it, I guess." She also had a small
garden spade in her bag. She had grabbed it from the back porch—where
the Stewarts' few plants were in severe distress—just before leaving the
house.

"When did you start doing all that?"

"When didn't I? I mean, Mom was always blogging or taping from
the day I was born. She did a show on her pregnancy. It was like she
wanted to save every moment of her life."

"And yours, too."

"I suppose." She looked out the window. The sky was growing darker,
some big storm about to blow up from the Gulf. In fact, the cemetery
now looked much as it had the day Megan Stewart was buried. "What's
really weird is that I might have the chance to ask her."

Jillianne kept her eyes on the winding road. "So you think that's really
your mom up there?"

"You don't?"

"Honey, I just— Well, my momma taught me that all good people sit with Jesus. It took me a long time to sort of, you know, get past that." She smiled sadly. "Not that you can't work for NASA and be religious. There are a lot of people at the center who do both. But I had to choose sides, you know?"

"So you're on the side that says those people up there are alien whatevers."

"I don't want to be on a side, young lady. I suppose if it was someone I knew and loved, I'd feel different. Sorry, I mean . . . well, I don't know what I mean. But I think we're here."

Rachel hadn't been completely sure that the "Megan" she had talked to was really her mother—

Until now. It was just like Daddy said: *You don't know what you've got until it's gone.* If Megan's intimate knowledge had brought Rachel ninety percent of the way to full belief, Jillianne's gentle skepticism had carried her the final stretch.

Of course, there was still Megan's body. . . .

Her grave lay twenty meters off the road, in a flat, open area surrounded by other graves, of course, most of them recent, many of them marked with crosses and angels. Rachel slid her bag over one arm, tucking her Slate under, then followed the familiar trail. Jillianne stayed with the car.

Rachel and Zack had their cemetery rituals, visiting every year on Megan's birthday in November, and on Mother's Day. And now and then, just on impulse.

There was a simple stone with Megan's name and years. And one thing that had always freaked Rachel out: the empty plot next to it. "That's for me," Zack had told her, the first time she asked about it, early one summer morning almost two years ago.

"That's seriously creepy, Dad."

"Don't worry, I'm not planning to occupy it any time soon."

"But doesn't it bother you to think that someday you're going to be there for a thousand years or whatever?"

Since Zack rarely wore sunglasses, he had blinked in the brilliant sunshine. "It's just not that big a deal."

"If it's not that important, why do we keep coming back?"

"You got me." He had closed his eyes for a moment, thinking. Then smiled, as if he'd solved a big problem. "Wait. It's because coming here gives us a place to think about your mom."

"We could do that at home."

"No, there are too many distractions. This is just . . . a special meditation zone dedicated to her, okay?"

Rachel had remembered that. She was never comfortable offering prayers, anyway. She didn't like going to church and, after a series of heated arguments, had persuaded Zack to let her skip religious education.

But meditation? Thinking good thoughts? She had been able to do that.

Though not today. She examined the grassy surface of the grave, then knelt to run her hand across it.

It didn't seem to have been disturbed. But how to be sure?

She took the little spade out of her bag and jammed it into the sod. It went in easily—of course; with all the rain, the ground was soft, soggy.

She chopped out a square two feet on a side, then began sliding the tip of the blade around the edges. She had just started to peel up a corner of the sod when a man said, "Rachel Stewart, what are you doing?"

Startled, Rachel sat up.

Harley Drake was a few feet away, his powered wheelchair finding slow if silent going. "We've got to stop meeting like this."

"What are you doing here?"

"Hiding," he said.

"Really." She went back to her excavation.

"Really? I just wanted to check on something."

"What?"

"You'll laugh."

"I don't think so."

He was at the grave now. He looked uncommonly serious. "I just wanted to be sure the grave was still intact. Weird, huh?"

Rachel managed to peel the square of sod off the grave. Her hands were dirty, so she wiped them on the grass. "You're nuts."

"Before you make judgments, tell me what you're doing. Because it almost looks as though you're worried about the same thing."

"What? That aliens stole my mother's body so they could fool everybody?" She knelt again and quickly dug a hole of sorts where the sod used to be.

"I wouldn't put it quite like that, but, well, yeah."

Rachel smiled. Poor Harley. "Nope." She picked up her Slate and dropped it in the fresh hole. With several swift moves, she covered it with loose soil.

Harley watched this. "Uh, that's a pretty expensive item. . . ."

"My father used to say it was really just a paperweight."

"Now it's a muddy paperweight."

She put the sod back in its place, then walked on it.

"All that blogging and stuff, that was my mom's world. I need to take a break."

"Unplugging? That's not the worst idea you've had lately."

They both laughed. In moments, the laughter turned to tears—even hardcase Harley Drake. Rachel knew it had nothing to do with her disposal of the Slate. She gave him an awkward hug. "Her old body is still under there, Harley. But that other part seems to be up in space."

"You're sure about that?"

"Yeah."

"It makes things really difficult, then."

At that moment, Harley's phone rang. "I don't believe this." But he answered it, listened for a moment. "Wow, okay. Yeah, I'll be right in."

"What's going on?"

"Your father. The rest of the crew is on the surface, but not him."

"He won't leave without my mother."

"Guess not."

"What's going to happen?"

"I have no idea, but I think you need to come with me."

This is *Destiny* mission control. The team here is following a number of unexpected developments, beginning with the anomalous loss of contact with the *Venture* spacecraft on the surface of Keanu at 103 hours, 34 minutes mission elapsed time and associated venting on the NEO's surface. Mission manager Shane Weldon has issued the following statement: "We consider this to be an extremely serious situation." He adds that the orbiting *Destiny* spacecraft is still providing downlink. We will continue to bring you timely updates as warranted.

NASA PUBLIC AFFAIRS COMMENTATOR SCOTT SHAWLER

"Maui got this twenty minutes ago," Shane Weldon said.

On the main screen, the white crescent that was Keanu still showed the traces of the detonation as a faint, symmetrical cloud.

With Rachel tagging along, Harley had rushed to mission control without stopping at the Home Team. But he had found Sasha Blaine already waiting, lost in the group grope, since at least a dozen people crowded the usually sacrosanct area near the flight director and capcom stations. Bynum was here, too, of course, and so was Gabriel Jones, still, to Harley's eyes, looking like a phantom.

"Is this real-time?" Bynum asked.

"Just watch the damned screen," Jones said. His voice sounded weak, and the idea that the Johnson Space Center's director would snap at a representative from Washington was further confirmation: Jones was out of it.

Even in real time, what happened next made Harley's heart go irregular. There was a flash of light from beyond Keanu's bright limb—

something exploding or erupting on the side away from the Earth-based telescope.

But instead of dissipating like the debris from past events, a small object fell away from Keanu. "What the hell is *that*?" someone said. Harley could not have phrased the question any better.

"Keep watching, everyone," Weldon said.

Then it happened again, though this time the eruption seemed to come from Keanu's south pole. But the result was the same . . . a bright object that, like its predecessor, separated from the NEO.

Within seconds, both objects had left Keanu behind. The Maui scope smoothly tracked with them; Keanu fell out of frame, leaving two white blobs on the screen.

Several people began talking at the same time, all asking the logical questions. *How big are they? How fast are they moving?*

And Harley's new favorite, "Where are they going?"

"People, please!" Weldon said. "We don't actually know much more than you do."

Into the sudden silence, Harley said, "Is there better imagery?"

Weldon simply nodded, then jerked his head to one of the operators.

One of the objects suddenly filled the screen. "It's still nothing but a blob," Bynum said.

"Correct," Weldon said. "We have other sites besides Maui tracking this, and no one has seen any edges or definition on this thing. At the moment, all we can say is that it's a blob moving at thirty-two thousand clicks an hour."

"Two blobs," Jones said.

"Were they simply fired, like bullets?" Sasha Blaine said, speaking up. "Or are they accelerating?"

"We haven't seen any maneuvering yet," Weldon said. "So far, we're treating it like a launch."

"What could those things be?" Bynum said.

He looked genuinely baffled, and for once Harley couldn't blame the man. "I can only think of two things," Harley said. "Pure mass, like ice or rock, or a vehicle, which could be a spacecraft or a missile."

"If it's a missile, is it a counterstrike?" Bynum said.

"You'd have to look at it that way."

Even a chunk of rock could be a devastating weapon. Harley had fond memories of a Robert Heinlein novel he had read as a kid in which the Moon had gone to war with Earth—and won it by pounding the home planet with . . . rocks.

"First orbital data," Weldon announced. "From NORTHCOM." He fumbled for reading glasses and bent to his screen, Jasmine Trieu, Gabriel Jones, and others pressing on him. "Apogee is four hundred eighty thousand—Keanu distance. Perigee thirty-six thousand. Inclination TBD."

"Don't we have assets at thirty-six thousand kilometers?" Bynum said.

"Only most of the world's communications satellites," Harley told him. "And a few intel birds, too."

"What if they attack those satellites?"

"We lose a lot of capability," Harley said. "I'd love to hear a size for these things."

"Are they even the same?"

Hearing this, one of the controllers pushed back and took off his headset. "Maui thinks both are on the order of one hundred meters wide, roughly spherical."

Harley turned to Sasha. "So if it's a chunk of rock a hundred meters in diameter, and it's traveling at orbital velocity, how much damage does it do if it hits Earth?"

"I don't have to run numbers," she said. "It's just a meteorite. Nasty and capable of doing tremendous damage if it hits a city, or different but equally awful stuff if it's a water impact."

Travis Buell stood up. "Shane, I've got Bangalore on the line and they say it's urgent."

"Well, what are you waiting for?" Jones said. "Put it the fuck up there."

The main screen split, the left half showing Vikram Nayar, the *Brahma* flight director, looking at least twenty years older than his age.

"I'm getting word from Maui," another controller said. "Maneuvers!" The message was unnecessary; both blobs had dropped off the screen. Harley didn't think the remote-tracking hardware had suddenly gone tits up.

On screen, Nayar was looking at a piece of paper that had just been handed to him. "We have more useful information on the objects," he said, finally. "Their trajectories are diverging. But both objects are going to impact Earth."

Weldon rubbed his head. "When and where?"

"In four hours, the first predicted impact will be on the Indian sub-continent at approximately twelve point five degrees north, seventy-seven degrees east."

"That's Bangalore, isn't it?" Sasha Blaine said to Harley. His grati-tude for her speed at recognizing the importance of the information was short-lived, because Nayar then said, "On the order of thirty minutes later, second impact North America, twenty-nine point eight degrees north, ninety-five point five degrees west."

"That's pretty close to us," Josh Kennedy said, his voice failing for the first time.

"The impacts are too coincidental to be accidents," Nayar was saying. "Although these figures are imprecise and could be off by many kilome-ters, it appears Bangalore and Houston mission control are the targets."

"We have to assume we are," Weldon said. He turned to Gabriel Jones. "You'd better order an evacuation."

"Where do I tell people to go?" Jones said. "If this is a big rock and JSC is ground zero, that mass and velocity—hell, it's going to take out all of Houston."

"If JSC is ground zero, anywhere is better than here," Harley said.

"We have ten thousand people just at the center!"

"That's why you'd better get started," Weldon said.

"Fine." Jones nodded at the mission control team. "You guys, too."

"We can't," Josh Kennedy said. "We've got a spacecraft to land."

Jones was adamant. "You could all die here!"

But Weldon said, "Our crew will die without that vehicle. We can't let that happen." He smiled. "Besides, Gabe, we've been through this before. Hurricane Horace, remember? Shelter in place."

Harley surely did; a decade back, during his ASCAN year, Hurricane Horace had aimed itself directly at Houston, right in the middle of one of the last shuttle missions.

Mission control was operating the International Space Station at the same time, though those functions were shared with Russia. But the shuttle could be directed only from Houston.

And as the city—and ninety-nine percent of the staff at Johnson Space Center—took to the highways heading for higher ground, a skeleton team remained in Building 30 . . . sheltered in place.

Horace ripped through the Houston area, causing massive damage on the city's west side. JSC was spared a direct hit, though roofs were torn off, windows were broken, and power lines were ripped away. The shuttle continued to have support.

But this would be a greater challenge. Building 30's walls were brick and mortar, capable of withstanding severe weather. They would be little protection against a kinetic energy strike, which would unleash incredible amounts of heat and energy. This time, the mission controllers involved in a shelter in place stood a good chance of dying.

Not that you could tell, from the hushed atmosphere.

"Well, then, God bless you all," Jones had said, wisely realizing the futility of his argument.

Weldon was approaching him. "Harls, you better get back to your team."

"Yeah, time for the great minds to earn their meal money."

"I was thinking you should offer them the chance to get out of here."

It had not occurred to Harley that his group of academics and quasi scientists might not be eager to take part in shelter in place. "Right."

Blaine pushed him and his chair toward the door. Once they were in the hallway, Harley said, "Assume these are hostile. Are they kinetic-energy weapons?"

"Are they going to change direction at the last moment and strike

Washington or New York? Wade Williams will be so happy—it'll be like his movie."

"He'll just have to take his happiness on the road."

Blaine stopped and looked down at him. "What about you, Harley?"

"You know, there were two things I liked to do before my accident and only one of them was flying. I haven't been able to do either since, and it doesn't look as though I'll start any time in the future. So I'll take my chances here."

"That's brave of you," Blaine said. "What about Zack's daughter?"

Oh God, Harley thought. *Yes, what about Rachel Stewart?*

That conversation had consumed much of the intervening hour. It started in the visitors' gallery; progressed to the hallway, where Sasha Blaine left them to return to the Home Team; then ended back in mission control.

The bottom line: Rachel Stewart wasn't going anywhere. "This is the only place in the world where I can be in touch with my father," she said.

"There won't be much contact if it turns into a giant smoking hole in the ground."

"If that's what the Keanu-ites are doing, my father won't have a chance, either."

Harley Drake was a big believer in the right of any human being to make his or her own giant fucking mistakes, and the younger said human being learned that, the better. Some vestige of adult responsibility made him question the convenience of that either-or judgment. After all, the important lesson might well be that your decision got you killed. But no matter how he examined it, he still came back to the same conclusion: If Rachel wanted to stay, she should stay.

Besides . . . if the Keanu Plasma Thing was what it appeared to be, Rachel and Harley would be no safer sitting in a traffic jam on the 8 Beltway.

And here . . . the main screen displayed a computer-generated image of *Destiny*, flying tail first, sharing space with several ground-based images, one showing a small white dot . . . *Destiny* as seen from Hawaii. Two others showed what it now called the Objects, now completely diverged.

One was being imaged from Hawaii; the other, if the bug in the screen corner told the truth, from a facility in Russia.

"Getting word from Maui," one of the trajectory flight controllers said. "They can put a definitive upper limit on the diameter of the Keanu Objects, which appear to be the same size. Well under two hundred meters."

Hearing that figure, Harley felt sick. In his years as an astronaut, and especially the past two years as an accelerated student of events astronomical, he had spent a good deal of time examining the Arizona meteor crater, primarily because he'd visited it for training, and just because it was so cool.

Which was why he knew that the big hole in the ground outside Flagstaff was something like 150 meters deep and close to a kilometer across . . . and that the impact—which vaporized vegetation and living things for tens of kilometers around—was triggered by a hunk of space rock around fifty meters in diameter.

One quarter that of either of the Keanu Objects. The damage if one of them struck wouldn't just be four times greater, but some geometric multiple of that, comparable to a good-sized nuclear weapon.

Meaning that JSC and Building 30 stood no chance.

If an Object struck nearby, that is. There was still time for the both of them to change course . . . or to be much smaller than this two-hundred-meter figure, or to turn out to be less dense than iron.

The activity at the consoles never changed, though the pace of door openings and closings increased, with Brent Bynum the most frequent visitor, usually trailed by one of his deputies and several of Jones's, all of them either talking into cell phones or touching Slates.

Harley wouldn't have believed it possible, given Bynum's expression when Keanu launched its Objects, but the White House man was even grimmer. "DOD is screaming. They want to shoot them down."

"—Because putting a nuke on *Venture* was such a brilliant move," Weldon said. Harley couldn't tell if the flight director really thought it was stupid—or futile. Or just didn't want to be distracted from the upcoming *Destiny* landing.

"Don't worry, Shane," he said. "Even if it was the best idea since the shitless dog, even if the president authorized them to shoot, they can't."

Bynum wasn't so sure. "They've taken out satellites. And we have all these missiles—"

"Our missiles are offensive weapons that can't be retargeted for exo-atmospheric intercepts, at least not in the next couple of hours. We do have some anti-ballistic missiles, about a dozen of them in Alaska and California. They were put there a decade ago when we were nervous about North Korean or Chinese birds. But even if the Objects came across the northern Pacific, where our ABMs might see and hit them, they don't carry nukes. And I don't think they're capable of locking onto a target that's plasma."

"I guess that's a relief," Bynum said, though his expression remained grim and pale. His phone buzzed again, and he left.

"I knew there was a reason I wanted you in here," Weldon told Harley, "rather than back with the freaks and geeks."

"I thought it was just because you didn't want to die alone."

Harley was impressed by the way Weldon and Kennedy and their teams never wavered from the immediate task before them: configuring *Destiny* for a crash landing on Keanu.

It helped that they had reestablished contact with Tea Nowinski, and with Taj, Lucas, and Natalia. All four were now on the surface, in suits; they had been forced to leave the rover on the ramp. Zack Stewart's situation was still unknown. There had been a brief burst of communication, but nothing since.

Just then Shane Weldon turned to Harley. "Mr. Drake, I think your kids need you."

"What's going on?"

Weldon tapped his headset. "Blaine says there's a problem. Get those people straightened out and out of here, then hurry back. I want you around when Bangalore gets it."

Leaving Rachel in mission control, Harley powered for the door. What now?

> I have been born more times than anybody except Krishna.
>
> MARK TWAIN, FROM HIS AUTOBIOGRAPHY

Zack Stewart felt the double shock moments after he reached the clearing surrounding the Temple. He almost missed the events; the interior environment inside Keanu had gone insane. He had the gusting roar of wind in his ears and the sight of Keanu plant life literally melting, dissolving, then re-forming all around him. It was like being in a carnival house of horrors.

And the air—it smelled like rotting vegetation mixed with burning plastic.

Combine that with the freakish "sky," which had darkened and was rent with odd flashes that reminded Zack of lightning, but minus the thunder.

The Temple loomed larger with each flash, however. It looked like a haunted house from a black-and-white horror movie, if you allowed for the fact that it was several stories tall and resembled no structure ever seen on Earth.

But that was his goal. That was where the Sentry trail led.

That was where Megan was. Camilla, too, though Zack wondered if he would have been as eager to abandon his crew and slim chance of a flight home just for the strange little girl.

Well, yes. But the issue was irrelevant, anyway. He was here, now, chasing both.

As he stumbled into the clearing, he remembered Taj and Tea's warnings about some kind of magnetic field . . . perhaps he was hypersensitive because of the alert, or possibly the field's intensity had increased with the wacky activities in the general environment, but Zack had gone only ten steps toward the Temple when he felt the hair on his neck tingling, lost feeling in his fingers, and generally slowed down. He stood in place as long as he could, feeling like a Van de Graaff generator in some junior high school science experiment.

One further step brought blinding pain. The Architects had erected an electronic fence around the Temple, and they were not going to allow Zack to use this route.

He backed away, then began to work his way around the perimeter of the clearing. He probed again—with the same result. Then a third time. No luck.

With the shifts in lighting, the wind, the unfamiliar lines of the Temple, it was easy to lose track. Where was the front door to this thing?

He calculated that he had been forced to a point completely opposite his entry. This time the "field" either compressed, or opened, to allow him to move forward.

In the shadows in front of him he could see what appeared to be a door, though twice as high and three times as wide as he would require.

When he was still fifty meters away, however, he noticed something unexpected on the ground, which was otherwise rutted and stubbly.

There were two mounds of steaming goo . . . as soon as Zack got close, he recognized them: they were what was left of two Sentries, likely the same ones that had scooped up Megan and Camilla.

It was as comforting to know that he was on the right track as it was disturbing to know that the Architects were still so casually destructive of their servants.

Would he find the masters of Keanu inside this structure?

Well, no matter what lay inside the Temple, Zack would have to confront it—the building was the only shelter he could see. And with the wind continuing to howl, debris filling the air, the temperature dropping, and worst of all, the air getting thin . . . he would require shelter, if nothing else.

Thirty meters, then twenty. Suddenly he was in the shadow of the building, face-to-face with a marker that sat in the center of what could only be a door. Its surface was no smoother than that of the rest of the Temple structure. It seemed to be an assembly of differently colored and textured substances, whether rock or metal or even wood, he couldn't tell. It was possible that it was more of a sculpture or carved surface. Maybe the shapes and heights of the pieces gave directions.

In any case, Zack searched for a handle and saw none. (Given the size of the thing, a handle would likely be out of his reach, anyway.)

So he began pressing on various parts of the door. He even tried to probe the obvious edges.

Nothing. He shouted "Hello!" and "Hey, I'm here!" and "Please open up!"

Still nothing. The door stayed locked.

He looked at Taj's Zeiss radio/camera. In frustration, he aimed it at the marker, adding, "This is Zack Stewart, for Bangalore or Houston, transmitting blind." *And deaf,* he wanted to add.

"If you hear me, you can likely see this . . . it's what we're calling the Temple of the Architects. My wife and one other revived person have been brought here. I'm searching for access. Unless I'm missing something very important, I'm locked out."

He counted to ten, heard nothing. Then, just to be sure, he counted to ten again. He added a third ten.

Still nothing. And his frustration finally reached a boil. He picked up the Zeiss, fully prepared to test its alternate use as a hammer. How long would it last when he slammed it against the marker—?

"Zack, this is Houston, Jasmine Trieu back at you. Do you copy?"

"Houston . . . Zack Stewart here. It's great to hear your voice, Jasmine!"

The lag might be only seven or eight seconds, but it felt much longer. Then he heard: "We've got a lot to catch up on, Zack. Can you talk?"

Zack looked up at the impervious Temple door. "Houston, I've got nothing but time."

Megan Doyle Stewart was not at all sure she approved of her newly re-born state. Yes, she'd been given a second chance at life, but why? What for? She had gone almost directly from car crash in Florida to the Beehive on Keanu.

Yes, something of "Megan Stewart" had existed for those two years in between . . . bodiless, blind, deaf, a state that would have terrified the living Megan, taking her buried-alive fear to a horrific extreme.

Yet she hadn't felt fear. Instead she had . . . well, soared, flown, skipped from memory to memory. She had become unstuck in time and space, recalling and reliving her first kiss with Sean Peerali and meeting Zack at that party in Berkeley and late nights editing and dragging her tricycle across Main Street. . . .

But whereas dreams were mixed-up, twisted replays of a day's activities, these moments seemed real, a record of what she had seen and heard and felt at the time.

She had even experienced "memories" from different points of view . . . other people in those same scenes. And in at least one instance—that she could recall now; it might have been a dozen or a hundred—she lived a moment from some other person's life altogether.

The more she thought about it, the more fascinating it was . . . right up to the inevitable instant when she realized that unless her luck changed radically, and soon, she was going to be right back in that . . . postlife environment, a matrix of memories, a file in some cloud computing system.

In any case, since reawakening, she had not had much time to dwell on the larger eschatological issues, being more concerned with adjusting to the environment, with functioning as an organic being again . . . and with the pain and joy of reconnection with Zack and Rachel.

Who were now, apparently, lost to her again.

No one had told her about the detonation atop Vesuvius Vent. She had actually *felt* it, as a noise combined with a flash combined with a sickening tremor.

Thankfully, it had lasted only a second or two. All of her senses had actually shut down, like filters on a camera turned to the Sun.

Still, it felt as though she had been thrown off the top of a building, only to be grabbed the instant she cleared the ledge, but not before seeing the twenty-story fall that awaited her.

She had been able to tell Zack that she knew, that the event was bad news. Or was it bad? It was . . . *important*. That was what the message from the Architects said.

It was like one of her early news reports, before marrying Zack, covering the collapse of a good chunk of the Antarctic ice shelf.

In some ways, it was bad . . . it was expected to raise global ocean levels by several feet, enough to ruin some coastal cities . . . but not instantly, not so quickly that people couldn't move out of harm's way.

And given that she was far inland in Colorado at the time, not of immediate concern to her.

Still . . . it was a Significant Event.

As soon as she had told Zack, however, something had happened to her . . . she had felt herself growing extremely fatigued, almost faint.

She knew that one of the Sentries had grabbed her; she had seen the creature approaching in her peripheral vision but had been powerless to run, scream, or do anything, in fact, but shut down.

(Which made her wonder just what other "improvements" the Architects had made in her resurrected body.)

She awoke in a heap inside the Temple—and alone. Camilla wasn't with her.

She was in a large room that was so big, shadowy, and empty that it gave her the creeps. It was like being in a monster's cave. The Evil Ogre's castle.

With no door or windows.

The floor looked like wood in that it had a grain or cellulose-style pattern. But it was too hard to be wood. There was a trail of some kind that led from Megan's resting place toward a wall, some kind of nasty spooge that had the apparent texture of a snail trail. Megan had not been able to force herself to touch it.

The ceiling was out of reach; it looked to be the same material, minus the patterning, but with squiggly shapes that let in light.

The walls looked like the exterior of the Temple, varicolored and oddly shaped bricks that, when touched, seemed about to crumble . . . but didn't. Megan could compare it to something from Zack's world: the thermal-protection tiles of the old space shuttle. Those silicate cubes were incredibly light and felt like plastic foam . . . yet were such perfect insulators that you could bake one to a thousand degrees in an oven, then pick it up with your bare fingers.

Maybe the Temple needed to be insulated. Megan remembered being jogged several times during her "ride," prior to being rolled onto this floor. And although the floor felt solid—like the sort of marble you found in Houston mansions—Megan's bare feet detected a low-frequency vibration, like the drone of a power line.

The room wasn't empty, either. It was stuffed with furniture. It would have been too much to ask, she guessed, for anything as simple as a table or chair. There were solid, symmetrical platforms at varying heights, but none lower than her eye level. Other objects were spherical, cylindrical, or, to use a word Rachel had loved, *blobular*.

Some were solid colors, though none Megan would have allowed in her home. Others had stripes or patterns. The surface of one particular cubelike object was different every time Megan looked at it.

And several of the objects transmitted the same hum that could be felt in the floor. It reminded Megan of mission control, with all its computers and screens . . . but it looked like a catalog photo for home decorators from Mars.

Oh yeah, there were no sanitary facilities . . . and of more immediate concern, no food or water.

She wondered about Camilla. She knew the girl had been taken . . . even if she was in an apparently benign environment like this, she must be terrified.

Thinking of Camilla reminded Megan of Rachel, and Zack. And the utter futility of her circumstances. She had heard the phrase *better off dead* most of her life . . . for the first time, she believed there might be something to it.

She leaned against one of the flat-surfaced objects and slid to the floor. Barefoot, largely naked, except for the surprisingly durable underlayer of the second skin, she could literally feel the vibrations of the wind against the Temple walls.

Which made her wonder just how durable this imposing-looking structure really was. How durable *could* it be? It had "grown up" in the past two days!

Then she felt something different . . . not a gentle wavelike motion that seemed to be caused by the storm outside. This was a deeper, more powerful vibration. A tremor.

It was coming closer, too. And more frequent.

One entire wall of the room slid open, revealing a dark chamber beyond. She heard more thumps, scrapes, and an awful chittering sound.

In spite of the darkness in the chamber, Megan could see the shadow of something huge and multi-armed.

Megan got to her feet. She knew there was no point in running—

—But she tried.

Before Harley opened the door to the Home Team, he heard what sounded like Britain's House of Commons in full roar. Then Blaine said, "We need you."

The immediate image did nothing to cheer him; the tableau reminded Harley of a bar fight paused in midpunch. Wade Williams and his little friend Glenn Creel were, in fact, nose-to-nose with Lily Valdez and some other person Harley couldn't place.

The heated argument Harley had heard through the door simply stopped. All parties looked at him like guilty schoolchildren when the teacher got back early. "Do you people realize we're about to try the craziest maneuver in the history of spaceflight?" Harley said.

"We do," Sasha Blaine said, indicating the big screen behind the potential pugilists. *Destiny* was now so close to Keanu that the NEO landscape filled the screen.

"Then please tell me what the hell is going on?"

Blaine smiled and blushed. "We think we've cracked the Architects' code."

"What do you mean?"

Wade Williams geared up for a sound bite. "It turns out those markers were transmitting and receiving information—"

"No, Wade, that's imprecise," Lily Valdez said. "We managed to isolate what we think are two reciprocal functions."

Williams looked at Creel for his usual support. "Isn't that what I just said?"

"Not quite," Sasha Blaine said. She turned to Harley. "All we've done is isolate what appears to be packets of information flowing to and from the markers. The Bangalore team was able to record a burst of both when Zack and Taj made their first approach. Logic and precedent suggest that the message could contain warnings or instructions about entering the Keanu interior—"

"Probably asking us to remove shoes and headgear," Creel said, largely for his own amusement.

"Truly, we know nothing!" Valdez was quite adamant.

"O ye of little imagination," Williams said, unwilling to concede the point. "We recorded the burst, and can reproduce it. That, young lady, is communication. If we ran across a Martian who took one of our messages and fed it back, we'd think we were on to something."

"We aren't the Architects," Harley snapped. "How the hell does this work?"

Blaine said, "It's just a weird frequency—"

"—Not entirely unlike *Brahma*'s terahertz radio," Williams said.

"Fine," Harley said, growing exasperated. "You're ready to simply feed their own signals back to them on command?"

Blaine polled the room visually. "Yes," she said.

"Any other thoughts on what would happen? Ranging on a scale of one to ten, one being nothing and ten being Keanu blows up?"

Valdez answered quickly: "Two, some kind of response, likely automated. We have to operate on the assumption that the Architects are at least as advanced as we are, and to return to Wade's Martian scenario, we would respond if our signal returned in a nonreflective manner."

"Good," Harley said, not knowing what value this would be. "If we decide to try it—"

"—Oh, you'll be trying it," Williams said.

But this time Harley wasn't ready to yield the floor. "There's a larger issue on the table." He told them the center was being evacuated, that only a limited crew would remain in mission control. "As far as NASA is concerned, you are putting your lives in danger by staying. And you are, in fact, free to leave now."

The Home Team room remained silent.

"What, and fight all that traffic?" Wade Williams had said. Several of the others laughed.

"Do you all feel this way?"

Lily Valdez said, "We may not play nicely all the time, Mr. Drake, but we're bright enough to know the situation. We're needed here."

Harley could have kissed her. Clearly he was getting softhearted. Well, if he was softhearted enough to allow Rachel Stewart to ride out the upcoming impact with him, he was in no position to try to dissuade these people from remaining . . . especially not when he needed them. "Fine. In the time we have left, why don't you tell me what those dang things are saying?"

He never learned. As he was turning to Sasha Blaine's Slate, the speaker relaying real-time air-to-ground communications with the astronauts on Keanu went live.

Capcom Jasmine Trieu was talking to Zack Stewart.

"We're only with you for a few minutes. Comm is through *Destiny*."

Zack found he was blinking back tears. *Steady,* he ordered himself. *Be strong. Look forward. Look at the task. Don't think about where you are and what you're losing.* "What happened?"

Trieu gave him the short version, ending with news that *Destiny* had survived the blast, though *Venture* and *Brahma* had not. That Tea and the others were on the surface awaiting a long-shot rescue. (Trieu didn't phrase it that way, but Zack made that determination.) "And what is your status?"

So he gave mission control his short version. "Bottom line, I'm stymied."

"Wait one," the capcom said. The persistent and by now infuriating lag made that statement unnecessary.

Then Harley Drake came on the line. "Yo, Zack . . . I'm patched in. Rachel is with me, by the way."

"Say hello for me."

"She's listening. But since time is short, we want to get you this idea: Home Team thinks the markers are not only antennae of some sort, scooping up data . . . but might also serve as locks for the doors."

"I kinda figured that out for myself. The locked part, anyway."

More lag time. Zack realized he was hungry and out of breath. Neither one was a good sign.

"We're going to feed you a signal that we want you to play into the nearest marker. Our hope is it will start the unlocking process."

For the first time in days, Zack got furious. "When did we start making decisions based on *hope*?"

Now the lag stretched. Zack was immediately sorry—the whole mission plan had vanished soon after the landing on Keanu. He was in a bad way, risking his life on an alien environment . . . but at least he had the advantage of making his own decisions and living with the direct consequences.

The team in mission control felt just as responsible but operated in the dark. It was certain to drive them crazy. "Hey, guys, belay that last remark," he said.

Naturally Harley talked over him. "—Ignoring that, because I know you'd want it that way. We all want the same thing, Zack, which, right now, is for you to get through that door. So stand by for this signal. We will play it, you will hear it just as you're hearing my voice . . . ideally the marker will pick it up."

"What does it say?" He owed himself that much information.

"It won't be *open sesame*, it will repeat what the original markers transmitted . . . with one significant change."

"I hope that change doesn't say, 'Shoot this guy.'"

He waited. Then he heard Harley say, "Well, my friend, that's a chance you'll just have to take. It will take about a minute to boot this up. In the meantime, let's talk about step two. You get out of the Temple and return to the surface."

Zack noted that Harley didn't mention *with Megan*. Or what the plan would be if the unlock signal failed. "Tell me straight, Harls: Do I really have a chance to make it to *Destiny*?"

Zack waited, knowing that no matter what Harley said, Zack's fate was controlled by the state of his EVA suit, still lying at the former campsite. Would it still hold pressure? Did he have enough oxygen in his tanks to get back to the surface?

"We don't have to worry about launch windows. Once we set *Destiny* down, we only need to get the crew off the surface. Obviously time is everyone's enemy here. Tea could drive the rover back to the floor of the vent and pick you up."

Zack knew immediately that that wouldn't happen. "Come on, Harls. An EVA by Tea and rover is going to take hours and put four lives further at risk." Optimistic projects were nice, but what he needed now was cold-eyed realism. "Have you talked to her about this?"

More lag. Then, "Not yet."

Zack wondered about that—he was afraid Tea was actually able to hear this conversation. But, since he was using a *Brahma* channel routed in some cockamamie way to Houston, maybe not.

"Okay, we're ready. The next voice you hear won't be a voice . . . we may go LOS right after this, but we will be listening and hoping. Hang in there, buddy."

Zack waited. Keanu itself was still vibrating . . . it reminded Zack of some gigantic beast shuddering in a troubled sleep.

Then the tones began. The sound was a mash-up, what might result from a mixture of whale song, old Internet dial-up, and clicks. It was eerie enough to make Zack feel more uncomfortable—quite a trick, given his circumstances.

He could only wait. And wonder what he would do if it failed. Give up? Try the damaged EVA suit? Say good-bye to any chance of seeing Megan or the others again?

He realized that at least three minutes had passed. No further word from Harley . . . no apparent unlocking signal.

"Hey, Harls . . . Zack transmitting in the clear for Rachel. If you're wondering why your father is doing what he's doing . . . it's because I've spent my life trying to find answers to big questions, like, 'What are those lights in the night sky?' It was why I became an astronomer and why I wanted to be an astronaut.

"So here I am, one of the first humans ever to see and experience life beyond Earth. I can't just walk away from it. The worst thing would be to try to come home now, and die on the way.

"And I really can't leave your mom.

"Just so you know, if the tones don't work . . . I'm going to break a window. If I can find a window."

Still no word from Houston. And no response from the Temple. It was if the last ten minutes had not happened. He was right back where he started.

In that case, before looking for this non-existent and, if existent, difficult-to-reach window . . . at least try the door.

He pushed. Well, that was in the lower part of the center. How about in the right corner?

Pushed again. Nothing. No sign of movement at all.

Then the opposite corner, another push.

Fuck it! Nothing!

He stood back, hands on hips, tears of rage brimming in his eyes.

And the goddamn bottom of the Temple door rose up like his father's garage—

"Bangalore is in the batter's box."

"Shouldn't that be the strike zone?"

"Don't get cute. We're next."

"How is my attitude going to change anything? If we all die, you can still go to heaven no matter what I do."

After loss of signal with Zack Stewart, Harley had returned to mission control, to hold Rachel's hand, if nothing else. (She had heard the air-to-ground exchange between Houston and her father. There had not been pictures.)

She had said, "Will you stop worrying about me?" Which only made Harley worry more.

But there was no additional word from Keanu . . . Tea, Taj, and the others on the surface were still waiting for *Destiny*.

Everyone went on hold because Bangalore was in the kill zone.

Someone had punched up a news feed—Sky TV out of England— that showed the flat landscape and multicolored structures of Bangalore's southern suburbs in the early light of dawn. "What time is it there?" Harley asked.

"Six A.M. tomorrow," Rachel said. She was making good use of her presence here, listening and learning. For whatever ultimate good that might do her.

"Have they said where mission control is?" Harley knew the Indian center was in the suburbs but had no idea how close it was to the camera, which seemed to be on a hill overlooking the city. The glass and silver towers of Bangalore's financial core lay in the foreground.

"It's where that dome is." Actually, there was a collection of radomes—plastic bubbles providing protection for radar dishes—on the lower left of the screen, what appeared to be some kilometers distant.

"Too bad they can't get closer," Harley said.

"I wouldn't," she said.

Half the screen still showed the interior of Bangalore mission control, with most of the consoles deserted. There was a cluster of operators, all in white shirts, around what Harley took to be the lead director's station.

A heavyset, white-haired man in glasses sat at that console, obviously speaking to someone, likely Taj and his surviving crew, perhaps.

"One minute," the TV news voice said. "Oh my!"

The sky brightened. The camera tilted up, revealing what looked to Harley like a needle of fire from the sky. Just a trail on your retina—

The shot from Bangalore mission control stopped.

The wider, distant image had bloomed white—brightness overwhelming its processor.

"Bangalore is dark," Travis Buell said, unnecessarily.

But then the hilltop image returned . . . to Harley's relief, it didn't show a molten crater a kilometer across, just a plume of smoke where the antenna farm—and Bangalore mission control—used to be.

"Is that a mushroom cloud?" a controller said, voice quavering.

"Yes, but not nuke-sized," Harley said. "Any release of heat and energy will create a cloud like that. Don't assume it's a nuke!"

"Which gets to my question," Weldon said. "What was that thing?" He turned to Harley. "A meteorite would have done a lot more damage, right?"

"Much more."

"So what's the deal? It's kind of important to all of us."

"Did you notice how long that terminal phase was?"

"What do you mean?"

"I think it was slowing."

"All I saw was a streak of light," Weldon said, waving a hand and offering those nearby a chance to contradict him. "It looked just like a warhead reentering over Kwaj." Weldon had done a tour on Kwajalein Atoll as an Army officer, pre-NASA. It was where American nuclear missiles were aimed during tests.

"I've seen those, too," Harley said. "And this was different."

"Maybe it really was plasma," Josh Kennedy suggested.

"Then it isn't much of a weapon of mass destruction," Harley said, pointing to the screen. "It looks like the control center is gone, but not much else." Several windows in the screen were showing other news channels, each with its slightly different title. *"Tragedy in Bangalore!" "Strike from Space?"*

"Tell that to the *Brahma* team," Kennedy said.

"Well, hell, Josh . . . we can tell it to ourselves. How far out?"

"Fifteen minutes," Buell said. He was starting to annoy Harley.

"We made our choice," Weldon said. He patted Jasmine Trieu and Travis Buell on the shoulders and talked to the comm team behind them. "Make sure you keep checking their frequencies. Taj and his folks need us now."

"And we need divine help," Kennedy said.

Sasha Blaine entered mission control, bringing the entire Home Team with her. "This will be cozy," Harley said.

"He told us to come." Blaine nodded toward Shane Weldon.

"I was kidding," Harley told her. "I'm glad you're here."

Weldon was saying, "It puts a few more walls between you and whatever happens outside."

Williams, Creel, Matulka, and Valdez had at least been confined to the visitors' area. (Harley wondered if that shiny glass would be transformed into knifelike shards in the next few minutes.) Rachel was standing with Harley and Sasha. "Maybe we should all hold hands," the girl said.

Blaine was quick to comply, and she made sure Harley couldn't escape her grasp.

But Harley remained engaged in the operational aspects. He couldn't help it; he didn't do emotion and sentiment. "What's on the networks?" He knew they had covered the Bangalore strike . . . they had surely heard that Houston was next up.

"On screen," Weldon said. Four different images showed Houston from a variety of angles. There was a shot from an office tower downtown, two from news helicopters (one of them north of the Johnson Space Center), and one from a traffic airplane flying east along I-10.

"Wouldn't you know it?" Travis Buell said, clearly exasperated. "A cloudy day." The images were indeed obscured by low clouds. The aircraft shot bobbled as its pilot fought through choppy air.

"You want it sunny when you die, Travis?" Weldon snapped, triggering a wave of hysterical laughter.

Buell didn't care for the comment. "I just want to see what's going on!"

"What's going on," Harley said, "is that a blob from space is about to whack us. Anything beyond that is just guesswork."

The young astronaut didn't care for that response, either. He pushed back, disconnected his headset, and, elbowing his way past another controller, walked out.

"One minute to projected impact," Jasmine Trieu said.

"You can spare us the countdown, thank you, Jazz," Shane Weldon told her.

"There it is!" Rachel's voice.

The fixed camera in downtown Houston had tilted up—there was a bright sphere just like the one that had destroyed Bangalore mission control, falling fast. Weirdly, it was headed away from the camera . . . which was downtown.

But toward JSC.

Harley felt Sasha Blaine's grip tightening. He reached for Rachel's hand, looked into her eyes. "Here we go."

The plasma blob flashed through the other screens, then vanished.

Nothing happened.

Then the whole building shuddered, as if belted with some giant hammer. But only once, and for a fraction of a second. The lights dimmed and the screens flickered. But they, too, stayed on.

After a moment, someone said, "Is that all you got?" But there was no laughter.

Harley looked at Sasha and Rachel. Both of them were wide-eyed, hopeful. Then everyone looked at the television images on the big screen.

Allowing for unsteady mounting—the cameras seemed to be getting buffeted by some kind of shock wave or wind—all showed images much like Bangalore: a small mushroom cloud rising above a landscape.

Weldon was shouting. "Does anybody know where, exactly, that thing hit?"

Kennedy had an answer. "KTRK is saying NASA Parkway in Seabrook."

"Can we do better?"

He could. "Look at the KHOU feed." On the screen a Google Map of the JSC area showed a big fat X to the east of the center itself.

"Did they miss?" Rachel asked, giggling.

"No," Sasha Blaine said. "They hit the target dead-on."

Weldon was not a shouter, especially not at people who didn't work for him. Today was an exception. "What the hell are you talking about?"

Blaine swallowed, like an actress thrust onstage in an unfamiliar play. "Bangalore took a direct hit and was destroyed. Its relay antennae were on its roof.

"Houston's plasma bomb hit two miles east, at the corner of this facility. Where your antennae are."

There was silence in mission control. Finally one of the communications operators said, "She's right. That impact was directly on the antenna farm. We're in backup mode."

As the other controllers resumed breathing, and working, Harley turned to Sasha Blaine. "You're pretty smart for a girl."

Sasha Blaine kissed him. "I'm just happy we're still alive!"

Even as Harley pondered the insanity of a personal relationship with Sasha Blaine, especially one conducted in Rachel's presence, Weldon was once again on task. "Okay, everyone, we have obvious comm problems. Let's find a workaround. We need to be able to talk to *Destiny*."

Then he turned to Harley and Sasha. "If they weren't trying to destroy us, what the hell was the point?"

Sasha shrugged. Weldon had accepted her completely, a rare honor for someone who had not trained "the MOD way." "Maybe just to show they could."

"Well, then, are we supposed to surrender now?"

Harley ceased to listen. He had his eyes on the big screen.

So did Rachel Stewart. "Harley, what's that?"

One television camera showed a close-up image of the shattered Bangalore mission control center . . . the smoke had cleared and showed what appeared to be the plasma blob from Keanu still intact.

And rotating.

Gabriel Jones and Brent Bynum entered, along with their retinue. "Are you watching this?" Bynum asked.

Jones had regained his equilibrium. Once again, Harley was impressed by the way NASA people allowed sheer professional curiosity to trump personal tragedy. The speculations came quickly. Maybe it was a sample return craft, like one of NASA's Mars probes. Someone asked, "What if it gets bigger?" Another man wondered if the Object in India was burrowing deeper—

Shane Weldon was shaking his head. "It would disappear, wouldn't it? If it were trying to burrow into the Earth?"

"And why would it do that?" Harley couldn't help asking questions, either, though he directed his at Rachel and Sasha.

Sasha was looking at the screens and the news footage. None of the four feeds showed anything but a vapor cloud over the Houston impact site. "Do you suppose our Object is rotating, too?"

"I wish you guys would take this discussion somewhere else," Josh Kennedy said. "We've got a spacecraft to land."

Entering the Temple was like entering a cathedral, something Zack had done at Chartres, during his one and only trip to Europe. This alien structure had similarities, at least by Zack's frazzled standards. For example, here was a nave, a smaller, narrower room that led to the chamber containing the altar. Or was that the transept? For one of the few times in his life, Zack told himself he really should have paid more attention to medieval architecture.

Stick to your training. Concentrate on what you can see, hear, feel, identify.

The floor was made of the same material as the doors and walls. As he walked, slowly but directly, into the nave or transept, Zack realized that sounds were deadened.

It was dark, but not like the total darkness of an underground cave. It was more like the let-your-eyes-adjust near-darkness of a warehouse. Somewhere some light was present . . . and not just behind him, where the door remained open.

He looked at the Zeiss unit. It was a camera . . . Holding the instrument two inches off the ground, he flicked it on. Yes! *And there was light!*

Another advantage. He could not only sneak up on the Architects, he could blind them.

Things were just getting better and better. All he had to do was find Megan, and her captors.

Assuming they were captors. *So, Zack, don't assume—*

He was at the threshold of the main chamber. He glanced back . . . the giant door was now about the size of his hand held at arm's length. A long way to run. But what was the point in running? He had only one choice—

Forward. Into the larger chamber. *This is exploration, right?* Going where no one has gone before? Hell, most space exploration would have to be via remote vehicles, given lack of oxygen (like Mars), or extreme surface pressure (like Venus) or too freaking hot (Venus again) or too much gravity (Jupiter and beyond). And those were just the solar planets . . . five thousand extrasolars, some of which he had discovered himself, only expanded the envelope of deadly environments.

He could have been doing this like some tele-operator in a sci-fi movie. Which at least had the advantage of being somewhat safer—

The immediate difference was the air. It was cooler, blowing somehow.

And smelled . . . just like the Beehive. Zack put out his left hand, found the wall.

It *felt* like the Beehive. Moist to the touch.

Zack wiped his hand on his undergarment—which would, he realized, never be remotely clean again.

Then he pressed the front of the Zeiss to his thigh and clicked it on.

He aimed at the wall . . . well, no surprise; it looked like part of the Beehive, but with what appeared to be several large cells as opposed to many small ones.

These were large enough to have held Sentries. Was it possible he had just walked into their incubator? Not the smartest move he could have made.

But it was difficult to tell. He didn't want to wave the light—*yeah, don't give up that element of surprise*—so he could not get true perspective.

He clicked off the light and turned back to the chamber proper. Zack's spider sense told him it used up about a third of the Temple's interior.

Well, there was no sense in waiting. *Sometimes you just have to go off the high board or jump out of the airplane.*

If only he could feel more like a diver and less like a soldier approaching Omaha Beach on D-Day. . . .

Vulnerable and blind, he stepped farther into the main chamber. He had ruined whatever night vision he had by flashing the Zeiss lamp.

Nevertheless, he knew there was something in front of him, something quite large.

He could smell it—some kind of scent, almost floral, but thick and, with each careful step, more intense.

Now he *heard* it, too. Over the increasingly draggy scrape of his own soles on the floor, there was a deep, slow hiss that sounded like a whale breathing. There was also a chittering sound from up near the ceiling.

As if the whale had a hummingbird flying around its head.

Stop anthropomorphizing. Deal with what's really here.

Because it was here. If it was possible to see something blacker than pitch black, that was what Zack was doing: a large *thing* sat no more than five meters in front of him.

What the hell. He raised the camera. Thumbed the light switch.

The first image he registered was of ceiling and walls, which for an instant seemed to be teeming with maggots. As Zack's eyes adjusted, he realized that he was seeing swirling dots and squiggles in no recognizable pattern.

What immediately consumed his attention, however, was a creature close to ten meters tall sitting—this was exactly the word—on a bench or chair. It had a head and four arms, but only a pair of legs. The face was too high up, too much in shadow, for Zack to count eyes or noses.

Assuming it had eyes or a nose.

Was it covered in armor? Or a space suit? Possibly. Maybe it was just . . . clothing. Zack always wondered why most sci-fi aliens went naked. . . .

He had to assume this was an Architect.

And, if it noticed Zack at all, it was being patient—or totally indifferent.

Zack had no time for that. "Down here!" He waved the light, expecting the next few seconds to be his last, wondering, foolishly, if he would be resurrected on Keanu.

Fucking hell if the big creature didn't turn right toward him, rotating its upper torso and face—which was either some kind of shiny, almost waxy and ill-defined collection of planes and reflections . . . or a mask.

A pressure suit mask? No, the Architect was wearing the same kind of second skin that had covered Megan and Camilla!

It was a Revenant, too!

Revenant or not, the Architect moved with frightening speed. Things this big did not, in Zack's experience, move that fast. Which suggested a hellacious physical structure, including extremely fast-twitch musculature.

Just the one swift move, however. Then the Architect held all four arms close to its chest. The posture, for no good reason, reminded Zack of an Asian bow . . . the kind of gesture one might see performed by a solicitous waiter or shopkeeper.

As if the Architect wanted to know, *What do you want?*

The human race's chance for a well-managed First Contact had been missed when Zack and crew encountered the first Sentry. It was too late to trot out the classic "We come in peace." (Zack was no longer sure why humans had come to Keanu. To beat other humans, maybe.) Now he had to be practical, forceful. To hell with nuance—

"Give me back my wife!"

This is *Destiny* mission control. The uncrewed *Destiny* orbiter is currently at thirty-eight kilometers altitude, still on the far side of Keanu. Mission manager Shane Weldon and lead flight director Josh Kennedy have confirmed that, given the sporadic contact with astronauts Nowinski and Stewart and the corresponding lack of contact with the *Venture* lander, they will attempt to "snowplow" *Destiny* onto the surface of Keanu. . . .   NASA PUBLIC AFFAIRS COMMENTATOR SCOTT SHAWLER

The digital clock in mission control showed twenty minutes until burn. Harley heard confirmation that uploads had been completed, that every antenna but one had been retracted—and that the big circular solar arrays were going to be rotated sideways. (Seen nose-on in its nominal configuration, *Destiny* looked like a hat from the Mickey Mouse Club.) "They'll be edge-on to line of impact during the snowplow," Shane Weldon had said, briefing not only Gabriel Jones and Brent Bynum, but Harley as well. "That will minimize damage, we hope."

"What if we lose both arrays?" Jones asked. Harley knew that *Destiny* depended on Houston for guidance updates in the best of times, in a mission that followed a flight plan. This situation was far more challenging.

"Then the crew is going to have to get off Keanu in a huge hurry. They only have a couple of days' battery power if they can't use the arrays."

Bynum made a face. "What the hell is a 'snowplow'?"

"That's pretty much what *Destiny* will be doing." Weldon said, unsuccessfully keeping contempt out of his voice. "Sounds better than *crashland*, don't you think?"

Harley agreed, but talk of the landing made him ask about the equally tricky business of taking off from Keanu. Weldon turned to Josh Kennedy for this answer: "The gravity is so low that once we fire the main engine, *Destiny* will just pop off the surface. It should be clear of any surrounding terrain in a few seconds."

"Sounds like you've thought it through."

"I sure as fuck hope so," Kennedy said, startling Harley with the uncharacteristic profanity.

Neither Kennedy nor Weldon needed any distractions, so Harley backed away. He knew his presence in mission control was not vital—except to him. He lived for the real-time tension of a critical event, whether it was launch or docking or touchdown . . . and in this case, the first-ever attempted "snowplow" of a vehicle that was never designed for it. This controlled adrenaline rush was what he remembered about flying jets. Mission control was the one place he could experience that rush again, if only for a few moments. . . .

But he no longer belonged here. He had been put in charge of a back room—a vital, unique resource. And whether or not he had been the ideal choice to lead it, it was his job.

As was keeping an eye on Rachel Stewart, who had been slumped in a chair in the visitors' gallery. Gabriel Jones had found her. Harley was afraid that could prove to be awkward for the girl, a suspicion confirmed when he entered the gallery and heard: "—Remember that daddies are human, too. We'll be selfish, we'll be distant, we'll be off chasing some dream of our own, but it doesn't mean we don't remember our daughters, that we don't love them—"

Eyes closed and face wet with tears, the man was kneeling next to Rachel, holding her hand. Rachel's eyes were wide and her face sent Harley a clear message: *Rescue me!*

"Gabriel," Harley said, as gently as he could. "Bynum says he has a question for you." This was an outright lie, but a useful one.

Sniffing, forcing a smile, Jones rose, patting Rachel on the shoulder. "Take care, young lady. And know that we are doing everything we can to get your daddy home safely."

The moment the door closed behind Jones, Rachel turned to Harley. "God, that was creepy."

"He just lost his daughter." Harley knew that Gabriel Jones had lost his daughter years ago. "You're not a middle-aged man or colleague. He could be . . . weak and emotional with you."

"And that's supposed to make me feel better?"

"It wasn't for you."

Sasha Blaine and the other members of the Home Team were as wilted as Rachel Stewart—or, for that matter, as Harley. As he wheeled his powered chair down the corridor to his domain, passing two of the other backroom groups, both with doors open, both deathly silent and populated by exhausted people, Harley realized he was hitting his own redline. He needed a whole list of things, from a bath to a decent meal, but number one was rest.

Maybe once *Destiny* was safely down and Tea and the other survivors got aboard . . .

First, of course, *Destiny* had to land. Snowplow. Slide into home.

Then? Zack Stewart. The moment Harley entered the room, Sasha turned to ask him, "When will we be able to use *Destiny* to link with Zack?"

"Not until that thing's safely on the surface," Harley said. "And maybe not even then." *Destiny* likely made a better relay satellite in orbit. On the ground its systems would be trying to punch or receive signals through denser rock and soil.

For that matter, it might not have antennae at all. It could go deaf, dumb, and blind. And the same would apply to poor Zack.

Well, Harley thought, *let's burn that bridge when we come to it.*

On the Home Team screen, the feed from one of *Destiny*'s forward onboard cameras now showed a clearly defined image of a snowy, rocky landscape, with actual mountains or, at the very least, high hills dead ahead. "It's like flying," Sasha Blaine said.

"Too low," Harley said. "If I could feel my feet, I'd be pulling them up." Like most people who heard one of his little jokes about his infirmities, Blaine pretended she hadn't heard it.

Nevertheless, *Destiny* was low. Jasmine Trieu was saying, "Altitude fifty meters, down at ten . . . ten seconds to snowplow."

Harley realized that because of lag, *Destiny* had already made it—or smashed into the surface.

Suddenly the picture went blank. "Oh shit," one of the Home Teamers said.

Wade Williams spoke up. "Do they have telemetry?"

Harley had been thinking the same thing, concentrating on the figures on the bottom and side of the screen showing altitude, rate of descent, and a dozen other factors. The screen flickered—a momentary loss of communication, or a sign that *Destiny* had ripped open as it spread itself across the landscape of Keanu?

But then figures returned to the screen. Altitude and descent showed zero. Other figures seemed nominal; at least none of them was red.

"They made it," Sasha Blaine said.

"Houston, this is Tea!" The astronaut's voice was barely recognizable through the crackling and hissing in the speakers, but her joy was impossible to hide. "We saw it all, baby! Perfect landing about half a kilometer east! I think you lost one of the solars, but the other one is still intact! We're heading there now!"

Harley was seeing imagery from some camera on *Destiny*, a view of the surface of Keanu, but tilted ninety degrees.

The denizens of the Home Team room remained silent . . . possibly uncertain of the protocol, more likely just exhausted beyond belief.

"Feel free to applaud," Harley said. He rolled to the door and opened it. Distant cries of "Woo-hoo!" could be heard. For the first time in two days, Harley Drake felt that Tea, Taj, Natalia, and Lucas had a chance to make it home.

There was going to be life after Keanu.

For some of them, anyway.

Rachel Stewart watched the successful *Destiny* snowplow with vague interest that bordered on resentment. It was great that Tea Nowinski and the others had a way home. But what about her father? Where was he? What was mission control going to do for him?

And no one was talking about her mother anymore.

Besides, there was something else going on that struck her as more interesting.

The main viewing screen in the center had shown the *Destiny* landing, and now switched between several semiuseless views of either tilted landscape or blackness. Rachel could see the camera team at work at its console. Everyone was desperate to actually see Tea and the others on approach.

Okay. But on the smaller screen, four different news feeds were visible, and no one but Rachel was paying attention.

Too bad. Because Mr. Weldon and Mr. Kennedy and even Dr. Jones and that Bynum guy would have seen that the Bangalore Object was not only rotating, but actually sucking up whatever happened to be around it.

The Houston Object was still hidden, partly from the debris cloud . . . but also by the Gulf Coast's gift to summer, a tropical downpour.

Nevertheless, the shots of various talking heads—all of them with their eyes wide, all waving their arms—told Rachel that something freaky was happening.

For a moment she regretted burying her Slate in her mother's grave. But only for a moment.

She decided she wanted to see and hear better. So she slipped out of the gallery and brazenly walked onto the floor of mission control, taking up an empty seat at one of the forward consoles on the right side, where she had an unobstructed view of the news feed.

She was a fourteen-year-old girl. Her simple presence in mission control was an anomaly . . . but because she'd been hanging around for the better part of two days, she had grown transparent. None of the remaining men—and the one woman—noticed her at all.

Weldon did tune in to the news out of Bangalore. "Anybody have any idea what in God's name is going on there?"

Capcom Travis Buell, who, after losing connection with Bangalore, had become the designated TV watcher in the center, said, "They're calling the Bangalore site some kind of sinkhole."

Weldon, Jones, and the others surrounded Buell at that point, so Rachel couldn't hear what they were saying. But it was clear they were agitated: Bynum kept pointing toward one of the walls, with Weldon more gently indicating another corner.

They were talking about the Houston Object.

The TV news heads were still going on about Bangalore. "—as if it's collecting material," one of them was saying. "No one has been able to get close enough to say for sure, but the rotation is creating some kind of vortex, for want of a better word. It looks though soil, grass, debris, air . . . it's all being sucked into it."

A second head—the anchor, Rachel remembered—took that very badly. "If it's sucking up material, what's to stop it from sucking up, say, a whole chunk of India?"

"Well, unless it's a chunk of super-dense matter—"

"—Or a baby black hole—" a third head said.

"—Which we've never seen—"

"—Any more than we've ever seen a hunk of super-dense matter—"

The anchor lost it. "People, come on! This isn't a lunchroom debate at Caltech!"

The first, more reasoned head then said, "Unless it's some exotic matter, it can't absorb or 'suck up' more than a few tons or dozen tons. It doesn't appear to be some kind of, I don't know, doomsday weapon."

The second head couldn't resist: "Come on, David, we don't know what the hell this is."

It wasn't anything specific anyone on TV said. Maybe it was a combination of four images hitting her eyeballs combined with fatigue and those cryptic words from her mother. But Rachel Stewart suddenly knew that she had to get out of mission control.

She slid off her chair and, still invisible, left mission control.

She wasn't entirely sure she could walk to the impact site. She was a bit fuzzy about its actual distance from mission control, but she knew it couldn't be more than a couple of kilometers. She had walked distances as great as a single click in her life, on occasion, when forced. So how hard could it be to do two? Even in the suffocating heat of a late-afternoon thunderstorm?

"Don't be like this."

She turned and saw that Harley Drake, wheelchair and all, had followed her back to the Home Team. "Like what? Independent?"

"Just stop arguing." Harley was red-faced and in a bad mood. Fine. Rachel knew he wouldn't really yell at her. Her own father didn't do that. Mom, well, yes. This was all about Mom.

And maybe there was a better way to get Harley to give permission. "Don't you want to see what's going on out there?" She turned to Sasha Blaine, who was a few feet away, concentrating on her Slate and quietly trying to pretend she could not hear everything. "Sasha, how about you?"

Blaine looked at Harley before answering—as if asking permission to speak. "Frankly, I'm dying to go out there."

"What if it's radioactive?" Harley said, though he didn't sound convincing.

"The local fire and police will have the place surrounded, anyway, won't they?" Blaine said. "If it's dangerous, we won't get close."

"You're putting a lot of faith in some overworked men and women in a very unusual situation."

Blaine indicated her Slate screen. "There are people all over the Bangalore Object. They haven't started vomiting or losing their hair." Rachel couldn't see much . . . the feed was from a phone, and Blaine's screen was small. Nevertheless, it showed dozens of men in white shirts—the uniform of Bangalore, from what Rachel knew—moving debris with their bare hands.

What was most surprising was that the slowly rotating whitish dome of the Object was literally a few feet from them.

Harley looked around the Home Team, whose members had broken into their normal pairs and triplets, conferring, arguing, talking on phones.

Then he faced Rachel and Sasha. "Fine, whatever you want. I need air, anyway."

The rain had let up for a few moments, though dark clouds to the south and east promised a new downpour. "We'll take my rig," Harley said, with no argument from Sasha or Rachel.

"Good. My rental is a kilometer away." And Harley's van was in one of the handicapped spots right outside mission control.

As Rachel walked around the van to the other side, Harley advised Sasha Blaine, "Watch out for my junk."

"Big talker."

Rachel was only beginning to contemplate the meaning of that exchange—good God, were they flirting?—when another group emerged from mission control: Shane Weldon and Brent Bynum, together with three of Jones's horse-holders.

"Where are you sneaking off to?" Harley asked them.

"One guess," Weldon said.

"Don't you have a vehicle to launch?"

Weldon tapped his earpiece. "Josh and the Orbit Two team are totally on top of things. They don't need me looking over their shoulders."

"Who are you, and what have you done with Shane Weldon?"

Bynum snickered. "Seriously," Weldon said. "I'm off duty for two hours."

"So why aren't you collapsed on a couch somewhere?"

Weldon smiled. "Why aren't you?"

Harley was attaching his seat belt. Weldon and his crew still hadn't reached their cars. "Race you," Harley said, in best astronaut tradition.

There was no chance for a contest. There was barely any forward progress once Harley's van left the JSC grounds and joined a polite and steady-but-slow flow of vehicles north on Saturn Lane. Blaine said, "Where are they all going?"

"The staging area for evacuation is the Harris County Courthouse. It's a few kilometers west of here."

"They're still evacuating?" Rachel said.

"Inertia, maybe," Harley said. "It might also be wise because, ladies, we're in completely uncharted territory here. We have no idea what this Object is for, or what it might do."

"I have an idea," Blaine said. "It's spinning and churning up soil, right?"

"Soil, air, pavement, and pieces of buildings, yeah."

"I mean, think about what Keanu really is." She waited. Rachel certainly had no ideas. "A space probe, right? Just like *Mariner* or *Viking*. These Architects sent it here to take images and readings of Earth and the entire solar system. Well, now that they know there's life here, they're sampling."

"So these plasma balls are just some kind of advanced soil scoop. Don't they have dirt and water on Keanu?"

"Maybe not enough, or not the right kind."

Harley made a right turn onto Bay Area, a major street that paralleled the north boundary of JSC, then intersected Space Center Boulevard.

That thoroughfare snaked around to the south and east . . . directly toward the impact site. The traffic here was all one way, the other way.

Harley smiled. "It might be better to perform a flanking maneuver here." He drove right through the intersection of Space Center and Bay Area—a smart choice. Rachel could see that there was a roadblock a hundred yards south. No cars were getting through.

As Harley continued east on Bay Area, into the wooded lowlands flanking Armand Bayou, he glanced at Sasha Blaine. "Riddle me this: If our advanced civilization really just wanted to make a survey of this solar system, or a hundred solar systems, why would it send something as freaking large as Keanu?"

"Maybe it needs to be that large to survive a ten-thousand-year trip."

"Or maybe it isn't a space probe, and those Objects aren't sample-returners."

Sasha Blaine gave up the argument.

Just after crossing the bayou, as the traffic dwindled to nothing, Harley made a sharp right onto Red Bluff, and soon after, another right into Taylor Lake Village, a crumbling development from the 1960s.

"You do know where you're going," Rachel said.

"Used to have a girlfriend who lived here. She was married. Had to perform a few emergency evasive escapes."

Rachel had endured twenty minutes of being slammed around the backseat. Never a happy passenger, she was getting sick to her stomach. And impatient. "God, will you hurry?"

"What's the rush, Rach?" Harley said. "I don't think the Object is going anywhere."

"I just want to see it!"

Sasha Blaine turned around from the front seat. "You've had to listen to the two of us nattering. What do you think it is?"

It wasn't a question of trying to keep her feelings secret . . . it was more that Rachel didn't understand her own compulsion until Sasha asked her. "I don't know what it is," she said. "All I know is that my mother told me not to be scared."

The *Destiny* had come to rest safely—"No apparent leaks or holes, Houston"—but with one immediate problem. "The fucking hatch is underneath." Always a bit of a potty mouth, the tomboy's legacy, Tea Nowinski had developed strict air-to-ground discipline in her previous flights.

But the sight of *Destiny*, relatively unscathed except for the loss of one of its solar panels, with one edge of the hatch visible about three feet off the ground, overwhelmed her already-challenged verbal governor. "Any ideas?"

The lag seemed to stretch on, but Taj was ready to fill it. "Remember where we are, Tea."

He slipped past her, hopping close to the *Destiny*, which even on its side was twice his height. Tea found Taj's tone infuriatingly cheerful "I haven't forgotten," she said, about to add, *you fucking idiot*, when she realized what the vyomanaut meant. "Oh. Right."

Destiny had only a fraction of its ten-ton weight here. "Tea, Houston. We see your situation with, ah, hatch access. And we are recommending—"

"—That we simply roll it, copy, Houston." *Tea, you are the fucking idiot.* "Stand by for magic."

"Before you do," Houston said, "give us five. We want to vent atmosphere."

Of course: for uncrewed orbit operations, *Destiny* was pressurized to ten pounds per square inch, slightly less than it would be with a crew aboard. With all that pressure on one side, a hatch would literally blow open, possibly damaging its hinges.

Tea and Taj retreated fifty meters, to where Natalia and Lucas waited. "Thar she blows," Tea said, as a sudden gout of vapor erupted from *Destiny*'s base. Within a few minutes, it was gone. *Destiny*'s interior pressure was now almost a vacuum.

It took the four of them, two positioned on the side of the gumdrop-shaped *Destiny*, two on the canlike service module. The challenge wasn't moving the mass—which rocked slightly to the touch—it was traction. "We've got to dig in," Taj said.

"I wish I had my football cleats," Lucas said. Tea was happy to hear the World's Greatest Astronaut speak; he had fallen completely silent over the past hour, a sure sign of exhaustion and depression.

Natalia, who had also been sullen and silent, hopped to work, digging footholds for all. (She had been clever enough to bring tools from rover *Buzz*.)

"*Uno, dos, tres*," Lucas said . . . and the giant, bus-sized vehicle rolled twenty degrees, just enough to uncover the hatch.

"Goddamn, it worked!" she said. "Great idea, Taj!"

"Thank Zack," Taj said.

Tea dropped to her knees, looking for the handle as she tried to orient herself. When *Destiny* was upright, its main hatch opened to the left . . . with the spacecraft on its side, the hatch would open toward her, like a ramp. Which would be good.

Entry was simply a matter of finding the access handle—which was on the top of the hatch, from her perspective, and almost out of reach. "Houston, Tea, I'm ready to open 'er up."

She waited. Then Jasmine Trieu said, "Pressure is effectively zero. You're go for open."

The rectangular hatch, wide enough that Tea could not touch the ends if she stretched out her arms, opened easily. Tea climbed up on it, then stepped into the interior.

And almost fainted.

God, had it only been forty hours since separation? It felt as though she were visiting for the first time! There was the confusing inversion of local vertical and local horizontal—she entered the spacecraft along one of its sloping walls. The main control panel, and two unstowed couches, were directly over her head. She should have been used to that, of course; her last look at the interior had been as she dove headfirst through the hatch in its pointy nose.

Right now she was standing on a cabinet door that had not been designed—as parts of *Destiny*'s "floor" were—for stepping. Fortunately, with Keanu's gravity, Tea's fears were less about breaking or stepping through the cabinet than tracking alien ice and mud into the "house."

Taking slow breaths, she focused on the cabin lights and on key features: the stowed couches, the personal gear held in place by webbing along another part of the wall.

Better. She turned back to the hatch, where Taj waited. Natalia and Lucas were right behind him.

"All right, everybody. Last chance. Hot food, showers, massage. Well, none of that, exactly. But I'll think you'll enjoy the accommodations."

"*Destiny*, Houston for Tea. We need you to take a look at Panel Delta."

Tea reacted without thinking, closing up the flight data file and dropping it in the next seat. Panel Delta was where data on *Destiny*'s environmental systems was displayed.

It was only an hour after she and her colleagues—survivors of the human race's less-than-nominal First Contact mission—had sealed themselves inside *Destiny*. Taj and Natalia were now awkwardly camped out on the sloping "floor" next to four rigid and empty pressure suits; Lucas was wedged atop the two stowed couches.

And Tea was in T-shirt and shorts, perched above them at the command operator's position.

The moment she had been able to close the door and restore pressure,

Tea had not only removed her worn-out EVA suit, but had also stripped off her fantastically nasty undergarment. She then cleaned herself with a wad of wet wipes and shrugged into a flight suit, telling the others, "Be my guest."

Taj had objected. "What if there's a loss of pressure?"

"Then I'll die comfortable," she said. "Besides . . . your suits have different hose fittings. You can't recharge from these tanks. You might as well clean up and change clothes, too."

To spare the others the awkwardness of donning coveralls last worn by dead comrades, Tea had opened a cabinet and pulled out spare garments intended to be worn the last day of the mission. She hoped this was the last day of the mission.

Pogo's size XL hung loosely on Lucas, and Tea's spare didn't fit tiny Natalia much better. Zack's fit Taj as though tailored . . . which caused Tea to think about her absent friend and commander. As the others laid waste to the stored food and water, Tea radioed a quiet query to Houston about word from Zack and was only told, "Last contact was two hours ago. Nothing since then. Nothing expected."

Now Houston had her checking environmental systems. She quickly learned why. "Houston, I'm seeing a pressure drop . . . barely over seven hundred millibars, and I think it's gone down a point since I've looked." She was too tired to do the math, or to wait for Trieu to confirm those figures. "How long before we're sucking vac?"

"It's still on the order of hours, possibly a day or two," Trieu told her. "But it means we have to get you off the surface ASAP."

Taj had heard this, and so had Lucas and Natalia. The vyomanaut was already climbing into the seat next to Tea. "How much time?"

Houston answered for Tea. "You will be going LOS in the next ninety minutes. We want you off the ground before then."

"No more than we do," she had told them.

Just then, strangely, the spacecraft rolled. It was worse than one simple motion . . . it actually seemed to yaw a bit, too, causing Tea's already-sensitive stomach to protest. "Okay, anyone, what the hell was that?"

Natalia said, "I thought this was solid ground!"

The nearest window to Tea showed nothing but black sky overhead. "Taj, take a look—"

The vyomanaut already had his nose up to the square window in the hatch. "There's a lot of vapor outside!"

Lucas pulled himself up to the couch next to Tea. "Are we venting?"

Tea didn't think so—at least, no more than before the movement—and a quick glance at all the panels confirmed it. "No indicators. Haven't heard anything."

Taj was getting agitated. "I think Vesuvius is active again—"

That was all Tea needed to hear. She clicked her radio. "Houston, *Destiny* . . . Let's get to that departure checklist!"

To Zack, it seemed as though the Architect considered his request to release Megan.

Then it moved again, its portside appendages swiftly lashing out, touching the interior walls to Zack's right. A third of the way up, just above the height of Zack's head, a panel opened up—

And a body slid out.

Zack moved reflexively . . . and a good thing, too: it was a writhing, scratching, loudly protesting human female.

Megan.

They both collapsed. Fortunately, Keanu's gravity ensured that they wouldn't be hurt.

It took a moment before Megan realized who had caught her. "Oh my God," was all she said.

Zack had never heard anyone so relieved. "Are you hurt?"

"I don't think so."

They regarded each other. "I keep hoping I'm eventually going to figure this out," Zack said.

"Me, too."

Zack turned to the Architect, who, after releasing Megan from a hole in the wall, had resumed exploration of other cabinets higher up in the chamber, using two or three of its appendages at the same time. "Any ideas?" Zack shouted.

"I think he can hear you."

"And you would know."

"Yes." She seemed to be regaining strength. "Both of us know."

"Listen, darling . . . I'm just about out of time and energy. I haven't slept in three days, I have barely eaten . . . I've seen stuff I wouldn't have thought possible. And I've given up my ride home. So there's a clock on me. I don't know whether it will be days or hours, but if you and the Architect have anything to share, please do it now."

Megan knelt and slipped her arms around him, cradling his head the way she'd held Rachel as a child. "Ssshh," she said, almost cooing. "I know. I do know. You were . . . incredibly brave to come here."

"You're the brave one—"

"Hardly. I was in an accident, then these guys brought me back. I didn't choose any of it. But I would have, to see all this."

"Yeah. I wish I felt luckier."

She hushed him, just like Megan of old. "How many people ever get the chance to . . . change the history of the world? Or a couple of hundred worlds?"

"Yeah, well, my team hasn't done a very good job so far." He glanced up at the busy Architect. "I'd like to tell our . . . host here that that bomb was a major mistake."

Megan leaned her head close to his again. "I think you just did."

"You think, or you know?"

Megan looked at the Architect herself. The giant being looked back. "I know. I mean, I figured my new body had some improvements."

"You know things you shouldn't."

"Even more as time goes by. It's like I'm being prompted. I can't just offer things up. But hear the right question—bam! Here's an answer."

Zack turned her face back toward him. He put his hand on her cheek . . . their first truly intimate touch, so familiar. "Who are they? What do they want? Just building or outfitting a ship like this would take the resources of an entire civilization!"

She took a breath, then closed her eyes and said: "Okay, trying my best: life is hard to find in the universe. Intelligent life is . . . incredibly rare. We've found more dead civilizations than living ones, and we haven't found many of those."

"You said *we*."

"Yes, *we*. I'm Megan. But I'm beginning to share some of their consciousness, too. This vessel . . . he's really old, on the order of ten thousand years. And our solar system isn't its first stop. There have been a dozen others."

"Does it really have the ability to reengineer its environment to suit whatever creatures it encounters?"

A pause. "Yes."

"For some of these other races, like the Sentries?"

"Other candidates, we call them." She blinked, as if listening.

Zack was about to seize on the term *candidates*—for what? But he had a more vital question. "And this vessel can magically access specific 'souls' of the dead of . . . any race?"

"Yes. Don't think of it as magic. It's technology humans don't possess. We know how consciousness and personality connect to bodies."

"But you found a handful of souls out of millions!"

"It was accessing data stored in . . . the closest I can come is *morphogenetic fields*. The universe is filled with it . . . with bioelectric data, all kinds of data. Information."

"Like the akashic records from the Vedas, the 'library' of all experiences and memories of human minds through their physical lifetimes."

"They're not using those terms."

"Neither am I, really. They were Taj's."

"And I keep thinking of Jung. I guess we all reach for the words and concepts we already know." She smiled. "This is like trying to explain the Internet to Benjamin Franklin. You know electricity, but you're a long way from computers and networks."

Zack looked up at the Architect, who seemed almost indifferent to his presence. "I feel like I'm standing outside the biggest library in the world, only it's closed."

"I'm doing my best."

"Oh, God, honey, it's not about you. It's just . . . look at this!" He gestured at the Temple interior. "Okay, why did your friends send this vessel?"

"We've found a . . . presence, a challenge, another entity, and it's been a threat to us. We came here looking for help. We think you might fill that role."

"Against another race?"

"Another type of being, the Reivers."

"The what? Sounds Irish."

"I'm sure it's Irish, Scots, Gaelic, whatever. It's the word in my head, and it means *bad guys*. It's not just that they're enemies, they are enemies bent on exterminating us, and all memory of us. We can't coexist."

Zack took her by the shoulders. "But, still, it's thousands of years in the past, hundreds of light-years from here, right? Does that threat still exist?"

"Yes. The Reivers don't live on the same time scale humans do. They'll be a threat for a million years."

"In that case, I don't know how much help we can offer. We could barely make the trip from Earth to here! When we did, it took us a day and a half to try to blow you up. We're rude, crude, and pretty damn stupid!"

"We've become too unattached, too machinelike. We can't be rude or crude, though we can still be stupid. But you're alive, and we're not."

Zack pointed to the busy Architect. "He looks alive to me."

"He's alive the same way I am." She paused. "But he's not the actual Architect. . . . Sorry, this is all mixed together in my brain." Megan actually took several steps. It was another habit that Zack found heartbreaking in its familiarity . . . he had always joked that his wife was the Sundance Kid, the legendary gunslinger who could hit anything as long as he was in motion. Megan thought better when she moved. "The race of Architects is old. If you think of humans as belonging to the past million years, try a hundred times as long.

"We don't have bodies anymore. The same technology that allows us to identify and copy souls in these circumstances means we can move a consciousness from one machine to another, or when necessary, to a . . .

a reconstruction like this." And here she gave a girlish bow. "It gives us immortality. But it costs us our ability to fight, to think creatively. To care about failure. To suffer."

"So he's a Revenant, too." Zack stepped back and looked up at the busy Architect. "What is he doing?"

"Setting switches."

"What the hell does that mean?"

"I don't know. That's one of your phrases, isn't it? 'Setting switches'?"

"Now you're channeling me?"

"I lived with you for eighteen years . . . I don't need to channel you."

"It means configuring a cockpit. It's what we did on *Destiny*."

"I know."

"So this building is a cockpit?"

"I think we both know it's not really a Temple." She thought for a moment. "How about, a command module?"

"Commanding what? Oh," Zack said, seeing the answer to his own question. "Keanu."

"Yeah. There are a lot of systems here. I told you there were other chambers. Some of them are bigger."

"What's in them? Uh, samples of these other races?"

"No one is saying." She pointed at the Architect. "But whatever he's doing, it's related."

Zack reached out, taking Megan's hand. He wasn't sure when he had leaped from reasonable skepticism to wholehearted acceptance that this was Megan . . . but he had. "You know what's funny about this?"

"Not a lot that I can see, darling."

"Megan, your entire life—you were the one who asked everybody all the tough questions. If you'd actually interviewed this guy, we'd have learned this stuff hours ago."

At that moment, the giant alien stopped what it was doing. It rose to its feet with a grace Zack found surprising. At full height, it towered over the humans, but only for a moment. "Now he's doing something else," Zack said, taking Megan by the arm and pulling her back toward the opening. "Is he leaving?"

The Architect was already halfway across the chamber, headed for what Zack would call the back wall. "Yes," Megan said. "We're not the most important thing he has to deal with."

"What could be more important than dealing with two members of this vital human race? Aren't we the key to his future survival?"

"The race is important. The two of us, not so much."

"And after all we've given up. Does he know we can't go home?"

"Oh, he knows."

The back wall opened, revealing the unchanged chaos outside the Temple. "We should follow," Megan said.

"Back out there? It looks dangerous."

"Yes."

But she wasn't waiting for him. She slipped out of his grasp and began following the Architect. Zack caught up with her in a few steps, as they found themselves once again outside in the near-darkness and buffeting winds.

To Zack's horror, the Architect seemed to stagger. The creature's staggering steps were just like those of the Sentry, before it collapsed.

"Is he all right?"

"No. Come on. We're running out of time."

My friends, all I can tell you is this: the wondrous rumors circulating about events on Earth's new moon portend Great Things. Signs are being fulfilled even as we meet here tonight. The Rapture itself could be at hand. Let us pray.

THE REVEREND DICKIE BOTTOMLEY, GREATER KANSAS CITY ALL-SOULS CHURCH, AUGUST 24, 2019

"This is as far as we go in auto mode," Harley said.

"Not a moment too soon," Sasha Blaine said. Rachel agreed. They had left the dirt road and been bumping across muddy grass for the past few minutes. The only thing that kept Rachel from throwing up was their lack of speed.

Harley had stopped the van on the shore of Clear Lake Park, which nosed into Lake Pasadena, the brackish pool of water just south of Armand Bayou. Half a dozen fire and rescue trucks flashed rain-spattered lights from NASA Road One a hundred meters to the south, and to their left. "I think we're inside the zone," Sasha said.

Their view toward the Johnson Space Center was blocked by the glowing plasma dome of the Object, doing its slow churn a few hundred meters away, just across the lake. It reminded Harley of the New Orleans Superdome, only illuminated from within—and filled with strange squiggly and angular shapes that seemed to be crawling across its surface.

Or on its inside, trying to come out?

"You did it," Rachel said. "You got us here."

"Don't thank me yet."

Rachel and Sasha helped Harley out of the van, a process complicated by the astronaut's insistence that he didn't need help. "Maybe not getting out," Sasha said, "but you're not going to get far in the rain and mud without us, so just put a sock in it."

The moment the wheels of Harley's chair began to sink into the soggy grass, the complaints stopped. Fortunately, today's rain hadn't completely transformed the soil into muck, though in this part of Houston it wasn't much of a transformation. Once they disengaged the power, allowing the chair's wheels to turn freely, Sasha and Rachel were able to push Harley forward, toward the road.

They kept to the trees, partly to avoid being seen from the road, partly for shelter from the steady drumming rain.

The slow flashes of light from the Object reminded Rachel of the time she and Amy and several other friends had sneaked into the Harris County Fair. The lights of the midway and the swooping, whirling, rotating rides had blinded them—they'd failed to see a security guard and gotten caught, escaping punishment only by becoming unusually giggly and flirtatious.

"Does it bother anyone," Harley said, "that the Object seems to have some kind of beacon?"

Sasha considered it. "It's not very beaconlike, though, is it?"

True enough; as Rachel and Harley watched with Sasha, the lighthouse-like light seemed to pulse in an irregular pattern . . . flash, dark, flash flash, dark. "I hope it's not a searchlight," Harley said.

"With a heat ray behind it," Sasha said.

"Stop it!" Rachel said.

"Sorry," Harley said. "Sometimes we forget . . . Anyway, we're here, as close as we can get. Now what?"

The rain had let up, though there was a strong breeze blowing in from the ship channel. "I want to go closer," Rachel said. She had already decided that the Object was not a weapon—or it would have gone off already. It was sitting there as if waiting. . . .

"Assuming that that's a good idea," Sasha Blaine said, "and I don't think it is . . . how? It's across this lake!"

Rachel pointed. "We can go across the bridge. All the cops and every-body are down the road."

"Granted," Harley said. "But then what? We're here . . . we've had as close a look as anyone else. You are not going to touch it."

"I don't know what I'm going to do, okay? But I think we should be closer. I think it's supposed to give us something or tell us something."

"It's a sophisticated piece of alien hardware! Why doesn't it just send us a signal?"

"I'm going to find out," Rachel said. "You can come along or wait here."

She broke from them and sprinted toward the causeway. But in the dark, the mud and gravel defeated her. She lost her footing trying to climb up to the road, slipped, and slid back to the bottom.

As she was getting to her feet—and Harley and Sasha approached, furious with her—a new light fell on the trio. "Hey, you people—freeze!"

Rachel thought she was going to pass out. Then five men walked forward, and one of them turned out to be Shane Weldon.

"We followed you," Bynum told Harley. Weldon, Bynum, and their pas-sengers all helped lift Harley up to the causeway.

"Not very closely."

"We had to stop to pick up some instruments," Weldon said. He pointed to one of his team, a young man with a boxlike object slung over his shoulder.

"Is that an actual Geiger counter?" Sasha Blaine said.

"Yeah. The best we could do on short notice," Weldon said. "We got that, a camera"—he raised a Nikon still camera like those astronauts used on missions—"and a spectrometer." Another of the party was struggling with a box twice the size of the Geiger counter. "That baby was built for lunar surface ops about ten years ago. I'm not sure it even works."

"Gotta love NASA planning."

"Don't worry," Weldon said. "I've got a real team putting together a set of instruments that will be able to tell what this thing had for breakfast this morning." He nodded toward the Object, which now loomed over them like a dome-shaped building.

"Speaking of breakfast," Sasha Blaine said. "What was the latest on the material this thing seemed to be ingesting? It appears to be sucking up water, mud, and even some vegetation."

"There might be some small absorption, right, Brent?" Weldon said, looking at the sodden, sullen White House man. "But nothing major. We don't feel as though Earth is about to be sucked into some kind of mini–black hole—"

"—At least, not this particular moment," Bynum said.

"Can we just go?" Rachel said. The entire party was now on the causeway, but they had not moved forward. Rachel was happy not to have been arrested, and grateful for the helping hands . . . but she felt she had to get to the Object as soon as possible. Or she'd lose her nerve.

Harley took Rachel's hand. "Okay, we're going—"

"No." Brent Bynum stepped in front of them, a pistol in his hand. "This is a hostile entity. None of us should be this close. I authorized it so we could gather data."

"Brent—" Weldon stepped forward.

"Stop right there!" Bynum screamed. To Harley the White House man looked unhinged. He could hardly blame him. "I'm . . . responsible!"

"No," Harley said. "I'm responsible. You and Shane told me. You had me sign the documents. I'm the official in charge of alien encounters. And I say we go." Bynum was wavering, unsure.

"Look," Harley said, "as far as the White House is concerned, I'm still in charge—and I'll be blamed." He held out his hand. "And take a step back, Brent. We've been reacting, not acting." Harley pointed to the Object looming in the near-distance. "Would that thing be here if we hadn't set off a goddamn bomb on Keanu? Give me the weapon. I don't want anyone to get hurt."

Bynum seemed happy to be rid of it.

As Harley dropped the piece into his lap and placed his hands on his wheels, he couldn't help noting that he was shaking.

And that everyone was immediately trying to forget what just happened.

Within moments, the party had carefully advanced across the bridge,
with Sasha Blaine looking over the railing for signs of Object-related
sucking. "So far, so good."

"Look," Harley said. Off to their right, on the other side of the lagoon,
still well north of the Object, half a dozen lights bobbed in the darkness.
"I hope they're on our side."

"This might just be the most dangerous fucking thing I've ever done,"
Weldon said.

"I certainly hope so," Harley said, to general laughter.

Let's review the bidding. There might be intelligent life on Keanu, which is no longer a NEO but likely a starship . . . at least one astronaut is dead, two others are missing . . . and both JSC and Bangalore have lost contact with the landing craft. And now two "objects" have slammed into the Earth's surface.

Am I missing anything? Has the entire universe gone insane?

POSTER JERMAINE AT NEOMISSION.COM

You're actually missing quite a lot. Stand by. POSTER JSC GUY, SAME SITE

"Two minutes, we're go for pop-up. Enabling RCS two and four. Go for main at plus two ten."

Tea Nowinski was strapped into the left-hand couch of the *Destiny*, with Taj to her right. Behind them—and, once *Destiny* translated to a nose-up, tail-down orientation, below them—Natalia and Lucas were simply stretched out on a "bed" of netting that held the discarded EVA suits. It was not the most comfortable situation, but the g-forces associated with a launch from Keanu's gravity field would be minimal. "About like a fast elevator," Jasmine Trieu told her. Tea didn't even need the straps at her seat. But she wanted them; they were a physical reminder that her vehicle was about to change locations.

"We show six-eighty on cabin pressure," Tea reported, knowing Houston could see the same figure, but just to remind the team of that looming problem. She could not get a handle on the leak. Pressure wasn't dropping in some straight line, suggesting some blockage somewhere. *Destiny*'s environmental system was pumping air into the cabin to compensate. That couldn't go on forever, of course. They had to get off Keanu, and back to Earth.

"RCS is go, main engine is go," Houston radioed, after the lag, which Tea now judged to be the most irritating thing she had ever experienced in her life. The reaction control system was a series of four small quads of rockets positioned equidistantly around *Destiny*'s service module. They were usually fired when *Destiny* needed to reorient itself.

Today, in this most unusual operation, they would actually lift the spacecraft off the increasingly unstable surface of Keanu. "We'd like to have clearance from the ground before we light the main," Josh Kennedy had told her.

"If you like it, we like it," Tea had responded. She saw the logic; even though the thrust of *Destiny*'s main engine would quickly lift the vehicle off the surface, there was no real way of predicting just how soon . . . it might scrape the ground for fifty or two hundred meters before getting airborne, certainly causing more damage.

"One minute."

"I hope we don't get any more movements," Taj said.

"No negative thoughts, okay?" Tea told him.

There had been concern about whether the RCS quads had come through the snowplow intact, or through that shocking movement caused by either melting snow or some other external factor. Quad number one faced downward at the moment, buried in Keanu snow. JSC's data showed that it was still intact—no fuel leaking, at any rate—but no one could know whether the small nozzles had been bent, and if so, how they would perform.

Fortunately, the pop-up burn didn't require quad number one, but rather numbers two and four.

"It will be nice to see home again," Natalia said, trying to correct for Taj's gloom.

"For some of us," Lucas said.

"Thirty seconds," Tea said, knowing she sounded snappish, not to mention a couple of seconds ahead of the actual count. She couldn't help it. Ever since buttoning *Destiny*'s hatch, all she could think about was the horrifying truth that she was abandoning Zack. A colleague. A good man. A man she loved.

It didn't matter that he'd ordered her to do it. Who cared that she really had no choice? He was going to die, and for the rest of her life she would know it was her fault.

"Fifteen." She brushed tears out of her eyes, then put her hand on the controller.

It didn't seem to take long at all. Twin *whumps!* sounded in the cabin and Tea felt herself being lifted and, more annoyingly, flung forward. "We're up, Houston!" She thumbed the pickle switch on the controller, activating it and firing a burst from a smaller reaction rocket on *Destiny*'s nose . . . Houston had warned her that *Destiny* might go a few degrees nose-down when the RCS—aft of the combined vehicle's center of gravity—ignited.

It had, and Tea's immediate action seemed to correct it.

Destiny's main engine lit at that moment, delivering a substantial bang and jolt. The RCS shut down at that point. And they were off.

Tea had a window, but all it showed was the black of Keanu's sky. She looked instead at the instruments, especially the altimeter, which showed them already at fifty meters . . . seventy-five . . . "How high were those mountains?" she asked.

"Now who's the pessimist?" Taj said. He was craning to see out one of the other windows.

Before the burn reached its one-minute point, Tea knew they were clear. Not necessarily safe . . . there were still several tricky maneuvers to perform to put *Destiny* back on an Earth-return trajectory, at which point the concern would be the small matter of guiding the giant gumdrop command module through the searing, deadly plasma of reentry.

And, oh yes, before the air ran out.

But they were off Keanu. Away from whatever the hell was going on down there. Away from the vaporized bodies of lost comrades—and of two spacecraft.

Away from Zack and his reborn wife.

It had to be.

At three minutes plus, the main engine shut down. Tea radioed the news, then waited for Houston to tell them: "*Destiny*, copy shutdown. Pleased to inform you, you are now in orbit around planet Earth. You are free to maneuver to attitude."

Tea grabbed the controller again and fired a small tweak. She wanted to see where Keanu was. . . .

Not far, as it turned out. The altimeter showed *Destiny* at fifteen thousand meters and climbing rapidly. That was high enough to show the NEO as a crescent.

"Got your camera, Taj?" Tea said. She thumbed the radio switch. "Houston, are you seeing this?"

She didn't know how to describe it. Keanu's surface appeared to be melting . . . giant ripples swept across the surface, like waves on a lake . . . Entire sections of the ice were breaking up, like chunks of Antarctica during the Big Melt. There were small eruptions, too, shooting geysers into the sky . . . likely with debris.

Something was happening down there, and it wasn't the kind of thing you wanted to be close to.

"And, Houston, we would welcome, uh, separation data."

Tea's message overlapped with Jasmine Trieu's answer to the first, about the imagery. "What does it look like to you, *Destiny*?"

"I think the place is coming apart!"

Part Five
"FOR THE DEAD ARE FREE"

We are such stuff as dreams are made on
And our little lives are rounded with a sleep.

WILLIAM SHAKESPEARE, *THE TEMPEST*

Following the Architect was like chasing Frankenstein's monster through a blizzard . . . Megan clung to Zack's hand as they both ducked flying debris and tried to keep the giant creature in sight.

It wasn't easy. The light was low, the equivalent of the moments before sunset. The wind was strong and gusting and would have forced them to shield their eyes even absent clouds of tiny particles.

"I hope Camilla's safe," Zack said. "When was the last time you saw her?"

"She was scooped up the same time I was," Megan said. "I assume she was taken to the Temple, but I just don't know. I keep feeling we should stay and search for her."

"Me, too," Zack said, "but finding her won't solve the immediate problem. Might just make things worse for all of us."

The Architect led Zack and Megan out of the Temple and across the by-now-familiar scorched cornfield, then took a sharp turn into what seemed to be a huge ovoid tunnel. The Big Smart Alien, as Zack dubbed him, was no longer staggering—perhaps he'd found his legs again after centuries or millennia in storage.

"Any idea where this leads?" Zack shouted to Megan.

"Another chamber." Megan spoke without waiting for that instant prompt from the Architect, though once she spoke, she realized the chamber was called the Factory. For building what?

That answer, if it came, was lost in a stumble.

She had been having a tough time keeping up with Zack. Yes, the terrain was rugged. Yes, she was exhausted. But the third stumble was convincing. . . .

Her legs were failing. Worse than that, her eyes were, too. It was as if—horrible thought—she were aging several years every few minutes.

She was too weak to frame the question . . . too busy clinging to Zack as they entered the passage to the Factory chamber.

The airflow here was compressed—it was literally a wind tunnel. "The wind is in our face," Zack said. "Which means pressure behind us is less than where we're going."

"Is that bad?"

"I don't see a lot of good in it, no."

"We could stop."

"What's the point? There's no food, no water, no answers back there. Only with your friend Gargantua up there."

Making matters slightly worse, the surface was rugged, not just ridged and uneven, but rough and even sharp in places. Megan was barefoot. Zack was in his stocking feet. They were going so slowly now that they were losing ground. "We can't take much of this . . . it's like walking on coral," he said.

Distracted by the struggle to simply remain upright, and conscious, she didn't reply. "Are you still in touch with him?"

She forced herself to say, "Ask me something."

"Well, not that I can do anything about it, but just for science: How the hell is the human race supposed to help the Architects in their war? Half of those who came here are dead . . . The rest have gone home."

"Others may join you."

"Others? Here? How?"

"The, uh, transfer device is already active," she said. "I'm sorry, but that's the phrase in my head." She stopped and turned to him. "Okay, they'll bring humans here. Then they'll carry them back to their world."

"Won't that take thousands of years?"

"Yes."

"We don't live that long."

She thumped him on the chest. "No. It's your descendants."

"I don't like the idea of condemning fellow humans to a life sentence aboard Keanu."

"They will have the opportunity to affect the future of intelligent life in the galaxy for the next hundred thousand years. Isn't that worth some sacrifice?"

"Are these people volunteering, or being drafted?"

"I don't know. I'm . . . I'm sorry." Her head slumped. "I really don't feel good."

He slid his arms around her and held her close. She was trembling. "Look, maybe I can get a message to Houston . . ."

"I think you left your radio behind."

"I'm an idiot."

"I don't think it matters." Either Zack misunderstood—and how could he understand something that Megan herself was not ready to face?—or he was focusing on the practical. He turned her so they could resume forward motion, however slowly. "What happens if I say no to this big recruitment the Architects are making?"

"You've already said yes."

"How?"

"By your actions." She could see the answers now, though she took no real joy in the discovery. "The decision is made."

"It's not fair."

"The universe isn't fair," she said. "Zack, I'm dying again."

Zack freaked out. "No, no, no!" he shouted, holding her as if his touch could save her. "You're just worn down. Let's rest."

"I know what's happening to me!" she said. "This body wasn't meant to last! It was only temporary, to give you someone to . . . talk to." She was already mourning for her own lost life, for the experiences she would never have, for the faces she would no longer see, voices she would no longer hear, touches she would never feel.

For no more Zack. For Rachel never again.

Now she knew loss.

And the part of her that was linked to the Architect could only scream, *Why? Why now?*

But there was no answer.

Moments later, they emerged from the tunnel into a chamber that dwarfed the previous one. . . . But whereas the human-friendly environment looked, at its most stable, like a terrestrial jungle, this looked like a circuit board . . . or an urban cityscape, all silvery towers and boxes mixed with coils, vents, bridges. There were broad passages between some of the structures. Others were packed as tightly as Manhattan brownstones.

And much of it was still taking shape, being assembled before their eyes.

"What is this place?"

"The Factory," Megan said, barely able to speak.

"What does it build?"

"Environments. Life-forms. Supplies. Everything."

"Well," Zack said, "at least it will be easier to walk." He indicated the ground, which had now formed itself into flat, bricklike shapes much like those in the tunnel between Vesuvius Vent and the membrane.

"And the environment is still human-friendly." Zack had half-expected to start gasping the moment he and Megan cleared the tunnel. "What about those people the Architects need?"

Megan swayed. Zack caught her. "I'm sorry, all I'm doing is asking questions that can wait. You need food. We need shelter . . ." He trailed off. "Did you hear something?"

Megan stood up, alert. "Yes."

It was a human voice screaming in terror . . . the voice of a child! "That was Camilla!" Zack said.

The Architect was due south of them—if north could be defined as the tunnel mouth—and busy with his own tasks. The sound came from their right. "Stay here," he told Megan, and began edging along the rocky wall.

"No, thank you," Megan said. "I'm coming, too."

"No signs of radiation, at least." Shane Weldon looked up from the Geiger counter. "But I wish we had some other ways of looking at this thing."

"Do we even know what we're looking at?" Harley said.

By the time they had crossed Lake Pasadena, Harley, Rachel, Sasha, and the mission control group had been joined by dozens of other people, all approaching the big bright dome of the Object from different directions . . . including one trio in a rowboat.

Harley said, "I just wish I knew where all these folks were coming from."

"I think they were the same ones outside the center," Rachel said. "The ones in the RVs."

"I think you've just got a lot of the JSC community here," Weldon said. "People who live along the lake."

"I didn't realize so many of them were nuts."

"Only in a good way," Weldon said. "There are lots of places in the U.S. where you'll find people who are fascinated with spaceflight . . . but right here you've got a group that is not only curious, but involved. Naturally they'd be compelled to see something like this."

What they were seeing now was a whitish sphere perhaps fifty meters in diameter, embedded in the ground and slowly rotating . . . dirt, debris, and even water seemed to be bubbling up around it. Visibility was still limited; the only light at the site came from the Object itself, and from the flashing red lights of emergency vehicles a hundred meters away.

"Well," Harley said. "Look away. I am not going any closer."

Not that that was an immediate option. The Object had impacted north and west of the NASA Parkway bridge over Lake Pasadena. JSC's antenna farm had indeed been obliterated, but the damage was far less than Harley expected. "We should be seeing a crater here, don't you think?" He addressed the question to Sasha Blaine.

"Yes. It's almost as if it landed."

"That's exactly what it did!" a familiar voice proclaimed. Emerging from their left, having apparently walked from JSC, came another group led by Wade Williams. "What the hell . . . it came from a spacecraft. Logic says it's another vehicle of some kind."

Williams was clearly winded by the walk. He leaned on a tree as others from the Home Team caught up. "Gee, Harley," Shane Weldon said. "If I'd known your whole crew was coming, I would've chartered a bus."

"They're free agents, Shane. They can go wherever they want."

Williams heard the exchange and stepped in front of Weldon. "You asked us to give you advice on alien activities and objects. Isn't this where we're supposed to be?"

Weldon never passed up a challenge to his authority. "It's where one of you might be useful. Suppose this thing blows up? Then where are we?"

"I don't know about you, Mr. Weldon, but I suspect I'll be dead." That drew laughs from the Home Team group, even those who weren't members of Williams's claque. "And I suspect I could turn this argument back on you: You're the mission manager. You've got a whole bunch of very important mission control types here. If this thing goes tits up, the program will suffer, will it not?"

"Hey, everybody," Harley said, annoyed that, once again, his job was to be referee. "Why don't we see whatever we can see . . . then go back where it's safe?" There was no sign that his suggestion was acceptable, but there were no further exchanges, either.

Helped by Creed and Matulka, Williams began to make his way down the slope toward the Object.

Weldon turned back to his team. Brent Bynum was busy with his

BlackBerry, of course. Harley wondered what the White House thought about the Object. Or what they were telling everyone. It wasn't likely to be the truth.

"This is real-time, folks. Do we follow them? What's our plan? Deferral is not an option."

"If the Object were a weapon, we'd be dead by now," Sasha said.

"Likely," Weldon said. "But if not a weapon, then what?"

"Uncrewed space probe," Harley said. "Or crewed."

That caused Weldon to react. "What do you mean?"

"Maybe one of them is aboard," Harley said. "Or more than one of them." He hadn't really considered the possibility until this moment . . . but suddenly it seemed logical. The Object was far larger than any reasonable space probe. So maybe it was a lander . . . an "Earth Excursion Module" for Keanu's inhabitants.

"Maybe this is the *message* my mother told me about," Rachel said.

"I think Rachel's right," Sasha said, taking the girl's hand.

Harley looked at the two women, one thirty-two, one fourteen, and wondered how they had come to be friends in such a short time. He could never manage that. He had had a lot of girlfriends, but no real female friends.

No matter; however this situation played out, it was clear he was going to have to learn the art of friendship—with Sasha Blaine, maybe—and parenting, with Rachel. The only thing he knew about kids was that he had once been one.

He wondered, briefly, what it might be like to be married to Sasha . . . but why was he thinking about personal stuff when he was two hundred meters from an alien spacecraft?

He was tired. He was overstimulated. And he was stuck in this fucking chair.

"Hey, Shane, hold on a moment." It was Brent Bynum, looking more harried than Harley had ever seen him, emerging from the shadows with his Slate.

Weldon turned away from his colleagues, glancing directly at Harley, as if to say, *Now what?*

But once he'd glanced at the device, he brought it directly to Harley. "This is trouble," he said. "Bangalore."

Harley saw a fuzzy image of the other Object, in full daylight, suddenly expanding to two or three times its size. Text on the image said, "20 MINS AGO THEN IT LEFT."

"It left?" Harley said. "Assuming that's correct, where did it go?"

"No idea," Weldon said. "But I think this means we should go—"

Then it was if the whole world suddenly groaned. "What was that?" Sasha said.

The strange sound lasted perhaps three seconds. It was gone now. "It came from the Object," Harley said.

The Object had stopped spinning.

Rachel said, "Why is it doing that?"

"Doing what?" Weldon said.

Rachel ran to Harley. "It's growing."

Harley could see it for himself. The fuzzy white dome and its strange internal components lost definition, becoming almost transparent . . . reminding Harley of what clouds looked like when you punched through them in an F-35. . . .

Then something passed through them all, an electric shock combined with a flash of light. Everyone around him cried out.

And began to rise.

Harley Drake knew the feeling: it was just like being in zero g. Only now he was inside a huge sphere along with several dozen, possibly a couple of hundred, human beings, trees, blocks of earth, birds, and at least one dog.

As he tumbled, separated from his chair, from Sasha, from Rachel, he could see Houston, and soon all of Texas, falling away below them.

I have broken agency rules and risked my job by posting here under a screen name, but to hell with it: this situation is beyond the control of any agency or nation. We are in a game-changer, folks. And there's no point in hiding. My name is Scott Shawler, and I am JSC Guy.

POSTED AT NEOMISSION.COM, AUGUST 24, 2019

There was a dirt perimeter around the growing "Factory zone" that reminded Zack of the warning track in a baseball stadium. It was smooth enough to show footprints . . . human, barefoot, child-sized.

"I think we've found her," Megan said. Her voice was weak and wheezing, not good at all.

"Someone else has, too." Zack pointed to another set of tracks, long slashes alternating with splash marks that ran parallel to the footprints, and eventually on top of Camilla's, obliterating them.

"Got to be a Sentry," Zack said. "Do you see or hear that thing?"

Megan was scanning their surroundings, too. "No."

"God, where is she?"

"You aren't going to call for her, are you?"

"With one of those killing machines out here? Hell, no!" Zack squinted at the structures. The low light and unusual features made it tough to see. "I just hope she's hiding. . . ."

Out of the welter of tracks that showed Konstantin's final struggle, he noted the beginnings of another trail. "There." Camilla's tracks led directly into the Factory.

Taking Megan by the hand, Zack began to follow them. If he'd had any energy—if he'd thought Megan could keep up—he would have started to run. "If you can offer any insight into why this thing is on the loose, now would be the time to share."

"They aren't machines. They're intelligent beings."

"Then what did we do to deserve their hostility?"

"They're no longer responding to commands, that's all I know."

Zack listened again. The dominant sound was the steady wind. Far off Zack could hear some kind of pounding, like piles being driven, and a low-cycle buzzing.

But no little girl. "I guess we should keep moving," he said. Megan made no protest as he tugged her into one of the broad but still shadowed passageways. "Could you ask your Architect friend why he isn't helping us?"

"Don't assume he's benevolent, or on your side. Or even cares."

"I've got to say, none of this would encourage me to ask a couple of thousand humans to sign up for a one-way voyage."

"I think he's got troubles of his own. Remember . . . the Architect is a resurrectee, too."

"And all you resurrectees stick up for each other." Wait! Farther into the Factory . . . not just a scream, but actual words. In Portuguese?

"I heard her, too," Megan said.

Tired and hobbled, both of them nevertheless started running. They soon discovered that their passageway ended in a shimmering wall that looked as though it were being assembled by the omnipresent Keanu molecular machines. They backtracked, found a connecting passage, and took it.

"So now we're rats in a maze," Zack said.

Camilla shouted again.

"She's closer. . . ."

"It sounds as though she's right next door," Megan said.

The both heard another voice, this one harsh, guttural. "Is that who I think it was?" Zack said.

"Yes."

"Tell me again about how intelligent these things are?"

"They were chosen for their size and mobility," Megan said. "But the ones we're seeing aren't necessarily typical of the species. It's like you hired human mercenaries and then complained that they couldn't change diapers." She tapped her fingers on her forehead, as if trying to improve the flow of information. "The big problem is they weren't optimized for the same atmosphere as humans. It's preventing them from following orders any longer."

"You mean, a civilization that can build this vessel, send it across the galaxy on a fishing expedition that lasts ten thousand years . . . can't manage some nasty-looking alien it picked up?"

"They don't have total control." She was shaking her head. "At least, that's what I think. I'm not getting answers. . . ."

"Now I wish I had a weapon." He stopped. They had reached a nexus where five different passages intersected.

"Any insights as to which road to take . . . ?" Megan suddenly started laughing.

"What's so funny?" he asked.

"Think about it. All the many choices we've made in our lives . . . all those other roads. Look at where they took us! How many roads are left?"

At that moment, Zack Stewart realized that they had, in fact, reached a final destination.

They were in a plaza. Like everything Zack had seen in the Factory, it was freshly formed . . . and already crumbling.

One structure opened into the plaza. Its interior was filled with panels and screens covered with changing figures. But Zack and Megan had no time to examine them . . . there was a more compelling image:

The Architect, all eight meters of him, dead at the base of the open structure . . . sliced and diced like Pogo Downey.

Zack looked at Megan, who was looking away from the body. "No wonder you weren't getting answers."

Zack could be clinical and objective about the mangled Architect's body—it wasn't sufficiently human to arouse empathy. But the smell made him want to gag . . . and so did the realization that he and Megan were now truly on their own. Not that the Architect had been a very useful guide . . . but he seemed to be in charge of operations, or at least the flow of information.

Now what did they have?

In one of the passages to his left, he saw Camilla, terrified, runny-nosed, a child in a situation no child should ever imagine, much less face.

Directly across from her, in one of the passages on Zack's right, stood a Sentry. It had an appalling bluish ichor—the Architect's blood?—on its appendages.

"Zack, darling," Megan said.

He didn't answer. He was too fascinated by the Sentry . . . it was actually trembling, as if struggling. It turned its head back and forth, scanning. "I'm going to tackle the bad boy."

"No, you're not. I want you to pick up Camilla and go back to the tunnel, back to the Temple, anywhere but here. . . ."

He looked at her and was terrified by what he saw. Megan was pale, shrunken and hunched, as if suffering abdominal pain.

"Hang on—"

"Don't say that! It's over for me! Let me distract the Sentry while you get away—"

"I'm not leaving you—"

"You don't have any choice. I may not last ten more minutes."

He wanted to argue, but the evidence was compelling. She could barely stand. And yet her eyes blazed, reminding him of the angriest she had ever been at him . . . for some offense he could no longer remember. Or chose not to remember. "I lost you once. I can't do it again!"

Suddenly her eyes were no longer fierce, but filled with tears. "You have to. Just remember . . . 'the dead are free.'" She flung herself at him, for the shortest, most heartfelt hug of their nearly twenty years together, as well as a last kiss. "Now get the girl and go!"

Without waiting to see what Zack did, Megan charged directly at the Sentry.

Which turned its attention to her like some jungle beast. Then it opened itself and engulfed her.

Zack forced himself to look away and run toward Camilla.

He scooped her up. She hardly seemed to weigh anything, which was good.

It was time to run.

"We're coming up on the terminator," Tea said.

A series of posigrade rocket burns had pushed *Destiny* out of the immediate clouds of debris surrounding Keanu, eventually dropping the vehicle into a lower orbit around Earth.

Of course, when even the perigee of that orbit was more than four hundred thousand kilometers, *close* was only a relative term.

The maneuvers also put *Destiny* on the dark side of Keanu. They could see the lopsided halo of the debris cloud shining in light from the Sun, of course . . . but the NEO's surface was black, hidden, unknowable.

For a few moments, anyway.

"*Destiny*, Houston. Still showing you on track for retrofire in thirty minutes."

"Copy that, Houston. Hope you can take some time off then." Jasmine Trieu was still on duty as capcom—a fifteen-hour shift, if Tea had it right.

"I'm happy to stay here as long as you need me," Trieu said. "Right up to splashdown, if necessary."

"We'll be getting some sleep before then," Tea replied. Retrofire would put *Destiny* into an orbit with a much lower perigee . . . one that would intersect Earth's surface about three days from now. "You should, too."

Trieu's answer was delayed by the lag, of course. Tea looked around the cabin. Lightly attached to the floor by bungee cords, Natalia Yorkina was sound asleep, eyes covered by Tea's mask.

Lucas and Taj were yawning but kept busy bouncing between a laptop and one of the windows as they updated Russian mission control—the backup for destroyed Bangalore—on what had happened to *Brahma*.

Tea didn't care what the rest of the world knew, or didn't. She had no idea whether her conversations with Houston were being carried live.

She just wanted it to be over, to take the memories of Keanu and the resurrected Megan Stewart and the vaporized remains of *Venture* . . . and Zack Stewart's sad, knowing smile . . . and hide them somewhere, like photos in a family album, to be opened at some happier time.

"Oh, *Destiny* from Houston. A bit of news. Tracking shows increased delta V for the NEO."

"You mean it's moving?" Tea had spent her entire professional life in engineering, most of that in NASA. She understood the need for precise usage . . . but there were times, like now, when she just wanted someone to use plain English.

"Tea," Taj said. "Look out the window."

While Tea waited for Jasmine Trieu to clarify her last statement, she floated up to the window, where dayside Keanu was coming into view.

She gasped.

Narrow swaths of Keanu's surface were gone, exposing a shiny white surface. The NEO looked like an apple someone had started to peel. "What the hell?"

"Some of the snow and regolith are boiling away," Taj said.

"I think that pretty soon it's going to look like a big fat pearl," Lucas said.

"Well," she said, "we knew it was really a ship of some kind." A ship that seemed to be shedding an accretion of debris gathered over ten thousand years. Shedding a skin to enter a new phase.

"*Destiny*, Houston, confirming: There have been eruptions on Keanu that are consistent with, uh, propulsion. It seems to be leaving Earth orbit."

It was going farther than that, surely. "Houston, *Destiny*, I think our NEO is going home."

It would be seven seconds before she heard an answer, but Tea Nowinski didn't need it.

She was going home, too.

> But of the tree of knowledge of good and evil, thou shalt not eat. For in what day soever thou shalt eat of it, thou shalt die the death.
>
> GENESIS 2:17

Dragging Camilla, Zack emerged from the Factory tunnel to the Temple chamber into a shower. Rain was falling and blowing sideways. It wasn't a downpour, nor was it a tropical gully-washer like those he'd experienced in Houston. It was more like a rainy day in the Pacific Northwest... but warmer! It actually felt good to have some of the grime wash away.

It felt better to let some of the water trickle into his mouth. He could not remember the last time he'd had a drink. He actually scooped some out of a shallow puddle and offered it to Camilla. "This could kill us," he said. "But without it we're going to die of thirst."

This small gesture toward survival took Zack's mind off the idea that the same Sentry that had killed his wife and the Architect was on their trail.

No sign of him so far. The respite allowed Zack time to consider his next move. *Now that you've done such a great job solving the water problem.*

Through the mist he could see, a kilometer distant, the top of the Temple rising over what, for lack of the proper term, he would have to call trees. He had no special desire to return there, but it was the only possible shelter he knew—and the only door he might be able to close.

"Come on," he told the girl, knowing his words weren't being understood, but hoping his gestures conveyed the message.

Camilla didn't respond. She was looking past Zack, behind him—

Toward the tunnel.

Zack turned . . . and there was the fucking Sentry. The colloidal bubble dribbling out of the creature's tool vest and down its torso was bloody. It made Zack want to rip the being apart with his bare hands.

That not being an option, he picked up Camilla and, hoping the Sentry had not yet seen them, plunged into the nearest stand of trees.

Camilla whimpered. It wasn't loud, it was understandable . . . but it was potentially fatal. As Zack glanced back, he saw that the Sentry had heard the girl.

And was after them.

Knowing they would be faster if he dragged Camilla rather than carried her, Zack dropped the girl and led her through the trees. They had some advantage here . . . the trunks were close together. They could slip through, but the Sentry would have a more difficult time—

Until the creature simply slashed at several trees, clearing his way.

There was no point in looking back. Zack kept his eyes forward, always on the Temple. "Stay with me," he said. "Keep going." He was speaking to himself as well as to Camilla.

The clearing around the Temple loomed. The crash and crunch of trees being torn up told Zack that the Sentry was probably fifty meters behind.

Get ready to run—

They broke into the clearing, where Zack took three steps, tripped, and sprawled on his face, taking Camilla down with him.

That was it. He had fucked up and now he was going to die, like Pogo, like Megan. . . .

With the last of his strength, he rolled toward Camilla, who was lying on her back, eyes closed, as if she had already given up. "Run," Zack said, making shooing gestures. At least he could get the girl away safely, not that the poor child was likely to survive long here, alone.

But Camilla refused to move.

Okay, then, time to face the truth. Zack rose to a crouch, looking around for stalks or husks of whatever vegetation had been cleared for the Temple. He still believed that a sharp stick might be useful—

Crack! The top half of several trees less than a meter away disintegrated into a shower of sticks and knifelike shards, slashed away by the Sentry.

It had caught up to them.

The creature was growing in apparent size, its protective bubble expanding around its middle pairs of arms without hindering them. Now Zack could see that the semiliquid came from its vest. No matter . . . the Sentry was winding up for a killing slash at the prone Camilla. Without thinking, Zack reached for one of the shards at his feet and flung it at the Sentry.

The jagged spear bounced off the creature's major right-side appendages, but not without leaving a wound.

The Sentry whipped all of its left-side arms at Zack, who fell flat on his back dodging the attack.

He found himself looking right up into the Sentry's face. It wasn't horrific, just cold, implacable, like that of an executioner about to trigger the guillotine—

This is it, Zack thought—

But the Sentry didn't make the killing blow. It suddenly twitched to one side.

Camilla had flung herself at the creature and was clinging to its right leg.

As the Sentry turned to brush her off, Zack had enough time to locate a sharp, sturdy spear.

With a whimper, Camilla went flying.

When the Sentry turned back, Zack stabbed it in the vest, pushing through the colloidal bubble. Which collapsed in a shower of watery goo.

For a long, anguished moment, the Sentry stood in what could only have been shock and surprise, its appendages waving in confusion, a greenish ichor bubbling out of its torso, then its throat.

Then it collapsed and began to curl into itself, rolling into a ball that began to hiss and steam.

"Camilla!" Zack ran to the girl. She was crying, badly scratched, but not seriously injured. He picked her up.

Within a few minutes they had worked their way around to the rear of the Temple, the side that had opened for the Architect. It was still open, revealing the empty chamber where he and Megan had first encountered the being.

Where he had left his radio.

He thought of Megan. As a working reporter, as a mother, she was famous for making realistic assessments of situations. Her most overworked phrase was, "Hoping won't make it happen."

Zack was out of hope. He did not expect to leave Keanu. He did not expect to survive more than a few days at best.

But if he could get in touch with Houston, if he could somehow tell them what had happened.

If he could talk to Rachel—!

He left Camilla at the threshold of the chamber, making it as clear as possible that he wanted her to stay put. Then he began searching. . . .

It took only a few moments to locate the Zeiss right where he had set it down.

Five minutes later, he was ready to smash it. He could not make it work! All the buttons were operating as before—the power indicator lit. But there was no link, no response, nothing.

Where was Camilla?

Leaving the radio behind, he ran out of the Temple, calling, "Camilla!"

Off to his left, a few steps into the forest, a hand appeared.

Zack found that the girl had plucked some purplish soft gourd off a tree.

"Hey, don't eat that!"

Too late . . . Camilla had already bitten off a good chunk. Zack reached for her, hoping to get her to spit it out, but the girl scampered away, chewing happily.

She climbed up one of the trees, parking on a branch just out of reach, and like a primate avoiding a keeper, happily finished the fruit.

Zack watched Camilla carefully. She showed no signs of instant rejection . . .

And she was starving. "What the hell," he said. "Eventually we're going to have to do this." He went back to the tree and plucked his own piece of Keanu fruit. The texture was like a green pear; the taste reminded him of mango.

He must have liked it, because he devoured it right down to a core.

After a while, still feeling full—not poisoned—but terminally exhausted, he led Camilla into the Temple, where they curled up against the farthest wall.

His last thoughts, as he lost awareness, were sad ones. He would never see Megan or Rachel again.

We have entered a new age.   PRESIDENT'S REMARKS, AUGUST 24, 2019

. . . and I don't like it much.   POSTER JERMAINE AT NEOMISSION.COM

Lucas Munaretto woke in great confusion. He was floating, though wrapped in a light sleeping bag. The *Destiny* cabin was dark, except for the gentle glow of several LEDs on the instrument panel. The windows had been covered. For a good few moments, he thought he was still aboard *Brahma* approaching Keanu.

Then he remembered, and wished he hadn't.

He could see his fellow travelers, all asleep in their own bags . . . Tea, her hair an unbound halo, somehow appropriate for the sacrifices she had made, and the skill she had shown in getting them all aboard *Destiny*, off Keanu, and now falling toward reentry. She would be a hero once she returned to Houston . . . sadder, yes, but with an unlimited future.

Then there was Natalia Yorkina, wrapped too tightly, of course, like a woman in pain. Given nagging equipment failures—Lucas had done an EVA in an overheating Russian suit, and it almost drove him mad—she had done well. From the mysterious exchanges between Zack and her, and the quick disappearance of her Revenant, Lucas suspected a dark secret that would haunt Natalia. But only he and Taj could embarrass her, and neither would. Natalia would return to Russia and some make-work job with Roscosmos, slipping into anonymity.

The largest figure in the cabin was Lucas's commander, Taj, who had submerged his intense dislike of American arrogance in order to bring most of his crew home safely. Taj would be publicly acclaimed in India;

Shiva only knew what kinds of criticism he would face in private, both for the extraordinary losses of spacecraft and Chertok, and for allowing Zack Stewart to make so many vital, and possibly flawed, decisions. Ultimately, though, Taj would be promoted . . . he would go back to the Indian Air Force to command a fighter wing, or he might stay on as a leader in ISRO.

No, all of the others would be happy to reach Earth. Only Lucas Munaretto felt that he had left something undone.

Camilla, of course. He had never been that close to Isobel and her family . . . Camilla's birth had occurred when Lucas was away training for his space station mission.

He never knew the girl, not really. Was that why he had been so useless to her in her second life? He had held her, yes, comforted her, fine, given her voice with the others, great, told her her mother loved her, all good. But that was all. He had not learned what she saw, what she felt. He had made no move to bring her back, had stood by helpless as she was taken.

And yet he did not know whether she was still alive, or as she had been before. What was he going to tell Isobel?

Then there was Zack Stewart . . . abandoned on an alien world, left to die.

No, the only failure was the World's Greatest Astronaut. He should have stayed.

He knew he would carry that guilt all his days.

Zack woke with Camilla curled into a crouch and facing him. He had had
terrible dreams of being chased, and then being shaken, like sleeping
through a thunderstorm.

The light streaming into the rear of the Temple looked different . . .
brighter somehow.

Leaving Camilla to her sleep, Zack walked outside.

No wonder he had dreamed of a storm. The environment had obviously gone through a radical change in the past few hours, from the
vaguely Amazonian jungle to what could now pass for North American
forest.

There was no more rain, no wind blowing. The glowworms were back
in the sky, a network of bright yellow-white light.

But something was happening in the chamber. Zack could hear . . .
voices?

He ran around to the front of the Temple. Coming toward him was a
ragged stream of people! He had never been good with crowds and numbers, but there were hundreds of them. Many appeared to be from India;
the men were all wearing that subcontinent's uniform of white shirt and
trousers, the women and children in colorful garb.

There were also several dozen who could only be from America. All
looked stunned and disoriented . . . "Hey!" he shouted, no doubt terrifying those at the head of the column.

He made it worse by running directly at them. Those in front parted to let him pass. "Hello! I'm Zack Stewart! Do any of you speak English? Where are you from? Say something!"

There was a moment of confused silence. Then an Indian male in his late fifties stepped forward, pushing his glasses back on his nose. "Yes, hello, Commander Stewart. I am Vikram Nayar, and I worked at Bangalore mission control. Am I to understand that we are now inside Keanu?"

"Yes! You are! But how did you get here? How did so many of you get here . . . ?" He remembered Megan's stories of the Architects and a "recruitment," but hadn't expected it to happen at all, much less this soon.

Any possible answer was lost in the growing clamor, as those slightly farther away began repeating Zack's words, in several languages, and others shouted more questions.

"Hey, everybody, coming through!"

A handsome if incredibly disheveled man in a lopsided wheelchair was being pushed through the crowd by a man wearing NASA badges. "Harley Drake," Zack said.

"Zachary Stewart, I presume?" He looked at Zack and, with some effort, held out his hand. "Nice place you've got here."

"It's a little underfurnished." It was a relief to just banter with Harley, but only for a moment. "Okay, what the hell happened?"

"The short version is, Keanu decided to scoop up some human talent. We were like fish in a goldfish bowl for the past twenty hours . . ."

"Just floating—?"

Then Zack saw another familiar face. . . . Rachel. "Daddy?"

His daughter leaped from the crowd into his arms. "Oh my God," she said. "I knew it, I knew you'd be here! That's why I went to the site! No one believed me, but—"

Zack tried to shush her, with no success . . . and no sense of failure. He was happy just to hold her.

But then Rachel said, "Where's Mom?"

All Zack could do was shake his head.

"She's gone, isn't she?"

Zack could still find no words.

Rachel took a big breath, one that usually presaged a breakdown. But this was an older, stronger girl. "I knew it. I knew she wouldn't last. . . ." Then her resolve failed, and she became a sobbing child again.

Who could blame her?

Harley gently separated them. "We've all got a lot to catch up on, but I'm guessing food, water, and shelter are the first priority."

"Not to mention figuring out just why the hell we were brought here." The voice belonged to Shane Weldon, who raised his hand. "Hey, Zack."

Well, if Harley had wound up here along with flight controllers from Bangalore, why not Weldon? "Welcome, everybody!" Zack said. He directed them to the Temple, and the "orchard" beyond. There were several minutes' worth of discussion about scouting parties, rationing, water.

While part of his mind worked with relative efficiency on these matters, Zack tried to process his new reality. He would never see Earth again. He had found and lost Megan, likely forever. He would spend his remaining days, months, years, engaged in a brutal quest for simple survival. No more television, good food, sports, cars, science, medicine.

Only what Keanu offered, what the Architects had arranged.

It was like being dead without actually dying.

Finally he was able to turn to Harley, saying, "I just hope someone here speaks Portuguese."

"I have no idea what that means, but I'm sure you'll explain it." Harley turned to a tall, red-haired young woman while Zack took Rachel's hand, all of them watching the crowd march on the Temple.

They're like new souls entering heaven, Zack thought. Or at least its shadow.

We think we're beyond the orbit of Jupiter, but no one knows for sure. There's been no communication with Houston or Earth of any kind for the past six months.

We're just beginning to explore Keanu. This place is big and strange.

I miss my friends.

RACHEL STEWART TEXT, TYPED INTO A SLATE THAT ONE OF THE CHILDREN FROM BANGALORE CARRIED. MESSAGE RETRIEVED FROM ENHANCED CASSINI SPACE PROBE DATA.

Acknowledgments

Thank you, Marina Black, Dan Aloni, Matthew Snyder, Simon Lipskar, Glynis Lynn, Izzy Hyams, Nellie Stevens.

D.S.G.

Thanks as well to Cynthia Cassutt, Andre Bormanis, Greg Bear, and Ginjer Buchanan.

M.C.

Don't miss the next book by
David S. Goyer and Michael Cassutt

HEAVEN'S WAR